Abra Pressler writes romance novels from her home on Ngunnawal country in Canberra, Australia. She grew up on Wiradjuri country in West Wyalong, New South Wales, and studied Creative Writing at RMIT University.

Love and Other Scores

ABRA PRESSLER

MACMILLAN
Pan Macmillan Australia

Pan Macmillan acknowledges the Traditional Custodians of Country throughout Australia and their connections to lands, waters and communities. We pay our respect to Elders past and present and extend that respect to all Aboriginal and Torres Strait Islander peoples today. We honour more than sixty thousand years of storytelling, art and culture.

First published 2023 in Macmillan by Pan Macmillan Australia Pty Ltd
1 Market Street, Sydney, New South Wales, Australia, 2000

A catalogue record for this book is available from the National Library of Australia

Typeset in 12/16.5 pt Bembo MT Pro by Post Pre-press Group, Brisbane

Printed by IVE

The paper in this book is FSC® certified. FSC® promotes environmentally responsible, socially beneficial and economically viable management of the world's forests.

For Rebecca—every draft, every tear, every victory.

And for Dad, the 2022 West Wyalong Open Men's Champion.

'What is the single most important quality
of a tennis champion? . . . Desire.'
—John McEnroe

PROLOGUE

GABRIEL

The ball whizzes past my face. There's a breath, a moment of silence, before it hits Phoebe's racquet with a *thump* and flies back to the Froebel siblings on the other side of the net.

Lukas Froebel runs forward, racquet extended, but his foot lands short and he needs to stretch to reach the ball. I know his forearm won't have its usual kick so I step forward and meet the ball with a well-timed backhand, sending it crosscourt. It zips between Lukas and Freyja, landing by the baseline.

The scoreboard changes: 15–0.

Phoebe pats me on the shoulder. 'Nice one.'

We reset. Phoebe's serving. I hunch over, knees soft and head up, ready to launch. When I first turned pro, I hated playing doubles in charity matches. Too many players had more power than accuracy in their serve and the back of my head would cop it. Slapstick humour always earns a good laugh from a crowd, though.

Phoebe serves again. Freyja, the younger of the Froebel siblings, has a vicious backhand. Tonight, her swing is calmer, and I return it easily. Lukas hits a moonball, and it flies well above my head, but Phoebe runs backwards to meet it at the baseline. She grunts in frustration as she smashes the ball across the net. It bounces out of reach, even as Lukas strains his racquet upwards. 30–0.

'I hate moonballs,' Phoebe growls as we reset.

I nudge her shoulder. 'Chill, it's a charity match.'

She gives me a hard look. Phoebe's always been wildly competitive. She can't stand to lose, but she hides it graciously when it happens.

I hand her a spare ball and the crowd quietens as Phoebe prepares to serve. Just as she raises the ball, someone calls from the grandstand, 'Marry me, Gabriel!'

The crowd vibrates with laughter. The hair on the back of my neck stands up at the attention. Across the net, Lukas grins at me.

'Quiet, please,' commands the umpire.

As the crowd's tittering dies down, the umpire nods at Phoebe to continue. This time she serves without interruption.

Two months ago, a fan-run Instagram account held a vote on the hottest players currently on the professional tennis circuit. Objectifying? Sure. Were we all invested in where we ranked? Of course.

Lukas came second.

Mortifyingly, I took first place.

My measly hundred-thousand Instagram followers shot up to over half a million in less than two days and #Mad4Madani was trending on Twitter in eight different countries. Suddenly, people were trawling through my social media accounts to figure out where I was and who I was dating. When they found nothing, the internet decided I was single and ever since, my direct messages have been out of control.

Phoebe serves again. Freyja hits the ball back with the effortless grace only thousands of hours of practice can create.

I return the ball to Lukas with little urgency or power. When it's easy like this, it feels like a dance. With my feet square and my knees slightly bent, I position myself at the net, ready to volley, trying to anticipate Lukas's next move.

What I don't expect, however, is to see Lukas's left leg rise into the air as he swings the racquet behind him. A classic between-the-legs shot. The ball flies back over the net as the crowd erupts in laughter.

Lukas revels in the attention, waving to the fans and flashing a cheeky smile. He's as much a showman as an athlete, and at six-foot-three with handsome Scandinavian features, he's a crowd favourite.

Phoebe stumbles forward, scooping her racquet under the ball in a risky attempt to save the point, but it hits the net.

'Take it easy,' I say as she passes me. We're a few days out from a major title; there's no need to go hard. 'You don't want to overdo it.'

Her mouth tenses into a long, tight line. 'I'm fine.'

I turn back to face the Froebels. Freyja watches Phoebe with a calculating gaze as my partner walks back to the baseline. Immediately, I regret commenting on Phoebe's play, criticising her on the court. Phoebe's one of Freyja's biggest competitors and she'll be looking for signs of weakness.

I glance at Lukas and wonder if he's sized me up during the match. I've held back, and I'm sure he has too. As if reading my mind, he gives me a sly smile as he wipes the sweat off his brow with the hem of his shirt. Six glorious abs shine in the arena light. Behind me, I hear the click of a camera shutter.

Always the showman.

Brisbane is notoriously hot—everyone who attends tournaments in Australia struggles with the heat—but tonight the breeze is cool and smells like eucalyptus. It makes my skin prickle. Phoebe prepares to serve and the crowd dies down. I can hear the buzzing of the court lights overhead, the drone of cicadas, the beating of my heart. I'm hyper-aware of my breathing and take long, even breaths. It's almost blissful. Seconds stretch as the moment slows down.

Phoebe serves and Freyja returns. It's long. Too long for me to intercept. I hear Phoebe's shoes squeak along the baseline and wait for the sound of the ball hitting her racquet—

—but it doesn't.

Instead of the *thump* of ball on racquet, I hear Phoebe let out a shriek of pain.

I turn but my body feels sluggish, like I'm trying to walk in a swimming pool. Phoebe's on the ground, clutching her knee. Tears stream down her face.

I run to her side, my racquet falling to the ground.

'Gabi.' Phoebe grips my forearm so tightly it hurts. Behind us, I can hear someone calling for the medic. 'Gabi, I can't get up.'

1

NOAH

I'm running late.

Technically, I'm running on time, and it's the trains that are late—delayed by the sweltering heat and the warping tracks—but Mark won't accept that excuse.

Heat rolls off the ground in waves. It's two in the afternoon and already more than thirty-eight degrees. Tomorrow, it's supposed to be forty-two. They say if things continue the way they're going, it won't be long before Melbourne sees fifty-degree summer days. Fuck my life when that happens.

Further down the platform, two girls in short sundresses pass a water bottle between them. I'd bet my last dollar it doesn't contain water. One has a beach bag slung over her shoulder, colourful towels spilling out of the top. A warm breeze pushes down the platform, ruffling the hems of their dresses. In contrast, I'm in black dress pants, black belt, black button-up shirt and shiny lace-up Oxfords.

One girl laughs at something the other said. They look around my age, but our lives are probably completely different. They'll spend the afternoon lazing at the beach. I'm heading to a shitty job to make a shitty buck.

The train rolls in to Flinders Street Station and, after waiting for the passengers to disembark, I slide into a vacant window seat. Finally, sweet, sweet air conditioning.

As the train lurches forward, I rest my elbow on the window ledge and watch the station disappear.

'*This is a Frankston-bound train, stopping all stations to Frankston*,' says a perky robotic woman over the loudspeaker.

The train slips into a tunnel—

'*The next stop is . . . Richmond*.'

—and emerges again. To my right, Rod Laver Arena is awash with banners promoting the upcoming tennis tournament. Cleaners scour the grounds. A handful of staff are setting up a garden display in the shape of a tennis racquet by the large arched entrance.

As the train loiters at the station, I watch the electronic poster ads roll. First is a woman in mid-swing, her gaze determined. *Two-time winner Phoebe Song*, the poster reads.

The poster rolls again to reveal a fiercely attractive blond man leaping into the air in pursuit of the ball. His shirt rides up and gives just a tease of his well-defined stomach. *Lukas Froebel. French Open Champion*.

The final poster promotes a man named Pejo Auer. He stares down the camera with a playful smile, his thick arms crossed over his chest. *World Number One*.

The doors close again and the train lurches forward.

Across the carriage, a baby gurgles. I watch as the woman

leans over her pram, making animated faces as the baby squirms with delight.

I wonder if my mum looked at me like that. It's always been clear my dad didn't want me, but I wonder how Mum felt when she found out she was pregnant. If she was happy. Excited, even. Or if she felt resigned to 'figure it out' like she seemed to do with everything else in her life.

Pulling my phone out of my pocket, I scroll through my messages.

Don't worry about me. I'll be fine.

She sent that text message over two years ago. We haven't spoken since.

'*The next stop is . . . South Yarra*,' the robot woman says over the intercom.

Putting my phone away, I push Mum from my mind. Gotta tackle one thing at a time.

I get off the train and walk out into the affluent suburb of South Yarra. Tendrils of jasmine fall from the balcony of an apartment, swaying in the warm summer breeze. As I walk past a suspiciously chunky puddle, I get a whiff of something nasty and hold my breath until I get to Chapel Street.

There are two faces to Chapel Street. Designer clothes outlets, expensive hair salons and handmade jewellery boutiques dominate the north end. Further south, Chapel Street's clean, preppy exterior morphs into something darker. The money is dirtier. The nightclub floors are sticky. I walk past a twenty-four-hour establishment, silent and dark on a weekday. Once, I grazed my knee stumbling out the door of that club and was hauled back onto my feet by a drag queen. She'd pressed me to her latex bosom while flagging down a cab before chivalrously loading my drunk arse into the back seat.

The bar I work at is located in the basement of a beautiful old building nestled down a narrow side street. As I unlock the door, the smell of stale beer wafts out. *Just like home.*

Turning on the handful of TVs that surround the bar, I flick through the channels until I find a sport I can stand. Cricket. All I can glean from the game is that Australia's playing India and we're batting. The score is a weird fraction. I've no idea who's winning.

A poker table stands in the middle of the room, chips and peanuts scattered across it. I wipe the surface down, stack the chips and drag the table back to the storeroom.

When I started working here, the bar was called the Peacock Lounge and was owned by a bloke named Graham. The décor was incredible, and the bar smelt like sandalwood and expensive cologne. Booths with emerald-coloured velvet seats faced an elevated stage where there was always an array of musical instruments. Graham could play all of them. On Thursdays, he would take the stage and people would come in droves to watch his one-man performance.

Then Graham got sick, and Mark bought it, and changed its name to Mark's Place.

As soon as they handed him the keys, he installed six garishly large TVs, wedged the piano into a narrow storage area at the top of the stairs, razed the stage and installed a pool table. The bar went from being one of the most unique venues in Melbourne, a place where you would end your night, to being just another bar where you could drink a beer and watch the footy.

Mark's supposed to be here for opens, but he's often late. When it's just me, I don't mind the job, but it's not like I haven't looked for something else. The job market is tough. I dabbled in phone sex for a few months because, why not—I'm an adult. I was told I had a nice voice, and it was fun; but when Graham offered me a job at the Peacock Lounge, it became too difficult to manage both.

I'm an hour into my shift—and still no Mark—when Peaches comes in. I know it's her the moment she steps through the door. No one makes an entrance like Peaches O'Plenty.

The late-afternoon light glows around her hourglass figure as she descends the stairs. Today, Peaches wears a skin-tight black catsuit and the latex hugs her in all the right places, emphasising her over-padded arse and long, shapely legs. Her poker-straight blonde wig brushes her lower back and as she comes closer, she twirls, just because she can, and I glimpse a flash of a red undersole on her black high heels.

I nod towards the shoes appreciatively. 'They're new.'

'And they're real, baby.' Peaches slides up to the bar. Her eyelashes must be an inch long. She flutters them as she leans forward, giving me a good view of her cleavage.

'Found yourself a good gig?' I ask, keeping my eyes on hers. They're a beautiful light blue.

'A *regular* gig,' Peaches emphasises. 'Working over at the Rosewood.'

I raise my eyebrows in surprise. 'A high-class establishment for a high-class woman.'

'Aren't you sweet?' She reaches forward to take my hand in hers. This week, she's sporting hot-pink stiletto nails with diamantes on the cuticle. 'I'll have the usual, baby.' She adjusts her catsuit. 'Fuck, it's hot out there. My puss feels like she's in a sauna.'

'Thanks for sharing,' I remark. For most of the year, Melbourne is beautifully grey and mild. It's nice. But for two months, Melbourne is as hot as fuck and it's awful. Most people leave and holiday along the golden shores of Sorrento and the Bellarine. Those who need to stay suffer through summer.

Peaches places a twenty-dollar note on the counter. 'You apply for university yet?'

I ring up her purchase and hand her back the change. 'No.'

She frowns, a brow wrinkle forming under a thick layer of foundation. 'Why not?'

'Not sure what to study.' It's a lie. The truth is I didn't finish school. If I had, then I'd be applying for a music program, but you can't apply for university without a graduating certificate.

'Choose *something*,' she implores. 'If you don't like it, move on. We both know you can't stay here forever.'

'I'll figure it out.' I hand her the drink: gin and tonic. 'What's this new gig at the Rosewood, then?'

She rolls her eyes as she takes a sip, noting the change of subject. 'A bit of stand-up. Some singing. I'm on Thursday, Friday and Saturday nights, which suits me fine. Thursdays I do Drag Queen Storytime at Windsor Library, so I have time between gigs to spend with my favourite bartender.'

'I'm so lucky,' I drawl.

'. . . But he doesn't open until four, so I just drink at any old watering hole until then.'

I flick Peaches with the edge of my tea towel. 'Get out of my bar, you wench.'

Peaches laughs and takes another sip of her drink. 'I could talk to the manager at the Rosewood. You'd fit right in.'

The Rosewood is a gorgeous bar and nightclub on the edge of the city with all the charms of a Victorian pub: beautiful architecture, historical significance and tiny bathrooms that smell like piss and mould. During the day, it's a well-known brunch spot. In the evening, it hosts a range of live acts and performances. All the big drag names perform there. Seems Peaches O'Plenty is one of them now.

I wipe my rag over the bar. 'You think so?'

'Babes, with a face like yours, you'd have more shifts than you could handle at the Rosewood. And we could hang out once work's over.'

She's teasing me, but my throat feels scratchy with sudden emotion, and I cough to clear it. I didn't realise we were close enough that she'd want to hang outside of this 'bartender–customer' dynamic we've got going on. It's weird because I don't even know Peaches's real name and if I saw her on the street out of drag, I don't think I'd recognise her. We've known each other for just under a year, and in that time, Peaches has fed me tidbits about her life as one would a stray cat: she's thirty-nine, works part-time as an IT consultant, and owns a two-bedroom apartment in St Kilda which she shares with her toy poodle, Monster.

She leans forward, her breasts spilling out of her top. 'So, you'll let me talk to the Rosewood for you?'

'Fine,' I relent. It's not like Mark would care if I left, and I could use the extra money.

'That's the spirit,' she says. 'Imagine all the fun we'll have working together.'

I scribble down my number on a napkin and pass it to Peaches. She folds it and slips it into her absurdly tiny handbag with a smug smile.

'I'll have my people call you,' she says, and I roll my eyes.

'You're insufferable.'

2

GABRIEL

I drag my sore and severely under-caffeinated body through the airport. I barely slept last night. All I could think about was Phoebe and if she was okay—and if she was okay, why wasn't she messaging me back? So clearly, she wasn't okay. I'd spiralled like that until two in the morning when my brain finally shut down.

Now I'm in the security line for a 7 am flight to Melbourne feeling like death warmed up. I check my phone to see if she's messaged back, but I'm still on 'unread'. Just like I was six hours ago.

Papa sighs as we move through the line at a snail's pace. Rafael Nadal and Novak Djokovic have private jets and their own security gates. As Papa and I make our way through the airport, shoulder to shoulder with the general population, I wonder if I should have texted one of them for a ride. Rafa's usually good for it.

A security guard makes me take off my shoes to check

for a bomb or gunpowder residue. Papa waits on the other side of the scanner, scrolling through messages on his phone. Victor, my media manager, stands beside me, glaring daggers at the security agent as she hands me my shoes back.

'Right to go,' she says, and I slip my sneakers back on. Victor follows behind me, slinging his satchel over his shoulder as it comes off the conveyor belt.

'Have you heard from Marco?' I ask Papa. Marco is Phoebe's coach of over ten years and well known on the tour for developing her formidable 190-kilometre serve.

Papa shakes his head as he scans the departures screen. Today, his locs are tied into a bun on the top of his head, and a few wiry salt-and-pepper fly-away hairs sprout from his scalp. He won't trust anyone but his barber in France to retwist them so until we get back to Paris, he's rocking the loose look. 'Come, Gabriel, we're at gate eighteen.'

My iPad dies halfway through the two-hour flight, and I sink back into my seat. I check my phone again to see if Phoebe's messaged—nothing. Beside me, Papa turns the pages of his novel.

'Stop jiggling,' he mutters, nudging my leg with his.

I realise I've been tapping my foot and still it. 'Sorry.'

'You'll do well at the tournament,' Victor assures me from my other side. 'I've *manifested* it.'

'Manifested it?' I repeat.

'Yep,' he says, and I realise he's being completely serious. '*And* the tarot cards agreed.'

Tarot. Manifesting. I'm all for luck, but that's a bit ridiculous. I turn to Papa, hoping he'll be the voice of reason, but he's got his headphones on. To him, we might as well not exist. 'Since when are you into that kind of stuff?'

'Since the pandemic. Some people baked bread, I got really into astrology. Sometimes I do it before your big matches, just to settle my nerves.'

Boredom prompts me to ask, 'What else do the tarot cards say?'

Victor leans to one side, reaching behind him, and produces a well-used pack of tarot cards from his back pocket. 'Want to ask them?'

I shrug. It's not like there's anything else to do. 'How do I do it?'

'You ask the cards a question.' He goes to hand them to me, but at the last second pulls away. 'Be serious about this, Gabriel. If not, the cards will know.'

'I promise,' I say, and mean it. My sincerity is more for Victor than it is for the pack of cards—I don't care if I offend literal pieces of paper—but it seems Victor really believes in this stuff, and I don't want to be disrespectful.

Satisfied, Victor hands me the cards. 'Hold them between your hands and push your question into them with your mind.'

'Do I have to tell you the question?'

'No, you telepathically tell the cards.'

Right. Okay. Sure. Telepathically tell the cards. For a second, I fumble around for an appropriate question. Finally, I settle on *Is Phoebe going to be okay?* and mentally push it into the deck.

I hand the cards back to Victor and he shuffles them, then flips down the tray table.

'Now, there's no such thing as a bad reading,' he says as he starts laying out cards facedown. 'And I also don't read reverse.' I don't know what that means but I don't want to ask. 'Do you have the question in your mind?'

I nod. Suddenly, I'm super curious about the reading.

'Eight of Cups,' Victor says as he flips the first card over. 'Disappointment. It might feel you've been abandoned or left behind but it also represents the desire to escape our lives, if just for a moment.'

I lean in closer. I know disappointment—I've lost matches and had tough draws—as much as I know victory, and the demands of professional tennis are relentless. New cities, new tournaments, play your best, win that title—or lose it—pick yourself up, keep going. 'What's the next card?'

Victor cracks his neck, like he's physically preparing himself for the revelation. He flips the next card. 'Death. It represents the end. A major change is on the horizon. New beginnings.'

I don't like those connotations at all. Tennis players are notoriously superstitious, and while I do my best not to buy into the hype, the Death card rattles me. Victor flips a third card and sucks in a breath.

'Five of Swords. It represents conflict, competitions and defeat.' He looks over the cards spread before him. 'The cards suggest that a major change is coming. You may feel defeated.'

Not exactly the reading I want going into a major tournament. 'I thought you said there were no bad readings.' I pick up the Death card. 'This looks like a bad reading, Victor.'

He plucks the card from my hand. 'Death is not literal, Gabriel. It represents the closing of one chapter and the start of another. In many readings, it is invigorating.'

Just as he slips the card back into the deck, the plane lurches as it hits a patch of turbulence. I grasp the armrest and shoot Victor a *you did this* glare, but he avoids my gaze.

No bad readings, my arse.

I check my phone as soon as we land, but my five messages are still unread.

'Focus on the tournament,' Papa says as he picks the luggage off the carousel. 'She'll be fine.'

'I *am* focused.' I grab my tennis kit off the belt. I have four racquets in circulation for this tournament. All Wilsons. My favourite has a green accent, and got me to the third round of Wimbledon on a wild card, and the semi-final of the US Open three months later. I may not buy into tennis superstitions but there's no way I'd risk leaving it in Paris. 'That doesn't mean I'm just going to stop worrying about her.'

Papa fixes me with a hard gaze. 'Don't argue with me, Gabriel.'

I wasn't, I want to snap back, but if I lose it at Papa now, there's no way we'll make it through the next two weeks. I bite back the words, even as they sizzle on my tongue.

Victor finds our shuttle driver and we load our luggage into the back. In Paris, I have an assistant, another trainer and a nutritionist, but when we're attending a big tournament, it's only me, Papa and Victor. When we travel for smaller titles, it's just me and Papa. I prefer it when Victor is with us. Being the centre of Papa's universe can be overwhelming.

When I first turned pro, my *maman* and my sister, Claudia, would tune into *every* match, no matter the time difference. Now that I've been on the tour for nine years, they keep up to date with highlight reels. Sometimes, when I call Claudia, we don't even talk about tennis—just life and university and who she's dating—and for a brief moment, with her, I'm not Gabriel Madani, the tennis player. I'm just Gabi.

We take the shuttle into Melbourne. The sky is vast and blue and there's not a single cloud in sight. Cool air billows from the van's air conditioner, and the driver chats about how Melbourne's set for a record heatwave next week.

Fantastic. Can't wait to play tennis with a touch of heatstroke.

We check into the hotel and a bellboy whisks our small mountain of luggage into a service elevator. By the time we open the door to our river-view apartment, our bags wait in the narrow hallway.

'What a beautiful view,' Victor announces as he steps up to the floor-to-ceiling windows. The mid-morning sun glitters over the Yarra, the wide brown river that runs through the middle of the city. Silver trains weave their way along the labyrinth of tracks leading to a large train station. I catch my reflection in the window; my curls are frizzy and out of control, and my brown eyes are rimmed with dark circles. I look, and feel, a mess.

'It feels great to be back in Melbourne, doesn't it?' Victor sighs in a way I'd describe as *dreamy*.

'Fine, I guess. I'm going to take a shower.'

I love the Australian Open—the heat, the crowds, the taste of summer zipping across my tongue—but right now, this feels like any other hotel room, in any other city, for any other tournament. Even though I've travelled to Melbourne several times, I've never seen what lies outside of Melbourne Park—the complex where the tournament is held. Mostly because I train like a dog, and also because Papa and Victor don't like to let me off the leash.

It's hard to tell friends back home that, although I fly across the globe chasing titles, I've never seen the Pyramids, or toured the Statue of Liberty or snorkelled in the Great Barrier Reef. It may sound glamorous, but I'm here to work—to win—not play tourist.

The hot water rinses away the layer of grime from the plane journey, and I quickly wash my hair to tame the frizz. As I walk back into the hallway, I see Papa out on the balcony, his phone pressed against his ear. He's pacing. Not good.

'Hungry, Gabi?' Victor asks. I turn to see a platter of sandwiches and a bowl of salad on the kitchen table.

'Yeah.' My wet hair drips down my neck and I grab a spare towel from the linen cupboard to plop my curls. Ironically, Phoebe—the girl with the poker-straight hair—taught me how to plop and seaweed my curls when she stayed at my house before the 2021 French Open. 'Who is Papa talking to?'

'Not sure,' Victor replies. 'Come eat.'

As I stare at my uninspiring meal of mediocre club sandwiches, I vow to eat the biggest, messiest, *cheesiest* burger Melbourne can muster once this tournament is over.

'Eat,' Victor repeats as he grabs a packet of salad dressing.

'Your father's booked the rooftop courts for this afternoon, so you'll need something in your stomach.'

I bite into my sandwich, but my attention drifts back to Papa. I try to read his lips through the window, but he keeps turning away as he paces.

Suddenly, he ends the call. I turn back to my food, feigning interest in lunch and not the conversation on the other side of the glass. Papa steps back into the apartment, the balcony door closing behind him with a *click*. When I glance up, his face is grave, though he always looks sour. *Maman* says Papa's got a resting 'disapproval' face—but something in me knows this is bad news.

'That was Marco,' Papa says. 'Phoebe's torn her ACL.'

'Shit,' I say without thinking. A torn ACL isn't great, but it's not the end of the world. 'Hopefully she'll be back for Wimbledon.'

Papa frowns at my swearing. I'm not supposed to swear. Not casually. It makes it more likely that I'll swear on the court. Papa's all about politeness in tennis. No swearing. No tantrums. Always raise your hand in apology if your ball hits the net cord.

'There's an excellent surgeon in Melbourne so they've decided to fly down,' he continues as he takes a seat at the table and reaches for a sandwich. 'She will recover here, and then go back to the US.'

Immediately, I perk up. If Phoebe's staying in Melbourne, I'll be able to visit her. Depending on how well her surgery goes, she might be able to attend my matches.

'Gabi,' Papa continues, immediately squashing that tiny bloom of hope, 'Marco says she's decided to retire.'

'What?' I blurt out. 'No! She's only twenty-nine!'

'Twenty-nine with a knee reconstruction and now an ACL,' Papa counters. 'Most don't get as far as she has.'

'That's not fair!' Anger quickly overrules my disbelief. How is this happening? Phoebe and I have always done big tournaments together; revelling in our victories and sharing the sorrows of loss. She's been my rock more times than I can count, and now it's over? Just like that?

Papa squeezes my shoulder. 'Don't be upset. It's the nature of the game.'

I shrug off his hand. I don't want to be placated, and I hate that he's telling me how to feel. Everything in my life is his construct. His plan. Move your feet like this. Hit the ball like that. Do an interview for this magazine. Don't get upset. Don't get angry. Be gracious. Be kind.

'I *need* her there,' I say. Phoebe's my best friend, my lifeline. There's no way I can get through this tournament without her.

Victor reaches across the table and takes my hand, his soft gaze and sympathetic smile ice to my father's fire. 'I know this is a lot to process, Gabi, but things will be okay.'

'Don't,' I say, pulling my hand away. I'm not in the mood for their good cop–bad cop routine. Papa and Victor share a meaningful look.

'Come, Gabi.' Papa pushes away from the table, still holding half a sandwich. 'Put your shoes on. Let's go to the court.'

Training's the last thing on my mind, but I do as he says to buy myself a sliver of alone time. I close the door to my room and grab my phone. Still nothing from Phoebe, but I have two messages from Lukas Froebel.

Wanna hit the beach later?

Also, u heard from Pheebs?

I leave Lukas on 'read' and pull up my chat with Phoebe, cringing at how many messages I've sent, but once you've got five unanswered messages, what's six?

Papa said you're retiring. Is it true?

Phoebe's the only person I've told about my sexuality. I'm not out on the tour, I'm not out to Victor or Papa, or my family back home. Lukas is my friend, but he's also my biggest rival. Phoebe is like an older sister, and she has been since we met at a teen training camp ahead of Wimbledon Juniors twelve years ago. I'd watched Phoebe rise through the rankings, and by the time I was sixteen, I was on the circuit too, hungry to match her success.

We go to award nights together; we do media together; we catch taxis to the airport together. For years, she happily played her part in our 'suspiciously too close' friendship, and speculation about my sexuality stayed out of the tabloids.

Even when she dated actor Aaron Waterstone, my commitment to the role of 'dumped ex who still wants to be friends' was Oscar-worthy. When they broke up last year, rumours swirled that she'd decided to finally give 'the long-suffering best friend' a chance. It was great fun.

'Gabriel! *Allez!*' Papa calls from the kitchen.

Quickly, I change into training gear: an old Nike top, shorts, a pair of thick white socks and my headband.

Besides my rising popularity as an eligible straight bachelor, my hair has, annoyingly, become a thing. During the US Open, the ESPN commentators jokingly awarded me 'Best Hair of the Tournament'. I'd never considered my hair anything special until a fan page uploaded a slow-motion video of me returning a serve to Dominic Thiem sync'd to 'Buss It'. My hair was loose, sweaty, and the curls bounced around my shoulders as I moved. Suddenly, people were calling me the 'Fabio of tennis' and my Instagram blew up.

After that fiasco, I'd had to make an entirely new Instagram account just so I could see messages from my friends. So many people slid into my DMs, it was overwhelming.

'If you're going to engage with people like that, you need to be careful,' Victor had said during one of our 'now that you're famous' meetings. 'Ask them to sign an NDA. You don't need girls screenshotting your messages and sending them to gossip magazines.'

I'd promised him that girls could message me all they wanted; I'd never respond. He'd seemed satisfied with my answer, at least.

Training is brutal. The sun beats down on us. Papa serves and I return, but there's no bite in my forearm. We spend time warming up and getting used to the conditions before we work through our paces. By the time we're done, I'm dripping with sweat.

'Focus on the backhand,' Papa calls. 'Make sure you're following through with your shots. Bent elbow, full swing.'

During Wimbledon, Lukas knew I had a poor one-handed backhand and he exploited it. Ever since, Papa's worked on improving my technique. If I can master it, it'll take my slicing skill to the next level and provide more power and control over the ball. And, it might just take Lukas by surprise the next time we meet.

Papa serves, but I miscalculate the power behind the ball. I position myself to return with a one-handed backhand, but as soon as the ball hits the strings of my racquet, my hand buckles and I lose it. The racquet bends as the ball veers into the net.

'Again,' Papa calls from across the court.

'Softer this time,' I say.

He doesn't serve softer. He sends the ball flying with the same amount of power and speed. But this time, I'm prepared. I soften my elbow and knees and when the ball hits the racquet, I feel in control. Driving through the backhand, I hit the ball crosscourt, making sure to follow through with the full stroke. The ball bounces on the inside corner and then out.

'Better, Gabriel,' Papa shouts back. 'Curve your arm.'

I know, I want to reply, but don't.

We play for another hour, although 'play' is a loose term. Papa hounds me with never-ending serves and I return until my left arm is aching. It's real Luke and Yoda stuff, and by the time Papa calls the training session, I'm hot and sweaty and irritated.

This is nothing, I remind myself as the sun beats down on us. *The tournament hasn't even begun.*

3

GABRIEL

Victor calls me over to his laptop the moment I set foot in the apartment. Papa left after training to check out the gym and pool on the ground floor. Victor's set up his office on the glass dining table. Behind him, there's a whiteboard with photos of my opponents tacked around the edges, each connected with little red twine, like he's planning a sinister fight club.

'They've released the draw,' Victor says. I slide into the seat beside him and peer at the laptop. 'You're up against Derbin in the first round. He won a qualifier. Show Court Nine at 11 am. If you win, you'll face either O'Lachlan or Ujo. That will be at Evonne Goolagong Arena.'

Nathan Derbin is from Ireland; he's twenty-four and number fifty-three in the world. He's never won a grand slam but had a decent run in a few ATP tournaments last year.

'I can take Derbin,' I mutter as I follow the draw on the screen. As the name indicates, qualifiers have already played three matches to qualify for the Australian Open. You'd think they'd start the tournament tired, but when I qualified for the Australian Open seven years ago, I was in great form and hungry for my next match. 'Where's Lukas?'

'He's on your side of the draw with Rhodes in the first round.' Victor taps Lukas's name on the screen. 'Hagiwara will likely win his first round to meet Lukas in the second.'

If things go right for both of us this tournament, Lukas and I will meet eventually. It'll be the first time we've played against each other since I crashed out of Wimbledon last year when he beat me in straight sets.

It was the worst match of my life; I'd left the court embarrassed and overwhelmed, and even now, just thinking about that match makes the hair on the back of my neck stand up. I'd avoided Lukas's calls and messages for weeks before I'd licked my wounds enough to face him. It's one thing to lose a match, but it's another to have your arse handed to you by one of your closest friends on international TV.

Beside me, Victor prattles on about matches and show courts, but I'm not really listening. The apartment suddenly feels small, and I'm having trouble focusing on anything except how unnaturally cold the room feels. Papa will be back soon, and he'll want to talk about strategies and what I did wrong against Derbin last time. After everything that happened with Phoebe this morning, I feel too raw to be picked apart any further.

'I'm going for a walk,' I interrupt Victor. Sweat pricks my forehead. I just need *space*. Space where, ideally, Victor and Papa are not.

Victor's pale brows rise and he closes his laptop. 'You're going out? Like . . . out on the street?'

'I just need to clear my head. Make a game plan. Zone out a bit.'

Victor's mouth purses. 'We should arrange an escort.'

I shake my head. No. No escort. I'm a twenty-five-year-old man who should be able to take a walk without minders. 'I will share my location with you. No one will recognise me, it'll be fine.'

Victor doesn't look convinced, but I don't care. I'm going.

'At least put a hat on,' Victor calls as I grab my wallet and hotel key card. Ah yes, the curse of my famous hair. 'And make sure your phone is charged.'

I leave the apartment, taking the stairs down to the lobby so I don't run into Papa in the elevator.

The hotel lobby is an expanse of shimmering marble. There's a sunken bar to the left of me, and the entrance to an indoor pool and spa on the far wall. A taxi loiters in the half-circle driveway by the large double doors, its engine rumbling. A dark-haired man smiles from behind the reception desk as I pass.

A small group of people wait by a nearby tram stop and I jump on the first tram that comes by, not bothering to buy a travel card. It's busy and I shoulder my way into the carriage, barely finding my footing before the tram lurches and I stumble backwards, falling onto someone. A man in a suit turns to look over his shoulder, clearly annoyed.

'Watch what ya doin',' he says in a hard Australian accent. 'Hold on to the bloody rail.'

'I'm sorry,' I stammer, finding the words in my rusty English as I grab the rail above my head. An older woman in a priority seat gives me a tight smile.

My plan is to get off at the first stop that looks interesting, and for a while, all I see are business complexes and highways. No one gets on or off. But then, the tram turns onto a narrow road lined with retail shops, restaurants and bars. The street hums with excitement.

'*The next stop is . . . Chapel Street*,' says a woman's voice over the intercom.

The tram stops in the middle of the road and I hop off, weaving my way through stationary cars to the footpath. I put on my cap, keep my head low and follow the crowd, telling myself, *No one's going to recognise a tennis player who's had only a handful of decent wins.*

But Victor's voice comes back to me like the buzz of a persistent mosquito. 'It only takes one social media post with a location tag for someone to find you at a restaurant and stab you,' he'd said as we'd flown into New York last year.

I don't want to get stabbed, so I adjust my hat and turn on the tracking on my phone, sharing my location with Victor. Hopefully he won't be a nark and tell Papa.

Chapel Street gets busier the farther south I walk. It's late evening now, but the sun is still strong and in a matter of minutes, I'm sweating. I wanted space to clear my mind but there are people everywhere. Maybe this was a bad idea. Maybe I *do* need an escort. I pass a man who gives me a double take, and then looks a third time. Does he recognise me? My heart's beating so fast I can hear it. How do *actual* celebrities do this? My resolve shatters and I search desperately for a side street, a refuge, *anything*.

A few metres away, there's a chalkboard sign on the footpath: *Try our new Hazelnut Expresso Martini*.

Yes, espresso with an 'x'.

An arrow points towards a bar located in the basement of an old Victorian-style building. *Perfect*. I go down the few steps into the sunken courtyard, avoiding the barren pot plant full of cigarette butts that sits precariously on the edge of the stairwell. I push the heavy wooden door and the sound of saxophone creeps out. Weirdly, the door jams before it opens fully. Stepping inside, I realise why—there's a dusty old piano wedged in the space behind the door.

The bar smells like sour beer and something musty, as if it's been closed for weeks. There's no chatter or conversation, just quiet saxophone and the sound of cutlery clattering.

I take a deep breath and descend the staircase. About halfway down, I make eye contact with the bartender; he's my age, lanky with a mop of long chestnut hair. He smiles at me as he polishes a fork.

'Take off yer cap if yer coming in,' he calls, his broad Australian accent running the words together. When I don't move for a long moment, confused by his direction, the bartender uses the fork to point to a sign by the bar.

No Hats!

Cautiously, I raise my hand and take off my cap. With a held breath, I wait for a spark of recognition.

It doesn't come.

Perfect.

'Are you open?' I ask.

The barman's expression changes. His brow furrows and his lips purse. I've learnt that people look like that when they're trying to place my accent.

'Sure.' His deep, resonant voice echoes in the empty pub. 'What can I get you?'

Though there are plenty of free booths, I take a seat at the bar, facing the bartender. He reminds me of a young Leonardo DiCaprio, all floppy hair and charm. He grabs a glass from the shelf above him and looks at me expectantly.

'A Coke,' I say, and then quickly add, 'please.'

'A Coke?' he repeats in disbelief. '*Just* a Coke?'

'Zero sugar if you have it. But if you only have diet, then a regular Coke is fine.'

The bartender gives me a strange look. 'No, we've got it. Want a glass or just the can?'

'Glass. Please.'

'Lime?'

I nod.

He opens the can and pours the Coke into a glass, adding a squeeze of lime. As he slides it towards me, I notice a red scar runs diagonally down his palm.

'That'll be four dollars,' the bartender says abruptly.

Merde. Four dollars?! Everything in Australia is so expensive. I fish out my wallet and hand him a bright pink five-dollar note.

The bartender hands me back a dollar coin. I glance at the tiny tip glass beside the cash register and reach towards it.

The bartender smacks his hand over the top of the cup. 'Don't tip me.' My dollar coin hangs in the air between us.

'My boss takes all the tips. Besides, you don't need to tip in Australia. Keep the dollar.'

I put my dollar back in my wallet, feeling like I've somehow offended him. 'Thank you.'

'No worries,' the bartender says with a chirpiness that seems to come naturally with Australian accents. 'Where you from?'

It's small talk, but it seems like he could use someone to talk to. There's no one else in the bar, and it looks like he's the only one on staff.

I take a sip of my Coke. 'France. My name is Gabriel. My English is not great.' When you spend most of your teens playing tournaments across the world, you're bound to miss *a lot* of school. I've learnt English through playing and travelling, but I wouldn't consider myself a confident speaker. Especially to reporters.

'I'm Noah, and I promise my French is terrible. Are you here on holiday?'

'No,' I reply. 'Work.'

'Work?' he echoes. I can tell he's trying to figure out exactly what work would bring me all the way from France. 'What kind of work?'

'International relations.' It's the first thing that comes to me. I suppose it's true enough.

Noah studies me like I'm a puzzle he wants to solve. 'That sounds like a fun job; are you staying the summer? It's hot as fuck now, but Melbourne's really lovely in the evenings.'

'I don't mind the heat. Growing up, my family spent our summers in Algeria. Melbourne has the same dry heat.

It's nice.' I don't know why I'm telling him this; perhaps it's the way his eyes haven't left mine since I walked in, or maybe because I know I'll likely never see him again—but something about him makes me uncharacteristically chatty. 'Are you from here?'

Noah's mouth tenses slightly as he polishes a spoon. 'I moved here when I was eighteen from a small town two hours north. You know, small city, big dreams.' Before I can ask him about what specific dreams, he adds, 'So how long do you think this job will take?'

A day? Two weeks? 'Hard to say. The company will schedule a flight for me as soon as it is over. No time for sightseeing.'

Most of the time, Victor books a flight to the next tournament the moment I come off the court after my last match.

'Well, that's a bit shit.' Noah finishes polishing the spoons and begins on the knives. He rolls his sleeves up past his forearms and my eyes are drawn to the flex of muscles; the veins that run up the back of his hand. Why is that so sexy? 'If you were staying a little longer, I'd offer to show you around.'

A nervous laugh escapes me before I can stop it. Is this flirting? Am I being flirted with? 'That would—'

The door opens at the top of the stairs.

'Shit,' Noah says quietly. I glance up to see a man lurch down the steps. His greasy dark hair hangs limply over his pallid face and his sunken eyes are bloodshot.

Without thinking, I get up to help him down the last few steps, only to be hit with the sour smell of sweat and booze. The man pushes me off forcefully and I fall against the bar, hitting my back against the hard edge and knocking over my drink.

'Gabriel, don't,' Noah protests as the stranger staggers into the office, slamming the door behind him. Noah helps me into my seat. The last of my Coke drips onto the floor. 'Shit, are you okay?'

'I'm fine,' I manage, even if my lower back disagrees. I rub the sore spot and notice Noah's eyes following the movement. 'Who was that?'

He sucks a breath between his teeth. 'My boss. He gets like this sometimes. You should probably go.'

'Are you going to be okay?' I don't want to leave him here, especially if he could be in danger.

'Weirdly, I deal with this a lot,' Noah says. 'I'll be right behind you.'

Under the topaz lights of this basement bar, his eyes shimmer like emeralds. A part of me wants to stay with him, to suggest maybe we go find another bar and continue this conversation—

—no.

I'm here for a reason. Tennis. Tournaments. Glory. Not dreamy bartenders with sexy forearms and hairstyles from the nineties.

'Thanks for the Coke,' I say before walking up the stairs and heaving the heavy door open. Sunlight streams into the dark bar, illuminating dust particles suspended in the air. Outside feels completely different; it's like I've stepped out of a cinema after a marathon movie session only to realise it's still daylight.

My phone buzzes in my hand. It's Victor.

Your father is asking for you. You know I'm a bad liar.

I tap out a reply before shoving the phone back into my pocket. As I come to the intersection of the busy street, I raise my hand to adjust my cap only to realise it's not there. I must have left it in the bar.

For a second, I think about returning to find it, even though I have a dozen others just like it. The cap's not special, and certainly not anything worth going back for.

It's a cap, I think, *get a hold of yourself.*

Tennis. Tournaments. Glory.

4

NOAH

I think about following Gabriel right out that door. Instead, I lock it behind him, trapping me and the beast in together. As much as I dislike Mark, I don't want him accosting customers or accidentally stumbling into oncoming traffic.

I count the money and tally the receipts in the bar. Between Peaches, Gabriel and a handful of others, we've barely made a hundred bucks.

The office door opens again and Mark walks out with a vice-like grip on the bottle of whiskey he must have pinched from the storeroom. He downs a large swallow.

'Are you playing poker tonight?' I ask, trying to keep my tone casual even as fear prickles down my spine. I learnt from my dad that he hated being treated like he was a drunk, so I'm wary not to upset Mark.

'Maybe later.' He leans over me and glances into the cash register. God, he reeks of sweat and beer and I swallow down the bile that rises into my throat. Out of the corner of my eye, I notice a black Nike cap resting on the bar. Gabriel's cap. He left it here.

'Is that all we took today?' Mark demands.

'People don't pay in cash anymore. It's all on card,' I lie. To see the full balance, he needs to log into the EFTPOS account using the laptop in the back office. Right now, he can barely stand, let alone remember—or type—his password.

Mark's grubby fingers grab several bills from the till before he slams the tray closed. 'Go home.'

Don't have to tell me twice. If I hurry, I might be able to catch up with Gabriel. Quickly, I pull off my apron, check my reflection in the mirror behind the bar, and grab my satchel from the back office.

In the time it's taken me to clock out, Mark's moved to a booth. Tennis plays on the big screens. Mark's greasy head lolls against the velvet-cushioned booth. For a moment, I wonder if he's passed out.

Mark wasn't always like this. When he first bought the bar, he was just an arsehole on a power trip and was delusional about how hard it is to run a bar well.

His drinking started subtly, socially, but soon the late-night partying and private poker games began to eat into the profit. A few weeks ago, I walked into my shift to find bottles missing and money gone from the till, and all I thought was *How have I found myself in this situation* again?

It's like I'm a fucking magnet for this kind of shit.

'You okay?' I ask Mark. I want to try to find Gabriel, but I also don't want to leave him like this. 'Rough few days?'

God, am I really trying to communicate and show *empathy*? To the same man who once called Peaches the f-word slur and banned her from the bar?

Seems I've given Mark far more credit than usual, because he waves me away with a grunt. I'm so low in his view that I'm not even worth words.

'See you tomorrow,' I reply. I don't even want to remind him that Monday is payday.

Instead, I make a plan to update my résumé as soon as I get home.

Locking the door behind me, I hurry down Chapel Street. Weaving through the crowd, I keep my eye out for a head of curly hair, but the streets are busy and the trams more frequent. By the time I get to a tram stop, I've accepted that Gabriel's gone; lost to the bustling churn of Melbourne. Oh well.

A tram pulls up to the stop and I jump on board. Immediately, I regret it. With all the hot, sweaty bodies crammed into the narrow cabin, it's stifling. The air conditioner rattles above me, its breeze barely cooler than the air outside.

I ride the tram from Chapel Street, up the wide streets past the National Gallery of Victoria, and into the city. The last of the day's sunlight dapples through the thick canopy of plane trees that line the city streets. Outside, a busker in a Batman costume plays the saxophone on the corner. The melody of 'Careless Whisper' slips through the opening in the tram doors before they slam shut.

Getting off the tram once it veers into Carlton, I begin the long trek up Lygon Street. Famous for its blocks and blocks of mouth-watering eateries and upmarket bars, Lygon Street is a vibrant mix of culture and community. Party lights hang from awnings, flickering in the twilight. Waiters stand in the doorways of their restaurants, menus tucked under their arms. Each of them attempts to catch my attention as I pass, but I wave them off politely.

The vibrancy of Lygon Street peters out as I walk further north. Narrow streets sport rows and rows of thin Victorian houses that scream, *We're cramped, we're old, and we're very expensive.*

Mine is the third in a row of eight: a white terrace house with a striking yellow door—because, individualism—and a huge bush of crimson roses that dominates the small front yard. I do my best to avoid the bees that buzz around the flowers as I open the gate and grab my keys from my satchel.

'Just me!' I call as I unlock the door.

'You're home early,' Margie replies, her voice echoing down the hallway.

The lounge room is at the far end of the house, and Margie's slightly deaf and in her mid-sixties, so she keeps the front door locked. Cool air rushes out as I step inside, so I quickly close the door behind me. The house smells like vanilla and spices. One of Margie's favourite candles glows on the hallstand. Just in case she's forgotten it's burning, I blow out the flame as I slip off my shoes.

'Mark took over,' I call back as I throw my satchel into my bedroom. Sadie, Margie's caramel-coloured cavoodle, wanders down from the lounge room to greet me, and I give her a quick scratch behind her ears.

'Dinner's in the microwave,' Margie says.

'Thanks, Marg!'

Our yell-greeting complete, I peel off my sweaty work clothes and deposit them into the laundry basket. After a quick shower, I pull on a pair of old shorts and a vintage Carlton footy club t-shirt I thrifted.

I run the microwave for a minute before opening the door to find a plate of silverside and vegetables. It's hot enough, so I take it over to Margie's little kitchen table and dig in.

When I first moved in, I used to hate that she left me a plate. It felt like pity. Fed up with being fed, I confronted Margie about it only to be told that she *enjoyed* making me food—and of course, then I felt like a major dick.

Before I met Margie, I'd been sleeping rough, working the phone lines, and living off sandwiches from the servo. Margie's dog-sitting ad had popped up on a house-sharing website one afternoon, and I'd applied without hesitation. A place to stay with a cute dog? It was a no-brainer. When she accepted my application, I thought it'd be two weeks off the streets, but when Margie got back from visiting her daughter, Lucy, we got to talking. Turned out, as an older woman living alone, she was more than open to finding a roommate who could offer a sense of security and help a bit around the house. Cheap rent for a bit of security work and vacuuming? Sign me up.

Sure, maybe we're unconventional roommates, but we make it work.

Margie doesn't know about anything that happened before I came to stay with her—my violent dad, his alcoholism, our late-night escape—though I think she can sense that my situation wasn't ideal. But she doesn't ask, and frankly, I don't really want to tell.

'You have a nice day?' Margie steps into the kitchen to grab a drink. Her salt-and-pepper hair is set in curlers and her robe is tied tightly around her waist. Sadie sits patiently by the door, hoping for a tidbit as Margie rummages through the fridge.

'It was fine,' I reply. 'How was yours?'

'Good. I received an email saying there's an information session for uni admissions next week,' she says as she grabs a bottle of lemonade. 'I can forward it to you.'

'I'll have to check if Mark wants me at the bar,' I say. 'But thanks.'

Like Peaches, Margie's big on me starting university. To her, going to university is the start of any successful career. Not only does she have a doctorate, but her three children went to university and now they're all over Australia doing interesting and successful things. She doesn't understand why I put it off.

My phone vibrates in my pocket. Pulling it out, I'm surprised to see there's a message from Mark.

2moro 2pm – 8pm? I haev poker one @ 8.

A couple of spelling mistakes but not bad for a guy who looked like he had more alcohol than blood in his system an hour ago. *Sure*, I write back and leave it at that.

'Want a shandy?' Margie asks as she cracks a can of beer.

'What's the occasion?' She hardly ever drinks unless there's something worth drinking for. 'I'll have the leftover beer.'

'Good lad,' she says as she pours a dash of beer into her lemonade. 'It's awful hot outside, and the tennis is on. Makes me crave a shandy.'

Margie mixes the lemonade and beer with a spoon and then slices up a lime from her backyard as a garnish. She places the beer can in front of me and ruffles my hair as she passes.

'Come watch the tennis,' she says. 'It's the last of the qualifying matches.'

I scoff and put on my most camp accent. 'Do I look like I know sports?'

She looks down at my thrift-shop Carlton Football Club t-shirt.

'It's *vintage*,' I protest. And it was two dollars.

'You know, some of the players are quite easy on the eye, Noah,' she says as she walks back to the lounge, Sadie hot on her heels. '*And* the men take off their shirt sometimes.'

I don't know why she thinks a glimpse of a sweaty male torso will convince me to suffer through hours of hit-ball-over-net. Like, porn exists.

'I'll pass,' I say as I finish my dinner. 'I'm gonna go work on an application for a new job. Forward me the email for the information day, would you? I'll put it in my calendar.'

Margie beams from her recliner and picks up her phone. 'I'll do it immediately.'

I don't have any intention of attending the information session, but at least it will get her off my back. For now.

5

GABRIEL

When I get back to the hotel, Papa's gone and Victor's leaning over the balcony railing. The port-wine stain that runs from his ear to his shoulder is a stark red mark on his white skin. There's a cigarette between his long, thin fingers, and a trail of smoke curls up from the glowing end. Lost in thought, he brings it to his mouth and takes a deep drag before flicking ash into the wind.

I realise he hasn't heard me come in, so I lean forward and tap twice on the glass. Victor startles and stubs out the cigarette, crushing the butt in the glass dish at his side.

'I thought you were quitting,' I say as he steps back into the apartment.

'So did I.' He runs a hand over his bald head. I've seen photos of Victor and Papa when they were two scoundrels on the tennis circuit—Victor, with his high cheekbones, blue eyes and long blond hair, could have been mistaken for a distant relative of the Hemsworth brothers. 'How was your walk?'

'It was good to get out.' There's no way I'm telling him what happened.

'No issues?' he pries.

'No stabbing, no harassment. No one even recognised me.'

Victor mutters something under his breath as my phone vibrates in my hand. It's Phoebe.

Hey from me. Sorry been radio silent. Just out of surgery. Went well.

Immediately, I shut myself in my room and type, *Are you okay? Sorry for the million messages . . . I was worried.*

Phoebe: *It's okay lol. I've been dealing with some things.*

Gabriel: *Are you really retiring?*

Three dots appear, indicating she's typing again. But then they disappear. Reappear. I wait impatiently for the message to come through.

Phoebe: *Can you meet me at the hospital tomorrow? I'm in the Parkville Ward @ Prince Albert. Level four.*

Gabriel: *Okay . . . I'll see you tomorrow. Midday?*

Phoebe: *Sounds good, I'll let my nurse know.*

Phoebe sends me a *Grey's Anatomy* GIF just as someone knocks on my bedroom door.

'I ordered sushi,' Papa says, pushing open the door and peering in.

Three words and my bad mood lifts immediately. I know Papa's trying to make amends for the words we exchanged at the airport and his brutal training session earlier, and I'm a sucker for sushi.

He's bought a veritable feast—we're talking *tamago* and salmon *nigiri*, *maki* and *gunkan*. We load our plates and settle in front of the television.

The hotel television has a limited selection of channels: we can choose the cricket, a backyard renovation show, or a re-run of *Kindergarten Cop*. We choose *Kindergarten Cop*. The movie is almost finished—Arnie rescues the kid who climbed the tower to escape his abusive dad—though the plot is of no interest to Victor or Papa. They spend ten minutes talking about how Arnold achieved his physique.

'It's all about visualisation.' Victor nudges me with his socked toes. 'Arnold *visualised* that he could look like that, and so that's what he worked towards.'

'Don't think Arnie would be much of a tennis player with that physique,' I reply through a mouthful of *nigiri*.

'It's about picturing the goals you want to achieve.' Victor was never a tennis player; he worked at a small PR agency in Paris when he was assigned a new client—a little-known tennis player named Bernard Madani who'd had a handful of wins since turning pro and desperately needed to refresh his brand.

I stifle a groan. 'You're right. I've never imagined what holding the championship cup would be like.'

Victor tuts at my sarcasm.

'Not that,' Papa pipes up. 'Visualise the championship point. The cup is nothing; it's a ceremony. The championship point is the last point in the match when you stare down your opponent, and you will them to give up. Visualise that moment. Visualise what you'll do when you're tired and run-down and your opponent doesn't want to roll over. When they've suddenly got fire again, but you've got nothing left to give. Think about how you'll feel when you're playing a five-set match into the early hours of the morning, and the championship point is the only thing standing between you and the trophy.'

'Your father's right,' says Victor. 'You have to have confidence that you can get to the end, and then push past it, even when your body doesn't want to.'

'Play could continue, and four more championship points could come and go before the match has ended,' Papa continues.

'Coffee is for closers,' I parrot.

Papa leans over me to swipe the last hand roll off the plate. 'Sushi is for closers.'

'You know I had my eye on that,' I mutter. The credits of *Kindergarten Cop* roll across the screen.

Later, I curl up in bed and read more about Arnold Schwarzenegger's training on my phone—his routine, his philosophy and diet. Of course, he was a professional body builder. His entire career was about aesthetics. I'm nothing like Arnie but I have to admit that Papa's speech about visualisation and the championship point hit me harder than I expected, and now uncertainty swims in my gut like an eel. What if I face the championship point, and I'm not ready? What if I squander it, lose it, and can't get it back? What if, at the last second, the championship is ripped from me? How do I face my player's box? How do I face Papa? Myself?

I've won tournaments before, but the Australian Open is one of *the* championships. A quarter of a grand slam.

It's different.

For once, I wish there was someone I could talk to about this stuff other than Phoebe. She's sympathetic, but she's also a stoic. She'll say stuff like, 'That's the way it goes' and

'Never let them see you sweat'. I wish I could text Lukas but anything we say to each other is filtered through the lens of tennis. He's a friend but he also catalogues any insecurity he perceives and stores it until we meet on the court.

Tennis is as much a mental game as it is physical, and once your opponent's found your weakness, and they're under your skin, it's hard to dig them out.

The Prince Alfred Hospital is like any other: clean polished floors that reflect the fluorescent lights, a lingering sickly sweet chemical smell, and polite smiles from busy staff. We're directed to Phoebe's room after they cross-reference her visitor's list: it's a private room in a far wing of the hospital designed for 'people of note'.

Phoebe's thumbing through a fashion magazine when Papa and I arrive. I notice a bouquet of red roses in a glass vase on her bedside table before I see all the drainage tubes creeping out from under her blanket.

'Oh, thank god you're here,' she says, relief clear on her face. 'Gabi, my phone fell on the floor fifteen minutes ago, and I don't want to bother a nurse. *Puh-lease* can you get it for me?'

Trust Phoebe to focus on the most important things. Shaking my head, I lean down and find the phone underneath her bed.

'How are you feeling?' Papa asks in heavily accented English. He doesn't speak English as often as I do anymore, and it shows.

'Better, thanks, Mr Madani.' She folds the magazine in her lap and gratefully accepts her phone. 'Surgery went well. Hopefully I'll be on a flight home soon, but I'd like to try and see a few matches before I leave.' She looks at me. 'How are you feeling about the Open?'

'Good,' Papa replies for me. 'Gabriel will face Derbin in the first round.'

Phoebe gives me a cheeky smile. 'You can take him, Gabi.'

'Thanks.' I want to tell her how much I'm struggling to get in the right headspace; how nervous I am about not having her at this tournament—all the things I'm afraid to say to Papa.

Papa looks from one of us to the other. He's never been overly social, and now that he's made small talk, he's scrambling for conversation.

'I'll get coffee,' he says. 'Leave you to talk.'

After Papa leaves, I fall into the armchair beside Phoebe's bed. She looks tired. Worn out. Like the game has beaten her. I remember when she had no problem biting back at critics who said her plus-sized body wasn't compatible with professional sport. I remember when she won a championship on Monday and owned a photoshoot for *Vogue* on Tuesday.

Being stuck in a hospital bed is no way to retire, and a part of me aches for the on-court send-off she deserves.

'So, how bad is it?' I ask. 'Career-ending bad like everyone's saying?'

Phoebe lets out a heavy sigh. 'I mean, kinda.'

She pulls the sheet away. Her knee is wrapped in stained bandages, but a dark-blue bruise travels up her thigh. The surgeons have attached a small brace to the joint to keep her leg straight, the rods penetrating her knee in a way that makes my stomach churn.

'It doesn't look that bad,' I lie. 'You could play again.'

Phoebe laughs even as her lower lip trembles. I watch as she tries to hold back a sob but fails. Fat tears roll down her cheeks as her chin puckers. I reach over and take one of her hands, threading her fingers through mine. 'You're a terrible liar, Gabriel.'

I don't know what to say, so I just hand her the box of tissues on her side table.

She grabs a handful and dabs at her eyes. 'I just pictured my retirement differently, you know? I want the fanfare, I want that final match.'

I want that for her too. How can one second—a moment in time—ruin a person's entire career? Thirteen years playing professional sport and it's all over after a fall during a low-stakes charity match? It's unfathomable.

I feel awful for thinking it, but what if it had been me? What if I was the one in the hospital bed facing the end of my career? Everything in my life is tennis. Everything I do is for tennis.

If it all ended, who would I be?

'You've recovered from knee surgery before,' I say. 'There's no reason why this has to be the end.'

'Gabi, I'm pregnant.'

I wait for her to break into laughter. To smile and say she's 'got me', because she can't be pregnant, she—

'Do I need to get the nurse?' She laughs through the tears. 'Gabi, you've gone pale. Honey, you know you're not the father, right?'

It's a stupid joke but at least it lightens the mood. 'For real? Pheebs . . . you're really pregnant?'

Phoebe nods. 'I'm about seven weeks. I found out just before I came to Australia. Obviously surgery is not ideal, but we're both fine.'

'How did this even happen?' At Phoebe's sly grin, I rephrase. 'I didn't even know you were dating anyone after A—'

'Aaron and I are working things out,' she cuts me off. 'We've been back together for around six months, but we've kept it out of the media. It feels different this time.'

I had no idea she was seeing Aaron again. A small part of me is offended she didn't tell me—but to be fair, six months ago I was playing Wimbledon with single-minded focus. The world could have collapsed around me and I wouldn't have noticed.

'Well, it doesn't mean you have to retire. Serena did it!'

Phoebe gives me a meaningful look. 'I'm no Serena, Gabi. Aaron and I are excited to slow down a bit and refocus our priorities with the baby. Besides, I've won my grand slams, I've gone to the Olympics. Not to mention our absolute domination in mixed doubles. I hate to admit it . . . but there's nothing left for me there.'

Me, I want to say. *Me! I'm still here. I still need you!*

She smiles and rubs her thumb over my knuckles. I can feel her calluses, a testament to how hard she's worked. The sun moves out from behind a cloud and the light graces Phoebe's face, makes her dark eyes shine with warmth. Something inside of me aches. I'm going to miss this woman so much it physically hurts.

'It's time to give the other girls a chance.' Emotion crackles through her voice. She squeezes my hand. 'It's time.'

'I don't want to do this without you,' I admit.

'I'll still be cheering you on. Just from the sidelines.'

'But you won't be there. Not like you normally are.' There'll be no more drunken rendezvous after we both crash out of a tournament; no more award ceremony red carpets; no more late-night practice sessions; no more rushing through tournament crowds to watch each other's matches. I know she'll still support me, but it won't be like it was before.

What is wrong with me? She's going through so much, and I've sat here for the last five minutes wondering what it means for *me*.

'You're going to do amazing things, Gabriel, with or without me there,' she says. 'I need a break from the game. The tour. The lifestyle. I'd appreciate it if you kept this to yourself for now.'

'I will,' I promise. 'I'm pro at keeping things out of the media.'

Phoebe perks up at the change of conversation. 'Oh, can we talk about Andre now?'

'Andre is the last person I want to talk about,' I say, even though Phoebe's vibrating with excitement to talk about my love life. The story with Andre is rather pathetic: after being thoroughly humiliated by Lukas at Wimbledon, I'd drunkenly texted one of the security guards who'd given me his number for *purely professional reasons*. We'd met up at a bar and shared a few drunken kisses before going home—he had an early shift, I had a flight to Paris.

'It ended as fast as it started, and I haven't heard from him since.'

That's not the whole story, but I can't bear to tell Phoebe what really happened—that I overestimated my ability to do 'no-strings attached' and found myself thinking about him more than I cared to admit. I'd put my feelings on the line and told him I wanted to see him again—I'd be in London by September, maybe we could get drinks again?

I'd been immediately rejected.

Mortified, I deleted his number, and for weeks I was anxious my messages would appear on online gossip sites and Victor would find them. He'd tell Papa, and I'd never get to come out to them on my terms.

I'd been careless with my heart and my career, and it couldn't happen again. And as much as I may want *something* with *someone*, between the tour schedule and prep for the clay season, I don't have time for romance.

Phoebe, however, has the most annoying habit of seeing straight through me. 'There's nothing wrong with having a bit of fun.' She pauses. 'Have you told your father about, you know, liking guys yet?'

'No, I'm a—' I can't find the right word, though *coward* seems to surge up my throat, and I barely manage to catch it. I've tried to tell Papa I'm gay four times in the last two years, and each time I've baulked at the last minute. It is hard not being out to my family, or to the public. My paternal grandparents are conservative and while I think my father would understand and support me, there's a vicious little voice inside me that says, *But what if he doesn't?*

'Being gay doesn't affect how I play tennis, so why does it matter if I'm out or not?'

'You're right, it doesn't,' Phoebe says. 'But we weren't talking about tennis. We were talking about your life, Gabi.'

'It's one and the same.'

Phoebe makes a face and I know she doesn't believe me. I can't help but think back to yesterday; how a heated look from Noah had made my chest feel tight, had made a zip of adrenaline run through me when I'd thought he was flirting.

Phoebe continues, 'I know we aren't talking about tennis but . . . you coming out could do a lot for the sport, you know. And the kids who look up to you.'

Unlike me, Phoebe's always weaved social justice into her tennis. She's spent years representing plus-sized women in sport, and she was a spokesperson for the #StopAsianHate movement that swept the French Open last year. Her Instagram is a powerful force for good. Phoebe knows what words to say. She knows how to convince people of her point of view. She's brave and outspoken.

'I'm not like that,' I say, and sometimes I wonder if saying that makes me a bad gay.

'I just want you to be happy, Gabi. I want you to be free to explore connections without fear of being outed, and to find someone who realises how special and wonderful you are.' She caresses my hair affectionately, but I shrug her off, embarrassed. 'What you do is your choice, but I see how much you're hurting right now and I—' She swallows down her emotion. 'Well, it's just hard to watch.'

Of course, Phoebe would see what I'm desperately trying to hide; how much I'm struggling with the *want* building up inside me—for the championship, for a life I can't allow myself to believe could be mine, and, worst of all, for a quiet bartender I met barely twenty-four hours ago. Why can't I stop thinking about him? Why can't I ignore the pull of that dingy little bar?

'Stop being mushy.' I'm finally at my limit for all this emotional nonsense. 'Besides, I'll never find someone special on the tour. I have grand slams to win.'

The tour pace is relentless, and hardly conducive to dating.

Phoebe threads her fingers through mine and brings my hand up to her mouth, kissing the knuckles. 'When you find the right man, you suddenly have all the time in the world. Trust me.'

I shush her loudly as a nurse passes the doorway. 'If anyone sends an anonymous tip, we're in trouble.'

Phoebe chuckles. 'If there aren't rumours that you're the father of my baby by tomorrow morning, I'll be disappointed.'

'You're not, are you?' Papa asks from the doorway, a tray containing takeaway coffee cups in his hand. His eyes are wide and the colour's drained from his face. If it wasn't such a serious moment, I'd have burst out laughing at his horrified expression. Instead, my stomach clenches in fear; fear that if he had walked in a few moments earlier, he would have heard *everything*.

Phoebe drops my hand quicker than Sam Groth serving a ball. 'No, Mr Madani, Aaron and I got back together in June.'

He actually exhales in relief. 'Well, congratulations, Phoebe. I thought I'd walked in on a little secret just then.'

A nervous bubble of laughter escapes me. 'No! No secrets here.'

Papa looks from Phoebe to me, clearly aware that he's missed something. Phoebe bites her lip, trying to hide her smile.

6

NOAH

It's forty-one degrees in the city. The air is stagnant; there's no breeze, no reprieve. Just heat. From inside the carriage, I watch commuters crowd towards the doors as the train pulls up to the platform, desperate to board. It's common courtesy to move to the side and let passengers get off first, and I glare at a sweaty businessman who dares to push past me as I disembark at South Yarra station.

While some establishments might prepare for a trickle of customers once they open, I . . . polish cutlery. I wipe down the shelves. Dust the tops of the televisions. Check the undersides of chairs for bubble gum: *Clean! Just like last week!*

Eventually, I make my way to the piano at the top of the stairs. It's a Brodmann baby grand, stylish and petite. Mark had planned to throw the instrument out on the street for anyone to take until I'd gently talked him down; even in its current condition, it would fetch eight grand on the second-hand market. Of course, Mark had only half listened to me. He'd listed it on Gumtree for almost double what I'd suggested, and it's sat here ever since.

After wiping down the lid and fallboard with a damp cloth, I pull the bench from where it's tucked away under the keys, and with my heart hammering in my chest, take a seat.

I find the ledge of the fallboard and pull it up, revealing the keys. My fingers fall into the C position. I'm just checking the piano is in good working order, I tell myself. For the listing.

I press down on the keys, and a slightly out-of-tune C-chord rings through the bar. The piano desperately needs maintenance but that's unsurprising given its condition. On a whim, I play the first few notes of Tchaikovsky's *Swan Lake*, one of the first pieces I learnt. Truthfully, I expect it to feel weird. I haven't played seriously in ages, but to my surprise the *feeling* of playing comes back to me quickly. It's muscle memory, I guess.

Soon, whatever nerves I felt when I first sat down at the piano begin to melt away. It feels like it used to; I'm confident and skilful and finally *good* at something. At school, I was never the art kid, or the sport kid, or the English kid. I never had a natural talent for anything—until I began playing the piano. The more I practised, the better I got.

My fingers move nimbly, the vibration of the keys travelling up my fingertips to my hands, my arms. The piano meets every note, like it's sat here for the last four months just begging for someone to play it again, and now we're caught up in a dance neither of us wants to break. The music moves through me, just like it used to, just like—

'Working hard, I see.'

I jump, and the fallboard drops over the keys with a *bang*, the lip barely missing my fingers. Whirling around, I see Peaches leaning against the doorway, looking smug.

'Hey, you.'

'Shit, you scared me half to death,' I gasp, heart still racing.

Today, Peaches sports an apple-green bob that curls around her jawline. Her flowy white-and-yellow daisy dress is ruffled by the warm breeze that blows through the open doorway, and she's switched her black pumps for a pair of canary-yellow strappy heels.

'Please, don't let me stop you.' She nods towards the piano. 'Play on.'

I roll my eyes and stand up, pushing the bench back underneath the piano. 'The usual?' I ask as I descend the stairs.

'You know me, darling,' she says with a smile. 'You should really start me on a loyalty card or something.'

I slip behind the bar and make up her gin and tonic. 'Mark doesn't value loyalty.'

'He should.' Peaches takes a sip of her drink and lets out a satisfied little sigh. I can't help but notice her hot-pink nails. 'As always, your talents are wasted here. When did you learn to play the piano?'

'I started lessons when I was thirteen.'

'Can you play anything else?'

'A couple of things.' I grab the vodka bottles from the shelf to dust them. You know business is shit when your vodka is on the shelf long enough to get dusty.

'You're being cagey about this, darling. Why?' Peaches asks over the lip of her glass.

'I dunno, it's just . . .' It's hard to find the words to describe how piano saved me at school. My best memories were school performances when I'd play so fast my fingers would hurt, and for a moment—a single, glorious moment—people would talk about how well I played, and not about anything else.

'My dad drank a lot; my home life was less than ideal growing up. The dream was always to play professionally—in a band, or maybe in an orchestra—but,' I glance around Mark's shitty sports bar, 'since moving to Melbourne, things haven't gone to plan. Maybe I was a little naïve but I thought there would be more . . . opportunity.'

Peaches's gaze slides back up to the piano. 'Play me a little.'

Heat floods my cheeks. 'I'm not sure.' It's one thing to play alone and another to play for an audience, even if it is only Peaches.

'Just a little,' she presses. 'I'll keep asking until you do.'

Of that, I have no doubt. Maybe it's better to just get it over with. 'Fine.'

Peaches whoops in excitement as we make our way back up the staircase and huddle together on the landing. I take a seat at the bench as Peaches closes the door, flicking the 'open' sign to 'closed' for good measure.

'You know, I've always wanted to play in a little jazz band,' Peaches muses, swishing her drink around.

'Can you sing?' I ask as I roll up my sleeves.

'I can hold a tune or two. Do you know any jazz-singing drag queens, darling? It'd be a hoot.' She swallows down the rest of her drink and leaves the frosty glass on top of the piano.

That makes me smile. 'Can't say I do.'

My fingers hover over the keys as I run through the scores I've memorised before settling on the 'Boogie Woogie Stomp', an upbeat and repetitive swing by Albert Ammons. At first, I start out a little wobbly but soon my fingers dance across the keys, quick and sure. Then the swing kicks in. Something takes over my body and I lean over the keys as the song unravels beneath me. I love this feeling. God, I can't believe I ever stopped playing—everything in me screams that this is what I'm meant to do.

'Hot damn, kid,' Peaches says. 'You're bloody good.'

But then, I miss a note, then two or three, and wind down the piece. Peaches claps beside me and the sound echoes around the empty bar in a way that's kinda creepy.

'That was incredible.' She sounds a little breathless. It's a simple melody with repetitive chords, a song I learnt one afternoon at school, but I'm not about to tell her that. 'You have a real talent, Noah.'

My face warms at her compliment. Shit, I might be blushing. 'Thanks.' I turn back to the keys, running my fingers over the smooth surface. 'I was scared I'd lost it.'

Peaches squeezes my shoulder. 'Playing music is like riding a bike, sugar. You always know how.'

We make our way back down to the bar. I take a half-full tray of washed glasses from the dishwasher and begin loading them back onto the shelf under the bar when my fingers brush against something soft. Frowning, I pull out Gabriel's black Nike cap.

Peaches frowns. 'Someone leave that here?'

I turn the cap over in my hands. 'Yeah. It's not really my style. You want it?'

'Please, have you ever seen me in a cap?' Peaches knows full well I've never seen her out of drag. 'You're one to talk about style. Don't you own a pea coat?'

I scoff in mock offence. 'They'll come back in fashion! Besides, mine is vintage.'

'Just because you bought it at Savers doesn't mean it's vintage.'

I turn the cap over in my hands, studying it. Gabriel probably doesn't miss it. A small part of me had wondered—even hoped—he might come back for it; that he'd left it here as an excuse to return.

With a huff I stash it under the register. One cute guy gives me googly eyes across a bar, and suddenly I'm creating this complex romantic narrative where he's formulating ways to 'accidentally' run into me on purpose? I really need to get laid.

Peaches leaves soon after, and Mark rears his drunken head around seven. It's later than I expected, which is good because I'll get paid for a few hours' work, but bad because he's had more time out on the town. A few of his buddies are with him. One of them, Troy, is a real estate mogul developing a new entertainment complex in Dandenong. They're bulldozing a heritage cinema to make it happen, and every other day I'm invited to 'Save Dandenong Cinema!' events on Facebook.

The other friend introduces himself as George. Tall and broad and in his mid-forties, he reeks of strong cologne and cigarette smoke.

Mark pushes open the door to the back room, and I sense that he's upset about something. A moment later, the televisions flicker on, and my heart sinks. Damn, between Peaches and the piano, I forgot to turn them on.

'I told you to keep the TVs on!' Mark shouts as he re-emerges. 'How many times do I have to tell you? We're bleeding money, Noah.'

'People aren't coming in because of . . .' I glance to see what's on the TV, 'someone playing tennis on a slightly bigger screen than they have at home.'

'Agreed,' says Troy before Mark can reprimand me for my backchat. 'This'd be a great nightclub. Hidden down in the basement, just off Chapel Street. A rebranding, good PR campaign and some models on opening night and you'd be laughing.'

I dread to think about droves of people scuffing up the beautiful hardwood floors. I love clubs as much as the next young gay kid, but there's something special about this place.

'The bar could be heritage-listed,' I say to Troy. 'I looked into it before—'

I stop myself from finishing my sentence: *Before Mark bought it*.

Graham had wanted the place to go to someone who would respect it. I'd investigated getting it heritage-listed to ensure it wouldn't become just another grotty nightclub—not that I have anything against them. But Peacock Lounge was *special*. It deserved a buyer who respects it. I have no idea if Mark was just a good bullshitter or if he was the best egg in a rotten carton.

Troy rolls his eyes. 'Most people don't care about heritage unless it's in a museum. They want new and fresh, not old and decrepit.'

'It used to be a jazz bar,' Mark says as he swipes a bottle of bourbon from behind the counter. 'No one gives a fuck about jazz, except for fags and old birds.'

I bite back my retort as Troy and George laugh. Mark pours them each a bourbon neat and then grabs the pack of cards from behind the counter.

'You're good to clock off, Noah. I'll close up,' Mark says. Troy settles in their usual booth and George goes into the back office to put on loud house music. It's too much for the speaker system, which buzzes on every hit of the bass.

I take my leave, still seething at the fag comment. It angers me that people still think and speak the way he does—he and his mates are the epitome of the average upper-class dickhead, rooted in old money, racism and homophobia. As I climb the stairs, I take a breath and will myself to let it go.

Stepping out onto the street, I squint as my eyes adjust to the brightness. The evening sun still holds a warm bite. A tram passes me, its bell dinging as it approaches the stop at the end of the block. I'm too late to catch it but the track runs all the way up the street and into the city, so I begin walking, weaving through the crowds of people, with a loose plan to catch the next tram that comes along.

'Noah!' Someone shouts my name from across the street.

I turn, scanning the crowd. Very few people know me here. Immediately, my pulse quickens. What if—

'Noah!'

Fear makes the hairs on the back of my neck stand up, and I begin to walk faster.

'Noah, over here!'

This time I hear the hint of an accent. Whirling around, I see a figure waving on the other side the road. *Gabriel.* For a moment, my brain freezes at the sight of him and it takes me a second to believe he's actually there, but suddenly he's jogging towards me, the wind tousling his loose curly hair. He's wearing a white tank top and a pair of fluoro-orange shorts, and the muscles in his thighs flex as he runs. Gabriel's fucking *ripped*. How hadn't I noticed that yesterday?

Probably because you were too busy making googly eyes at him, I think.

'I forgot my cap,' Gabriel calls as he jogs across the road. 'I hoped you were working. Is the bar closed?'

Just that he'd *hoped* I'd be working makes my cheeks warm. Or maybe it's this damn sun, still relentless even in the dying hours of the day.

'Mark's got a private function on,' I say. 'But I can go back and get your cap if you'd like. It's really no trouble.'

He hesitates, eyes darting down the road. 'No, don't,' he says, no doubt remembering how much of an ogre Mark was yesterday. 'I have a lot of caps, Noah.' The way he says my name; the way his tongue curls around the vowels, makes my stomach flip. 'But while I am here, would you like to have a drink with me?'

The words come out of Gabriel's mouth so quickly, a string of heavily accented French, that it takes me a moment to work out that he's maybe, kinda, sorta asked me out.

'A drink?' I repeat, like a fool.

Gabriel shoves his hands into his pockets and looks almost bashful. Flustered, even. 'If you would like.'

My heart, my traitorous little gay heart, does a half-skip at his words because yes, I would like it very much. Even as I remind myself that there's no indication whatsoever that Gabriel's queer—and that developing romantic feelings for straight guys is a recipe for disaster—I feel giddy.

'Yeah, why not. I know a place.' I'm astonished at how calm my voice sounds even though, on the inside, my intestines are twisting themselves into knots. 'Follow me.'

7

GABRIEL

It's not every day your best friend gets injured, tells you she's pregnant and then retires from the sport you grew up playing together. With my papa's ruthless training schedule and the first round of the tournament starting tomorrow, to say I'm a little on edge is an understatement.

Worst of all, I can't stop thinking about Noah and the hot ball of *want* that's burning a hole through my stomach. It's not logical, it's not anything I should allow . . . it just *is*.

Maybe if we spend a bit more time together, I'll pop the fantasy my brain is constructing without my permission, and finally focus on the tournament. That's the theory I'm testing, anyway.

But I have to admit, it's . . . *nice*. Nice to talk to someone who doesn't know who I am, or what I've done, or how much money I have in the bank.

The place Noah knows is a rooftop bar two blocks away from where we met. English ivy curls around the exposed iron beams that frame the bar, giving it an industrial, slightly apocalyptic 'the plants have taken over' feel. Giant palms and elephant ears are spaced along the walls, shading the low-lying tables from the evening sun. A cool mist filters down from the sprinklers that line the rafters.

We order—an IPA for Noah and a Coke for me—and find a seat.

'Cheers,' Noah says, raising his beer glass. I tap the edge of my glass to his, making sure our eyes meet, before taking a sip of Coke.

'How was work?' Noah asks. I like the way he talks about *work*, like it's just another day at the office and not one of the biggest slams of my career.

'I start tomorrow.' I pause before adding, 'I'm nervous that I won't be able to do a good job. That I'll . . . fail.'

'They wouldn't have had you come over if they didn't think you could do the job, would they?' Noah reassures me with a dimpled smile. 'I'm sure you'll do fine.'

'I hope so.' That's not how this works, but I'm not going to correct him. It's freeing to discuss tennis so openly, and there's something about Noah that makes me want to talk about myself, if it'll mean he tells me about himself in return. 'But I worry people have put their faith in me, and I won't be able to deliver what they want.'

Noah takes a sip of his beer. 'If you tried your best, then they gotta accept that and move on. I know that sounds stupid and clichéd, but shit happens.'

'Shit happens,' I repeat in agreement. 'And your job? Your boss is . . .'

Noah's expression darkens and he fidgets with the coaster

beneath his beer. 'He crossed the line when he pushed you and I'm sorry about that. I've got a new job in the pipeline but I love that bar. It killed me when Mark bought it.'

There's something Noah's not saying, and I want to tease it out. 'What would you do with the bar if you could?'

Noah gives me a look that says, *How much time do you have?*

'Tell me,' I prompt him.

He huffs out a laugh, and the end of his fringe flicks up. 'I'd revamp it into a jazz bar. Bring it back to its roots, you know? Revarnish the floors, get the piano tuned, serve decent cocktails, and get rid of those bloody awful TVs. We'd have live music every night. There wouldn't be a place like it in all of Melbourne, and there'd be people queuing out the door to get in.'

Passion dances through his words. It's beautiful to hear him speak about the bar with so much enthusiasm. Hot, even.

'But that's a pipe dream,' Noah says over the lip of his beer glass and his ambition deflates like a balloon. 'I could never afford it.'

'Is that your dream?' I ask. 'To open a bar?'

He presses his lips into a long, thin line and shakes his head. 'I dunno. I don't really have any dreams. Right now, I'm taking it one day at a time.'

'That is untrue. You just described a dream.'

'I described a *fantasy.* Not the same thing.' Sensing I'm not going to let it go, Noah turns the conversation back on me. 'What's your dream?'

I lick my lips, tasting the zing of lime from my Coke, and do my best not to squirm under his sudden interrogation. 'Recently, one of my dreams was to ski down a very hard track in the French Alps—I'm still not quite ready to take it on, but maybe next season.'

Noah considers my reply for a moment. 'I thought dreams had to be . . . big. Life-changing, you know?'

'Small dreams lead to big dreams.'

'Guess my current dream is to get a new job, then.' He drums his fingers on the table as if considering my words. 'What are you doing tomorrow night?' I must look particularly startled because he adds, 'You deserve to be shown the city by a local, you know? And I know all the best bits.'

Excitement blooms inside me. I've never really *seen* Melbourne, but a voice that sounds a lot like Victor's tells me this is a risk. People are dangerous and have different ways of getting what they want. But if Noah had wanted to hurt me, something tells me he would have done so already.

Or he's running a complicated and dastardly take-down plan that requires him to get close to me.

He smiles, and his dimple appears again. A sweet little pucker. I don't think he's got a dastardly plan, but at the same time . . . I could be down for something dastardly.

The thought makes me take a long drink. Didn't I just say to Phoebe that I have a grand slam to win? I'd pushed away her concerns about romance, convincing myself nothing would disrupt my focus. Now here I am, sitting at a bar, struggling to comprehend all the ways I *want* this.

If Phoebe finds out, she'll never let me live it down.

But she doesn't have to find out.

Besides, it's not like Noah's *interested* in me. Australians are notoriously friendly. This is standard friendly Australian hospitality. As long as I don't catch feelings for him, I'm safe.

'I'll be free tomorrow night,' I say. 'Seven o'clock?'

'Works for me.' Noah pulls out his phone. 'Can I add you on Insta?'

I hesitate. He notices.

'Or are you one of those guys who is too cool to have social media?' He eases off. If only he knew about my hair's Instagram page. 'It's okay. We can go old-school. Phone numbers. Texting.'

'No, it's fine,' I say as I pull out my phone. 'My Instagram is . . . um, hungrygabriel73.'

Noah laughs. 'A food account?'

It's my finsta. I have 112 followers. Mostly, they're people on the circuit and a few friends from school and home. 'It's just me and my friends documenting what we eat. Other stupid stuff,' I explain.

Noah types my handle into his phone, and it must appear because my own phone buzzes a moment later. 'I love stupid stuff. I'm NoAgenda.'

'Funny.' I accept him. There's nothing in my bio to suggest I'm anything but the person Noah thinks I am: a French guy working in International Relations who travels a lot. I click on his profile. His picture is a crude drawing of a cat, and his first and only photograph is of a dog. I click on it. The caption reads, *Always wanted to come home to a cute girl*.

'Wow, were you in Tokyo recently?' Noah asks. I realise he's doing the same thing. 'And New York too?'

'Yeah, I travel a lot but it's always just a couple of days here and there. I never stay very long.'

His mouth twitches as he puts down the phone. I follow his lead, glad to be done with the social media deep dive.

'Well, I better make my tour memorable. I'm gonna show you such a good time you're never gonna want to leave.'

My face goes hot at his words. I down the rest of my drink as my thoughts begin to spiral. What if Noah knows who I am, and he's playing a game of gay fish, throwing out lines like that just to see if I bite? The last thing I need on this tour is to wake up to rumours of my sexuality on gossip sites.

All because I couldn't resist a flirty bartender.

I need to get a grip.

I have a tournament to win.

Noah smiles at me across the table, eyes sparkling in the dying sun.

Just don't catch feelings, I remind myself as Noah drains the last of his beer. *You can do this.*

My first opponent is Nathan Derbin. He's number fifty-three in the world, and beat Marcus Allman in a gruelling five-set match during the qualifiers. In his spare time, he loves playing Dungeons & Dragons. I know because he's invited me to several games while on tour. One day, I tell myself, I'll take him up on his offer.

It's forty-two degrees on the first day of the Australian Open. The crowds are heavy, and play starts at exactly 11 am. We're on Show Court Nine, an open-air court on the left side of Melbourne Park, which means no air conditioners, no fans and no shade. It's us against each other, and both of us against the sun. This match needs to be quick if either of us has any chance of recovering to play well in the second round.

I make my way onto the cerulean astroturf, adjusting my clay-red Nike shirt as I meet Derbin by the net. One of the ball boys tosses a coin. I call heads and decide to serve. Papa's gaze follows me from the side of the court, his expression unreadable behind his dark glasses. I can't lose this match. I can't face boarding a plane and having to sit beside him, feeling the disappointment rolling off him in waves.

Derbin must lose.

I serve. The ball flies over the net and Derbin moves quickly to return it. We're off. Adrenaline races through my veins as I lunge forward to scoop the ball with my forearm. Nothing beats the thrill of the first point of the game, or the first match of a big tournament. There are eight matches that stand between me and the trophy: two weeks of sweat, blood and tears. But it all starts with this point.

Derbin miscalculates his backhand, and the ball lands out.

'Out,' calls the linesman.

'Fifteen–love,' the umpire says.

As we move through the first set, it's clear Derbin's not used to the relentless heat. On the sidelines, the audience cool themselves with Australian Open-branded fans but on the court, there's no relief.

I wipe the sweat from my brow as Derbin prepares to serve, squinting as he raises the ball to the sky.

'Fault,' the linesman calls as Derbin's ball hugs the centre service line.

He wipes the line of sweat from the top of his lip and prepares to serve again.

'Fault!'

Across the net, Derbin shakes his head and makes for his water bottle and towel. I do the same, rinsing the cottony dryness from my mouth.

I've trained most of my life in this dry heat. My grandparents have a tennis court on the top of their building in Algeria, and my father and I spent more afternoons than I can count practising under the beating sun during my childhood, playing in the smoky dusks and warm mornings.

Derbin loses the next three games. I'm up 4–0, but he steals the fifth game back in a flurry of rallies that push us both to the edge. We're panting by the end, sweating so profusely we drip onto the astroturf.

I feel the sweat travel down my spine and into my arse crack as Derbin prepares to serve. He raises his racquet into the air. I blink.

Derbin drops his racquet. And then his knees buckle.

'Break, medical break!' I manage to shout as I watch Derbin hit the ground, his body collapsing under him. The audience gasp, and someone jumps the fence to try to help.

'I'm a nurse!' she says to the umpire as she and I both hurry to Derbin's side.

The ball boy douses Derbin's towel with water from his drink bottle and presses it to his forehead as I help the nurse roll Derbin into the recovery position. Derbin coughs and vomits onto the court. Bile splashes onto my trainers.

Quickly, I grab Derbin's other towel from the box and shield his body from the prying eyes of the crowd. A ball kid does the same as we wait for the medics to arrive.

'This is so fucking embarrassing,' he groans. 'Fuck, did I vomit on you? I'm so sorry, Gabi.'

'Don't worry about it, it happens to everyone,' I assure him. It happened to me in 2016.

When the medic arrives, the nurse helps Derbin into the sit-down stretcher. As he's wheeled off the court, the crowd applauds, and Derbin gives them a weak wave.

While I don't like the circumstances of the win, I'm into the second round. I take a deep breath as I quickly gather my towel and water bottles from my station. The pressure's off, for now at least. Zipping up my tennis bag, I hoist it over my shoulder and plan a hasty exit—

—only to come face to face with Percy Jones, champion tennis player turned commentator. Wherever he goes, so does the camera.

'Welcome back to Melbourne Park, Gabriel,' Percy says in his thick Texan accent. 'That's your first round done and dusted; how do you feel?'

The most important thing about these wrap-up interviews is to stay diplomatic. Don't badmouth your opponent. Win graciously. Be a little funny if you can.

I put down my tennis bag and push back my hair. 'Um, well, it's a hard one because we didn't get to play the match all the way through, but Derbin is a skilled player, and it could have gone either way . . .'

Hungrygabriel73: *I finished work earlier than expected. Can we move dinner to 6.30?*

NoAgenda: *Sure. Meet me at Flinders St Station. On the steps. I know the best place.*

Hungrygabriel73: *Ok* ☺

NoAgenda: *I'll be the one wearing the avocado-print shirt.*

Hungrygabriel73: *Really?*

NoAgenda: *It's the best—I got it for $2!*

Hungrygabriel73: *Maybe a reason for this price.*

NoAgenda: *You will regret those words when you see it!!*

8

NOAH

'The famous avocado shirt,' Gabriel teases as he descends the staircase at Flinders Street Station and finds where I'm hidden beside the stairwell. He looks stylish as fuck in a white linen t-shirt, a pair of denim shorts, sunglasses and a khaki-green Lacoste cap.

I look down at my black avocado-print button-up, the shirt I told him I was wearing as though this was some kind of blind date and not the third time we'd seen each other in person in as many days. 'What? I needed to stand out from the crowd.'

His dark gaze takes me in. 'Mission accomplished.'

My chest grows tight. This isn't the first time he's left me breathless; Gabriel is gorgeous with a deep bronze complexion, thick curly hair and a jawline so sharp it could cut glass. The way he's looking at me over the top of his sunglasses makes my mouth dry and my shirt feel way too tight.

Gabriel quirks a brow as if he's oblivious to the panic he's awakened inside of me. Maybe offering to show him around the city was a bad idea. 'Shall we go?'

I swallow the lump in my throat as I push myself off the wall. 'Yes, um, it's not too far from here. Follow me.'

It's peak hour and swarms of people cross the busy intersection outside Flinders Street Station. Gabriel sticks close to me; so close that I feel the gentle brush of the back of his hand as it passes mine, once, and then twice. Every now and then, I get a whiff of Gabriel's citrusy cologne as it dances between us, tantalising me. All I can think about is how the cologne must smell against his skin and—damn, what is wrong with me? Suddenly, the crowd thins out and it's almost a relief to have space between us again.

'What's the secret place?' Gabriel asks as we continue down the street.

'You'll find out.'

He huffs a little. 'I don't like surprises.'

A busker plays an upbeat Dua Lipa cover on the other side of the street, and everything feels so *electric* and alive. Our hands touch again, and this time I glance at Gabriel. He looks at me, too, and I swear there's a spark between us: current charged by the pure vibes of a summery Melbourne evening.

'We're here.' I stop at the mouth of a damp, narrow lane full of graffiti.

'Um,' he says as he glances down at an upturned milk crate and a soiled poster for a stand-up comedy show. 'Are you going to murder me?'

I like the way his accent makes the question sound so innocent. 'Yes, Gabriel, I plan on murdering you in this brightly lit CBD alleyway during peak hour, so please don't scream too loud.' When he doesn't laugh, I grasp his forearm and tug him in. 'I'm joking. Come on. No one is murdering anyone.'

Gabriel sucks in a breath but follows me into the laneway. As we walk, the scummy brickwork transforms into, well, magic. An elaborate gang tag turns into a modern interpretation of the Virgin Mary, crimson roses curling around her portrait. Further down the alley, there's a painting of a French bulldog, a sunflower with curling yellow petals and an octopus fighting Godzilla.

Gabriel darts forward to stand in front of a pair of large painted wings. 'I've always wanted to do this,' he says as he hands me his phone.

'It's peak tourist,' I remind him as I snap a picture, ignoring the handful of unread messages that linger in his notification bar.

We walk past a long mural depicting a haunted graveyard, which eventually transforms into a landscape of rolling hills, sunbeams and rainbows. At one point we stop to watch a woman on a ladder paint a giant curling dragon around a second-floor window.

'Every time I come here, the art's different,' I tell Gabriel. 'It's like a living canvas.'

The smell of onion and garlic drifts down the laneway. 'Come on,' I lead Gabriel towards the street, 'I want to show you my favourite place in Melbourne.'

Across the road, the word *GYROS* flashes on a neon sign above a small brick shop. A queue curls around the block as a young man with a booming voice calls out order after order through a small window.

'This is a Melbourne staple: hole-in-the-wall gyros,' I assure Gabriel. 'It's worth it.'

'I'm sure it is,' he replies. Gabriel takes out his phone and I see a message from someone named Lukas appear on the screen. My thoughts instantly spiral. Who is Lukas—a friend? A colleague? His boyfriend?

I pull up the menu on my phone and hand it to him, making him abandon the message he's typing to Lukas. 'Have a look. You can't go wrong. Everything's good here.'

Gabriel peers at my screen. 'What do you recommend?'

'I mean, you could go classic. Marinated lamb, garlic sauce, Greek salad . . .' He hands me back the phone. 'Or you could try the spicy chicken—a bit of a deviation from the usual, but—'

'You've convinced me,' he interrupts. 'The lamb.'

'That was easy,' I laugh. We move forward in the line.

'I'm easily convinced.' He turns to me, sinking his hands into his pockets. God, he's so effortlessly cool in his billowy linen t-shirt that standing next to him in my lame avocado-print shirt is making me self-conscious. 'What did you do today? Did you get the new job you were thinking about?'

'Not yet,' I say. 'But I walked my housemate's dog, did my laundry. Boring things.' The line moves forward again. 'How was your first day?'

'It was . . .' He pauses, as if looking for the right word. 'Surprising. In a good way.'

Before I can respond, we get to the window. I lean over and relay our order to Angelos, the chef, shouting over the noise of the kitchen, and then his daughter swings by with an EFTPOS machine. Gabriel stands behind me, looking stunned at both the efficiency and the chaos of the entire process.

I grab two milk crates on the other side of the alleyway and tip them over, indicating for Gabriel to sit.

'Peak Melbourne culture is eating gyros on a milk crate in a dirty laneway,' I explain as he eyes our seats with suspicion. 'Don't ask me why, it just is.'

'I see.' Gabriel sits down beside me, and our knees brush. He looks up at me, as if he wants to say something. 'Noah, I—'

'NOAH!' the chef, Angelos, calls from the window. He grins as I approach him, sweat dripping down his brow. 'Good to see you!'

'You know I can't stay away, Angelos.' I take the gyros, the heat of the wrap seeping through the thin paper.

'Enjoy, my friend,' Angelos says before he turns back to the crowd and shouts, 'ZOE!'

Returning to Gabriel, I hand him one of the wraps. 'I desperately hope I haven't hyped it up too much.'

Gabriel unwraps his gyros carefully and waits until I've taken a bite before taking one himself. Then he takes another one, and another, and soon he's practically inhaled it.

'Amazing.' He groans. 'It's like . . . the best gyros I've ever had, *anywhere*.'

Pride bubbles through me. 'I told you.'

I take another bite and sauce drips from the bottom of the wrap and onto my finger. Without thinking, I raise my hand to my mouth and lick off the juice. When I look up, I realise Gabriel's watching me.

Heat rushes to my face and I stand up. 'I'll grab us some serviettes,' I mutter, and without waiting for his response, I stride towards the window to grab a handful of serviettes from the dispenser.

Suddenly, Angelos bursts into the laneway, waving his phone in the air. 'Boys, we must get a photo!'

Gabriel looks at me, confused.

'It's easier just to say yes.'

Angelos fidgets with his phone for a moment, figuring out how to use the front-facing camera. Eventually, Gabriel helps him get us all in frame, and takes the picture.

'Thank you, my boy!' says Angelos. 'This one is going on the wall!'

Gabriel smiles kindly, patiently, like he's a celebrity meeting an adoring fan. When Angelos leaves, Gabriel turns back to me. 'What's "the wall"?'

'It's his favourite customer wall. Famous people, regulars, people he thinks are cool.' I indicate the window where, inside, dozens of photos are tacked above the gyros wrapping station. 'Now we'll be up there too. Maybe we'll go next to the photo of Chris Hemsworth.'

'One can only dream.' He slips his glasses back on, and I realise, *Fuck I like him*. Like, *really* like him. 'What do we do now?'

I check my phone. It's only eight. 'Do you think you still have room for dessert?'

Gabriel grins. Seems he's living up to his Instagram handle: Hungrygabriel73. 'Always.'

♪

@CelebSpotr: Spotted! Tom Holland spotted in Tribeca—looks like the movie is back on!
@CelebSpotr: Spotted! Meg Ryan and Tina Fey having coffee in London. Low-key but chic as usual. Tina asked for her order to be remade.
@CelebSpotr: Spotted! Tennis cutie Gabriel Madani demolishing a kebab with a friend in Melbourne.
@CelebSpotr: Spotted! LeBron visiting home town with family. Looking chill.

9

GABRIEL

The last rays of the sun stream through the glass roof of the old arcade, scattering rainbows onto the delicate mosaic flooring.

Noah opens the door to a small but chic bakery and the heavenly scent of vanilla and cinnamon hits me. Trays of doughnuts line the vintage glass cabinets: cinnamon, classic glaze, jam-filled, custard-filled, chocolate glaze. As we browse the selection, the flavours get more eccentric: 'Summer Fields'—a classic glaze with musk filling; 'Piña Colada' with rum and coconut filling; and the 'Mike Wazowski': a green-iced doughnut with a large fondant eye where the hole should be.

'I'm thinking the "Coyote Ugly"; the whiskey-glazed caramel,' Noah says. 'Get two and split them?'

What calories Papa doesn't know about won't hurt him. Besides, it's not like I won't burn them off tomorrow. 'I'll have the Nutella and pretzel.' I reach behind to grab my wallet. 'I buy this time.'

After I purchase the doughnuts, Noah leads me through a secret passage beneath Flinders Street Station that opens onto the delta of the Yarra River. We sit on the edge of the boardwalk, our legs dangling above the water but not quite touching the surface. Lights glitter on the river; the sun is now almost gone and the sky is a marble of navy blues and baby pinks. Noah grabs his doughnut from the bag and, without ceremony, breaks it in half. Custard oozes down his fingers as he hands me half.

'Mind the fingers,' he says.

I take the half from him. 'What do you mean?'

Noah grins as he sucks custard from his fingertips. I don't know why but something in me goes hot at the sight of his lips wrapping around his finger, I—

—I need to get a grip.

'It's a way of apologising for using my fingers,' he explains. ''Cause it's not very polite.'

'Oh, it's okay.' Strange Australian sayings.

As I bite into the doughnut, I'm immediately hit with the strong whiskey-flavoured custard. Then comes the sweetness, the sugar, the cinnamon. As we eat, Noah points out a few landmarks: the casino and its flame towers; an island named Ponyfish; the lights of the MCG.

'Melbourne Cricket Ground,' Noah explains helpfully. 'I'm not big on sport, but it's a big deal here.'

I grab the Nutella doughnut and break it in half the same way Noah did. As we both bite into it, he groans in appreciation.

'Your pick wins,' he murmurs through a mouthful of doughnut. A gentle breeze tousles his hair, and he pushes a stray lock behind his ear. Noah has a very lovely profile; long, dark lashes, a thin angular nose with an upturned tip, full lips, chiselled chin.

'You wanna do something tomorrow, too?' Noah asks, and before I can answer, he has brought up a list of tourist experiences on his phone. 'We could do the Skydeck, or a tour of the MCG? Looks like they just built a new sports museum if you like sports.'

'I don't mind tennis,' I admit. 'But you don't like sports.'

He chuckles, shaking his head. 'This isn't my tour of Melbourne, Gabriel.'

For a moment, I wonder if Noah's playing with me. If he knows exactly who I am, and this is all a ruse.

I hate to be the one to scream, 'Don't you know who I am?' but seriously, if Angelos knew who I was, and deemed me worthy to go on the wall next to Chris Hemsworth, then what game is Noah playing?

Suddenly, I'm frustrated. Frustrated that he might be playing this long con and I can't tell if he is or not, frustrated that I'm suddenly the kind of guy who thinks, *Don't you know who I am?*, but most of all, I'm frustrated that I think the possibility of a guy liking me for me isn't an option.

Tennis.

Tournaments.

Glory.

Everything's getting confusing, fast. The only option I have is to extract myself from this entire situation. I get up. 'Noah, I have to go.'

Noah stumbles to his feet, clearly taken aback by my

emotional one-eighty, which makes two of us. 'Oh, okay. So I'll text you about the MCG tour?'

'I'll message you,' I promise, even though I know I won't, and because that thought feels so completely arsehole-ish, I add, 'I had a nice time.'

Immediately, I don't know why I said it like *that* because this wasn't a date. There was no way this was a date, and Noah's not gay and I'm not falling for a straight guy, and—

Tennis.

I take a mental breath.

But then Noah smiles, his face lit by the lights that reflect off the Yarra, and says, 'I had a nice time, too,' and the warmth in the pit of my stomach spreads, into my chest and arms, and lower—

Oh dear.

This is not good.

Papa's still awake when I get home. He's sitting on the lounge nursing a glass of port like a disapproving parent waiting for their recalcitrant child in the early hours of the morning. Except I'm an adult, and it's nine-thirty.

'Enjoy your night?' he asks as soon as I step through the door. I wonder if he can smell the doughnut on me; if he knows I've been seduced by sugar and carbs and betrayed my high-performance diet.

Victor suddenly bursts from his bedroom with a sheet mask stuck to his face. 'You're home!' he exclaims. 'How is Lukas?'

Lukas?

Victor's hard gaze is unwavering, and I realise that he's *lied* to Papa for me.

'Y-yes, he's good. We went out for dinner and saw a bit of the city,' I say. Twenty-five years old and I'm still making up stories about where I've been and who I've been with. 'I'm going to shower and go to bed. Big day tomorrow.'

Papa nods and turns back to his port, seemingly happy to let the conversation go. I close my bedroom door and press my head against the wood grain. Everything suddenly feels so confusing, I just want to scream. I came here to play tennis; I'm into the second round, and yet all I can think of is—

The room's stiflingly hot, so I open the window and let in the cool night air before flopping onto the bed and pulling out my phone. I know Lukas texted me earlier about meeting up to hit a few balls around, and I left him on 'read'. As I open my phone to reply to him, I'm shocked to see that Noah's messaged me.

Maybe I don't have to cut him off completely. Maybe I can keep texting him while focusing on tennis.

NoAgenda: *So I might have a new job. Dare me to quit the old one tomorrow?*

Hungrygabriel73: *Double dare.*

NoAgenda: *Wow, way to up the stakes.*

Hungrygabriel73: *Where is the new job?*

NoAgenda: *A queer bar in the city. My friend works there.*

Queer. I can't help but focus on the word.

Hungrygabriel73: *Are you*

No. Too forward. I delete the words. Try again.

Hungrygabriel73: *Sounds like a fun place—do they only hire gay people?*

What in the world is wrong with me? Get a grip, Gabi. I delete that message, too.

Hungrygabriel73: *Sounds like my vibe.*

I hit *Send* before I talk myself out of it. My response says both something and absolutely nothing; it's flawlessly crafted to ensure plausible deniability should my words appear in the press.

NoAgenda: *It's my vibe, too.*

NoAgenda: *I think it's important there are places where people can feel safe to be themselves.*

Then he sends an emoji of the Pride flag and my stomach clenches. This is dangerous territory. Besides my fling with Andre, the only other person who knows I'm gay is Phoebe. Letting Noah so close feels like a recipe for disaster—but at the same time, I want to know what it feels like to be myself, just this once, without any of the other baggage that comes with fame.

Hungrygabriel73: *I had a lot of fun tonight. Thank you for showing me the city.*

Does that sound sappy? Maybe that's too much. I cringe as Noah types, and then stops, the three dots disappearing from the screen.

NoAgenda: *Me too.*

I realise I'm smiling at the screen. Smiling at the stupid cat drawing Noah uses as a profile picture. I wish he'd use his own photo. I wish I could see him right now.

NoAgenda: *Listen, I'll be frank—I'd like to see you again.*

My heart falters. I read the message again, and again, until another comes through.

NoAgenda: *If you'd like that.*

NoAgenda: *If your work allows and you're not getting on a flight home tomorrow.*

I can't help but smile at his message. If I want this friendship with Noah to have any chance of moving forward, I have to put myself out there. How much longer am I going to allow being afraid to stop me from getting what I really want? And right now, I want to explore this; whatever it is.

Hungrygabriel73: *I'd like to see you again, too.*

And then, mustering up my courage, I add an emoji of the Pride flag to the end of my sentence, and send it back. Noah sees it. He heart reacts the message.

I guess that's that.

NoAgenda: *So MCG? Tomorrow?*

Hungrygabriel73: *Can I let you know? I'm not sure what will happen at work.*

NoAgenda: *Sure. The MCG tour is on a few times a day and now that the tennis is on, you can get a ticket to the general grounds for free when you book. Might be fun?*

'Gabriel, Gabriel, Gabriel,' Victor tuts as I emerge from my bedroom, hair wild and my body severely in need of caffeine. 'The cards are not happy today.'

There's no way I can humour Victor's bungled tarot readings without coffee. Especially after what happened yesterday. 'Are they still plotting my demise?'

'Worse,' he mutters. So much for no bad readings. 'There's a storm brewing on the horizon. A conflict. A battle.'

The coffee machine whirrs to life and golden nectar drips slowly from the spout. 'O'Lachlan will be hard to beat,' I say.

Victor shakes his head. 'I've already asked the cards about your match—they responded favourably, of course. This is telling me about what's in store for your immediate future.'

I take my coffee from the machine and walk to Victor's side. There are three cards on the table in front of him: the Wheel of Fortune, the Emperor and Judgement.

'An inevitable rebellion against authority or rules,' Victor translates.

I scoff and grab a banana from the fruit bowl. 'It's not like I'm going to the dark side.'

'You are a young Padawan, and I've heard you fighting with Obi-Wan.'

'They're cards, Victor. Also, I didn't tell you to lie to Papa about where I was last night. You could have told him the truth.'

That makes him sit up straighter. 'You're right. What *is* the truth, Gabriel?'

He only says my name when he wants to make a point. 'That I was out for a walk,' I say lightly.

'Long walk.'

'Big city.'

He snorts and shakes his head. 'I know how intense your father can be, and Lukas was an easy scapegoat. He agreed to go along with it.'

I'll have to thank Lukas later.

'Do I have to arrange for someone to sign an NDA?' Victor asks as he packs away the cards. 'I don't care what you're doing, just as long as you're being safe.'

'What? *No.*'

Victor pins me with his intense blue-grey gaze as he reshuffles the cards. 'I understand why you might not want to tell your father the truth, whatever it is, but you can tell me. If there's any chance of . . . *fallout*,' he uses the words carefully, 'then I should know. And she should sign an NDA.'

She. I'm sure it's just a slip of the tongue but it's a stark reminder of everything I have on the line.

'There's no girl,' I tell him, and hope my tone is firm enough that he'll back off. 'I just need a bit of space. I lost track of time; it won't happen again.'

Victor looks me up and down and, finally, nods once. 'All right.'

The security guard opens the gate to the training court, keeping control of the spectators as I slip past him. Lukas is on the other side of the court, signing photographs and tennis balls and caps. Dropping my training bag at my station, I suck down a mouthful of water and slip my racquet from its cover.

'Hey, you dirty little liar,' Lukas taunts as he jogs over.

'Thanks for covering for me last night,' I say quietly. 'I appreciate it.'

Lukas fishes a couple of balls from his bag and stuffs them into his pants pocket. 'I get it. Shoot me a text if you want to hit the beach on our off days. Freyja and I hired a couple of boards, rented a car and went out surfing. The beaches here are incredible.'

I pull on my headband. 'I'll let you know.' I nod at the court. 'The usual?'

We have a set program when we practise together during tournaments. Lukas and I have trained together since we met at Indian Wells when we were ten. Lukas, already a strong player in the juniors' circuit, was a ballboy in the 2008 Federer versus Fish match. Papa and I had come over to watch the tournament and work with the tennis academies in the States for the summer, and Lukas and his twin, Freyja, had moved from Stockholm to Florida permanently to train.

Some people might think it's silly to train with your rival, but hey, Serena trained with Venus and it worked out well for both of them.

Lukas nods. 'I'll serve.'

As I make my way to the baseline, I see Freyja and Lukas's coach slip into the court, taking a seat near our bags. Freyja's close behind, dressed in her court gear with her blonde hair in an intricate braid. She must have just played.

I wonder how she feels about Phoebe's absence. Happy, no doubt, and probably a little guilty for being so happy. She's yet to win a slam and now there's one less competitor on the circuit.

Lukas and I train for the better part of half an hour, and he throws in a trick shot here and there. Lukas wouldn't be Lukas if he didn't put on a show for the crowd, and the large audience that's made its way to the practice court is very appreciative.

'Your second serve is still flat,' Freyja tells Lukas as we make our way back to our bags. Lukas's coach nods in agreement.

'Hey, hey, don't trash-talk me in front of my opponent,' Lukas whines.

Freyja turns to me. 'Heard about your match against Derbin. That sucks.'

'It is not fun to win like that,' I reply. 'How did you do today?'

'I won,' she chirps. Freyja's always been a woman of few words. Succinct, just like her tennis. She plays a hard, precise game and she doesn't joke around. It's the complete opposite of Lukas's playing style, but when they pair up, somehow their doubles partnership works.

'I miss Phoebe,' she continues. 'It would have been nice to beat her.'

Knowing Freyja, that's a warm compliment. Pulling off my headband, I shove it into my dirty laundry pouch and zip the cover on my racquet.

'What are you doing tonight?' Lukas asks. 'You coming to watch me?'

I raise an eyebrow. 'Did you watch me?'

'*Yes.*'

'On the TV,' Freyja elaborates.

Watching Lukas is the only thing my father would allow me to do without his supervision, I consider. And at least this time, it wouldn't be a lie. 'I'll be there. Hope you lose.' I shoot him a grin.

'I'll make sure they save you a seat in my corporate box.' Lukas smiles back as he throws his bag over his shoulder. 'How does it feel to walk through these grounds and see *my* face everywhere? I *own* this park, Gabriel.'

'I saw your face directing people to the toilets,' Freyja says dryly as we exit the training court. 'Very glamorous.'

'He's still upset about being named the second-hottest player on the tour,' I reply.

Lukas bristles. 'Next season, I'm growing out my hair. I'll be the next Björn Borg, just you wait.'

10

NOAH

Something feels off about today. For one, it's cooler. Maybe the sudden drop in temperature has me on edge. But there's also this *feeling* in the air. It's an uneasiness I can't quite describe. Things begin to go wrong: Sadie vomits in the hallway as I leave for work. The train runs late for no apparent reason. I step in gum and it's all soft and stringy. They're small things but they all seem to stack on top of one another until I can't shake the sense of dread.

It's probably all in my head. That's what happens when you have an incredible night—the next morning feels . . . lame. Nothing compares to the moment I turned to Gabriel and saw him staring back at me, with city lights shimmering in the water behind us, his dark hair framing his face. I wish I could go back there. I wish I could live in that night, that moment, forever.

But I can't, and right now my reality is a shitty six-hour shift. The letter outlining my two weeks' notice is tucked safely in my satchel, and I plan to hand it to Mark at the end of the shift before grabbing an Uber home to get ready to meet up with Gabriel.

There's music playing when I arrive at work, I hear it faintly through the heavy wooden door. Strange, but Mark's been known to leave it on. Grabbing my key, I unlock the door. It doesn't budge.

Frowning, I try my key again and the door audibly unlocks. Shit. Mark must have had a serious bender last night if he hadn't bothered to lock up.

Preparing myself to find the place ransacked, I push the door open.

Instead, I'm hit by the stench of something rancid.

Flicking on the lights, I try to pinpoint what the source of the smell could be: a dead possum, deep in the labyrinth of building vents, or a backed-up toilet. It smells weirdly . . . familiar. As I descend the staircase, I realise what it is . . .

It's Mark.

My satchel falls to the ground. I rush towards where Mark's slumped over a table. His skin is pallid and cool. Without thinking, I haul him out of the booth and onto the floor. His vomit follows him, dripping across the hardwood floor.

'Mark!' I yell into his face. My fingers search for a pulse on his neck, slippery in his chunky vomit and saliva, but I don't really know *where* I'm supposed to place my fingers because there's nothing. He's unnaturally cold and there's just *nothing*.

'Mark!' I hit his face. Hard. I'm not sure if I'm supposed to do that, but it's all I can think of. He doesn't respond.

Scrambling back to my satchel, I grab my phone and quickly dial triple zero. As the phone rings, I hold my fingers under Mark's nostrils, trying to feel if he's breathing.

'*Ambulance, fire or—*'

'Ambulance,' I tell the operator immediately. I hear the phone reconnect, and an officer comes on the line.

'Ambulance. What's your location?'

'A bar called Mark's Place, on Prince Close. Just off Chapel Street.' I wedge the phone between my shoulder and ear as I turn Mark on his side. 'Hurry; I don't think he's breathing.'

'Okay,' says the operator. 'We're going to commence CPR. You need to listen to me very carefully.'

♪

Never knew how to do CPR until today. Didn't think I'd do it on Mark. Didn't think it would be the thing that saved his life. Didn't expect to save anyone's life, really. Who does?

The paramedics carry the stretcher up the stairs and roll Mark out of the bar. He's barely conscious but after twenty minutes of CPR, they've deemed him stable enough to be transported.

The red and blue lights of the ambulance flash. A few people stand on the corner and watch as Mark is loaded into the back of the vehicle. One of the paramedics claps me on the back.

'You right, mate?' he asks. 'You did a good job. Saved his life.'

'Yeah, I, um . . .' I look down at the keys in my hand. 'I think I'm just going to close up.'

He hands me a brochure that says *What to do after a medical emergency* and squeezes my shoulder. Then the ambulance siren whirls and the vehicle pulls away from the kerb.

I look back to the bar. The door's wide open and music still plays on the speaker system. Someone needs to clean up in there and it's obviously not going to be Mark.

With a sigh, I head to the office in search of the cleaning gear. My shoe hits a bottle. It clinks against another one. Looking down, I realise the floor's littered with empty beer bottles—there are at least a dozen scattered around the small office.

Carefully moving the bottles out of the way, I grab a large rubbish bag and find the mop and bucket. Then, I start the tedious task of cleaning up.

Fun fact: baking soda is great at absorbing smells, especially in patches of vomit. Growing up, we always had a box on hand in the cupboard, wedged between the flour and sugar, even though my mother never baked. Occasionally, I'd walk over a spot in our carpet and feel fine powder between my toes.

It's almost four in the afternoon when I've finally finished cleaning the vomit and tidying up. Nothing will save the velvet cushion on the booth, but it's the best I can do. I close the door to Mark's Place behind me, throwing the rubbish bag in a dumpster in the alley, and let out a long breath.

One way or another, I know that's the end of that chapter of my life. I'm nervous to start the job at the Rosewood, but it's gotta be better than giving your non-responsive boss CPR in a puddle of his own vomit.

Unsure what to do with myself, I walk for several blocks until I come across a park. I find a shady place under a gum tree, its thick trunk comfortingly solid behind me.

After a while, I pull the brochure the paramedic gave me out of my pocket. *Our priority is to get the patient to hospital as quickly as possible, but here are some services that might help—*

I'm sure Mark will be okay.

When Dad went to hospital the first time—and every time after—I hadn't wanted him to come home. When I was about nine, I remember trying to pray after an influential school scripture lesson. Surely God just didn't know what my dad was doing, or what he was like. If I told God, he'd know it was wrong and he'd make my dad go away. I was naïve, but I was also nine, and as time passed and my prayers went unanswered, my opinion of religion soured. Eventually I turned away. After all, I've always had daddy issues—why not just lump my beef with the heavenly father in with those?

I pull out my phone to check the time and, realising it's close to five, pull up my chat with Gabriel.

You still keen to hang?

Gabriel responds after a few minutes.

Meet me at the hotel I'm staying at—Southern Apartments. As soon as you can?

I look down at my clothes. They're dirty, and I probably reek of sweat and vomit. I reply, *Will do. Give me 30 or so.*

Quickly, I duck into a shop on Chapel Street and buy the cheapest clothes I can find: a pair of boxy tan shorts, a rust-coloured t-shirt, a pair of white canvas shoes and white socks. Then, I throw it all on the counter and ask the shop assistant if I can change in the store's dressing-room. She agrees with a chuckle, and after stuffing my disgusting work clothes into a spare bag, I drop them back at Mark's Place for him to do with what he sees fit. Finally, I pop into a pharmacy to spritz some free cologne before catching the tram to Gabriel's hotel.

Gabriel's in the lobby when I arrive at six. He's leaning against a wall, eyes cast down as he taps out a message on his phone and I can't help but wonder who he's texting. He's wearing a pair of ripped jean shorts, a grey Adidas t-shirt and a pair of chunky white sneakers. Today, he's pulled his hair into a high messy bun, stray curls falling over his eyes and down the nape of his neck. He looks good.

More than good.

Gabriel glances up from his phone, sees me and smiles. Suddenly, I don't care who he's texting because they're not here with him. They're not the reason why he's smiling. It's me. I'm the reason.

'Nice outfit,' he says, his dark eyes taking me in.

'This old thing?' I twirl for good measure. 'You would not believe how gross I got at work today. I thought I should change before I came over, and this was the best I could do from the sale rack.'

Gabriel laughs. 'You could have borrowed something from me.' He looks at my body again, analyses it, and my face flushes at the attention. 'You're thinner than I am. You'd have fit.'

The thought of wearing Gabriel's clothes feels intimate in a way I can't explain.

'So what's the plan?' I ask, desperate to change the conversation.

Gabriel shrugs off the wall and pulls his cap on. 'I bought two tickets for the MCG tour and then I thought we could go to the tennis and watch a match.'

'Two classic Melbourne experiences in one night? You're really blowing through our list.'

Gabriel slides his phone into his shorts pocket. 'Follow me.'

The request to 'follow me' consists of walking out of the hotel lobby to where a nondescript black car waits for us in the half-circle drive. Gabriel slips into the back seat, leaving the door open for me to join him.

'We could have taken the tram,' I say as I climb into the car, closing the door with a soft *thud*. 'It's peak hour.'

'It's also still thirty degrees out,' Gabriel reminds me, which is fair. While it's cooler today, I'd much rather chill in an air-conditioned car than wait for a tram in the sun.

Harry Styles plays on the radio as we weave through traffic towards the MCG. The large stadium glows against the slowly setting sun; the blue sky smudged with streaks of yellow and pink. I've never been a sports guy but there is something about this ground that makes the hairs on the back of my neck stand up.

We walk into the foyer and find a group of elderly tourists waiting by a *TOUR STARTS HERE* sign. The tour guide is an old, frail man with a plummy British accent, who regales us with tales of the cricketers who graced the grounds when the MCG was established in 1853—just eighteen years after the establishment of the city of Melbourne.

The guide shows us through the halls and to the famous Long Room: an enormous private members' club that looks down onto the ground and smells like wood polish and musky cologne. We walk by dozens of portraits of past presidents and secretaries, and the guide points out those of note—white men who did things that pleased other white men enough that they were immortalised in oils and put on display. Maybe it's because I don't like sports that much, but it all seems insular. Privileged. Exclusionary. I know enough to know that AFL was originally a game played by First Nations people, and I can't help but wonder—who are the faces missing on these walls?

We leave the private members' club and make our way down to the ground. Sure, it's just an oval of lawn with a hundred thousand seats surrounding it, but the other tourists in our group gasp. Even Gabriel seems rather mesmerised by it and before I realise it, he's toed off his shoes and is stepping onto the lawn.

'I want to *feel* it,' he says enthusiastically as he stuffs his socks into his Adidas Originals. 'Come on.'

Barefoot and feeling stupid, we step onto the lawn of the MCG and it's strangely . . . squishy?

'Ugh,' I groan as mud squelches between my toes. 'This is gross.'

'I know, I regret it,' Gabriel mutters. Grimacing, we return to the grandstand and put our now-damp feet back into our shoes. Behind us, the oldies laugh.

The tour wraps up and we wave goodbye to our new octogenarian friends. As we walk through the parkland towards Rod Laver Arena, the next stop on our tourist experience, we pass posters of various players both current and past, much like the ones that decorate Richmond Station. I see the blond Lukas Froebel, somehow still incredibly handsome despite being wrapped around a rubbish bin; Pejo Auer, world men's number one; Lorena Rodríguez, world women's number one.

Then there's Serena, Roger, Rafa. Names so big even I know them.

Gabriel presses his phone to the turnstile and pushes through. I follow and step into a world of saturated colour, bright lights and loud music. Above me, a screen displays the timing of the next match; Lukas Froebel plays Douglas Rhodes in just under an hour.

I catch up to Gabriel. 'Lukas Froebel plays soon. You reckon we could bunk off to Rod Laver Arena to watch?'

Gabriel slips his sunglasses over his face, though the sun's going down. 'I thought you didn't like tennis.'

I make a face, feigning offence. 'Excuse me, Lukas is my favourite player.'

Gabriel guides us through a barrier and around the side of Rod Laver Arena. 'You have a favourite player now? What country is he from?'

I scramble. *Froebel . . . Froebel . . .* With the fair features, I think he could be Scandinavian. Or maybe he's from the US. He's not Australian . . . but then again, with all the fuss the Australian Open's made about him, he *could* be. I take a pot shot. 'Denmark.'

'*So* close,' Gabriel says as he opens a door for me. 'He's from Sweden.'

A security guard approaches us and Gabriel pulls a pass

from his pocket, and we're allowed to continue. I frown. I didn't get a pass. Should I have got a pass? Looking around, I realise most people are wearing AO merchandise and lanyards.

'Where are we going?' I ask. 'No one's asked to see the tickets.'

Gabriel replies, 'The back way.'

Just as I'm about to ask him how he knows *the back way*, Gabriel presses the button for an elevator. It opens, and he ushers me ahead of him.

'Are you sure we're supposed to be here?' I pester. 'Shouldn't someone be with us?'

'Trust me,' Gabriel replies. The elevator doors open onto a hallway, but as we step out, I realise it's not actually a hallway at all: it's a ring that circles the entire arena. Every few metres, there's a brand name emblazoned on a door: Adidas, Nike, Rolex. Gabriel opens the Mysa Whiskey door and I realise we're stepping into a corporate box.

Is this Gabriel's company? Is the Open the reason he's here?

The corporate box offers a wide, unobstructed view of the court below with two rows of plush cinema-style seating. Towards the back wall, there's a full bar and I notice it's stocked with top-shelf liquor and expensive craft beers. Clearly, this isn't a cheap way to go to the tennis. And definitely *not* a part of the tour. I'm about to grab Gabriel and demand to know what's going on when we're approached by a bartender wearing coat-tails. *Coat-tails*. What in the business-class bullshit is this?

'Welcome again, Mr Madani,' he says warmly. 'Can I get you both a drink?'

'A Coke for me, please.' Gabriel turns to me. 'Noah?'

Well, when in Rome. I look over the liquor on the shelf, the choice too much. 'Whiskey and dry?'

'Good choice, sir,' the bartender replies. 'Mysa Whiskey is the finest whiskey from Sweden. Please take a seat. Our menu is on the table in front of you; let me know if you wish to order refreshments before the match.'

I follow Gabriel to the floor-to-ceiling window that overlooks the court, feeling utterly flabbergasted.

'You *gotta* explain, Gabriel,' I say as we sit in the plush chairs. 'Is this who you work for?' *What happened to the tour?* I want to add. *And what the shit is happening right now?*

His mouth purses. 'Not exactly. Noah, I need to tell you—'

Suddenly, the door to the corporate box swings open. Gabriel turns, and whatever he's about to say is quickly forgotten. I glance behind me to see a woman in a wheelchair push through the doorway. A burly man wearing all black sticks close behind her.

'Heya!' says the woman in the wheelchair.

Gabriel leaps out of his seat. 'Phoebe?!'

Phoebe? Instantly, Gabriel's by her side, and she's smiling up at him, the apples of her cheeks flushed red. I get the weirdest sensation that I know her from somewhere . . .

'A little Swedish bird told me you'd be gracing his corporate box tonight,' Phoebe says. 'I got permission from my doctor to stay out for a while.'

Then Phoebe's dark gaze zeroes in on me. 'Oh, hello.' She glances back up at Gabriel, suddenly nervous. 'I didn't realise you—' She pauses. 'Maybe I should go.'

'No,' Gabriel replies quickly. 'No, please stay.'

Phoebe.

My heart's beating hard as Phoebe wheels across the floor. I have no reason to be jealous—Gabriel is not *mine*—but Phoebe is gorgeous with her large dark eyes, rounded full lips and curvy frame, and jealousy is a wild and unforgiving beast that doesn't care for logic. I *am* jealous and it fucking hurts.

Gabriel looks back to me. 'Phoebe, this is my friend, Noah.'

Phoebe wheels forward. 'Nice to meet you, Noah.' She shakes my hand and then nods to the man beside her. 'This is Blake, my security.'

Her security?! I look between Gabriel and Phoebe. It feels like I'm getting pieces of a puzzle, but I can't make sense of the full picture.

As Phoebe gets settled, I look back to the court and take a long sip of my whiskey, washing the cottony dry feel from my mouth. *L. FROEBEL v. D. RHODES* is displayed on all the screens around the arena. I heard what Phoebe said earlier, and all the pieces suddenly fit: this is *Lukas's* corporate box.

I grab my phone from my pocket and google *Lukas Froebel.*

Instantly, Lukas pops up, easily recognisable by his spiky blond hair and dashing good looks. I scroll down the page until I find *People Also Search For.*

She's there.

Phoebe Song. The photo on Google is taken from a tournament, but it's her; she has the same muscular frame, the same long jet-black hair, the same dark mole on her right cheek.

The woman in front of me is Phoebe Song.

The Phoebe Song. US Champion Phoebe Song.

I feel like I'm having an out-of-body experience. I'm sitting in a corporate booth watching Lukas Froebel with a US-fucking-Champion and . . . Gabriel. A man I hardly even know.

A man who has very obviously lied to me.

I remember the name Lukas flashing up on Gabriel's phone yesterday when we walked through the laneways. Glancing over my shoulder, I make sure Gabriel's still talking to Phoebe before turning back to my phone and typing in *Lukas Froebel and Gabriel . . .*

. . . *Madani*, Google autofills.

Pressing enter, I wait for the page to load.

Photos flood my screen: Lukas with his hand slung over Gabriel's shoulder, each of them holding a racquet. Lukas and Gabriel in a photoshoot for *GQ*. Gabriel holding a trophy above his head, his hair and smile wild.

Gabriel, Gabriel, *Gabriel*.

I put my phone down and swallow the rest of my drink. Below us, ball kids step onto the court. The match is starting and I'm sitting in Lukas Froebel's fucking *corporate box* with two star tennis players.

Tennis players who garner media attention. Who are photographed and publicised online without their knowledge or permission.

Tennis players who *lied* about who they were this entire time, unknowingly putting me in danger.

Dad only needs a *whiff* of someone to track them down; and I've been so careful for so long. Caught up in my infatuation for Gabriel, I've let myself believe that maybe I don't have to constantly look over my shoulder.

God, I've been so blind.

Hurt and anger mix into a deadly cocktail. Biting back tears, I stand up . . . and run into Gabriel. Instantly, he reaches forward, bracketing my shoulders to stop me falling. 'Noah, are you okay?'

'I'm fine.' I run my hands down my shirt. They're suddenly really sweaty. 'Definitely. I'm peachy. Absolutely fine. I'm just going to go find the bathroom.'

I step out of Gabriel's embrace, but I'm not looking where I'm going and crash straight into Blake's bulky frame. Losing my footing, I stumble backwards. Blake catches me, his large hands hooking under my flailing arms.

'Noah,' Gabriel says as I push Blake away. I need to get out of here.

'I'm so sorry, I—' Deeply embarrassed, I dash out into the hallway, not bothering to look back. 'I have to go.'

11

GABRIEL

'Noah, stop!' I run down the hallway, trying to catch him before the elevator arrives. I knew that if I brought him to Melbourne Park to watch the match, there was a risk he'd figure out who I was, but the last person I'd expected to show up was Phoebe. 'Let me explain!'

To my surprise, Noah stops a few paces in front of me, whipping around like a viper. 'Leave me alone, Gabriel.'

I don't expect the viciousness in his voice. He turns and jams the down button for the elevator like he's a cornered animal, thrashing and scared.

I glance around to make sure there's no one else in the narrow hallway. The last thing I need is for this blow-up to appear on a gossip site. 'Please talk to me.'

'*Talk to you*?' Noah echoes. 'That's rich. You lied to me, Gabriel. I've asked you a dozen times what you do for work, and you *lied*. Even now, you—'

'I *wanted* to tell you,' I interrupt him. It's the truth.

I'd had the whole speech prepared until Phoebe had made her spectacularly ill-timed entrance. 'You obviously didn't recognise me. That doesn't happen often for me, and I admit I really liked it, just being able to be myself, but I know it was wrong.'

'God, you're *so* rich and famous, I'm glad I could fulfil that fantasy for you,' Noah spits back. 'Get your head out of your arse, Gabriel. You have no idea the kind of shit you've stirred up for me.' He begins pacing back and forth, waiting for the elevator doors to open. 'I can't believe I trusted you.'

There's an edge of emotion to that last sentence, like he's as upset at himself as he is with me.

'Noah, please, despite what you think, you know me. The real me,' I say, trying to grab his shoulders. 'You see me.'

I don't care if it sounds clichéd—Noah can't leave. If he leaves right now, I might never see him again and I don't know what I'll do if I can't make this right between us. 'Please, just give me the chance to explain.'

Contempt shines in his green eyes, and he looks at me with such disdain it makes my stomach clench. 'You're wrong. I have *no* idea who you are.'

The elevator doors open suddenly, and before I think too much about it, I barrel Noah inside and hit the button to close the doors behind me. Noah stumbles, his back hitting the wall.

'What are you *doing*?' he cries. 'Gabriel, this is ridiculous!'

I back off, giving Noah space. He's pressed against the back wall and panting hard. Maybe I've taken this too far, maybe this is making everything worse. 'You make me feel so *normal*, and I just—I just—' The words don't come out; I can't seem to get them past the big ball of emotions constricting my throat.

'Just what everyone wants to hear,' Noah deadpans, trying to move around me. What Noah gains in height, I make up for in body mass. I block him as he tries to move towards the elevator keypad.

'It's true. I play all over the world and make an obscene amount of money, and it's been that way since I was thirteen. But the reality is I don't have a friend who isn't on the circuit, and I've never even *dated* anyone . . . but when I'm with you . . .' I'm breathing so fast, it feels like my heart's trying to break out of my chest. 'It just feels normal. I *love* that it feels normal.'

I don't know what this is between us—whether he likes me romantically or otherwise—but I know I don't want it to end.

Noah presses the balls of his palms into his eye sockets, and sucks in one big, ragged breath and it takes me a second to realise he's crying. Tears stream down his cheeks as he begins to sob.

'I trusted you. I thought . . . I'm *so* stupid.'

'You're not,' I say, and really, the worst part of this isn't that I deceived him, it's that he feels bad about letting me in. 'I'm sorry I didn't tell you, but I—'

'My life is fucked up in ways you can't imagine, Gabriel,' he interrupts. 'And this . . .' He waves a hand in front of his face, but doesn't elaborate further. He lets out a long sigh. 'I should go.'

The elevator jolts suddenly and begins to descend to the ground floor. A moment later, the doors open and a woman steps in. Noah rushes out past her, and the woman gawks. There are so many people lingering in the lobby around Rod Laver Arena, I can't risk speaking to Noah here. I hurry after him.

'Let's talk outside,' I say, guiding him across the floor and opening a door to the back of the arena, an area blocked off to the public by a large hedge.

The crowd roars inside the arena. The sound of the cheering, the applause, is so loud I feel it vibrate through the ground.

Noah shakes his head, his floppy fringe skimming along his brow. 'I just . . . fuck.' He kicks at the astroturf, blowing out a breath. 'I just hate that you're famous. It makes shit so complicated.'

It's the most I've got out of him since he stormed out. 'It does make everything more complicated. I was scared that if you knew who I was you would only want to be friends for—'

'Money? Clout?' Noah scoffs but then he must realise I'm being serious. 'For the record, I don't, but I understand. I didn't have the best childhood, and when I moved here, I was looking for a normal life too. With normal friends, doing things normal people my age did. Then I found you. And it turns out you're the opposite of normal.'

'I should tell you the truth from the beginning.' I'm so emotionally exhausted that my English is slipping. Letting out a long sigh, I force myself to relax my shoulders. 'But I didn't lie earlier. You know me more than anyone else. No one else knows . . .' The words catch in my throat, it's a struggle to say them out loud. 'That I'm gay. Not even my family.'

Noah scrubs a hand over his face, wiping away the remaining tears. The crowd cheers behind us.

'I get it,' he says quietly. 'Your shit is complicated, mine is too. I hate that you felt like you had to lie about who you were just to feel like my feelings were authentic. It's manipulative. It's wrong.'

'I know it was wrong. I understand if you don't want to stay; I can call you a car.'

Noah's silent for a long moment, glancing between me and the open doors to the arena. 'I want to stay.'

Somehow, we both know he's talking about more than just this match, more than this evening. I know we've been friends till now, but the desire to be more is so overwhelming I want to take him by the shoulders and pull his mouth to mine.

'*But* I have boundaries,' Noah says, his tone firm. 'No more lying.'

'Agreed.'

'And no photographs together.'

I swallow down my nerves. The last thing I need is to be pictured with Noah, to have the rumours spiral. 'Agreed. There will be photos if you come to matches, but the media may not make a connection.'

Noah pauses, as if thinking. 'Okay. So, we just have to be careful while we're out.'

Careful. I can do careful. I've done it my entire life. 'We'll be careful,' I promise just as the crowd erupts again in the stadium. 'You want to go back in?'

'Yeah,' Noah says on the tail end of a sigh. I open the door and his shoulder clips mine teasingly as he brushes past me. 'You know you're gonna have to teach me the rules, right?'

'Basically, each player tries to hit the ball over the net, in a different spot from where the other player is standing,' I reply.

Noah gasps, mock scandalised. 'Sarcasm? Was the Gabriel I knew truly a lie, after all?'

'No lies,' I promise. 'You can google me all you like. And call me Gabi. All my friends do.'

Noah pauses just inside the door. He looks down at his phone. 'I don't think I will, if that's okay with you.'

'Call me Gabi?'

'No.' He chuckles. 'Look you up on the internet.'

I frown. 'Why not?'

'Because you can't google me. It doesn't seem fair,' he says. 'I'm sure Wikipedia has all your good and bad parts documented in astounding detail. You don't get a choice about what people know. I trust you to tell me what's worth knowing.'

What can I say to that? My heart feels like it's in my throat. *You don't get a choice about what people know.*

It feels like so much more than that. It feels like when I'm with Noah I'm someone entirely different from the person I appear to be to everyone else; I don't feel like Gabriel the tennis star or Gabriel the coddled adult–child who's never let off the leash. I just feel like *Gabi*.

And that's scary.

Because if I don't win tomorrow, I'll have to leave—and that feeling, the feeling of being someone I've never allowed myself to explore—will go away, too.

By the time we find our seats again, Lukas has won the first game and Phoebe's in deep discussion with the bartender over the menu.

'So, Noah,' Phoebe says once we've settled in again. 'How did you meet our dear Gabi?'

'Well, he walked into my bar a few days ago,' Noah replies. All I can think of is the conversation Phoebe and I had in her hospital room the other day, and how I'd said I had no time to date. I catch her eyes over Noah's head and I know she's enjoying this far too much. 'I guess we just hit it off.'

He makes our story sound so simple and well practised, like he's said it a million times—to strangers, and people at weddings, and my extended family.

And then I remember that nothing has actually been said or done; in fact, I have just spent the last two days lying to Noah's face—and the fantasy crumbles. It's not a meet-cute . . . it's just a *meet*.

'You're a bartender?' Phoebe continues.

Noah nods. 'Yes. Well, for now.'

'For now?' Phoebe echoes. 'Do you want to do something else?'

'I'd like to play music. Professionally.'

'Anything specific?'

'The piano.'

'Do you sing too?'

Noah laughs. 'Not well.'

I listen to the conversation with interest. I had no idea Noah played the piano, or that he wanted to do it professionally, but then I recall our conversation at the rooftop bar—how Noah said his dream was to open a bar with live music. I'm determined to hear him play before I leave. Not sure how to do that. Maybe get him drunk.

The bartender reappears with a platter of various canapés. My gaze slides back to Lukas down on the court. Without a doubt, the odds are in his favour. Douglas Rhodes is a nineteen-year-old from New York who had outstanding success as a local wildcard at last year's US Open, but now he faces the player who took out the championship.

When Lukas wins the first set, Noah leans over to me. 'When I said I knew nothing about tennis, I meant it. How long do they play for?'

'Up to five sets,' I reply. 'You win a set by winning six games, but the player must win a set by two games at least. Each game consists of four or more points, depending on how close it is. The points go love, which means nothing, fifteen, thirty, and then forty. Lukas just won the first set; six games to three. He needs to win two more sets to win the match.'

'Makes sense,' Noah replies in a tone that tells me it doesn't make sense at all.

'It will make sense the more you watch it,' Phoebe assures him. 'Just remember: game, set, match. Games make up sets, and sets make up a match. Depending on how close the match is, there are tie breakers at the end of sets, and at the end of games. This won't be a close game, though.'

'Douglas is very young,' I explain, just in case Phoebe's comment sounds callous. 'He hasn't been on the circuit long.'

The second set is about to start. Noah orders another drink from the bar and settles in. I feel the outside of his thigh touch mine as he relaxes back, the heat almost searing, even through our clothes. If Phoebe wasn't here, I'd put my arm around him. Or at least, I think I'd be brave enough to.

When Lukas wins the second set, Phoebe grabs her wheelchair from where it's folded against her seat. 'I'm going to head off and beat the crowd. Don't think there's much life in this game.' She looks at Noah, her smile saccharine sweet. 'It was nice to meet you, Noah.'

'You too,' he says. 'Thanks for explaining tennis to me.'

'You're welcome. I'm sure I'll see you at a match soon.' She gives me a knowing look. God, she is infuriating. 'Good luck tomorrow, Gabi.'

'Thanks, Pheebs.' I get up to hug her, and feel her squeeze my shoulders.

'He's lovely,' she says against my ear, quiet enough for only me to hear, and my stomach turns to mush. Warm, lovely, mush.

Phoebe leaves and Lukas wins the third set twenty minutes later. Douglas Rhodes loses gracefully, and the pair share a hug and a smile on the court. It was bad luck he had to play Lukas in the first round, but he still goes home with a hefty pay cheque.

'That was fun,' Noah says as we leave. 'I think I even understood some of it.'

'Let me drive you home,' I say as we wait for the elevator. 'There's a carpool for players and guests downstairs. It'll be faster than catching a train.'

It's a good thing we do; rain has started to fall over the city and the roads out of Melbourne Park are a flood of red brakelights. Noah tells the driver his address; it's north of the city, in a suburb called Carlton, and we wait in the bottleneck of traffic trying to depart Rod Laver Arena. Noah sits beside me and watches the rain trickle down the car window. His hand rests on the seat between us. I look down at his fingers and all I can think about is entwining them with my own. I want him—I—

The driver clears his throat as we stop at a red light and I come to my senses.

We're in public.

I still don't know where I stand with Noah.

I know why I shouldn't pursue this. Shouldn't risk it. But none of the reasons are loud enough to drown out the singing of my blood every time Noah looks at me.

'I'm playing in the second round of the tournament tomorrow at eleven,' I say. 'Would you like to watch?'

Noah turns to me, clearly surprised. 'I'd love to.'

My stomach flips. 'I'll arrange for my manager to find you at thc gate and—'

Victor, I realise. I'm going to have to tell Victor.

'And?' Noah continues.

'He'll take you to my player's box. It'll be less glamorous than Lukas's corporate sponsor, I'm afraid. I'm just a mid-list name.'

'You mean your face *isn't* plastered on water bubblers yet?'

I shove at his shoulder. 'It *is* the dream.'

A part of me enjoys his sarcastic little jabs; how they're bookended by a wry smile and a knowing glance; how we already seem to have little jokes between us.

'There's a chance you'll be photographed,' I say, recalling his boundaries. 'If that's an issue, I understand.'

He takes a deep breath, as if weighing up the options. 'I want to come.'

We break out of the traffic. With the sudden rain, the city streets are quiet. The driver rolls down the window to lessen the humidity, and the fresh earthy smell of the wet streets flows through the car.

Noah shifts his body towards me and our knees brush together. 'If you lose tomorrow, what happens?'

'I go home.'

His eyes slide from mine. 'So, if you had lost the first match . . .'

'I would have already left.' I drum my fingers against the car door, unable to control my nerves. 'We're planning to go to Brazil after this tournament ends, and then we start preparations for the clay season.'

He clears his throat. 'Will you leave tomorrow if you lose?'

'I don't *want* to,' I blurt out before I can stop myself, and the driver looks at me in the rear-vision mirror. 'But it's what they expect of me. It's hard to explain.'

'People rely on you.' Noah pauses. 'If that happens, I'll still be here next year. We can continue our tour then.'

Every year, tournaments roll around faster than I expect them to, but the idea of waiting a *year* to see Noah again already feels like a special kind of torture.

'Just this left,' Noah says to the driver. I look out the window and realise we're suddenly outside the city. The driver turns into a narrow street full of terraced houses. 'The one with the light on—yep, the yellow door.'

'I'll walk you in,' I say as we park.

Noah opens the door and steps out, droplets hitting his shirt. 'You really don't have to.'

'I want to.' If I lose tomorrow, this might be the last time I'm alone with him before we fly out. I can stand a bit of rain if it means another few seconds.

Noah opens the gate to the terraced home. Up the worn brick steps, bugs dance around the glowing porch light and I can hear the hum of a TV somewhere deep in the house.

'Well, as you can see, I made it home safely and your chivalry is appreciated,' he says as we step up to the screen door, though I can barely hear him over the sound of the rain on the tin roof. He turns, and blows out a long breath. 'It's been a weird night.'

'Again, I'm sorry.' It feels like I can't apologise enough.

'I know you are.' For some reason those words feel so validating. 'You can make it up to me by winning tomorrow, and maybe also with a six pack of doughnuts from that shop we went to.'

'Deal.'

Rain hits my back. I step in closer, narrowing the space between our bodies. Noah swallows, and I notice the way his throat moves, the way his jaw flexes. He takes a half-step backwards and his back finds the screen door. He looks at me, confused, and I wonder if I'm fucking this up, but then his dark gaze drops to my lips. Without thinking, I lean forward to kiss him. Noah's hands grasp my shoulders, fingers digging in, pulling me closer and closer and—

Our lips don't meet when I think they're supposed to.

'Argh!' Noah cries as he falls backwards through the doorway. I stumble forward, trying to catch myself on the warped remains of the screen door even as I realise what's about to happen. But it's too late; I can't stop myself as I fall on Noah with an *ooft*.

'OW!' he cries underneath me, wriggling—

Immediately, I try to get off him. Our bodies are too close together, but as soon as I get my hands under myself, I'm body-slammed by an overly enthusiastic dog.

'Sadie! Sadie!' A woman's voice bounces down the hall. 'Sadie, get off him! Oh dear, are you two okay?'

'I'm fine.' Noah winces as I crawl off him and submit to being licked by the dog. The older woman stares down at us both. 'I thought you'd locked the door.'

'Oh dear,' she murmurs as she steps over our bodies to examine the door frame, which is hanging askew. 'The door is so rusty, the hinge must have broken.'

'Top-notch security,' Noah mutters as he stands. We look at each other for half a second before I clear my throat.

'I'll, um, go,' I mumble. My face feels hot. 'I'm sorry about the door.'

Then, without waiting for a response, I turn away, hurry down the steps and through the gate and throw myself into the back of the car. With my ego, heart and shinbone bruised, I direct the driver back to the hotel and sink my head into my hands. What an absolute mess.

I grab my phone but immediately wish I hadn't. Phoebe's texted me.

Never find someone special, my ass.

12

NOAH

I think about the kiss all night. The almost kiss. The kiss that should have been. I think about Gabriel pressing me up against the door and how it felt to have his body against mine. I think about him as my hand slips under the waistband of my boxers. Except in my fantasy, he's the one touching me.

My phone wakes me, buzzing on my bedside table. Blearily, I pick it up. It's just after eight and the morning sun casts a warm light into my bedroom.

There are three messages and one email.

Hungrygabriel73: *I'm sorry about last night. I hope the door is okay . . . I am sorry I tripped. I hope you will still come today. My manager Victor will meet you at the gates near the station.*

Hungrygabriel73: *Please tell papa we've known each other longer than four days. Keep it vague.*

Hungrygabriel73: *See you after the match.*

Tripped? *Tripped*? Was that what happened? I remember him stepping closer. I remember he'd smelt of citrus and wood, like when I used to pick oranges from the tree in my backyard and the smell of the peel would linger on the tips of my fingers.

Had Gabriel leaned forward just to open the door? Is that why the hinge buckled?

I flick to the email. *Don't forget! University Open Day is coming up!*

Placing my phone back on the table, I drag myself into the shower. The warm water soothes the ache in my shoulders that's set in overnight. I wince as I roll my neck. It's one thing to fall on your arse, but it's another to be crushed by a professional athlete on your way down.

To be honest, I'm not sure how to feel about everything that's happening with Gabriel. On the one hand, when I'm with him, everything else feels kinda blurry at the edges. I can't remember the last time I felt the stomach-churning thrill of a crush.

But there's also a voice that reminds me he intentionally deceived me, and that's a pretty big red flag. And then there's the part where he's an actual celebrity, and I have to consider everything—photos, articles, publicity—that comes with that. It's a huge risk even to be seen with him, and I wish I'd known that from the start. It only takes one photo for the facial recognition software to ping and—

Don't think about it, I tell myself. *You can't keep living your life like this.*

I scrub a hand over my face, trying to untangle my thoughts. Why am I getting in over my head like we're star-crossed lovers? We aren't. Gabriel didn't try to kiss me last night; he was just opening the door. He stood close to me to get out of the rain. Every sign can be explained away, but my brain went ahead and constructed its own romance because I'm just that sad and desperate.

I resolve just to go to the tennis and try to have a good time.

After washing my hair, I then spend *far* too long wondering what one wears to the tennis. Eventually I settle on a pair of black shorts, a white t-shirt and a bright geometric eighties button-down I thrifted last month. Pulling on a pair of socks and my white sneakers, I check my appearance in the mirror before heading down to the kitchen to make coffee.

Margie's reading the newspaper on the dining table. She folds it down as I enter. 'Sorry about your date last night, Noah.'

'It wasn't a date,' I assure her. 'Does the door need to be replaced?'

Margie shakes her head. 'I should have had those rusty hinges replaced ages ago. I'll have someone do it this week.' She looks me up and down. 'You look very nice. Are you going out?'

'I'm meeting up with Gabriel.'

'*Gabriel*,' Margie says in a slightly singsong way. 'Looking very nice for your friend who wasn't a date.'

I give her a *drop it* look as my toast pops up. 'So,' I announce, changing the subject. 'The university open day is soon. I'm thinking about asking about their music program.'

Margie's face lights up and she puts down the newspaper. I sit down opposite her with my coffee and munch on toast. 'Really? I had no idea you played an instrument.'

'I used to play the piano in high school,' I say. 'I want to go in with a bit of an idea of what I could study, but I'm not sure music is the best idea.' Maybe I should focus on doing something real, something serious that will make me steady money. Like marketing or dentistry.

Margie reaches across the table and squeezes my hand. 'It's a *great* idea, Noah. If you're serious, I have an old piano in storage I could bring around. It'd be tight, but it might fit in your room.'

'Really?' I ask.

'I'd love to have music around the house again, but it'll need tuning. I think the last time it was played was around ten years ago.' She takes a sip of her coffee. 'So, tell me about this Gabriel. What's his story?'

♪

A bald man stands outside the gates near Richmond Station holding a sign with my name on it.

'Are you Victor?' I ask as I step off the tram.

He looks me up and down. 'I am. Are you Noah?'

'Yeah.'

'Prove it.'

'What?'

He nods to my pocket. 'ID. Prove you're Noah.'

Pulling out my wallet, I flash him my old driver's licence. It's expired, but that doesn't matter. He nods and hands me a lanyard with a pass that says *Player Guest*. 'Nice to meet you, Noah.'

'You too,' I reply. Truthfully, I'm not sure if his demeanour is prickly or just French.

It's late morning on the third day of the Australian Open and the crowds are thick. Victor leads me around the queues to turnstiles on the far side of the gate, where we flash our passes at a staff member.

Like me, Victor's tall and lanky, so he's easy to follow through the crowds. He has a port-wine stain that travels down the nape of his neck and disappears under his grey polo shirt, and a rather fascinating habit of talking with his hands.

'So, you're the bartender,' he says as we make our way towards Evonne Goolagong Arena, bypassing the lines of people waiting to get inside. 'How did you meet Gabriel?'

'Online,' I reply, keeping it vague, just like Gabriel wanted.

'*Online*,' Victor echoes in a particular tone. If he thinks I'm lying, he doesn't say so. Instead, he opens the door to a narrow hallway, and I walk down it apprehensively, unsure of where I'm going.

'This way,' Victor says, slipping past me to open another door that leads into what looks like a dressing-room. There's exercise equipment strewn across the floor, and multiple sets of the same clothes—a deep red polo and black shorts—laid out on a lounge. This must be Gabriel's playing gear.

There's a man sitting at a small table hunched over a laptop. He's got Gabriel's deep bronze complexion and the same dark brown hair, but it's flecked with grey and styled in locs, of which half are tied into a bun at the crown of his head. The rest flow around his shoulders and down his back.

This must be Gabriel's dad. My hands feel sweaty, and I shove them into my pockets to wipe them. Gabriel's *dad*.

'Bernard, this is Noah, Gabriel's friend,' Victor says as we enter the room.

Gabriel's dad stands, the chair scraping against the carpet as he pushes away from the table. He's tall; taller than Gabriel but with the same broad shoulders and chest. He strides across the room in three paces, his large hand outstretched to shake mine.

'Bernard,' he replies in a thick French accent. 'I'm Gabriel's father.'

I shake his hand, hoping he doesn't feel how clammy mine is. 'Nice to meet you. Gabriel's told me a lot about you.'

The corner of Bernard's mouth quirks. 'I can't say the same.'

Victor gives Bernard an admonishing look. 'Ignore him, Noah. We are always happy to meet Gabriel's friends. There's water and energy drinks in the mini-fridge, or you can go up to the arena and get alcohol from the vendors.'

'Just water is fine, thank you.'

He hands me the bottle with a smile. 'Let's go up to the player's box.'

I'd hoped coming up to the arena would be a breath of fresh air, but with the dumping of rain last night, it's stiflingly humid. Victor shows me to Gabriel's player's box; two rows of seats on the edge of the court.

'So,' Victor says as he settles next to me. 'What's your deal?'

'My deal?' I echo.

He turns to me. 'I've known Gabriel since he was a boy, and I've been on tour with him all his professional career. He's *never* invited anyone from the outside into his player's box.'

'I'm not sure what you mean. We're just friends,' I reply, even as my traitorous little heart flutters with the thrill of being the only one Gabriel's ever invited to watch him play.

Victor opens his mouth to say something, but then Bernard steps into the player's box, taking a seat directly in front of us. I suck down a gulp of water as the music in the stadium dies down.

I'd estimate the stadium is about half full, and more are still finding their seats. Across the court, a group of guys wear red, white and blue morph suits with the French flag tied around their necks.

'Welcome to our second-round men's singles match at the Australian Open.' The announcer's voice booms through the arena. 'Would you please make welcome our tenth seed, from Scotland, Matthew O'Lachlan.'

The crowd erupts into applause as Matthew O'Lachlan steps out onto the court. He's tall, handsome, with a short crop of dark hair. He waves at the crowd as he makes his way over to his station.

'And our fourteenth seed, from France, Gabriel Madani!'

I'd like to think Gabriel's applause was louder than O'Lachlan's, but that's my bias showing. The wind blows as he steps out onto the court, tousling his loose, curly hair. He casts his gaze upwards and for a moment, barely a second, we lock eyes, and it's electric. My body thrums. It sounds clichéd as shit, but when he looks at me, when he knows I'm *here* for him, it's like the rest of the stadium melts away. It's just us.

The moment is brief, and then Gabriel turns away and prepares for the match.

I try not to let on how little I know about tennis, especially as the play starts. Gabriel is in front of us for the first set, receiving O'Lachlan's serve. I recall the scoring system—he'd said love means nothing, then fifteen, thirty, forty. Gabriel's legs flex, and he moves so precisely, so effortlessly, it's like he's dancing. Watching him play tennis is one of the most beautiful things I've ever seen.

Before I've quite got my head around what's going on, Gabriel wins the first game. They switch sides, and Gabriel serves, but his first ball hits the net. I hear his father mutter something as Gabriel sets up to serve a second time.

It hits the net as well.

'Damn,' Victor says. On the screen above us, O'Lachlan wins fifteen points.

I take another sip of water, draining the bottle. It's so hot out here; the sun streams through the gap in the roof and the heat practically turns the stadium into a terrarium. Even Gabriel reaches for his towel as O'Lachlan wins the second game. They're one game apiece now.

To my relief, Gabriel wins the next game, and the fourth. They switch sides again, and Gabriel comes back to our end. He glances up at his player's box, but he doesn't meet my eyes.

Bernard turns and says something in French to Victor, who nods his agreement. I sit and fidget with my water bottle, feeling both awkward and overwhelmed at the same time.

'Do you speak French?' Victor asks.

I shake my head. 'No.'

'He doesn't speak French,' he relays to Bernard. I'm not sure if that means they'll stop talking in French in front of me, or if they'll continue now that they know I can't understand them.

Gabriel wins the next game, which makes Bernard happy. He claps for the first time in the entire match, despite Gabriel winning some impressive back-and-forth shots. *Volleys*, I think they're called.

'Madani leads four games to one,' the umpire says as they break again.

I feel my phone buzz in my pocket, so I pull it out. An unknown number flashes up on the screen. I don't want to be rude so I let it go to voicemail and the voice-to-text translation comes in a minute later.

Hey Noah, it's Bella from the Rosewood. I've emailed the shift schedule for the week. Look forward to meeting you officially!

The Rosewood.

Shit.

Mark.

After everything that happened yesterday, I completely forgot about Mark and the bar. God, I hope he's okay and just nursing a really fucking awful hangover in hospital.

I bring up Mark's number and shoot him a message.

Hey man, I just wanted to check that you're ok.

It feels kinda weird but what else can I do—we're not close by any means, but I still want him to know I care.

Beside me, Bernard rises to his feet to clap as I put my phone back in my pocket. I crane my neck to glance at the scoreboard, wondering what I've missed. Gabriel's won the fifth game. Now he's leading five to one. One more and he'll win the set.

Gabriel wipes his face on his towel and then calls for a fresh one. Across the court, O'Lachlan pants by his station, clearly overwhelmed by the humidity.

'This is what Gabi trains for,' Victor says, turning to me. 'We spend months in Dubai, Algeria, Morocco and Spain training in the sun, in the harsh conditions, in the humidity.'

'Japan is worse than this,' Bernard agrees. 'But the sooner he wins, the better.'

Gabriel wins the next game easily, closing out the first set. Only two more to go.

We break for a few minutes. Bernard goes back down to the dressing-room to fetch more water. Gabriel sits at his station and demolishes a banana. I wonder what he's thinking. What's he telling himself right now to get through the next two sets?

'Time,' the umpire calls and Gabriel gets to his feet, grabbing his racquet. He glances up at the player's box and I give him a little smile. I'm not even sure if he can see it across the court, but I swear I see him smile back.

O'Lachlan serves. Five minutes later, he wins the first game.

They break and switch ends. Gabriel's closer to us now. Sweat soaks his clothes and quite literally drips off him. God, I'm miserable just sitting in the heat. I can't imagine how he must feel playing in it.

Suddenly, Gabriel's down two games to love. Bernard drums his fingers against the railing in front of him. His shoulders are tense and every so often, he mutters something in French. Victor's silent beside me.

O'Lachlan wins the third game.

'Do you think O'Lachlan threw the first set?' Victor asks quietly. Do people do that? I suppose if you're so far down in a set, it makes sense to throw it and start fresh. Maybe Gabi's not as far ahead as I think.

'Maybe,' Bernard replies. 'Arrange fresh clothes.'

Victor nods and hurries away, and suddenly, I'm alone with Bernard.

I try to focus on Gabriel. He serves beautifully, and both players rally back and forth for a short while until Gabriel finally hits the ball across the court and O'Lachlan can't return it. The crowd cheers, and even Bernard seems happy with that performance.

Gabriel wins the next game, but then O'Lachlan comes back and wins two games in a row. I check my watch; it's close to midday and the sun is directly above us, beaming down into the stadium. How much longer can he play like this?

What if he loses?

He'll be on the next flight home.

'Where's Gabriel's next tournament after Brazil?' I ask Bernard.

'We have a break and travel back to Spain for the clay season,' he replies. 'Of course, Gabi is a favourite at Roland-Garros this year.'

Brazil, and then Spain, and then France. So much time on the road; so many countries to visit; people to see. It's hard not to feel like just a blip on his map.

Lost in my own crippling insecurity, I don't notice Gabriel lose the second set. The crowd cheers, and O'Lachlan soaks it all in. Gabi, on the other hand, returns to his player's bench with his shoulders slumped. I can see him talking to himself, and I wonder what he's saying.

Maybe Bernard and Victor are right. Maybe O'Lachlan did throw the first set.

This is anyone's game.

13

GABRIEL

A chant floats around the arena during the break, a riotous wave of: *Gabi, Gabi, Gabi*. A gentle breeze touches my face, cooling the sweat on my brow, neck and chest. Taking a deep breath, I suck down a final mouthful of sour electrolytes and take the court again.

O'Lachlan's come back.

It's one set all.

Three sets to go.

O'Lachlan serves. Immediately, I recognise that his game is purposely slow. Dropping the first and winning the second is an old tactic of his; give your opponent a head start and burn them out quicker. Finish them when they're tired and sloppy and questioning themselves. He's trying to trap me.

Not this time.

I return the ball, sending it down the sideline. O'Lachlan easily catches it, returning the ball crosscourt. I stride close to the net and hit a solid backhand. The ball bounces on the baseline.

O'Lachlan runs to get the shot, but he's not fast enough.

The crowd cheers. I shake my racquet in celebration. He won't get in my head.

Outlast. Outwit. Outplay.

Struggling against the sun, O'Lachlan's next serve is a double fault. Then he concedes another point in a poor volley; then another, and another.

For every point O'Lachlan makes, I make two. Then three. I refuse to lose this match. Losing means going home, it means leaving Noah and ending whatever's between us before it even starts . . .

We break play and I risk a glance up at my box. Noah's dressed in an outrageously bright shirt. The wind gently tousles his fringe. Our eyes meet. He smiles and my heart stutters. I'm not ready to leave.

O'Lachlan serves and the ball whips past me. I lunge for it, my shoe skidding on the court. Ace.

A few good shots later and we're neck and neck on the scoreboard. Somehow, he's clawed his way back to a tie breaker at the end of the third set.

And I've barely moved from the baseline; barely had a chance to get the ball in play before conceding the point. He's playing hard, recklessly.

We reset for the tie breaker. The set will go to whoever gets seven points first. No advantages, no weird points system, just simple round digits.

I stare at O'Lachlan over the net. I can't lose. Not yet. Not now. There's too much to stay for, and I've been on the circuit too long and worked too hard to bow out in the second round of a major tournament.

O'Lachlan serves. The ball hits the net and I can't help but think that his second serve percentage is taking a hit in this match. No doubt Victor will take that into consideration for our post-match debrief, and note it the next time I face O'Lachlan.

'Fuck,' I hear him cry. The score's 0–1.

I win the second point after a quick volley and the third after I lunge for a shot that goes crosscourt. The ball barely skims the net but lands in his service box.

0–3.

O'Lachlan glares at me as he prepares to receive.

I give him a little half-smile as I raise the ball to serve, trying to get in his head. He returns the serve fiercely, too quickly for me to regain my form. I lunge forward to catch the ball, but I don't get the right angle and it bounces off my racquet and into the net.

1–3.

'Come on, Gabriel!' someone calls from the audience. A smattering of cheers follows.

'Quiet, please,' says the umpire.

O'Lachlan wipes his brow on his sleeve as he hunches over, waiting for the ball.

When I serve this time, I'm ready for his vicious return. I pull myself back into position quickly, meeting his ball as he attempts to serve a hard backhand into my deuce court. I return the ball low and flat. He has no chance of chasing it.

1–4.

'Goddamn shit,' O'Lachlan mutters when he fumbles his first serve again. Whatever momentum spurred him to a tie breaker, it's gone now.

Second serves are all about getting the ball in play; they're more about accuracy than power. Try to ace your opponent on a second serve and you're practically handing the point to them. This isn't normal. In all our years on the circuit together, I've never known O'Lachlan to have so many second serves.

As predicted, O'Lachlan's second serve is surprisingly soft. I hit it down his sideline, and he fumbles to chase it.

Finally, after thirty-one hellish minutes in this broiler of an arena, I ace O'Lachlan and win myself the third set.

O'Lachlan crumbles not long after. I blitz through the first game of the fourth set; then the second and the third. He wins a handful of points, but it's clear he's in a funk.

I play an ace to get to fifteen–love in the last game; a drop shot to thirty, a ball down the baseline to forty, and finally, O'Lachlan hits the net and I close out the match. As the crowd cheers, I hit the playing balls into the stands and collapse onto the player's bench, heaving in mouthfuls of air as I fumble for my water bottle. A ball kid hands me a fresh one, icy condensation dripping down the plastic, and I take it with thanks.

Two days. I've bought myself another two days in Melbourne and fought my way into the third round.

I make my way over to my player's box where Papa,

Victor and Noah wait for me. Papa leans over the barrier to clap me on the back as I reach up to him.

'Good play, Gabriel,' he says, which is praise of the highest order.

I reach across him to take Noah's hand, squeezing it. 'Thank you for coming.'

'You're welcome,' he says, emotion overwhelming his voice. 'I'm glad you didn't lose.'

I laugh because we both know what was at stake. 'Me too.'

Papa nudges me and I let go of Noah's hand. 'Go get cleaned up. We'll talk downstairs.'

I grab my gear and see Percy Jones step onto the court. These on-court interviews are a part of my contract, and while they're not my favourite, I far prefer speaking to just one journalist than an entire room full.

'Gabriel Madani, you're causing a bit of trouble.' Percy's deep voice bounces around the arena. 'You're the fourteenth seed, playing like you're the second or third seed . . . and you just knocked out the tenth seed. How do you feel about that?'

'I'm just trying to play my best tennis under the conditions,' I say. 'I train a lot for the heat to prepare for this tournament, and I'm glad it's paying off.'

'You're known for having a very quiet player's box, but today it looked like you had a bit of support from a friend.'

My stomach churns. I'd thought no one would care about who was in my player's box, but once again I'm reminded how eagle-eyed people can be—especially journalists; how eager they are to find a story.

'Yes, a long-time friend from Australia,' I lie. I can't even look at Noah in the crowd, so petrified that my face will betray my real feelings and it'll be unpacked on a Twitter thread. 'I have been doing tournaments here for a while, but he's not been able to attend a match until now. It is good to catch up with him.'

If I fumble through my words a little more than usual, while struggling to translate in my head, who cares? I've just played close to three hours of tennis. Blame it on heat exhaustion.

'Well, good luck in the next round, Gabriel,' says Percy. 'We'll all be watching.'

With murmured thanks, I pick up my bag, wave to the crowd, and make my way off the court.

As soon as I hit the air-conditioned hallways, my body relaxes. To my surprise, Victor's waiting for me.

'Where is everyone?' I ask in French as I drop my bag. 'Where's Noah?'

'He went with your father,' Victor says. 'Come on, the media's waiting.'

I pull on a fresh t-shirt and throw my frizzy hair under a cap before I follow Victor into the press gallery. Press is, without a doubt, my least favourite thing about this job. I'd play another match against O'Lachlan under the ferocious sun if it meant I didn't need to front the media.

There are around a dozen journalists gathered in the press room when I step inside. Cameras turn on me, the red dots blazing, and the feeling of being watched by so many people makes me nervous. It's one thing to play in front of a crowd and another thing to *speak* to them.

I take a seat at a desk lined with microphones and smooth my hands over my shorts, wiping the sweat away.

'Gabriel!' A man raises his hand. 'Nigel from *The Guardian*. This was a great result for you today; how do you feel you played?'

I lick my lips and lean into the microphone. 'I think I played well but the court conditions were hard; it was very humid. The ball felt heavier.'

A woman speaks next. 'Fiona from Fox. You got so close to the final at the US Open last year; do you think you've carried the same momentum into this tournament?'

Last year, I'd lost the semi-final. 'The US Open was a good result for me; if I get as far as that this tournament, I will be happy.'

'You're twenty-five with no grand slam titles,' a younger man pipes up. 'As far as tennis is concerned, you are a mid-career player. Do you think this is the year you'll get a grand slam, if not here, then elsewhere?'

Stupid question. I lean towards the microphone. 'Every year is the year I might win a grand slam.'

'Noah seems nice,' Victor says as we walk back to the dressing-room after the press conference. 'Though I'm afraid we were not the best company for him. I hope he wasn't bored.'

After giving Noah a crash course in tennis while watching Lukas, he'd picked it up quickly. 'I'm sure he followed along.'

'I didn't realise you had friends in Melbourne,' Victor continues. 'It's good he came to see you play.'

He's prying. 'I have a life outside of tennis, you know.'

I don't mean it to sound rude, but I feel like it comes off that way.

'I know that, Gabriel.' Victor says my full name to get his point across.

When we get back to the dressing-room, Papa's packed up our gear and is talking to a member of staff to arrange a ride back to the hotel.

'Where's Noah?' I ask as the staffer leaves.

'He said he had to go back to the city,' Papa replies. 'Come on, they're bringing a car around.' He places a hand on my shoulder and steers me through the narrow hallway. 'You played well today.'

'Noah said he'd stay,' I mumble, spinning around. Maybe I can catch him on his way out.

'He seemed in quite a rush,' Papa says.

Did he get a call to go to work? Maybe he felt unwell after being in the sun all morning. There must be a reason why he bailed before seeing me.

We walk to the players' drop-off point and find the car waiting for us. As Papa loads our bags in the boot, I get into the back seat and pull out my phone.

Hungrygabriel73: *Hey, Papa said you left? R u okay?*

The car pulls away from the arena. Victor's fingers thrum against the vinyl of the door. No one looks at me.

No one says anything.

My phone vibrates in my hand.

NoAgenda: *I'm sorry Gabriel, your dad's right. I don't want to distract you.*

'What?!'

'I did it for you, Gabriel!' Papa says as we step into the apartment. 'Each time the play reset, you glanced at the player's box; even Percy commented on it. This guy is a magnet. It is not worth the distraction.'

Fear prickles up my spine. Was I really that transparent?

'He's not a distraction; he's my *friend*,' I shoot back. 'You know, things *normal* people have.'

'You are not normal, Gabriel,' Papa counters. 'You are *exceptional*, and every moment that you do not focus on what you can achieve is a moment that is wasted.'

He sounds so much like the voice in my head—the voice that makes me feel bad about things I really want to do—and it's overwhelming.

Victor stays quiet. I wish he would speak up. I wish he would say something; tell Papa how unreasonable he's being.

I wish he was on my side.

'I don't want to be exceptional!' I cry. My stomach feels like it's in my throat and every word is an effort to get out. 'I want to have a life. Every day it's the same; get up, train, play. I can't stand it. I can't stand *you*.'

There's a quiet rage in papa's eyes. 'I have done everything for you, Gabriel.'

'And I've spent years trying to live up to your expectations and I am *miserable*,' I reply. 'I'm a twenty-five-year-old man! I have no friends unless you approve of them. I've barely had a drink or a relationship, and I can't even *fucking* swear without being told off.'

'You're here to do a job. I don't want you to jeopardise your career over—'

'*What* career?' I cut him off. 'I'm past my best years! If it hasn't happened yet, it probably won't *ever.*'

'Gabi,' Victor says from the kitchen. He must recognise the comment from the presser earlier. 'Don't let them get in your head.'

I ignore him, too riled up to care.

'I'm no one outside of tennis, and that is your fault,' I tell Papa. The fury I've swallowed down for so long is coming up my throat, and I feel like I might vomit. 'You robbed me of my childhood with your blind ambition. You forced your dreams onto me and ensured I had nothing else to fall back on. Now I am nothing unless I'm on the court. I'm *no one* unless I win.'

'*Gabriel,*' Papa replies sternly. It's a warning. He wants to bully me back into obedience.

This is just a tantrum to him. Unacceptable behaviour which he must meet with discipline.

I look at Victor, searching for support, but he turns away.

They don't understand. Worst of all, they won't try to understand. My prize money makes this lifestyle possible, and they don't want the cash cow to complain.

Turning back to my father, I meet his hard gaze. 'You have failed as my coach and as my father,' I say coldly. 'I'm not a child anymore and I won't be treated as one.'

Then, I push past Victor and wrench open the apartment door. Papa calls my name, his booming voice echoing down the hall, but I don't stop. I don't know where I'm going, but I know I'm not staying here.

14

NOAH

It's early in the afternoon when I get home from the tennis. Sadie bounds down the hallway, her claws tapping on the polished floorboards. Margie must still be at work.

After Bernard told me, in no uncertain terms, to fuck off and leave his son alone, I'd taken my bruised ego home. *We're here for one reason,* he'd said in the claustrophobic tunnels of Evonne Goolagong Arena after the match. *Gabriel cannot afford a distraction.*

It's clear Bernard is not a man to be messed with. As much as I'd like to say I stood up for myself, the truth is I crumbled faster than an inner-city Victorian terrace, and fled Melbourne Park with my tail between my legs.

I have no idea where this leaves Gabriel and me—but I have no interest in getting between him and his father. Fuck, I've dealt with one shitty dad; I'm not about to add another to my list.

Besides, maybe Bernard is right. It's not like Gabriel's playing for peanuts; the winner of the Australian Open receives almost three million dollars. No doubt Bernard gets a cut of the prize money.

This is Gabriel's dream. It's everything he's worked for, and if I'm putting it in jeopardy, maybe I need to be the bigger person and pull back. Cut this off before someone gets hurt.

And what *is* this really—a fling with someone who jets off as soon as he loses a match? Is that worth all this drama? But as soon as I think that, I remember the way Gabriel looked sitting on the edge of the Yarra, the way my heart spluttered at his smile, and I know I'm kidding myself.

After being in the sun all morning, I dump my clothes in the laundry basket and wash the sweat and sunscreen off my body. The cool water feels like heaven.

Pulling on a pair of loose cotton shorts, I head into the kitchen to fix a sandwich. Sadie nudges me as I open a packet of ham, smearing her wet nose across my thigh. I feed her a little and she runs off.

I'm about to distract myself with something on Netflix when the doorbell rings. Putting my sandwich on the side table, I haul my arse off the lounge and go to answer it.

I expect to see a fluoro-yellow mailman's vest or maybe a kid selling raffle tickets but when I open the door, it's Gabriel. He stands on my doorstep, chest heaving. His eyes are wild and red-rimmed and his hair is a frizzy halo around his face.

'Gabi.' I can't hide my surprise.

'Hey,' he says breathlessly, and the butterflies that seem to have taken up residence in my stomach for the past few days take flight.

Sadie pushes past me, snuffling at Gabriel's shorts. He smiles and reaches down to pat her.

'I found the neighbourhood on the map. Then I walked the blocks looking for the yellow door and the rosebush.' Maybe it's the heat, but I swear I see a blush rise on his cheeks. He sounds delirious. Hell, he just admitted he practically *stalked* me on Google Maps. 'Papa told me what happened. I'm sorry. Can I come in?'

'Um, sure.' I move aside to let him past. Realising I don't have a shirt on, and it'd be impolite to have company half-naked, I go into my bedroom to find one. 'Let me grab a shirt.'

Gabriel's tongue peeks out to wet his dry lips. Heat prickles along my spine and before I can do—or say—something stupid, I retreat into my bedroom. Gabriel follows.

'Whatever Papa said, it's not true,' he says. 'I'm sorry he confronted you like that; it's not what I want.'

I open the drawer of my dresser, rifling through the mess of fabric. 'I don't know, he made it pretty clear I wasn't welcome.'

He has spent too long preparing for this tournament for it to be wasted because of you. Bernard's words come back to me. *Do not contact him again.*

'He's wrong. I wanted you there,' Gabriel says. 'I don't care what he says, and neither should you.'

'He's your dad, Gabriel.' I finally find an old black crew-neck and turn back to him. 'The last thing I want is to cause unnecessary drama or distract you from your training. Also—'

Gabriel steps closer and whatever I was about to say simply disappears. I feel the heat radiating from his body.

He's still wearing the same clothes he played in and he smells earthy. Primal.

'I played for *you* today. Not for my dad. Not for the championship. You.'

'Gabi,' I manage. His gaze drops to my mouth, and a muscle in his jaw flexes. His hand rests at the hinge of my hip. I feel the dry calluses on his palm drag against my stomach and try not to imagine how it'd feel to have him touch me in other places, too.

'I'll lose a thousand more times in my career,' Gabriel says, glancing up at me through thick, dark lashes. 'I'll lose for a thousand different reasons, but it'll never, *ever* be your fault.'

Fuck. Without thinking about it, I thread my fingers through Gabi's hair, cradling the back of his neck.

His thumb runs across my lower lip before it smooths down my jawline. God, is this really happening? He looks at me, his deep brown eyes raw and unfiltered, so full of emotion and *want*. No one's *ever* looked at me like this; no one's ever wanted me like this.

'Noah, I—' Gabriel's throat bobs as he swallows, and his eyes search mine.

We both know what he wants to do.

I can't let him overthink this. I curl my fingers into the back of his head and pull him closer.

'Kiss me, Gabriel.'

So he does.

Gabriel's mouth meets mine with unrestrained passion and urgency. My back hits my dresser and it *thunks* against the wall. The t-shirt I'm holding drops to the floor as Gabriel's mouth slides against mine.

Heat prickles up my spine as Gabriel tugs my body close to his, our hips meeting, chests touching. He strokes my cheek and deepens the kiss, tongue finding the seam of my lips. I open my mouth for him, of course I do, and his tongue meets mine. Whatever bravado Gabriel had a moment ago is suddenly gone. He kisses me tenderly, as if he's almost unsure, and the sweetness of it all makes me lose my mind.

'Noah,' he rasps as we come apart, our mouths millimetres from each other. Now that I've kissed Gabriel it feels like a crime to *stop* kissing him. To ever stop kissing him.

With a not-so-gentle nudge, Gabriel pulls me towards the bed. The back of my knee touches the frame and I fall onto my mattress, spread out and dizzy with desire. He grins down at me, his dark eyes practically feral. In one fluid movement, he pulls his polo over his head to reveal—

'Holy fucking shit.' He drops his shirt to the floor. I'd expected Gabriel's physique to be wicked, but nothing could have prepared me for what I see. Well-defined muscle ripples under his dark skin, almost-black chest hair covers his pecs and runs down to his navel before disappearing below the waistband of his shorts. All I can think about is running my tongue down the valley of his abs; pushing my hands through his chest hair and wrapping my arms around his shoulders, pulling him closer, feeling his body move against mine, and never letting go.

I don't know why I'm fantasising about it. Gabriel is right *fucking* here.

'Come here, baby,' I murmur as he kneels on the edge of the bed. Gabriel's breath catches at the endearment and he crawls on top of me again, our mouths finding each other. Like this, I can feel the length of his warm body against mine; my thin cotton shorts doing little to hide my growing desire.

My tongue slides against his and it's just—*wonderful.* I'm blissed out of my mind. Now that we're no longer fumbling for each other, Gabriel's kisses are deep and slow. He kisses me like no one has ever kissed me in my life, and maybe that's the point. Maybe he wants to ruin kissing for me. Because I already know I'll dream of his mouth and long for it well after he's gone.

I hitch my knee over his waist and Gabriel's body shifts, the crux of our bodies meeting together. He breaks away with a gasp, confusion and desire warring in his eyes.

'Fuck, Noah,' he groans. Gabriel moves, our shorts barely a barrier between us, and his eyes roll back. He does it again, lips parted, cheeks flushed, driving our bodies together.

'I don't have a condom,' I whisper. Or enough lube. Or the headspace for a discussion about how far we're both willing to go.

Gabriel opens his eyes again. They're wild and he's panting hard, chest heaving. 'Okay. I—' He clears his throat, clearly overwhelmed. 'It's . . . it's fine.'

I push his sweat-soaked hair from his forehead, letting the curls that frame his face rest on the shell of his ear. 'We can still—if you want.'

He nods, even though I'm not sure either of us is coherent right now. 'Anything. Touch me, please.'

I run my hand down his chest and stomach. His abs quiver under my touch, hips surging against mine in an action I'm not entirely sure is deliberate.

'Noah, I—' Gabriel swallows thickly and I kiss his bobbing Adam's apple and then continue down, kissing and sucking, even as my hand slips beneath the waistband of his playing shorts.

'God, Gabi, you're so fucking beautiful.'

As soon as my hands are in his pants, I realise I've made a mistake and take them out. Above me, Gabriel's eyes search mine, suddenly confused.

'What's wrong?' he asks in a panicked tone because when someone takes their hand out of your pants, I suppose it's normal to assume something is *very* wrong.

'Lube,' I manage to get out before reaching blindly for my bedside table. Opening the drawer, I find my almost-empty bottle of lube and squirt whatever's left into my hand.

He leans over to kiss me as I slip my hand back into his pants, stroking him once, twice, three times. He thrums like an instrument, every gasp and cry and mumbled word a note of the most beautiful song.

'Yes, baby.' I kiss wherever I can: his temple, his hairline, his jaw. His harsh, warm breaths hit my ear. 'Fuck, you're so hot like this.'

'Your *mouth*,' Gabriel grunts. Who knew he'd be a fiend for a bit of dirty talk? His arms bracket my head, shaking with the strain. Another hard stroke and Gabriel's hip surges upward, chasing more. He's close.

'That's it,' I soothe. 'Let go.'

He says something in French but it's garbled by a low moan. I turn my head to watch him, our noses brushing together as everything narrows down to a single point—me, him, and whatever this is between us. Gabriel comes on my hand with a heaving cry, his temple against mine, his body thrumming in my palm.

'I'm sorry,' he mumbles after a long moment. 'I should have told you I was close, I—'

'It's okay,' I reply, kissing his forehead. He looks sheepish, embarrassed even, and that's not the post-orgasm glow I want to foster. 'It was kind of the point.'

Gabriel rolls off me and collapses onto the other side of the bed, a loopy smile gracing his sweaty face. 'It's been a while. And I was all worked up.'

I find the shirt from before and wipe my hands on it before sliding back onto the bed. Gabriel frowns as I settle beside him.

'You didn't—' He reaches for my shorts, but I stop him, threading our fingers together.

'It's fine,' I say, because as much as I'd like to come, I kinda like this more—lying with Gabriel in this moment, the annoying is-he-isn't-he acrobatics my brain's been doing these past few days finally put to rest. 'I'll cash in an IOU another time.'

A frown flits across his beautiful flushed face.

'It means you'll owe me.' I run my hand down his chest again, feeling the muscles twitch underneath my fingers.

He laughs a little and pillows his elbow behind his head. 'I'll owe you.'

♪

I wake up before Gabriel, groggy and hot. It's just after five in the afternoon and the sun streams through my west-facing window, bathing us in warm light. Gabriel lies facedown beside me, hugging my pillow beneath him. His dark eyelashes flicker against his cheeks while he sleeps, and his lips are parted just slightly as he sucks in slow, even breaths. Not for the first time, I'm in awe of how beautiful he is.

I smooth back a few curls from his face and my fingers continue down the column of his throat, pushing his hair away. I discover a mole near his collarbone and a smattering of freckles across his neck and shoulders; markers of days spent training in the sun, no doubt.

'*Quelle heure*?' he murmurs into the pillow.

I thank my current overlord, the Duolingo owl, for my significantly improved French. 'Just after five.'

'Slept for a while.' He sounds genuinely surprised.

'You played tennis for three hours,' I say. 'I felt tired just watching you.'

Gabriel lets out a long sigh and stretches out on my bed. He reaches back to grasp my hand, brings it to his mouth and kisses across my knuckles. 'Thank you.'

My little gay heart swells. Fuck I'm a sap. 'You don't have to thank me; it, um, I wanted to.' Gabriel drags his mouth across my knuckles again and I swallow. Feelings jitter through my body, nervous and confused. Why am I confused? I got what I wanted—Gabriel in my bed, his mouth on mine. But now, it's clear that things have changed. And I'm not sure what that means—for either of us.

'You want something to eat?' I ask, swallowing down my feelings. Briefly, I wonder if Sadie's claimed my forgotten sandwich.

Gabriel shakes his head and rolls onto his back. 'No. I just want to lie like this for a while.' He runs his hands over his face, and groans. 'Papa is going to kill me.'

My stomach twists. I don't like this. While a part of me knows I'm little more than a drop in the river that is Gabriel's complex life, that there must be more to this argument than simply my presence, I don't enjoy being the one in the middle of a fight. 'I don't want to get between you two. Or the championship.'

He pins me with a serious look. 'I meant what I said earlier; you won't. Our fight was a long time coming. I finally told him things I've wanted him to know for a while . . .' He lets out a shaky breath. 'About how I feel and how he treats me.'

'Did you tell him you're into guys?'

Gabriel shakes his head.

His brown eyes are beautiful; the afternoon sun highlights flecks of amber in his irises. I feel his hand run up my back and rest between my shoulder blades.

'I want to tell him . . . I just . . . I'm scared he'll take it badly.' I feel like he's not telling me the whole truth but I can't push it. 'How did you tell your family?'

Ooft. Not the time to open that can of worms. 'Never did. I wasn't that close with my dad. I think Mum had suspicions, but I never told her.'

'No brothers or sisters?'

'Just me and my mum.' His fingers trail down my back and up again. It's distracting in the best way. 'You?'

'My *maman* and my sister, Claudia, live back in Paris. My sister is twenty. She studies law at university.'

'And your mum?'

'She is a manager at a tech company,' he says. 'Sometimes I think she has "suspicions", as you said.' His French accent hugs the word.

Gabriel curls closer to me, his thumb brushing over my exposed hipbone.

'So your next tournament is in Brazil.' I change the subject.

Gabriel nods into the pillow, his bronze eyes sliding from mine. 'I won't get home until March. When I was younger, I used to do all the tournaments I could. Now, it's expected of me. I wish I could take a step back. Choose where I go and when.'

I don't pretend to understand the intricacies that come with being a professional athlete, but it's clear things at home are more complicated than they seem. 'It sounds like you need to talk with your dad.'

Gabriel presses his lips together. 'I tried. We just fight. Doesn't make me confident to come out to him. And then there's the tour. Sponsorships. The fans.'

I flop back against the mattress and stare up at the roof. 'Sometimes it feels like everyone makes a big deal about being out and proud. There's so much pressure to live your authentic life that sometimes people forget how dangerous it can be. How much we risk.'

'I'm not ready,' Gabriel admits. 'For any of it.'

Rolling onto my side, I face him. 'Why don't you chill here for a bit? We'll make food and watch something on Netflix.'

'That'd be nice.'

'We can plan our tourist bucket list for tomorrow. Is there something you'd like to do?'

Gabriel's face lights up. 'Lukas told me about this one place . . .'

♪

Later, I find a packet of microwave popcorn in the deep recesses of the cupboard. As I pop it, Gabriel selects an episode of a cake-decorating show to watch. Sadie jumps on the lounge and settles against Gabriel, much to his complete delight and my absolute chagrin. Cockblocking dog.

Just after six, I hear the front door open. Sadie leaps from Gabriel's side and dashes down the hallway.

'Oh, hello you!' Margie says as she closes the door. 'Noah, are you in, honey?'

Gabriel looks at me, and then at the back door, clearly planning an exit route.

'It's just my housemate, she's cool, I promise,' I assure him as I pause the TV. 'I'm in the lounge, Margie! A friend just popped by; I hope that's okay.'

'Of course it is!' she calls back as she shuffles her way down the hallway. She appears with a handful of groceries, a cotton tote full of books, and her bike helmet skew-whiff on her head. She looks down at Gabriel and smiles. 'Hello again, dear.'

'Hello,' he murmurs, clearly embarrassed. 'Sorry again about the door.'

'That old thing had it coming, don't worry,' Margie replies. 'You did me a favour. Who knows who could have kicked down the door?'

Gabriel stands up to shake her hand. 'I'm Gabriel, by the way.'

I take the grocery bags from Margie and begin unpacking them on the kitchen bench, watching Gabriel and Margie across the open-plan space.

'Gabriel,' she repeats. Now that Gabriel's standing at his full height, Margie's entire demeanour changes. '*The* Gabriel. From the TV.'

Oh no. I abandon the groceries and step back into the living room just as Margie collapses into her recliner. Gabriel looks at me like, *I didn't do anything! Promise!*

'Are you okay, Margie?' I ask. She stares wide-eyed at Gabriel, her mouth moving around words that don't come.

'She's just a bit shocked,' Gabriel replies. 'It happens. Some water might help.'

I have no idea how often Gabriel's mere presence shocks people into stupors, but Margie comes back to herself quickly, clearly not happy being the centre of attention. 'Right, well. You played very well today, and it's lovely to meet you. I just, um, I just didn't expect you to be in my *home*.'

Gabriel laughs. 'Me as well.'

Margie turns to me. 'How long have you known each other? Why didn't you tell me, Noah? I thought you hated tennis.'

'I don't *hate* tennis,' I say, more to Gabriel than Margie. 'It's just a confusing sport.'

Gabriel shoots me a teasing glare. 'We met a few days ago. I walked into his bar.'

Margie smiles at us both. 'That's a bit romantic.'

Gabriel opens his mouth to protest. 'Don't even bother,' I cut in. 'She clocked me as a gay the moment I set foot in her house. At the very least, you're gay by affiliation.'

'Is this a *secret affair*?' Margie continues, clearly delighted by the entire situation. 'How scandalous. Of course, I'll keep it to myself.' She clasps a hand over Gabriel's. 'You must stay for dinner, honey. I bought a few lamb chops from the butcher on my way home and they're going straight on the barbeque.'

'Barbeques with lamb chops are very Australian,' I inform Gabriel. 'It's like the holy grail of authentic Australian experiences. An essential tourist must-do.'

He gives me a meaningful look, and like the Grinch, I feel my heart swell a few sizes.

'Well, I suppose I better stay.'

'Excellent,' Margie says. 'Oh, I'm glad I got a little more than I needed. You know, something told me, "Margaret, get a few more", and I thought, well, I better do just that, and golly, I'm glad I did.' She pushes me out of the kitchen. 'Help Gabriel set up the barbeque, will you, Noah?'

15

GABRIEL

The sun's setting over the city in whorls of crimson and gold by the time I get back to the apartment. I'd spent the evening in Margie's backyard, cooking lamb chops, playing with the dog and kicking an old soccer ball with Noah. My knees are grass-stained, my ankles are itchy from bug bites, and there's dirt under my fingernails, but I don't care. For once, my heart and mind feel full.

And now I have to face my father.

As the Uber drops me off at the hotel, I prepare myself. In almost a decade of professional tennis, I've never spoken to my father like I did earlier, and I don't know what to expect. The blow-up's so bad, it's got back to *Maman* and Claudia back in Paris.

QuelleClaudia: *I've heard you fought with Papa.*

Hungrygabriel73: *He started it.*

I consider calling *Maman*, but as I check the time on my phone, I realise she'd be starting work. It's not easy keeping up with each other when I change time zones every few weeks, but I desperately want her advice on how to mend things with Papa.

This isn't the first time we've had a fight on tour, but we've never blown up at each other during a tournament.

Digging my key card out of my wallet, I step into the apartment, expecting the worst, but to my surprise, it's quiet. Dark. Victor is smoking on the balcony, his cigarette almost burnt down to the filter.

He turns at the sound of the sliding door opening.

'Oh, Gabriel!' He sounds surprised to see me. 'You're back.'

'Where's Papa?' I ask, closing the door behind me.

'At the gym. He's been there for a few hours now.' Victor stubs out his cigarette in the ashtray. 'I think he's thinking things over in the sauna.'

Maybe I should go down and speak to him there. Apologise. Try to make him see things from my perspective.

'Gabriel.' Victor pulls me from my thoughts. 'Noah's a nice guy, and it's clear he cares about you a lot. Whatever you're doing, I trust you'll make the right decisions for you. Not for your father. Not for me.'

'I'm gay, Victor.'

The words spill out before I can stop myself. As soon as I say them, I don't know why I feared saying them before. It doesn't feel scary or wrong. They're just words.

Immediately, though, I realise that it wasn't the words I was afraid of—it was the response. Victor's response. He pauses a moment, as if he's trying to figure out if he heard me correctly.

'I, um—' he fumbles, reaching down for the packet of cigarettes and lighting another. He inhales deeply, the end glowing, and then lets out a long, smoky breath. 'Well, *okay*.'

'Okay?' My voice shakes. 'That's all you're going to say?' Suddenly, I'm crumbling. 'I tell you I'm gay and you just say *okay*? I feel like I've been carrying this *weight* with me for years and I—'

The words stop. The tears start.

Victor places his cigarette in the ashtray and pulls me into his arms.

'Come here, sweet boy,' he says in that same comforting tone I remember from my childhood; the same voice that picked me up off the court when I fell; the same voice that soothed me after a hard loss. I wrap my arms around Victor and cry into his shoulder, unable to stop myself, unable to dam the emotions that gush forth.

'Gabi,' he says, pulling back from me. His thumbs wipe away the tears on my face and he smells of the menthols he smokes, and aftershave, and home. 'You are so loved. I had no idea this was something that weighed so heavily on you. I'm sorry.'

'I just—' The words don't come. Truthfully, I don't know what to say. Victor smooths his hands over my hair, my face.

'You haven't told your father?'

I shake my head. Maybe that was why I flew off the handle today. Papa wasn't just rejecting Noah; he was rejecting *me*. 'I'm worried he'll take it badly.'

'He won't,' Victor assures me, and then gestures for me to sit on the flimsy outdoor furniture. He takes a seat beside me. 'A long time ago, the night after his spectacular loss at the US Open, your father and I were at a foam party in the Village. He introduced me to Elias—a friend he knew back in Paris—who had moved to New York to work in publishing. We had a fantastic night hopping around all these wonderful bars and clubs. A year later, Elias wrote to your father to say he was moving back to Paris and asked if he had a spare room—Bernard didn't, but I happened to, so Elias moved in with me. We dated for five years; saw the turn of the millennium, but then we broke up. Later, I met Louise—and, well, it was magic.' He folds one long leg over the other. 'What I'm trying to say, Gabriel, is that I know your father, but I've *been* you, and you deserve to live a life the way you want to live it. Your father only wants you to be happy, and part of his frustration today was realising you aren't. That's why I didn't get involved. It was important for him to realise that.'

'I had no idea,' I say, and it's the truth. I had no idea Victor dated a man before he met his current partner; I had no idea Papa had been the one to set them up; and perhaps most shockingly, I had no idea Papa had attended a *foam* party during a tournament—something he's expressed I'm *never* to do.

Maybe that's half the problem. We've spent so long on the circuit, so long surrounded by work, that we don't know each other outside of tennis. We've never really had the chance to just be father and son.

'It's up to you when or if you tell him,' Victor replies. 'But thank you for telling me.'

My shoulders slump and I sink back further into the chair. 'What about my sponsorships, the fans—the . . .' I struggle to find the words but what I want to say is, what about the places I might not be allowed to play, the comments people will leave online, the way I'll be treated on the tour moving forward? '. . . Everything.'

'Fuck them,' Victor replies. 'Let me handle it, Gabi. That's my job as your media manager. We'll manage your socials, and you can keep your personal account secret; we'll renegotiate sponsorships with companies that align better with your personal brand, if need be.' He leans across and takes my hand. 'You just focus on being you.'

Just focus on being you. That feels weirdly relieving. 'Okay.'

Victor picks up his cigarette. 'You best go find your father and ensure he hasn't worked himself into a cardiac arrest downstairs,' he says between puffs. 'Should I draft up an NDA for Noah?'

'No. Noah's reasonable; he'll be fine.' Signing an NDA makes things feel . . . official between us. When I'm with Noah, I feel gloriously normal, and I want to keep it that way.

Victor looks like he wants to say something, but settles on, 'As long as you're being safe.'

Leaving Victor on the balcony, I head downstairs to the gym and sauna. Papa loves saunas. He's had one built in our Paris home. I find them stifling and not at all relaxing—especially since I'm pretty sure I lost sixty per cent of my body's water playing tennis today, among other activities.

Papa sits on the far side of the wooden room, near the stove. He glances up when I step in but doesn't say anything. It's close to 8 pm. Briefly, I wonder how long he's been sitting in the steam.

'Hey.' I take a seat on the bench opposite him. 'Victor was worried you'd passed out in here.'

'I'm fine,' he replies curtly. His tone shocks me. I'd come in here to make amends, but I hadn't considered that Papa would still be sour.

'I can go if you want me to,' I say, trying not to let anger creep into my voice. Maybe it's too soon. Maybe we still need space.

'No, don't go,' Papa says as I move to get up. 'Sit, Gabriel.'

I sit.

And wait.

And sweat.

'I think we should skip Brazil,' Papa says after a long while.

'What?' I ask reflexively, my brain still processing his words.

'I think you need a break. Let's skip Brazil.'

'And what would we do instead?' I ask.

'Go on a holiday. Spend time at home. Prepare for the clay season.' He shrugs. 'It's your choice, Gabriel.'

My choice. There's so much I want to do—I want to see the Grand Canyon; I want to go skiing in the French Alps until the tip of my nose is numb, and then spend the night eating junk food in front of an open fire; I want to stay at home and read through my *maman*'s extensive library and go to Disneyland.

'I shouldn't have yelled at you,' I admit. 'I'm sorry I raised my voice.'

The electric stove pushes out more steam as Papa sweeps his long locs over his shoulder. 'You don't need to apologise, Gabriel. It is clear you have felt this way for a long time.

It was my fault for not realising it.' He stares into the distance, not exactly looking me in the eye. 'We have been pursuing tennis for so long because I thought it was our dream; I didn't notice when it stopped being yours and was only mine.'

'I still want to play,' I reaffirm. 'I just want *more*. More time at home instead of jetting around the world chasing minor titles. More time to just have you as my papa, and not my coach.'

'When I retired from playing, it wasn't my choice,' Papa says. 'I'd have done anything to keep going. I see so much of my talent in you, Gabriel, but I see how unfair I have become in my ambitions for you.'

A trickle of sweat runs down the ridge of my spine. I'm about done with saunas and emotionally draining conversations for the day, but I can see that Papa is really trying. I take a breath. 'First off, I want you to be nicer to Noah. He's my friend. I'd like you to get to know him.'

Papa's mouth tightens into a thin line. 'I regret what I said to him today. I should apologise.'

'And I want to train tomorrow afternoon instead of the morning because I'm going to the beach with Noah.'

Papa nods. 'It's a night match in two days; you can afford some time to relax.'

I wonder if now's the time to bring up the whole *being gay* thing, but I'm already tired of talking, and not keen to add any weight to our recently repaired bridge.

'Are you coming out soon?' I ask, cringing at my choice of words.

'Soon,' Papa confirms.

'Good, because Victor's stressed out that we're fighting—he's chain-smoking.'

That makes him laugh, like he's remembering a warm memory. It's nice that they have such a long history, and I'm glad I got some insight into who my dad was before me. Before all of this.

Victor's scrolling through his phone when I get back. It's late. A police procedural plays on the TV, but it's clear he's not paying attention.

'Gabi!' He jumps, clearly rattled as the door closes behind me. 'How's Bernard?'

'We patched things up,' I say. 'He'll be up in a bit.'

Victor doesn't look relieved at the news.

'What's wrong?' I ask. Dread settles in my stomach. What if someone recorded our conversation earlier—what if it's making waves on socials right now? *Shocking recording from Gabriel Madani's hotel balcony!* 'What's happened?'

Victor hands me his phone. My heart sinks. 'I got a media alert. It's about Noah.'

16

NOAH

I wake up in bed, sweating my arse off, when I see the text Gabriel sent me overnight. These Victorian houses are beautiful, but they were never made for the heat.

Or the cold.

Or Australia, really.

Hungrygabriel73: *Hey, I just saw the article. I'm sorry. Sometimes the press are like this. They find someone and they just latch on.*

Latch on? I frown as I text Gabriel back.

NoAgenda: *What article?*

NoAgenda: *Did someone mention me in an article?*

Gabriel doesn't reply. Maybe he's asleep; it's still early but I'm anxious. Impatient. Paranoid. Before I know it, I'm pulling up Google and inputting Gabriel's name. I swore I'd never do it, but I'm so nervous my fingers shake as I type.

Gabriel Madani dazzles during a sweltering second-round match, says one headline.

Gabriel Madani: what you need to know about tennis's hottest bachelor, says another.

Gabriel Madani's mystery guy: how to get the fit that sent the tennis world wild.

I click on the 'mystery guy' article just as Gabriel sends me a link to another on a different site. There's a photo of me watching Gabriel, sunglasses on my face—to be perfectly honest, looking cool as fuck—and underneath, the author's written: *Was I the only one OBSESSED with Gabriel Madani's friend's fit at the tennis today? Vintage 80s vibes, bitchy little sunglasses. Shop the fit here.*

I scroll past links to shop retro-looking cotton shirts, designer white sneakers and what they called *bitchy* little sunglasses until I get to the end of the article.

While no one knows who this dreamy stranger is—Gabriel simply mentioned he was a 'friend'—the Twitterverse is set on uncovering his identity.

Uncovering *my* identity.

I sit up in bed, grab my laptop and open Twitter. My heart's beating so fast it feels like I might go into cardiac arrest. I feel my phone vibrate against my thigh. I know it's Gabriel trying to get through to me, but I can't pull myself away from Twitter.

#retrotennisguy is trending and it's all about finding *me*.

@nighthawk87 Cute boy with floppy hair makes headlines and Twitter is in meltdown? Feels like my first crush all over again.

@red_velvet_cupcakes Anyone actually know his @?

@electricswitch to @red_velvet_cupcakes Why do you need to know? Respect his privacy if he doesn't have a public account!

@red_velvet_cupcakes to @electricswitch Wtf chill i just want to follow him.

@frugalguru The obsession with finding #retrotennisguy is everything that's wrong with social media these days!

I follow the stream of tweets and news articles written about my stupid fucking thrifted shirt and a pair of sunglasses I bought from a petrol station last year. There are tweets and shares, and heart reacts and people saying 'who cares' under Buzzfeed articles. I've gone viral.

I shut the laptop and push it away. There's a ringing in my ears, and I'm sweating. I don't know what to do; I don't know who I should call.

After *years* of lying low, of keeping my nose out of places it doesn't belong, this happens. Dad's bound to see it.

He'll know I'm in Melbourne.

My phone vibrates again and I realise Gabriel's trying to video-call me. I don't want him to see me like this, broken and crying and unable to think a sentence let alone speak one. I let the phone go to voicemail before pulling up our chat.

Hungrygabriel73: *I'm so sorry noah*

Hungrygabriel73: *Victor can try to make this go away but, in my experience, people will move on quickly.*

Hungrygabriel73: *Call me?*

Hungrygabriel73: *Are u okay, noah?*

I stare at the message for a long time, trying to make sense of my thoughts. All I want to do right now is to run; hide; disappear—again.

NoAgenda: *I'm just trying to make sense of everything.*

Hungrygabriel73: *I should have know this happen when percy asked me about it after the match. I'm sorry.*

He's typing so fast his grammar is suffering, but I know what he means.

NoAgenda: *It's okay.*

Hungrygabriel73: *This disappear by tomorrow, i promise*

God, but *what if*? What if someone knows how to dig up information about me?

Gabriel said he didn't care about my past if I didn't care about googling him—but what if it's systematically unpacked and exposed by people online, and laid out in front of him? My fucked-up childhood, my arsehole dad, my months of homelessness, my brief stint in sex work . . .

Everything.

I've always told myself I'm not ashamed of my past, but here I am—being ashamed over it.

My clothes are soaked with sweat, so I get up and shower. Sadie pads into the bathroom to keep me company.

Maybe I should leave after the Open.

Maybe I should leave before that.

Maybe I should leave now.

If Dad finds out where I am, the life I've built here could come crashing down around me.

The people I love will be in danger.

I'll be in danger.

I grab my phone and pull up my last message from my mum.

Don't worry about me. I'll be fine.

♪

Two years ago, I left Bendigo. For months I slept rough, jumping between hostels and homeless shelters, partying and taking drugs just to stay awake. I'd find places to sleep in public during the day; parks, beaches—places where it's socially acceptable to doze off. I'd go to the shopping centre to charge my phone at the outlets in the food court; sit in the library when I needed wi-fi; shower in public bathrooms or hostels and carry around my dirty laundry in my backpack.

When Margie's dog-sitting job popped up on the share-house website, it was early March, and the weather was already changing. It'd be a long winter on the streets and I knew I needed to find a more permanent solution before the weather set in.

The arrangement with Margie was a godsend, and the job at the jazz bar followed once I got a roof over my head. For the first time in a long time, it felt like everything was coming up Noah. I'd reinvented myself. I was a phoenix risen from the ashes of a burnt-out childhood and a shitty family, and there wasn't anything I couldn't achieve.

When Mark took over the Peacock Lounge and it became Mark's Place, I'd hoped everything would stay more or less the same, and that I could maintain the stability I'd fought so hard to create. By the time I realised it wasn't going to be great, I'd already adapted to the crushing weight of working for Mark.

I know, deep down, that I deserve better, but when you're in that cycle of abuse, it's hard to claw yourself out.

Once I'm dressed I go into the kitchen to make a coffee. It's only six-thirty and I'm already spiralling.

I shove my cup under the spout of the coffee machine and let it run. Holding my breath, I quickly google my full name and wait for the results to come up.

Luckily, there are at least a dozen Noah Burgesses on Facebook and a marketing executive with a prolific LinkedIn page and blog. The only thing slightly linked to me is a short article announcing me as the winner of a colouring-in competition when I was seven years old. As far as the internet goes, I might as well not exist.

So why am I stressing over Dad? I've lived with the fear he'll find me for over two years, but the fact is, Dad hasn't reared his head since I left Bendigo, and I'll be damned if I'll live my life haunted by the ghost of childhood past. If I stop living my life, he wins, and I've got a hot man to take to the beach and watch frolic in the surf. *No one* is taking that away from me.

Grabbing the keys to Margie's car, I throw an esky and my beach bag into the back. It's a little Hyundai Margie rarely uses because we cycle or catch public transport around Melbourne.

After swinging by a local café to grab us both a coffee, I drive through the city and arrive at Gabriel's hotel just before eight. To my surprise, he's in the lobby.

'I could hardly sleep, I was so excited,' he says as he falls into the passenger seat.

The tension eases out of my body. For the next few hours, it'll be just us, away from everything.

'Hey, about this morning—' he begins.

'It's fine. It'll die down.' I hand him the AUX cord. 'You're in charge of the playlist.'

He laughs as I turn out of the hotel driveway, my phone directing me to turn left. 'That's a lot of responsibility.'

Gabriel filters through his playlists while I find my way onto the highway; it's still early morning, and the traffic's light as we make our way out of the city. Eventually, Gabriel settles on Taylor Swift's latest album, which I'm *definitely* not mad about.

'I can't believe they called my sunglasses bitchy,' I say as we hit the open road.

'I like them,' Gabriel replies. 'They're *sassy*.'

I adjust said sassy-slash-bitchy sunglasses. 'I feel like that's just a synonym for bitchy.'

Gabriel laughs and pats my knee. His hand lingers for a moment, and it takes me back to yesterday and how it felt when his hands had dragged down my body; when he'd brushed the hair from my eyes.

'Did you work things out with your dad?' I ask.

'Yes. We decided to skip Brazil and go back to France after the Open is over,' he replies. 'I want to take time off.'

My heart stutters. I shouldn't get ahead of myself. Gabriel is here for a finite amount of time; it's selfish to try and make this anything more than it is.

'I told Victor I'm gay,' he says. I do my best to keep my eyes on the road.

'What happened?'

'He hugged me. Told me not to worry about the deals or the sponsorships or the fans.' He pauses for a while, as if thinking. 'Victor said he'll handle it. It was . . . good to talk to him about it.'

'That's fantastic.' I like how upbeat he sounds about the whole conversation.

Gabriel's hand slides up my leg. 'If I stayed for longer, would you like that?'

His sudden question, combined with his touch, makes me jump and I almost run the car off the road. 'Right,' I say once my heart rate's come down. 'Firstly, no lewd touching while I'm driving, and second: what?'

Gabriel smiles but removes his hand. 'If we're not going to Brazil, then I don't have to rush home.'

'You'd do that?'

'I'd do it for you, yes,' he says, and dear god, it feels like my heart is going to burst. *Focus on the road, Noah. Can you imagine the headlines if you were in a crash with your gay tennis star lover?* 'Do you want that?'

Of course I want it. 'I'd love for you to stay. I could ask Margie if she wouldn't mind if you crashed at our place.'

'I'd like that.' He says it so earnestly it almost hurts. Because he wants to stay here with me. He wants to get to know *me* and who I am and get to know my friends and where I come from. Not that I have any friends, I realise. Except for Margie. Is Peaches my friend? I wonder what Gabriel would make of Peaches and her huge platforms and glittery wigs.

'You'll have to show me around Paris one day.' I carefully take my hand off the wheel to take a sip of coffee. 'If I can ever afford the flight.'

'I'll pay for it.' Gabriel says it like it's nothing.

I choke on the coffee, swallowing what I can. 'Gabi, you can't just *say* that.'

'Why not?' He sounds genuinely confused, which only makes this worse. 'I have the money.'

I suppose as a professional tennis player, he is quite wealthy. 'It's not about the money, it's about the principle.'

'What principle? It would be a gift.'

'But I could never pay you back.'

'I am not asking you to. That's what gift means.'

Realising I'm getting nowhere with this argument—and that I'm arguing about a very generous offer—I shake my head and let Gabriel think he's won.

It's almost two hours drive to Anglesea. Gabriel stares out the window for most of it, captivated by the rolling green hills that hug the small port city of Geelong. A few minutes later, the first glimpse of the ocean appears on the horizon, a shimmer of dark water.

'It's a bit of a drive, but it's not as busy as the city beaches,' I say as we motor along the coastline, weaving through dense marshland, mangroves and bushes of blooming pigface.

'I don't mind.' He places a hand on my thigh again. 'It's beautiful.'

17

GABRIEL

I haven't been to the ocean since I was in Algeria. The smell of the sea—the brine, the freshness—reminds me of waking up with the windows open at my grandparents' place. It reminds me of late-night training on their rooftop when the wind would whip up whitecaps in the waves and scatter cool mist over the sweltering city.

'I need to buy swimmers,' I say once we park, spying a run-down surf shop across the road with a row of surfboards resting against the wall.

'Sure. We can make a stop,' Noah says.

It's so hot the tar sticks to the soles of our shoes as we walk across the road. The girl at the till looks barely eighteen; she's got a cool beachy vibe with her long blonde hair and a smattering of freckles across her nose.

'Heya,' she chirps. 'Lemme know if you need anything.'

Noah browses a rack of swimwear. I join him and find a little black brief that is cut so low that it leaves nothing to the imagination. Pulling it out, I dangle it in front of him.

'You like?'

Noah turns bright red. 'Jesus, no. Buy regular swimmers, please. We can't have *another* outfit incident.'

I put the briefs back onto the rack. 'Fine.'

'Just pick a pair you like and try them on,' he insists, clearly flustered.

There's not a lot to choose from so I grab a pair of navy shorts with a retro purple-and-white palm print on them. Noah nods his head in approval.

'Looks good. Let's go.'

I'm about to go into the change room when I see *them*. Frankly, I don't know how I missed them. It's not like one can just walk past hot-pink swimming briefs without picking them off the rack. They're practically *alluring*. Checking they've got my size, I sneak them into the dressing-room while Noah tries on a pair of sunglasses. Clearly, the comment about his current pair being 'bitchy' got to him.

I try on the hot-pink briefs first. I'd grabbed them for a laugh but as I pull them on, I'm surprised at how good I look. They hug my arse and look great against my dark skin. Discarding the navy shorts, I pull my clothes back on. Noah's going to have a heart attack when he sees me in these, and it's going to be delightful.

Before he realises my plan, I make a beeline to the counter and pay.

'No,' Noah hisses when he sees the pink swimmers folded up on the cash register. 'Gabriel, *no*.'

'You won't say that when you see them on me.'

His face is flushed red, and he keeps giving the retail girl apologetic little looks, though it's clear she's as amused by the situation as I am. He's embarrassed, I realise with a thrill. Finally, I've crawled under his skin just as he's managed to crawl under mine.

'Have a nice day,' I tell the shop assistant.

'You too,' she says with a grin.

As soon as we're out of the surf shop, Noah pushes my shoulder. I catch his wrist and pull him towards me.

'I cannot believe you just did that,' he huffs as he tries to evade my embrace. 'Bought *those*.'

'I think I look incredible in them,' I say. 'You will see.'

We make our way over to the public toilets and get changed. They're old but well-maintained and clean. I pull on my new swimmers and parade out of the cubicle.

Noah rolls his eyes. 'They're garish,' he says. 'But they do look nice on you.' His eyes roam over me again, and I feel a shiver run up my spine. I like the way he looks at my body. I like knowing he *wants* me.

I kiss him, rough and quick. He's warm and tastes like coffee. I pull away and Noah's mouth twitches as his brain processes the action. Before he has a chance to complain, I grab his hand and tug him towards the beach. 'Come on. I want to go swimming.'

The beach is a long, vast strip of white. The sky is cloudless and the most brilliant blue I've ever seen. Someone calls behind us as we make our way down the beach, and I turn just in time to see a border collie bolt past us, nearly knocking us over, its sights set on the water. When it finally reaches the surf, it leaps in. Its owner apologises profusely as she rushes after it.

We trudge up the beach, our feet sinking into the loose sand, and find a quiet spot away from the crowd and enthusiastic dogs to settle our bags and towels.

Noah rummages through his beach bag and pulls out a tube of sunscreen. 'Come here, I'll do your back.'

I sit down on the towel and try not to flinch when Noah rubs cold sunscreen between my shoulder blades. He works the lotion down my back, his hands moving in sweeping circles. When he's done, he tips my jaw back and kisses me, Spiderman-style.

'Do me next?' he asks against my mouth, except then he kisses me again, and I kiss him back, and the sunscreen bottle is forgotten.

We don't go into the water right away, too caught up in each other to bother with the surf. Noah's mouth opens against mine and I feel his tongue brush against my lips. Burying my fingers in his hair, I kiss him back harder. He's so good at this. I feel like I'm a bad kisser, unskilled and unrefined in my technique and far too enthusiastic.

He pulls me closer as his mouth moves against mine, and it feels like I'm drowning. I love the feeling of his body, how he takes charge, how he holds me to him like he never wants to let me go.

Noah breaks the kiss and rests his forehead against mine. 'Should we go in, then?'

To be honest, I'd be happy to spend the rest of the morning curled up on our towels and hidden away in our own little corner of this beach, but we did drive all this way to swim. Noah slaps on a layer of sunscreen and then we walk towards the water.

It's surprisingly cold but that doesn't seem to bother Noah. He dives into a cresting wave and comes up on the other side, wet floppy hair curtaining his eyes. I suppress a yelp as a wave hits the top of my thighs, splashing cold water against my cock.

'You just gotta jump in,' Noah calls from where he floats a few metres away.

Sucking in a breath, I dive under a wave and brace for the cold. Surprisingly, it's not that bad. I break the surface and swim out to Noah. When I reach him, he wraps an arm around my waist and pulls me flush against his chest. We're out far enough that the waves don't break over us and we can float in the placid water.

'Thank you for bringing me here,' I say as his fingers entwine with mine. 'When you come to Paris, I'm going to take you to the Alps. We'll rent a cabin and spend the day skiing, and at night, we'll lie by a log fire.'

Noah laughs. 'I can't ski, Gabi.'

'I'll teach you,' I say. 'It's easy, I promise.'

'I think you'll make it look easy.' Noah snuggles in, his chin resting on my shoulder to look back at the beach. 'You can't be serious about that sort of stuff, can you?'

'What stuff?' I ask.

He rears back to look at me. 'Stuff that happens after the tournament. I mean, I like what we have now for as long as we have it. But you could be out of the tournament tomorrow.'

'It doesn't mean we have to stop being friends,' I say.

'Friends.' He repeats the word like he dislikes the taste of it. 'Maybe I shouldn't go to your next match. Just to let #retrotennisguy blow over.'

'Is this because of Papa?' I ask, struggling to keep up with how quickly this conversation changed. 'Because he's sorry for what he said, sometimes he's just a little—'

'It's not.'

I grasp Noah's hip and pull him to me, our bodies knocking against each other as the current pushes us towards the shore. 'Then why? I want you to be there.'

Noah looks away, clearly embarrassed.

'Noah, why?'

'It's *my* dad, okay?' Noah admits finally. 'With the article going viral, I'm worried he might see it. I don't know what he might do. Growing up, he wasn't the best dad ever. He made my life hell. He was violent.' Noah glances back to shore, unable to look at me, and I study the water droplets that hang off the ends of his dark eyelashes. 'I've spent the last two years keeping a low profile. As much as I tell myself I'm not a kid anymore and that he's out of my life . . . when I saw that article this morning, I was scared. Scared that he'd find me and—'

He trails off, a little embarrassed. The urge to help Noah is overwhelming, even though I know I can't. He's already discovered a life in front of the camera comes with very little protection; people will demand more than you're willing to give, simply because they feel entitled to the information. 'Did you tell the police?'

Noah laughs mirthlessly. 'He *is* the police. A retired cop. No one believed us in Bendigo. Why would they believe us here?'

'I believe you.'

He gives me a tight smile. 'It's fine. I know how to keep myself safe.' He runs a hand through my hair, smoothing the curls back from my face. 'Forget him. He's not worth thinking about. In better news, I have a trial shift at the Rosewood tonight.'

'That's great!' I assure Noah, even though the issues with his father are definitely *not* forgotten. 'I'm excited for you.'

'Thanks,' he replies. 'I'm excited too. A new beginning.'

It's starting to get a little cold, and my stomach rumbles. 'Do you want to go back? Maybe we could get something to eat?'

Noah shakes his head and wraps his arms around my shoulders. 'Not just yet.'

He kisses me. I pull him closer. I can't keep him safe, or make all the drama and baggage in our lives magically disappear, but I can kiss him. I can kiss him until all he can think about is the way my mouth moves over his, and hope, somehow, that it's enough.

Noah's all sunglasses, sea salt and sex appeal as he drives, the first three buttons of his navy shirt open to reveal the top of his chest. ABBA's on the radio: 'Dancing Queen'.

As I watch him drive, I think about how lucky I am to have met him. How circumstances led me to his bar, of all places.

He looks at me over his sunglasses. 'So that's the beach ticked off. Any other tourist ideas?'

'Not really.'

'I'll try to think of something,' he replies.

'I could do anything with you,' I say honestly. 'Anything and nothing at all.'

For a long time, I didn't think I'd have something like this. The tour keeps me so busy it's almost impossible to date casually, let alone find someone who wants to spend time with me because they simply want to spend time with *me*; who isn't blinded by the money, or the fame, or the 'glamorous' lifestyle.

Noah's the kind of guy who picks you up a coffee without asking if you want one. He's the kind of guy who never asks for his comfiest hoodie back. He's the kind of guy who eats the green lollies and leaves you the red ones because he knows you love them. He's the kind of guy I've always wanted, but never dreamed I could have.

I wish I could live in this moment forever. I'd drive with Noah for hours, with salt lingering on our skin, grains of sand between our toes and ABBA playing on the radio.

But I can see Melbourne on the horizon, the skyscrapers like a shimmering mirage, and I know today must end.

'You better win tomorrow,' Noah says as he drops me at my hotel. 'I'm not ready to let you go just yet.'

18

NOAH

The Rosewood gives me a new uniform, and it feels weird to go back to work. Smoothing out my button-down shirt, I look at myself in the mirror. Black makes me look thinner than I am, and I think I rather resemble a ruler; tall and rectangular. I grab a pair of second-hand dress shoes and tie up the frayed laces before popping into Margie's office and saying goodbye.

'Good luck,' she says, shooting me a quick smile before going back to the essay she's marking.

The Rosewood is a fifteen-minute walk from my house, just on the edge of the city. It's a fine afternoon and the city is swarming with people soaking up the sunshine, so I'm not surprised to find the Rosewood buzzing when I arrive. Waiters navigate the crowds with trays of cocktail jugs and pints. I get to the front of the line and introduce myself to the bouncer as a new staff member. She looks me up and down before letting me through.

Inside, I can barely hear myself think over the chatter and music. Compared to Mark's Place, the Rosewood is a zoo of activity. A drag queen waits at the bar, her enormous foam glitter wig almost brushing the lights that hang overhead.

I weave my way through the throng to the bar, where I get the attention of one of the bartenders, a woman with blue hair and an eyebrow piercing. 'I'm looking for Bella!' I yell.

'You must be the new hire!' she calls in reply. 'Come out the back—it's quiet there!'

She opens the side bar and I follow her into a small back office which is thankfully much quieter. 'Take a seat. Bella won't be too far away.' She closes the door before I have a chance to introduce myself.

A moment later, another bartender steps into the office. He's tall, taller than me, with a mohawk and black kohl smudged around his eyes. 'Hey there, fresh meat.' The bartender grins. 'I'm Bella. Pronouns are she/they.'

Well, fuck my cis-gendered heteronormative brain. 'I'm Noah and he/him. Thanks for calling me in.'

She chuckles. 'As you can see, we're smashed. The upstairs bar is quieter and Peaches's act starts in an hour, so I'll station you up there with Kai.' Bella hands me an apron. 'We'll have the paperwork ready for you at the end of your shift. Pay is above award plus casual. Questions?'

None come to mind, so I shake my head. Bella leads me upstairs to a small theatre and I see Peaches on the stage, testing the audio beneath the blinding lights. She spots me.

'Darling, you've met the lovely Bella,' she says, crossing the floor in her giant platforms. Bella pokes her tongue out at

Peaches playfully as Peaches touches my shoulder. 'Sweetie, what happened to Mark's? It's been closed the past few days.'

'Long story,' I admit. 'I'll fill you in later.'

Peaches gives me a *you better* look before tapping Bella on the shoulder. 'Look after him for me, Bels.' Then with a wave she strides back over to continue testing her set.

Bella gives me a run-down of the point-of-sale system and sticks around as customers begin to file into the room. She ducks out when the lights dim, leaving me to handle the rest of the drinks.

I've never watched Peaches perform before; she lip-syncs to Britney Spears, does an act involving a lot of bubbles, riffs on the audience and finally plays a bizarre round of bingo where she raffles off a meat tray.

Kai, the other bartender, pops up towards the end of the show and helps me serve customers as they make their way downstairs. Peaches saunters over just after eight.

'G—'

'Gin and tonic,' Kai and I say in unison. We look at each other and smile.

'I see I'm getting predictable,' Peaches mutters as Kai makes the drink.

'So,' Peaches says, leaning over the bar. 'What's the deal with Mark, sweetness?'

I try to condense everything that happened that afternoon into words. 'I rocked up to my shift and found him passed out. I called an ambulance and left after they took him away. I've tried to contact him to make sure he's okay, but he never texted me back. He still owes me for my last shift, too.'

'Forget about him,' Peaches urges. 'I'm glad it happened; maybe it will force a bit of sense into his head. And now I don't have to skulk around that awful place anymore.'

As much as I loathe Mark, I love that bar. A part of me will miss it.

'I had no idea your set was so popular,' I reply. 'You had a healthy crowd.'

'Not a single spare seat tonight,' Peaches gloats. 'It's the meat tray that brings them in. No one can pass up the chance to win a tray of sausages and rissoles.'

Kai sniggers beside me. 'On Tuesday nights you should switch it up for a tray of tofu and greens. Get that Northside vegan crowd in.'

Peaches thinks about it for a second. 'Honestly, that's not a bad idea.'

♪

The kitchen slides me a schnitzel at the end of my shift and I eat in the back office while filling out my paperwork and admiring the large corkboard full of polaroids of staff. The polaroids are pinned to a crude drawing of the floorplan, indicating who is on which bar. There must be over twenty polaroid photos on the wall, with each person's name written underneath.

'We'll get a photo of you later,' Bella says as she steps into the cramped office and sees me looking. 'Come on, the shift's going for a drink.'

Grabbing my satchel, I leave my plate with the kitchen staff and follow Bella out the door.

'We don't drink inside?' I ask as we join a group of other bartenders waiting on the street.

'No, we don't drink at the Rosewood. It makes us look unprofessional,' Bella replies. 'Our normal hangout is down the block at the Old George Inn. It's a cute little pub. Cheap drinks.'

Peaches struts out behind me and slings her arm around me. 'What did I tell you, Bels?'

'What, you want a commission?' Bella retorts, then looks back to me. 'So, you coming or not?'

I check my watch. Ten o'clock. I'd promised to call Gabriel.

'I promised I'd meet up with someone, but next time.' It'd be stupid of me to reject another offer for a drink after work; it'd be nice to have a few more friends in the city.

'You gonna be okay to get home safe?' a woman from the group asks. 'We can call you a ride?'

I shake my head. 'I only live a few blocks away.'

Bella laughs. 'I'll remember that when I need to call someone in for a last-minute shift.'

I leave the group as they walk down to the Old George Inn. Once I'm at the end of the block, I pull out my phone to check my messages.

Hungrygabriel73: *How did it go tonight?*

He'd sent that an hour ago. It's late. I hope he's not asleep.

NoAgenda: *Really well—like so well. I just finished my shift. You still up?*

Hungrygabriel73: *Still here. In bed. Better than the old bar?*

NoAgenda: *Completely different. They invited me out for drinks just now, but I wanted to facetime you when I got home instead. While we're still in the same time zone.*

Hungrygabriel73: *I'm flattered.*

I come to the end of the block and stand by the traffic lights, waiting for the pedestrian crossing to flash green.

NoAgenda: *How was training?*

Hungrygabriel73: *Good. A bit brutal but good.*

Hungrygabriel73: *Wish me luck 4 tomorrow night.*

NoAgenda: *You know i'll be watching.*

The flash of red and blue catches my eye; a police cruiser pulls out of a gate down a side street and rockets off towards the city. I pause on the corner, Gabriel's chat still open in my phone.

I believe you, he'd said this morning.

It's been two years and my father still thinks he can control my life. He still thinks he has power.

He still thinks he can threaten me. Threaten people I love.

No more.

The police station is quiet when I walk in. There's a woman behind the main desk, and she looks up at me as I step through the large front doors.

'Can I help you?' she asks.

There's a thick plastic screen between me and the officer, no doubt a necessity of the job. 'I want to report an incident of stalking. And harassment. And violence.' I pause. 'It's complicated.'

She pushes a clipboard through the little gap in the screen. 'It often is. Fill that out. I'll have an officer come to take a statement.'

I take the clipboard and sit down on the old vinyl chairs that line the foyer. Fluorescent lights flicker above me.

The pen doesn't work right away so I scribble on the side of the page until the ink flows.

When I'm done, I hand the clipboard back to the officer behind the screen and sit down again to wait. Five minutes later, another officer calls me and I follow him down a long corridor and into what looks like an interrogation room. My hands start sweating as I sit down at the table and face the officer. He has a crop of reddish brown hair, and his moustache is tinged with ginger. It twitches as he reads through my paperwork.

'You've got a stalker,' he says, and makes a show of turning on the recording app on his phone. 'Start from the beginning; what do you know about them?'

I place my hands on the table to stop them shaking. A part of me still doesn't believe I'm doing this.

'He's my father.'

19

NOAH

Finding out there's a warrant for my father's arrest was not what I expected from the whole AVO process. The officer couldn't provide any detail about the arrest warrant—what it was for, or when it was served—nor could he give me any information about my mum. She isn't in the system.

Back to square one.

My mother told me my father had always drunk a lot. When they were in school, it was a social thing. He'd drink to excess with his mates, and everyone would have a laugh. When he became a police officer, he'd drink with the other recruits after a hard shift—or any shift.

There's not a lot of crime in Bendigo, so sometimes Dad would be asked to transfer to the city station for holiday or sick leave placements. According to Mum, that's when it got bad.

By the time I realised what was going on, my dad had taken a leave of absence from the police department for drink-driving. Caught going one-twenty in an eighty zone, he was two times over the limit when he was pulled over by a colleague. He never went back to the force after that. Don't think he could face it.

Growing up, Mum worked as a nurse at the local hospital. After school if she had a shift, I'd walk to the hospital and sit in the waiting room until she was done. Looking back, some of the nurses must have known what was happening; they knew why it wasn't safe for me to go home.

I was eight the first time he threw a glass bottle at me. I remember the sound it made as it shattered on the wall, and the pain when I stepped on a shard the following day.

People always say, 'Why didn't she just leave?' like it's so easy. Dad was an ex-cop. He'd have tracked us down. He had networks all over the country. All it'd take was a report that we were missing and a few calls, and he'd have his mates out looking for us. They'd have dragged us back home.

At least, that was what he told us.

Suspended in half-sleep, I hear the door lock and blearily realise Margie must be leaving for work, and that it's probably close to 8 am. Fumbling for my phone, I turn on the screen. A big red reminder screams: 10 AM UNIVERSITY OPEN DAY.

Shit. I *so* do not feel up to tackling that today. I force myself to get up and drag my lethargic body into the bathroom to take a long piss.

After spilling my guts to the police officer, it felt like someone had let a plug out of a bathtub and everything I'd been holding in for the past two years was sucked down the drain. I'd felt empty. I'd felt confused.

I had thought making an official complaint and applying for an AVO would make me feel vindicated. I thought it would feel like taking control of my life. But all it did was make me feel fragile, vulnerable. Condensed together in a single statement, the sum of my entire fucked-up childhood was sobering and sad. I'd cried walking home, grappling with the emotions that had risen to the surface.

Maybe I need to talk to someone. Professionally.

I grab fresh clothes and dress before running the coffee machine—double shot—and texting Gabriel.

NoAgenda: *I just want to let you know I submitted an AVO against my dad last night. Like a protection order.*

The coffee stops running and I take my mug and a banana out to the back porch. Sitting on the back steps, warm sun streams down on me and I close my eyes, relishing the feeling of it on my skin.

Hungrygabriel73: *That's amazing. What does it mean if you get it?*

NoAgenda: *He won't be able to come within a certain distance of me or my mum. He won't be allowed to contact me. If he does anything, anywhere, the police will be onto it.*

It doesn't leave me with immediate protection; it's not feasible to have someone watch my back twenty-four-seven on the off-chance, but it makes me feel a bit better.

NoAgenda: *I'm not going to live in fear of him anymore.*

Hungrygabriel73: *I'm proud of you.*

Finishing my coffee, I take Sadie for a walk around the neighbourhood until nine-thirty, then I drop her back at the house and take the tram down to the University of Melbourne.

There's a good crowd on the university lawns when I arrive. Stallholders have set up booths along a line of shady beech trees. Sunlight scatters through their leaves. I pass the stall for the Queer Union, noting their bowl of free condoms, and the various stalls for sports—netball, squash, competitive rock climbing, dragon boat racing—until I find the lecture hall.

Large urns full of coffee and hot water line the far wall. Slices of cake and sandwiches lie on silver platters beside them. I grab a cup of coffee and a piece of carrot cake because: free. A young woman hands me a leaflet as I enter the theatre, and I find a seat near the back.

Taking a sip of coffee, I flick through the leaflet. Each spread focuses on a different discipline, with all the courses on offer listed on the first page. I skim past medicine and law because who am I kidding? Business and marketing look interesting, but do I really want to chain myself to a desk for the rest of my life? Finally, I flick to a page that says *Music, Visual and Performing Arts*, just as a flamboyantly dressed older woman approaches the lectern.

'Good morning, everyone.' Her warm voice booms across the theatre. Frowning, she turns down her microphone. 'That's better. Well, thank you for coming today.'

The PowerPoint behind her transitions to the Acknowledgement of Country and then she talks about what life's like living on campus. I don't plan to live on campus, so I turn back to my leaflet. The Bachelor of Music Performance catches my eye.

'Most of you have your ATAR scores by now,' continues the woman. 'And likely you've already applied for the course of your choice.'

I was still a few months off my final exams when I left Bendigo. It didn't matter. I was failing anyway; didn't need to sit a week-long test to tell me what I already knew.

I check the entrance score for the Bachelor of Music Performance. Eighty-five.

I'd never have scored high enough to even qualify to study. This place isn't meant for someone like me.

The presentation finishes and as I file out, I see a few of the professors lingering by the morning tea spread, chatting to the students. I throw my paper cup into the recycling and head for the door. I've almost reached it when the same woman who handed out the leaflets approaches me.

'How did you find the presentation?' she asks.

'Good,' I reply, not wanting to be rude.

'What courses are you considering?' She looks down and sees the leaflet open to the music page and, to my horror, turns to shout back into the room. 'Sandra? Can you come over here? This young man is interested in music degrees.'

Mortified, I'm about to tell her not to worry and make a mad dash for it when someone, Sandra, I assume, excuses herself from the conversation she's currently engaged in and comes over to us.

'Let me guess—piano?' she asks with a grin.

I look down, unsure how she could tell. 'Yeah, I—'

'You've got pianist fingers. I can spot them a mile away.'

'Sandra is the head of student services for the music department,' explains the leaflet woman. 'She'll be able to give you all the information you need.' Then, she extracts herself to go and bail up some other unsuspecting attendee.

Clearing my throat, I thrust out my hand. 'I'm Noah.'

Sandra shakes it, smiling. 'Nice to meet you, Noah. So what degree specialisation are you thinking about—composition, music performance, musicology, musical theatre?'

'Composition,' I reply automatically. I'd never given it much thought before, but I suppose composition makes sense. I've always liked the craft of writing music and admire the way it translates from a page to the piano.

'Did you complete senior music?' she asks. Turns out, I did one better.

'A Certificate III in Music Industry at TAFE. But I never finished my VCE exams.'

Sandra's brow furrows for a moment. 'You didn't complete your VCE exams?'

'Things got . . . hard.' It seems the simplest way to say, *I escaped my abusive dad with just the clothes on my back*. 'I was only a few months off doing them.'

I expect that to put her off, but it doesn't. Straight away she says, 'There are *heaps* of options for people to attend university without having an ATAR. You could go back to TAFE and finish your exams, or you could do a bridging course. The music degree has an audition requirement, so as long as you performed well and had the scores from the bridging course, I don't see why you wouldn't be accepted.'

'What, really?'

Sandra shrugs like she hasn't just up-ended my entire life. 'Sure. Happens all the time. Usually for our mature-age students, but I can email you some information about the options.'

'That'd be great. Thank you.'

I provide my email and she types it into her phone. 'Nice to meet you, Noah,' she says when she's finished. 'Give me a call if you want to talk through the application process.'

I leave the open day—stopping by the Queer Union stall to grab a few free condoms—and walk home. Margie's bike is in the front yard, and I can hear her making lunch in the kitchen. The house smells like curry and onion, and something else I can't quite place.

'Heya,' she says as I step into the lounge room. 'How did the open day go?'

I drop my keys and the leaflet on the kitchen counter. 'Good. I spoke to a student advisor. She's going to email me more information about their music course.'

'Well, that's good to hear. I knew you'd find the day worthwhile.'

I take a seat at the dining table. There's a bit of grime in the groove of the wood, so I flick it out with my fingers. 'I don't really know what to do with my life, Margie. Is it wrong to be happy where I am for a bit?' I admit. 'To just want to stay in this moment until I figure something out?'

She places two curried egg and lettuce sandwiches on the table. 'As long as you *are* happy. University is a big decision. Looking back, I wish I'd taken my studies a bit more seriously. Not completely seriously, but a bit more than I did.'

'You weren't a star student?' I say with mock surprise as I bite down into her sandwich. 'I don't believe that for a second.'

Margie laughs. 'Hardly.'

Later that afternoon, after Margie and I have been to the shop for snacks to eat while we watch Gabriel's big match,

I sit on the plush lounge and pull up my mum's number again.

The police officer suggested I get a new number. Doing so means throwing away the SIM card I have and replacing it with a new one. It means losing my contacts, including the last message from my mother.

This is my last chance to contact her before I change the SIMs over.

Hey, I just want to let you know I put out an AVO on Dad. I hope you're okay and—

I delete the message.

I'm not sure if this is still the right number, but I'm in Melbourne and—

I delete that one too. Why is this so hard?

Mum—is this still your number? I don't need to know where you are if you don't want to tell me. I just want to make sure you're okay. I am. I've changed my number. If you want to get in contact, my new number is . . .

I type in the new number, then I press *Send*. I change my SIM card. I don't hear back.

20

GABRIEL

We're deep in the second set. I'm down a set, but up three games to love in this one. The American, Bailey Reid, is on the other side of the net. He's focused and fit and hungry for it. He just knocked off Indiana Rakefield, his thirty-one-year-old friend and countryman, in a five-set thriller.

It's the third round. Tonight, we're prime time. Rod Laver Arena. The crowd is loud and messy, and most of them are on Reid's side. I'm not one to worry about who the crowd supports or doesn't, but I can't lie: when they chanted his name as he stepped onto the court, a shiver ran down my spine.

I've only played against Bailey Reid three times in my entire career—and I've lost every time.

Glancing up at my box, Papa gives me a tight smile. Tonight, Phoebe's sitting beside him, and my stomach flutters at seeing her in my player's box.

It's a cool night. Dry. The ball is light off the racquet. A gentle breeze blows through the open roof and down through the arena.

I take a breath and gather my thoughts, preparing for my service game. The audience goes silent. Bouncing once, twice, I get a feel for the ball before serving. It lands in the top corner of Reid's service box. He returns it with a strong forehand, but I meet it easily, sending the ball flying across the net. He runs for it, but it's not enough. The crowd applauds.

In the next serve, I ace him.

Somehow, I close the service game quickly, and then I'm up four–love. Across the court, Reid shakes his head and swears. I have to keep this pressure on him, I have to wear him down. If I can snatch this set six games to love, it'll shake him.

Reid sets up for his service game, and I soften my knees, let my spine curve and prepare to receive. His serve is intense, fast and precise. In our last match, two years ago, he destroyed me with this serve: 6–1, 6–2, 6–0. But this time, I'm ready for it. I return the ball with just as much force as he served it with.

Every play I make, Reid's there. Every ball is returned. Every time I think I've run him off his feet, he makes the shot. The crowd applauds as he claws back a game.

Four–one.

It's my service game again. I let out a long breath and calm my thumping heart. Reid stares at me across the net. I serve, *hard*. He returns. The set descends into a flurry of volleys, of hard-earned points, and me falling flat on my face as I run to return a ball. I don't even get a point for my effort, either.

I close out the third set when, on the set point, Reid's ball hits the net. We're a set all, and I've just won six games to one.

I head to my bench and grab my towel. There's a five-minute break between sets, and I use it to refuel, to recentre and, most importantly, to towel the sweat off my body. Grabbing a fresh shirt from my bag, I try not to make a show of changing my shirt but someone in the crowd always whistles. In my mind, it sounds a lot like Phoebe.

After switching my shirt and swallowing a mouthful of water, I take to the court again. Glancing over at Reid, I realise he's berating himself. He's angry. Good. Let me get in his head.

I win the first two games and the match finally feels like it's swinging in my favour. Reid stumbles a little lunging for a ball, grabbing his ankle as he falls. Play stops. Reid rises to his feet and walks it off, raising his hand to indicate that he's okay. The crowd cheers.

Reid sets up for his serve. It hits the net.

I prepare again, knees soft, crouching.

Reid serves, but again it hits the net. A double fault. He throws his racquet down and swears, loudly. The umpire glances at him from her box, her mouth a tight, disapproving line.

I don't pity Reid. I know exactly what he's going through; he's trying to put the frustration of his stumble behind him; he's trying to reconcile our history together because he's beaten me so many times—why should this time be any different? Why isn't he playing as well as he'd hoped? Has he lost his mojo? No doubt somewhere, subconsciously, he'd thought I'd be an easy opponent. Barely a pebble on his smooth path towards the finals.

I'm playing better—better than I ever have—maybe because I'm no longer weighed down by the emotional baggage of living up to my papa's ambitions, or being chronically in the closet.

I'm playing for something, and someone, and a chance to stay here, even if just for a few days longer.

After eight games between us, I take the next set from Reid 6-2, and he throws his racquet towards his bench in frustration. The crowd jeers him and he walks off the court in a fluster. The umpire leans down to speak to him, but I don't catch their exchange.

I glance up to my player's box. Phoebe looks pumped, standing up on her crutches to cheer me on. The passion on her face sends a thrill through me.

As we break Reid calls a medical timeout to have someone look at the ankle he'd stumbled on earlier, and I eat a banana. Instagram always descends into a frenzy whenever I eat a banana. No prizes for guessing why.

The medic leaves the court and Reid stands up, loosening the tension in his ankle with a light jog back to the baseline.

I throw away the banana peel. I need to close this.

As we move into the fourth set, I win the first game, the second, the third in quick succession. He swears loudly again, his anger bubbling over, and gets a warning from the umpire.

I close the next two games in fifteen minutes, and then, Reid hands me the last game without scoring.

He's done.

The crowd erupts into applause. Papa's out of his seat. Victor's jumping around like a madman and Phoebe cheers with her hands cupped around her mouth. I fall to my knees, delirious with the win, and close my eyes as the glare of the stadium lights washes over me. I'm into the fourth round of the tournament—the round of sixteen, and just one match away from the finals. It's the best I've ever done at the Australian Open. I look up to my box and wish Noah was there, but I know I'll have time to celebrate with him later.

Taking a deep breath, I get to my feet and soak in the win. Approaching the net, I shake Reid's clammy hand.

'Hope the ankle is okay,' I say.

'Thanks, it'll be fine,' he replies sourly, patting my back. 'Good luck.'

Percy Jones makes his way onto the court as I wipe my face with my towel. Slinging it over my shoulder, I gather up the rest of my gear and step towards the cameras. He reeks of aftershave and cigar smoke.

Someone counts Percy in, and then the light above the camera turns red.

'We're at Rod Laver Arena with Gabriel Madani who has just triumphed over fifth seed Bailey Reid in four sets.' He turns to me. 'You're causing quite the upset this year, aren't you?'

'You played great,' says Phoebe as I step into the player's room and give her a hug. 'God, you reek.'

'Thanks for coming,' I say. 'I mean it.'

'I'm glad I could. I'm flying back to the States tomorrow.' She runs her hands down my shoulders, squeezing my biceps. 'I wish I could stay longer, but I know you'll smash the next match.'

I close my eyes, dread filling me. 'It's Lukas, isn't it?'

'Not quite. Alanzo Ruiz. He's up against Dylan Foster, the eighteen-year-old. But who knows, the kid might pull something out of his back pocket.' She nudges me. 'Lukas is up against Rod Lawson next round. They had a pretty tough semi-final battle at Indian Wells last year. Rod might come out on top. Or Lukas might get food poisoning. Hard to say.'

I snigger. 'Is that a threat?'

'I'm willing to do what I have to do,' she jokes.

Behind us, Victor clears his throat. 'Gabi, the media's waiting.'

Saying goodbye to Phoebe, I leave my bag in the player's room and reluctantly follow Victor into the media room. I might have won today, but I still hate speaking to the press.

The rapid-fire questions go like this:

'How did you feel on the court?'

'Good, a little wobbly at the start but I felt I played well.'

'How did you muster the energy to come back in the first set?'

'I don't try to focus on winning the first set; I try to build a good momentum.'

'How do you feel about possibly playing Alanzo Ruiz, the third seed, in the next round?'

'Good. We've played before a few times but right now I'm going to focus on my recovery.'

A young woman with a bob of black hair raises her hand: 'A new face was in your player's box recently; do you mind telling us who they are?'

I almost choke on my water.

'A friend,' I reply. 'That's all.'

'A friend who's caused quite the frenzy on Twitter,' she replies.

I lean into the microphone. 'His identity is private. Please respect that.'

Victor catches my eye. Immediately, I know I've said the wrong thing. I'm a fish who's just taken the bait.

'Thanks for your time,' I tell the room, rising from my seat. Victor practically steers me out of the room and into the hallway. I shrug him off.

'I thought you killed the story,' I say. After everything Noah told me at the beach, the urge to protect him is overwhelming.

'I tried,' says Victor evenly. 'But you know how they are. Once they think they have a story, they won't let it go.'

'What story do they think they have?' I demand.

Victor gives me a stern look. 'You know what story, Gabriel.'

Fear runs through me. It's weird how similar adrenaline and fear feel to the body; my hands shake, my voice goes wobbly. My skin prickles. They're hunting for confirmation of whether I'm gay or not; and it makes me feel sick.

'I'm here to play tennis,' I say. 'That's all. What I do in my private life is private. The *people* in my private life are private. You need to kill it, Victor.'

'People are always going to ask questions about something

like this,' Victor replies. 'It's a part of this whole package. Until you do something, or say something, you're never going to be free of it. What's worse: dodging the question, or embracing it? Celebrating it?'

'I . . .' I swallow. 'I can't do that, Victor.'

And I don't know why I can't.

Bad gay, I think. *You're a bad gay.*

NoAgenda: *Congrats on the win! Glad you're not leaving the country just yet.*

Hungrygabriel73: *I live to play another day.*

NoAgenda: *Dramatic much? Okay, SO I've cross-referenced my itinerary against TripAdvisor and it seems I'm doing a very bad job of giving you an authentic tourist experience.*

Hungrygabriel73: *Really?*

NoAgenda: *YES! so you must choose . . .*

NoAgenda: *Creepy tour around a maybe-haunted prison . . . ooorrrrrr . . . cuddling a koala.*

Hungrygabriel73: *KOALA!!!!!*

21

NOAH

Public appearances have strict rules, according to Victor's dating handbook, which he helpfully emailed me last night—all eighty-nine pages of it. The guide details the do's and do-not's of dating wonder child and tennis extraordinaire Gabriel Farid Madani. No hand-holding. No longing gazes, no 'accidental' brushing of the fingers and absolutely, *absolutely* no kissing in public.

'One tiny kiss,' Gabriel badgers as we step off the train and approach Melbourne Zoo. The old red-brick gate still stands; it's now a heritage building and a significant piece of Melbourne's history. 'In a dark alleyway.'

'Absolutely not,' I reply. 'We're just two dudes checking out the zoo together. Nothing gay about it.'

He lets out a huff as I pay for the tickets and grab a map.

'You're the navigator,' I say, thrusting the pamphlet into his hands. 'We gotta be at the koala enclosure by ten-thirty for the meet-and-greet.'

'They have *lemurs*,' Gabriel gasps as he unfolds the map. 'And giraffes! And red pandas!'

I slide my sunglasses over my eyes. Aside from helping to keep our identities secret, it's another bright day in Melbourne and it feels like the heat will never break. For eight days straight, the mercury has lingered at forty degrees, cooling in the evenings but returning with full force the following morning. With no chance of rain on the horizon, Melburnians can only stand the heat for so long before we melt, *Wizard of Oz* style.

I see a coffee stand on the other side of the entrance. 'Coffee?' I ask Gabriel, though I might as well have asked a fish if it likes water.

We grab two coffees from the cart and walk through the lush parkland. The zoo's bigger than I expected, but Gabriel's already charted a course that begins with the Tasmanian Devil and ends with something called a 'collared peccary'.

'I think it is a fancy pig,' Gabriel surmises as we peer over the Tasmanian Devil enclosure. The animals are sleeping in the hollow of a large log, looking like little more than a pile of coarse black fur. Gabriel, however, is enthralled.

As we make our way past the lions and tigers (no bears), I notice that Gabriel's limping. Not all the time, but sometimes. When I see it for the third or fourth time, I say, 'Is your leg okay?'

He looks a little embarrassed. 'Just a bit sore. It will be fine for tomorrow.' He thrusts the map in my face. 'Come on, I want to see the meerkats.'

We walk over to the meerkats' enclosure and watch as they scuttle around and chase beetles. Gabriel leans against the fence, completely entranced. I love his childlike wonder at things; I love how passionate and playful he can be when he lets his guard down; I love that I'm the one who gets to see this side of him. My pinkie finger brushes his and he glances at me, a half-smile on his face.

'Sorry,' I murmur, pulling my hand away. 'It was an accident.'

'Uh-huh,' he hums. 'Sure.'

'Oh!' I dig my phone out of my pocket. 'With the AVO, the police recommended I get a new number. I've just sent it to you in our chat.'

Gabriel pulls out his phone and adds my number to his contacts. We start walking to the next enclosure. 'What's the next steps after you get the AVO?'

'I'm not sure,' I reply honestly. 'As frustrating as it sounds, I just have to wait and see if he'll *do* anything. Against me or against others.'

Gabriel shoves his hands into his pockets as we walk. 'I keep thinking about everything you must have gone through. It makes me angry.'

'It makes me angry, too. I knew my childhood was different from other kids'—but I never knew how different.'

'What made you decide to leave?'

We stop at the baboon enclosure. One hangs from a branch as it lazily picks at a tray of fruit. 'I'd just turned eighteen. I was in my last year of school. When you turn eighteen, you know, it's a big deal. People have parties. Dad was out—at the pub or with his mates—I don't remember.'

Gabriel nudges up against me. It's like he's reminding me he's here; that he's someone sturdy, someone I can lean on when things get a bit too much. I realise I want to be that for him, too. Maybe I already am.

'Mum had organised this gigantic party in the backyard,' I continue. 'It was cold. Bendigo in July is *freezing*. We had this big fire in a drum, and we were playing music and drinking. My friends from school came around and Mum did her best to cater for all of us, but we ended up getting pizza delivered. It was great.'

'And then it wasn't?' Gabriel guesses.

'Dad came home around midnight. The party quietened down. People started going home. They knew what he was like, or they'd heard stories about him. Anyway, Dad was in one of his moods. He got angry at some kid, and then angry at Mum and me. I don't even know what the fight was about until he picked up a knife and lunged at me.'

Gabriel stays silent, letting me continue.

'Before that it had all been . . . well, he'd hit me. But this time—' I feel my voice break. It's been a while since I revisited these memories; I hadn't even given the police this much detail. 'This time, I know he meant to *really* hurt me. It wasn't like the other times. My mum fought him, and he pushed her to the ground. I got the knife off him but fucked up my hand pretty badly. Somehow, Mum and I escaped. Mum took me to the hospital and they stitched me up.' I show him the gnarly scar on my palm as evidence. 'No one asked questions, but I knew they all knew. Then she took me to the train station, waited with me, and the train to Melbourne arrived at 4 am. That's the last time I saw her. On the platform. Watching me leave on the train.'

I feel Gabriel's hand rub comforting circles on my back and then we're moving, or more precisely: he's moving me. We find a bit of parkland and he makes me sit on the cool grass. I don't realise I'm crying until his thumb wipes at my cheek.

'I'm sorry,' I blubber. 'We're not supposed to make a scene, and this is like the total opposite of that.'

I'd never put much stock in relying on anyone for anything, but here I am, hearing someone say they care about me and believing it; wanting to go to them for comfort, wanting to comfort them in return.

Gabriel smooths his hand down my arm and takes my hand in his, just holding it between us. 'What happened to your mum?'

'She promised she was going to leave as well, just as soon as I did. Take her car and drive north. We thought it made sense to split up. Disappear. It's been almost three years, and she's never contacted me.'

'You don't think she left?'

The other option is too hard to think about. 'I don't know. Sometimes I think about calling her—I still have her old phone number—but sometimes I think not knowing is better, you know?'

I know she didn't abandon me—Mum wasn't like that. I hope she really did disappear; she drove north and just kept going. But it'd be nice to talk to her, just once, just to tell her I'm okay.

'You must miss her.'

'She was the only one who ever believed in me.' The only one who ever loved me. The only one who ever gave a shit about me. We were two sides of the same fucked-up coin.

I check the time, not wanting to be late for the koala meet-and-greet because of an inconvenient meltdown.

'Hey, just chill,' Gabriel says, covering my watch with his hand.

'We're not supposed to hold hands.' I try to pull away, but he holds on tighter.

'I told you, I don't care.'

I attempt to reclaim my hand again, pulling it out of his grasp. This time, Gabriel lets himself be jerked forward and knocks me onto the grass. He laughs as he rolls on top of me, pinning me down.

'Gabriel!' I cry, trying to sit back up. 'Gabriel, this is *indecent*.'

'Oh no, I have fallen,' he says in the most monotonous French accent I've ever heard. 'Oh dear, what an accident.'

I roll Gabriel's dead weight off my body as he laughs, clearly pleased with himself. He crawls next to me, sweet-faced and unbelievably cute, looking like he just wants to be kissed senseless. God, I'd love to kiss this man senseless.

I poke Gabriel in the ribs and he squirms away from me. 'You wanna go check out those lemurs?'

'Definitely, yes.' He smiles, and quite simply, it's everything. It's the way the sunlight streams through the changing leaves in autumn; it's the way it feels to get into bed when you've just washed your sheets; it's the way wood smells when it burns, even though you know wood fires are a fucking environmental nightmare.

This man will ruin my life when he leaves, but in this moment, he is everything.

The lemur walk-through is a delight. They scatter throughout the enclosure, and at one point, one of the small creatures cuts in front of Gabriel to snatch a juicy fig from a platter. He stumbles backwards, running into me, and we laugh.

At ten-thirty, Gabriel holds his first ever koala—whose name is George—and I take just under a million photos (no exaggeration) for his Instagram. I find Victor's number in Gabriel's phone and shoot one of the best pictures off with the message, *Having an un***bear***ably cute time!—Noah.*

And maybe I send a few to myself, too. Just for safekeeping.

It's lunchtime by the time we leave the zoo.

'I'm training this afternoon. A private booking,' Gabriel says as we step onto the train and find a seat. 'You can come if you'd like. Dad's making burritos afterwards, and if you want, you could stay and watch a movie.'

Renting a movie, having dinner at each other's places—it sounds mundane, but so wonderful. 'I'd love that.'

Gabriel pulls out his phone. 'I'll text and let them know.'

At the apartment, Victor's cooked lunch: salmon bowls with white rice, vegetables and a creamy sauce that Gabriel's not 'allowed' to have, but he still sneaks a taste.

'When we are fuelling for a tournament, every macro counts,' Bernard says, clocking my dubious look.

'Once the tournament's over, I'm ordering the biggest, juiciest, cheesiest burger ever,' Gabriel replies. In the kitchen Victor pulls out four mugs from the cupboard and begins making coffee. Bernard takes the dirty plates from the table and stacks the dishwasher. Watching them work, it's clear they've spent a long time living together; their bodies move in sync through their lunchtime routine.

'Noah, do you take sugar?' Victor asks as the kettle whistles.

'Just one, please,' I say. On the far wall, there's a chart of all the players in the tournament, and where Gabriel sits in the draw. Studying the brackets, I trace his path to victory.

I turn back to Gabriel. 'Will you face Lukas in the next match if you win this one?'

'Unfortunately,' he deadpans.

'You can beat him,' Bernard replies as he starts the dishwasher cycle. 'You've done it before.'

'Have to get through Ruiz first.' Gabriel gives me my coffee and turns to the board. 'Then, I'll worry about Lukas.'

'Is it hard playing your friend?'

Gabriel lets out a long sigh. 'Unfortunately, yes, but it also means I know him. There are benefits and . . .' He searches for the word. 'Not-so-benefits.'

'Drawbacks,' I supply. Why is it so cute when he fumbles for a word?

'It's hard speaking English when you're tired,' he admits. 'It is mind-draining.'

'You're doing better than me,' I say, taking a sip of coffee. 'I lost all my hearts in Duolingo yesterday trying to figure out all the ways to ask a question in French.'

He nudges my shoulder, jostling me a little. 'That is actually very difficult.' And then quietly he adds, 'Thank you for doing it for me.'

His acknowledgement makes my cheeks heat. Gabriel's gaze meets mine and something electric passes between us;

desire licks up my spine. I wish, desperately, that we were alone.

We take our coffee out to the balcony and enjoy it in the afternoon sun. Victor has a smoke and declares more than once how badly he feels about smoking. We talk about Gabriel's next match, my new job at the Rosewood, and what we've been up to on the *tour de Melbourne*—doughnut shops, gyros in an alleyway, trips to the beach, meeting koalas. Bernard listens but says nothing. Victor can't stop talking about how well Gabriel's koala photo is doing on Instagram.

It all feels normal. Lovely and normal, and like this was always how it was meant to be.

Gabriel's booked a private court on the banks of the Yarra in South Melbourne. It's dark. Powerful lights illuminate Gabriel's body as he works on his serve. I watch, in awe of the power and grace of his body and how effortless he makes it look.

My phone vibrates. Yesterday, I downloaded the tournament app, and now I get push notifications for real-time scores.

'Looks like Lukas won,' I say as I pull up the app. 'Yep. In five sets.'

'Good,' Gabriel says, sauntering back towards me. 'Hope he's pulled something.'

I give a mock gasp at his bad sportsmanship. 'Leave him alone. He's my favourite player.'

Gabriel's arms encircle me, pinning me to the little plastic chair on the side of the court. He leans close, so close I can feel his breath on my face, and I feel the plastic chair buckle slightly. 'Oh really?'

I tilt my chin up, staring him down. 'I hope he wins this entire—'

He kisses me hard. I wrap my arms around him, full of need and desire after being so careful all day.

'Cameras, people,' I murmur against his lips. His tongue slides against mine and I lose all ability to think critically about the situation, or why we should *not* be kissing right now. I suck in a breath and pull him closer, even if it means half falling off the plastic seat and onto the artificial turf. It's worth it.

We kiss for an amount of time I'm not at liberty to describe or measure but eventually he pulls back. His pupils are wide with desire and his kiss-bruised mouth is a beautiful shade of red.

'I'm supposed to be training,' he murmurs. 'Dad was right; you are a distraction.'

'You're the one who kissed me.' I push him away. 'Go train. But do me a favour and at *least* take your shirt off while you do it.'

Gabriel snorts and it's the hottest thing I've ever heard. 'You are a horrible little urchin with its spike in my arse.' His accent curls around the words and it sends a tingle down my spine.

'Please, I have so little joy in my life, Gabriel,' I say, reaching for the hem of his shirt. 'Let me have this.'

Gabriel laughs and steps back. 'It will be weird for my partner though.'

'Your part—'

My question dies as soon as I see a familiar figure walking towards us. 'Gabi!' His Swedish accent echoes across the empty court.

Lukas Froebel.

I give Gabriel a dirty look. 'Why didn't you tell me he was going to be here?'

Gabriel just laughs like the spiteful little demon he is. 'I thought you'd be happy to meet your *favourite* tennis player.'

Lukas drops his gear beside us, looking more Greek god than mere man. He's over six foot, blond, tanned, with eyes like sapphires and a smile made for the cover of magazines.

'Hey, I'm Lukas.' He smiles like I don't know who the fuck he is; like ten thousand people haven't just celebrated his performance.

'Noah,' I reply. 'I'm Gabriel's friend.'

'Yeah, the kid on Twitter.' He laughs, his accent more American than I'd expected. 'Loved that shirt on you. Gotta tell me where you got it.'

'Savers,' I reply. 'It's, like, a thrift shop near my house.'

'Vintage, nice.'

Beside me, Gabriel holds his tongue and smiles like an idiot while I fumble through a conversation with a man who is so famous Japan makes vending machines with his face on them.

'Didn't you just play?' I ask, looking between them.

Lukas scoffs, tossing his racquet and catching the handle again. 'My warm-down is his training, that's how far apart in skill we are.'

Gabriel rolls his eyes and taps his racquet on Lukas's arse. 'Get on the court.'

Lukas swallows a mouthful of water from his water bottle and follows Gabriel onto the court. While Gabriel isn't training half-naked, it's still mesmerising to watch them play so close. The power behind the ball isn't something easily captured on the television, but in person, I can see Gabriel's arm ripple as he returns Lukas's serve.

Around half an hour later, a young woman enters the court from the side gate. She's wearing a yellow sundress and her long, straight blonde hair cascades around her shoulders. She sees me sitting on the sidelines and comes over, taking the seat beside me.

'I can't believe they're still at it,' she says. 'These two will kill each other one day.'

'They seem to have a pretty intense rivalry. I'm Noah, by the way. Gabriel's friend.'

Her bright blue eyes look me up and down; I can't tell if she likes what she sees. 'Freyja. I'm Lukas's sister.'

'Oh, cool. You played today, didn't you?' I'd promised Gabriel I wouldn't google him, but I certainly hadn't promised I wouldn't google other people.

'And lost.' She sighs, looking across the court at her brother. I wonder if there's a streak of jealousy between her and her sibling. It must be hard to be so similar, and yet, Lukas has enjoyed a markedly more successful career than Freyja. Not because she's a bad player, but because the women's draw has been dominated by strong players for so long and—

Damn. Do I know tennis now?

Freyja looks up into the night sky. 'I played like shit.'

Before I can respond, I notice Lukas tapping the rest of his balls over the net. Gabriel catches them easily and they make their way back to us.

'See you in the finals, Madani,' he says as he hauls his bag over his shoulder. Then, his unsettlingly blue eyes turn to me. 'Nice to meet you, Noah.' Lukas reaches forward to grab my forearm and pulls me towards him in a kind of awkward bro handshake. 'You'll have to show me the vintage shops around here. Gabriel will hook us up.'

'I will *not*,' I hear Gabriel say behind me, his tone slightly scandalised.

As Lukas and Freyja leave the court, Gabriel pulls off his sweat-soaked shirt and tosses it my way. I laugh as I duck out of the way, the wet fabric slapping audibly against the plastic seat.

'You're a gross man and I hate you,' I mutter as I pick the shirt up and fling it back to him.

He gathers his shirt and shoves it into the front pocket of his gym bag, then sheathes his tennis racquet like a sword. 'Come. Join me in the shower.'

My face goes hot at his words. 'For real?' I hiss. '*Here*?'

Gabriel throws his gym bag over his shoulder. 'I still have it booked for another hour, and no one knows we're here. Ironically, it's as private as it can get.'

The thrill of a scandal pulses through me as I follow Gabriel into the locker rooms. I really shouldn't; there have been so many close calls in the last few days, and there's so much on the line if we get caught. But every time I think about Gabriel naked, the feel of his skin against mine, all logical, sensible thoughts disappear. Gabriel's swaying arse is like a siren's call luring me to the deep, and goddamn do I want to dive in.

The changing rooms are basic—large, tiled showers, and a row of lockers on the far wall with a wooden bench in between. Gabriel dumps his bag by the doorway, presses me against the nearest wall, and kisses me.

I wind my arms around his neck, desperate to feel his body against mine. The first touch of his tongue has me whimpering into his mouth, and fuck, no one's ever made me whimper, so full am I of want and love and *everything*. Maybe it's just my dick talking, but whatever this is between us, it feels real.

A moment later, we're in the shower and everything's hot and naked and slippery—

'I one hundred per cent do not have a condom,' I groan as he presses me against the cold tile of the shower cubicle. 'It didn't even occur to me to bring one, though I bought, like, a whole packet.'

'A whole packet? That is bold of you,' Gabriel murmurs against my throat as he hitches my thigh to his hip. Between his body, the steam, and the washing-machine-on-spin-cycle that is my brain, I feel like I'm going to pass out.

I think I *am* passing out, because suddenly Gabriel's moving away from me, sinking to the floor. But then his mouth finds the hinge of my hip and thigh, and he kisses the little wrinkle in the junction, and I realise he's on his knees.

I'm embarrassingly hard when Gabriel takes my cock, and as his hand pumps me, I scramble to find the ledge of the half-wall behind me for support. 'Fucking hell, Gabi, I—'

'You'll have to tell me if I am not good,' Gabriel says, but I know I'll do absolutely no such thing. 'I've never done this.'

I don't have time to unpack any of that before Gabriel's mouth is on me. Tipping my head back, I breathe out and try to find some semblance of control to prevent me from coming too soon but then suddenly the heat of Gabriel's mouth is gone.

Gabriel reaches up from the floor to wrench the water off. I glance down; his curls are soaked, plastered to his face, and he's panting hard, face flushed, but he's grinning. 'Water, *off*,' he grunts then I laugh, and suddenly we're both laughing at the awkwardness of this situation.

Gabriel grasps the base of my cock and, while maintaining eye contact, directs it back into his mouth. I watch as his eyes roll back, dark eyelashes fluttering.

'Holy fuck,' I grunt. I drop one hand onto Gabriel's head, smoothing his wet curls, more to ground myself than to direct his movements. For all his talk of *not being good at this*, Gabriel is toe-curlingly amazing. He's enthusiastic, using his hands where his mouth can't reach, all tongue and lips and heat—

I gasp as everything narrows down to a single point, and everything feels both molten liquid and rigid stiff at the same time. I begin to shake. I think I cry out, but I have no idea what I say.

'Gabriel,' I breathe, suddenly lurching forward. 'Gabriel, stop, I'm—'

Gabriel's hand grabs my thigh, pinning me against the cold tile as I come down his throat. Slumping back against the wall, I try desperately to piece together some rational thought. 'Th-thanks,' I manage.

Gabriel smiles, rising to his feet. 'It was good?'

I blink up at the roof. 'I think you sucked my soul out of my body.'

Goosebumps erupt over my skin, so Gabriel turns the water back on. He rinses out his mouth and spits into the drain in a way that's both lewd and so fucking hot.

When I finally regain control of my body, I kiss him, soapy, sloppy and happy. Shower sex might be awkward as fuck, but shower head is simply divine, and I'm eager to return the favour. 'Want me to . . .?' I glance pointedly down and then meet his gaze again.

His eyes light up. 'I've never—'

I stand back, flabbergasted. 'You've never had a blow job?'

Gabriel shakes his head but won't look me in the eye. Maybe it was the wrong thing to say. Maybe I said it in the wrong tone. He's clearly embarrassed about it and now I feel like a bit of a dick. Of course. If he'd never given one, the chances were high he'd never received one.

'Baby, I didn't mean it that way.'

'It's fine,' Gabriel replies, even though I can tell it's not.

I grasp his shoulders, angling my body against his, and slide my hands up either side of his neck until I'm cupping his jawline. He looks up at me from beneath wet lashes. 'I was being a prick. Can I please suck you?'

Gabriel smiles. 'Since you ask so nicely.'

'I can be nice.'

I turn off the spray and Gabriel hands me a fluffy towel

from his pack. I wipe myself down, then fold the towel on the ground by the bench seating and drop to my knees.

Gabriel's hand runs through my hair as I swallow him, taking him as deep as possible. He swears, in French, then in English, and then language leaves him altogether and he groans, fingers holding my scalp so tight it almost hurts. His massive thighs tremble, and all I can think about is how incredible it'd feel to have them wrapped around my waist.

Gabriel gasps, shudders with his release, and when he goes still I pull away. Above me, he pants, his dark eyes wild and staring off into the middle distance. I grin, wiping the taste of him from my lips.

'I—' he tries, but words seem to escape him.

Somewhere deep in the pockets of his tennis bag, his phone rings. I quirk a brow in its direction. 'Let it go to voicemail.'

22

GABRIEL

Alanzo Ruiz knocked out fifteenth seed Dylan Foster in three sets—a strong demonstration. Ruiz is five-foot-seven, stocky, with a killer backhand and a defence that's hard to break. The media have dubbed him 'The Wall'. As far as media nicknames go, it's pretty flattering. And very accurate.

Ruiz's entire game plan is to tire out his opponent with strong defence and strong returns. It's a simple strategy and it's worked well for him over his career. He loves to outlast other players, slowly gaining points and creating momentum, even if it means he drops a set along the way. He's the master of the five-setter. When his opponent is sufficiently drained, Ruiz swoops in and closes out the match.

It's a quarter past twelve and there's a women's game being played on Rod Laver Arena: Helen Taylor from the US and Uma Aziz-Azir from the UAE are trapped in a tense stand-off as they both eye a place in the finals.

I set up camp on a stationary bike in the player training room, keeping my muscles warm until Aziz-Azir finally closes the match 6–4, 2–6, 4–6. The roar of the crowd vibrates through the skeleton of the arena. I can imagine the relief on Aziz-Azir's face now, the sheer joy of triumph that only comes with the final point.

I climb off the bike and change into my match kit, lacing up my sneakers. Grabbing my phone from my bag, I notice a message from Noah.

NoAgenda: *Good luck today. I don't know what else to say but please don't lose.*

Hungrygabriel73: *I'll try not to. x*

The truth is, I'm petrified of losing, of going home, of ending things with Noah. What had started as a fling—a *distraction*—is now . . . not that anymore. I don't know what we are. Our relationship is a complex gelatinous mass with no clear edges, but the fear of losing him eats at me. What if we don't get to see each other again for another year? What if things change between us in that time?

I can't do this. I turn off my phone and stuff it into my tennis bag, desperate to put distance between us. If I'm going to win this match, I have to focus.

It's the last round before the finals. I've gone further on harder draws, but Alanzo Ruiz is a real hurdle to overcome.

'Gabi!' Papa appears in the doorway. 'You're on.'

As I make my way through the hallways of Rod Laver Arena, Helen Taylor rushes past me, tears spilling down her cheeks.

'You played well!' I call after her, my voice echoing off the concrete. I've felt like that so many times—fallen short after giving my all, crying in the narrow halls of the arena, trying to figure out how I'd face my team.

Alanzo Ruiz stands by the entrance to the court, waiting to be called on. I tap him on the shoulder, and he turns, smiling. His big, toothy grin has been a staple on the circuit for five years.

Hey, I sign. *Nice to see you.*

Nice to see you too. It's wonderful weather, he signs. *Not too hot. Not humid.*

I like the sun, I reply, because my ASL isn't the best. Ruiz smiles and claps me on the back, acknowledging my effort.

Ruiz leans down to tighten his shoelaces, and I watch the subtle flexing of his forearm as his fingers loop and tie.

It's hard hiding my sexuality on the circuit. Ruiz, to my knowledge, has never had a public relationship. That's not uncommon. Most young players focus on the game.

Ruiz looks up, his dark gaze meeting mine, and I swear I see the hint of a smile. We're not close, but it's not the first time I've wondered if—

It's ridiculous to think I'm the only gay on the tour and I know some of the players in the women's draw are queer, but right now, keeping this secret feels like I'm a lone runaway train, hurtling down a track that's broken off halfway down the hill, and nothing and no one can stop the crash that's coming.

Some players come out publicly once they leave the professional circuit, or are already out before they gain fame, but when you're actively playing the game, it's like politics. To many, you're just a warm body with a racquet. Shut up and play the game.

Coming out now will change *everything*—and while I know a lot of good could come of it, I can't ignore the challenges. I still need time. I haven't even told my family.

Our names are called—mine first to help Ruiz time his entrance. I give him a smile and push past him, stepping out onto the court. I raise my hand to the cheering crowd, blinking against the bright stadium lights. It's a pleasant atmosphere tonight. Balmy. A gentle breeze rolls across the court. A moth flutters past my face, caught in the allure of a bright light.

Dropping my gear by my station, I suck down a mouthful of electrolyte water before unsheathing my racquet: my chrome-handled Wilson. Its strings are hard and taut. It's seen hundreds of games. Hundreds of wins. I'm desperate to give it another one.

Tonight, the strategy is to outlast. There's no point in trying to break Ruiz. His defensive game is too good, his backhand too strong. The only way I'll win this game is if I can exhaust him, control the ball, and time my points.

Ruiz doesn't disappoint. After five games—of which I win four—my knees ache and my wrist is sore. Ruiz may be down, but I know that's all a part of his plan.

It's my service game. I try to ace him and fail. The ball catches the net, dropping down to the court. My second serve is softer but Ruiz absolutely *sends* it back. I fumble forward and hear my racquet scrape against the ground. Standing up, I examine the frame. There's no warping, but the paint has chipped off.

On my favourite racquet, too. Damn.

I face Ruiz again. He stares across the net at me, hard and

intimidating. I grin back, trying to tip him off his game. He doesn't break.

On the next game, I win the set, but I've played right into his hand and my body is feeling it.

Ruiz doesn't even seem fazed as we head into the second set and just to prove it, he wins the first game. He is a meticulous, careful, even-tempered player. I'd rather be up against Lukas, whose erratic nature can turn against him just as easily as it benefits him, but trying to break Ruiz is, well, like trying to tear down a brick wall with your bare hands.

Every point is hard fought and I'm feeling the burn. Worst of all, Ruiz has me exactly where he wants me. For the first time, I have real doubts about winning. The scoreboard says I'm a set up, with two games of the second set in my favour, but as I meet Ruiz's gaze again, I know there's a lot left in this match.

I'm not winning.

Ruiz makes me run for the ball each and every point, the complete and utter *arsehole*, and my legs scream in protest. I'm two sets up but won the last set with a nail-biting tie breaker. Now we're deep in the third and Ruiz has won the last three games to my none. The momentum he has spent the entire match building is paying off.

This has been his plan the whole time, and the worst part is that I *knew* it.

I glance up at my player's box. Victor and Papa stare

back at me, quiet and emotionless. Bile rises into my throat. I swallow it back down and taste the burn.

The ball hits the net. I lose the game.

Four games to love.

Ruiz has broken me. I'm *broken*.

Stalking over to the bench, I grab my towel and sink into my seat. I need to refocus. I've beaten Ruiz before. *Outlast. Outplay.* I have to remember I've got further in tournaments than this when I've had *less* to play for.

But this match is *everything*—it's a pathway to a championship as I come into the peak of my career; it's a chance to put all the issues with my team behind me; it's a chance to fight another day.

And of course, this time there's Noah to fight for . . .

Getting up, I take a deep breath and taste the salt on the ocean breeze coming from Port Melbourne. I hear the hum of the stadium lights, and feel the droplet of sweat that trickles down the divots of my spine. Ruiz is already on the baseline, and crossing the short distance to my side of the court feels like a monumental effort.

Steeling myself, I serve.

The ball flies down the middle of the court and hits the back wall.

Ace.

Good. Okay.

I take another breath and set up for my next serve. I aim for the top corner of his service box, hitting the ball hard crosscourt. Ruiz catches it easily, drop-shotting it so it lands short. I run forward, not even thinking, and return it. It flies past him, hitting the corner of the court before bouncing out. My knee protests, and a deep throb of pain radiates from it.

Ruiz stalks back to the baseline, muttering under his breath.

Somehow, I claw back another point and then a game. Ruiz huffs and rolls his shoulders and I watch as a quiet discontentment pervades his body.

My momentum doesn't last long. Ruiz sticks to his game plan and slowly wears me down. I'm dripping sweat onto the court by the time he closes out the third set, 6–4, and I drag myself to my bench, completely and utterly broken.

Collapsing into my seat, I grab my water bottle and try to refocus. I'm *still* a set up. As much as Ruiz wants me to think he's outplayed me, this match isn't over.

I can't leave Melbourne yet.

So, as play recommences, I make a calculated choice.

A choice I may come to regret.

I play hard.

I play into his hand.

I picture my father on the sidelines, his eyes wide with fear and worry as I veer off our carefully constructed game plan.

But he's not the one down here, aching in more ways than one. If I let Ruiz take this to five sets, he's going to beat me. I'd rather push myself and win than play it safe and lose.

Play continues, and I chase down every ball, serving with precision, and biting my tongue when things don't go my way. I refuse to let Ruiz know I'm sore, even as my knee catches painfully again during one return. I refuse to allow any sliver of emotion to come through my game, no disappointment, no joy, no frustration. If there's any chance of me closing this set, I need to keep Ruiz out of my head.

I serve and Ruiz slices cross-court, his stroke fast and precise.

'Out!' the umpire cries as Ruiz's return skims the line.

Ruiz approaches the net, clearly checking the call for himself. *It's out*, I sign.

Ruiz looks to his interpreter, signing at them, and in turn, the interpreter speaks to the umpire. After a few tense exchanges with the umpire, he walks away, shaking his head. He signs something to his player's box. While my ASL isn't good enough to know what, anger's a universal language, so I can hazard a few guesses.

I swallow. The dry-mouth feel is back. The end of the set is looming; and I'm up by two games. It's Ruiz's service game, and the ball crosses the net at an alarming speed. I return it, and as Ruiz prepares his backhand, the ball hits the frame of the racquet and veers into the audience. A point to me.

Above me, seagulls squawk. Ruiz serves, and faults once. He serves again, and I make him run crosscourt. The ball bounces out, and he skids away.

Suddenly, we're at match point.

My empty stomach clenches as I glance at the scoreboard; I'm hot, sweaty, aching and desperate to close this match. My body's been pushed to the limit and I have no idea how much longer I can go on. I have to convert this point. I have to end this.

Ruiz raises the ball. He serves, and without thinking, I lunge forward. My racquet makes contact with the ball, a forehand that lands just inside the baseline. Ruiz runs for it, returns the ball with a backhand, and in a risky move I know Papa's going to berate me for, I get close to the net and hit the ball crosscourt, stealing the point and winning the match.

The crowd erupts as I fall on my back, exhausted. Closing my eyes, I let the celebration wash over me. I've won. I've done it. I imagine Noah's watching the TV right now, and I hope he can tell how elated I am—happy to be staying here, with him, for a few more days.

'Game. Gabriel Madani beats Alanzo Ruiz,' says the umpire over the speaker system, 'six–one, six–two, four–six, six–three.'

As I'm getting to my feet, Ruiz approaches the net, smiling. *Good game*, he signs.

I love to play with you, I sign back.

I think this is your year, he replies. *You can go all the way.*

As I wave to the crowd, I see Percy Jones scuttling onto the court with his camera crew. After placing my tennis gear back in my bag, I smooth my hair from my face and walk to meet him at the baseline.

'Great game again, Gabriel,' he crows in his southern drawl. 'You're officially into the finals—your first finals here at the Australian Open. There's a good chance you may face Lukas Froebel in the next round; what do you think about that?'

'This draw hasn't been easy for me,' I admit, and the crowd laughs. 'But if I am up against Lukas, then that is what it is.'

'What strategies are you bringing into these final matches?'

'None that aren't confidential,' I reply. 'Maybe some mind games.' The crowd laughs again. I shrug. 'I will do what I always do. Try to recover well, try to keep up my training, my diet, come back as fresh as I can.'

'Thank you, Gabriel—ladies and gentlemen, please give it up for our fourteenth seed, Gabriel Madani, who's into the quarter-finals at the Australian Open.'

Dove: Welcome back to Hello Hotline, your celeb gossip podcast with Dove and Laura. We've got a jam-packed show. We're talking about Beyoncé's surprise album news, a Hotline fave is possibly expecting a baby, and we have the goss on a hot new couple you will not believe.

Laura: And things are heating up Down Under. You guys have been obsessed with tennis star Gabriel Madani's mystery friend. And no, we still don't know who he is.

Dove: All I want to know is where he got that shirt from. That's what I'm obsessed with. You know, otherwise he's just another edgy boy with cute floppy hair.

Laura: So totally your type. A young Nick Carter.

Dove: I mean, I'd climb him in a heartbeat. Wouldn't you?

Laura: Oh yeah, he could wreck my life and I'd thank him.

Dove: You think they're a couple?

Laura: Like . . . well . . . Obviously, I don't want to speculate. As far as I'm aware, Gabriel's been linked to a few women, so I don't want that rumour to start here. Therefore, I'm going to intentionally say no, they're not a couple.

Dove: Yeah, like, of course we're not interested in outing anyone on this podcast. Plus, who really cares about tennis drama?

Laura: Great, thanks, Dove, that's one way to get us off the US Open PR list.

Dove: What?! It's the truth! This is a celeb gossip podcast, not tennis flavour of the week.

Laura: You've already offended me. Let's just move on to Beyoncé.

23

NOAH

Gabriel shrieks as Victor dumps a bag of ice into the bathtub. Wearing just a pair of black briefs, he scrunches his shoulders as he braves the shock, his skin ashen and prickled with goosebumps.

'I hate this, I hate this, I hate this,' Gabriel repeats as the ice floats to the surface.

Bernard appears at the doorway of the bathroom and says something in French. Gabriel rolls his eyes and slumps into the water in response. When Bernard's gone, I lean in close.

'What did he say?' I whisper.

'He said I deserved it for playing like an idiot.' He purses his lips as Victor returns with another bag of ice, and this time, it's unceremoniously dumped over Gabriel's head. I'd only managed to see the highlights reel on my way to meet Gabriel after my shift, but I thought he'd played well.

'I played . . . risky,' Gabriel explains. 'And pushed myself too far.'

'And now he's going into a quarter-final against Lukas,' Victor adds. He tosses me the eggtimer. 'You're on timer duty. Make sure he suffers for fifteen minutes.'

'What does this do, exactly?' I ask as a large chunk of ice bobs up against Gabriel's swollen knee.

'It helps muscle recovery and prevents inflammation.' Gabriel shifts slightly, wincing. 'Distract me. Please.'

'You wanna talk about what our next Melbourne adventure could be?' I bring up the TripAdvisor article. 'Oh, we could go to the IceBar!'

'Not funny,' he says through gritted teeth.

'We could go to Phillip Island for a day trip. Or is that too long?' I ask. 'The article has other suggestions. We could—'

'I don't care what the article says,' Gabriel snaps. 'I want *you* to show me why you like this city. I want *you* to show me around, not some app.'

'But the tourist experience—'

'I want the *Noah* experience.'

That is possibly the most romantic thing anyone's ever said to me. Still mindful of Bernard and Victor, I reach forward and catch his fingers, lacing our hands together.

'The Noah experience, huh? I'm sure I can manage something.' I lean down and swish the cold water. 'But now what do we talk about for the next fourteen minutes and thirty seconds?'

'I have an idea.' Gabriel leans forward in the bathtub. 'Victor!'

'Yes?' Victor's head pops around the doorframe.

'Do you still have your tarot cards? I want a reading.'

'A reading?' I echo.

Victor nods, disappearing to fetch a deck of tarot cards. When he returns, he sits cross-legged on the cold tiled floor—this is quickly becoming a bathroom party—and shuffles the colourful deck of cards eagerly.

'Victor reads my future before every game,' Gabriel explains. 'Ask him to read yours.'

'I dunno . . .' I've never really believed in this kinda stuff, but I also don't want to offend Victor.

'It's okay, I don't really believe it—it's just fun,' Gabriel reassures me even as Victor huffs.

'So far, the cards haven't lied,' says Victor.

'Okay,' I say. 'I'm game.'

Victor shuffles the deck then hands them to me. 'You have to trust the cards. Ask them what you want to know.'

I push my scepticism to one side and take the deck from Victor's hands. 'Do I have to ask my question out loud?'

'You *subconsciously push it into the cards*,' Gabriel replies, imitating Victor.

'Quiet, you, or I'll go and get another bag of ice.' Victor turns his attention back to me. 'The cards can help you chart a path forward. Think about somewhere in your life where you want clarity. There are no bad readings.'

Behind me, Gabriel scoffs.

'Ignore him,' Victor says.

'Should I go to university?' I ask out loud. It seems innocent enough. Behind me, I hear water slosh as Gabriel leans over the lip of the bathtub.

'Good question.' Victor takes the cards back and shuffles them again. 'Select three from the deck. Place them on the bathmat.'

I select three cards at random places in the deck and place them facedown.

'The Chariot,' Victor says, turning the first card over. 'It tells me you've overcome challenges in your life, hard ones, significant ones. You're bold and confident, able to adapt to the twists and changes of your life. You have a strong desire to be successful.' Victor smiles. 'It's funny you asked about university—a major milestone in people's lives, something you may feel you need to do to be successful.'

I look at Gabriel, and he looks at me. Victor flips the second card.

'Four of Wands, interesting,' Victor murmurs. 'The Four of Wands symbolises community. Family, but you're not necessarily related to them. They're people you can lean on for support, who cherish you and what you bring to the table.'

Victor flips over the final card.

'The Lovers. Romance is literally on the cards,' Victor says, looking up at me, and I feel my heart stutter. 'You're a very romantic person. You handle rejection with grace, whether this is in relationships or your career. But you tend to hold very idealised views. You may see your life as a series of milestones you must achieve, a perfect life, a perfect career, a perfect relationship. Such is the double-edged sword of the romantic.'

'It didn't answer my question, though,' I mutter, looking down at the cards.

'Didn't it?' Victor asks.

Before I can unpack the response further, the eggtimer

rings. Gabriel leaps up from the bathtub with a victorious cry, showering us in ice-cold water.

♪

The hall light is still on when I get home, which is weird. I check my watch; it's close to midnight, and Margie should be in bed. Closing the new flyscreen door, I make sure to lock it before toeing off my shoes and walking down the hall.

'Margie, are you still awake?' I call softly.

Margie jolts awake in her recliner. 'Oh, Noah, I was waiting for you.'

'You didn't have to wait up for me.' Guilt hits me. If I'd known, I would have come home earlier.

'I wanted to . . .' She eases to her feet. 'I wanted to see your face.'

Stepping past me, Margie ushers me back down the hallway and flicks on the light to my room, revealing an upright piano pushed between my bed and the far wall. It's an old Yamaha, made from warm oak, with a red velvet stool and a pedal worn down from use. I run my hands over the fallboard, feeling the ridges of wood.

'It's the only place it would fit; I know it's a bit tight,' she says as I turn to her, hoping my amazement and gratitude is evident in my face. 'And it will need a tune.'

'It's beautiful,' I murmur, raising the fallboard. My fingers find G and, well, the piano plays a note that is anything but a G. 'I love it, thank you.'

'It's yours,' she says. 'As long as you want it. When you go, take it with you.'

'What?' I gasp, running my hands over the keys. 'Are you serious?'

'It's spent the last ten years in storage, darling. It deserves to be played.'

Without thinking about it, I turn and hug her—something I've never done before. Margie wraps her arms around me and pulls me in tight.

'You're a good boy,' she murmurs against my shoulder. I bury my face in her neck and inhale the scent of lavender and musk that I know I'll always associate with Margie. 'You believe me, don't you?'

'I do.' It hurts to get the words out.

Margie smooths her hands over my shoulders as she steps away. 'I'm going to bed. Don't stay up too late.'

'I won't,' I promise.

Later, in bed, I send Gabriel a photo of the piano.

NoAgenda: *Look what Margie had in storage all this time! It's completely out of tune but the 1980 LU-101s are great for semi-professionals. It's a Yamaha with a German walnut cabinet; they legit don't make them like this anymore!*

Hungrygabriel73: *I have no idea what any of that means but it is a beautiful majestic piano!*

NoAgenda: *I'll have to record a piece for you when it's tuned. How are you holding up after the ice torture?*

Hungrygabriel73: *Still cold. In bed but still cold.*

Hungrygabriel73: *Wish you'd stayed to warm me up*

Hungrygabriel73: *That feels cringe I regret writing*

NoAgenda: *Wish I could have stayed too—are you a big spoon or a little spoon?*

Hungrygabriel73: *Don't know. Pros and cons of each?*

NoAgenda: *Little spoon pros are obvious—u are hugged. Big spoon pros are you get to do the hugging, initiate things but cons are you get a mouthful of hair.*

Hungrygabriel73: *I have a lot of hair. Feels like it's safer for me to be the big spoon.*

NoAgenda: *You do give off big spoon energy.*

Hungrygabriel73: *I could be ur big spoon.*

NoAgenda: *Gabriel.*

Hungrygabriel73: *Ye?*

NoAgenda: *Yesterday in the locker rooms. I don't want to get into our entire dating history but have you ever . . . been with anyone?*

He doesn't reply for a moment, and I panic.

It doesn't matter, I'm being rude and it's none of my business, I type, just as Gabriel replies, *I haven't . . .*

Gabriel's name appears on the screen a second later. He's calling me.

'Gabi,' I say, picking up. 'It's none of my business, I'm sorry I asked.'

'It's okay,' Gabriel whispers and I imagine him in his room, in the dark with the door closed, speaking under the covers. 'The truth is I'm a bit embarrassed.'

'Embarrassed?' I reply.

'I *should* have.' He sighs. 'Been with someone, I mean. I don't know . . . it feels like I've missed a boat that everyone else's been on.'

'You haven't,' I say, turning on my side and curling in on myself. 'If anything, you're about to board a *better* boat; having your first time with someone who cares about you. You get to avoid all the weird awkward embarrassing sex. All the emotions that come with it.'

'Do you care about me?' Gabriel asks.

I press my face into the pillow. 'You know I do.'

'I meant what I said about staying longer. After the tournament. We could go somewhere. Together.'

'What about after that?' There's silence on the other end, and it's like a punch in the gut. This is not where I expected the conversation to go, and I'm not sure if I'm really ready to discuss it, but we're here now. 'Is there going to be an after?'

'I don't know,' Gabriel whispers.

I know why he doesn't know. Because Gabriel's not out on the circuit; he's not even out to his dad. And being together—really being together, long-term—means changing his entire reality.

'I don't want to force—'

'You're *not*,' he replies fiercely. 'It's me. It's not you. It's never you.' He pauses and I wish I could just climb through the phone and be there beside him, touch him, hug him. 'I just need some time.'

Scrubbing my hand over my face, I force myself to take a breath. 'Of course. Take all the time you need.'

It's not what I want to say, or what I want to hear, but I have no idea how to navigate this situation; how to tell him I want more than what we have right now, without adding to the pressure he's already feeling.

I bite my tongue, waiting for him to speak again.

'Not long,' Gabriel replies after a moment. 'I just need to figure out how to tell Papa . . . and then everything else can come after.' He pauses. 'Can we still hang out tomorrow?'

'Of course,' I say. 'I'll text you the plan. I hope you're not too sore in the morning.'

'I'll be okay,' he says. 'Good night.'

'Good night,' I say. I wait for him to hang up, but it doesn't come. I don't hang up either.

'Are we really doing this?' Gabriel says sleepily on the other end.

I yawn. 'Guess we are.'

There's no way to know who falls asleep first, but I'm ninety per cent sure it's Gabriel.

24

NOAH

My mother texts me back.

I didn't think you still had this number. It's good to hear from you.

I sit up in bed, barely believing what I've just read. She'd sent the message just after 7 am. It's now almost nine. I read over it twice, three times, before it sinks in.

My fingers shake as I type, *Where are you?*

I wait for the response for fifteen minutes and then realise I can't spend my day waiting for my phone to buzz. So, I make coffee. Eat breakfast. The laundry's overflowing, so I put on a load before grabbing my joggers and Sadie's leash.

Making sure the door is locked when I leave, we walk towards Carlton Gardens. I say walk, but Sadie is a nightmare on the leash: lurching forward in excitement before stopping to sniff an electricity pole, darting around when she catches sight of a bird on a fence, or a lizard in a garden bed.

In Carlton Gardens, cockatoos graze on the yellowing grass under the shade of old English oaks; a group of women and their babies meet on a patchwork of picnic blankets; and I hear the unmistakeable sound of a ball hitting a racquet as two people play tennis on a bright green court on the other side of the gardens. As Sadie and I near the large fountain in the middle of the park, my phone vibrates in my pocket. I pull it out and feel my heart rise into my throat. Mum's texted me back.

I'm in Albury. Working at the hospital. Did you make it to Melbourne?

Albury is only three hours away on the train. If I wanted to, I could buy a ticket this afternoon and be there by tonight.

I take Sadie to the dog park and let her off the leash. A labrador bounds towards her and they take off, zooming around the park after each other.

Yes, I'm in Melbourne. I want to see you. I could book a ticket to Albury and—

Gabriel.

I'd promised him the 'Noah experience', and there's still so much left of the Open. I want to be there for him every step of the way.

I look down at my text message and delete a few words.

Yes, I'm in Melbourne. I want to see you. I could book a ticket to Albury sometime soon.

Mum texts me back instantly. *I'm planning to come down to Melbourne this weekend.*

Delight surges through me. After so long, I'm going to see Mum again. I'm going to hug her and she's going to smell exactly like Chanel N°5 and that fresh Rexona deoderant she always buys.

I'd love that. Let me know what time you can meet.

I will, she promises. *Soon.*

I give Sadie another twenty minutes in the dog park before calling her over and clipping her leash back on. It's a strangely cool day; the cloud cover is heavy and breeze rolls up from the south, bringing with it the smell of the ocean. Checking the weather app, I realise we're in for evening showers. Guess the heat had to break eventually.

When we get home, Sadie and I play in the backyard while I hang out the washing, keen to get it dry before the weather rolls in. Then I vacuum, mop the floors, take out the rubbish and generally do everything I can to be a fucking stellar housemate.

When the chores are done, I make myself another coffee and take the mug into my room, setting it down on my bedside table.

Pulling the stool out from the piano, I lift its fallboard and take the microfibre cloth off the keys. Running a scale, every note falls flat. The instrument clearly needs work before it's playable and while I can appreciate a nice piano, I've never had to maintain one.

Bored, I decide to video-call Gabriel and he answers, bare-chested and sweaty, panting hard from his training session. 'Hey.'

I swallow, trying to gather myself in the face of such unexpected erotica. 'Um, hey, is this a bad time?'

He rubs his towel down his glistening chest and it's

actually *painful* to watch him through the fishbowl-like lens of my phone. 'No, we just finished training.'

'How do you feel?' I ask. My mouth is suddenly *really dry*. 'Does your body feel good?'

He smiles, a breathy little half-smile. 'Yes, Noah, my body feels good.'

'I bet it does,' I murmur, not realising I've said it out loud until Gabriel tilts the camera up.

'What did you say?' he asks.

'I said I'm glad it does,' I reply. 'So, do you wanna go out tonight? To a restaurant.' Like a proper date, I want to add but don't. 'There's a place near mine that I've always wanted to try—are you up for that?'

'Sounds good,' he says. 'What time?'

'Six?'

'Don't stay out all night,' I hear Bernard say in the background. Shit, I had no idea his dad was listening in. I have to watch what I say.

'Be back by ten o'clock,' Bernard says.

'Ignore him,' Gabriel replies. 'Midnight will be fine. My match isn't until tomorrow night.'

It's nice to hear Gabriel and his father banter. Obviously, their relationship is complicated, but it's also obvious how much Bernard loves Gabriel, and how the professional and personal become conflicted.

'I'll have a car come pick you up at five-thirty,' I tease. 'My driver will see you soon.'

'I'll be sure to look out for him.'

'You should, he will be driving a Mercedes.'

'This is a fancy outing, then. I will have to dress up.'

'Please do. Only the best.'

He laughs, that dimpled smile coming back with a vengeance, and I long to kiss the corners of his mouth. If we continue with this romance after the tournament, I realise this will be my reality—seeing Gabriel only through a screen, not being able to touch, or kiss, or hug.

'I gotta go,' he says, running a hand through his damp hair. 'I'm going to sit in the sauna with Papa and strategise. See you tonight.'

I tell myself to stop thinking about his sweaty body as I hang up. But it's no use. The mind is willing, but the flesh is weak.

After pulling out practically everything in my wardrobe, at 1.34 pm I come to the frustrating realisation that I have absolutely nothing to wear. Nothing *feels* right.

Grabbing my keys and a cotton tote bag, I walk down the block and catch a tram to Sydney Road: the messy, beating pulse of the inner north. Sydney Road holds everything anyone could ever want within just a few blocks. There's a Vietnamese bakery wedged between a barber shop and a halal butchery that always has a line, as well as a shop that only sells unique bongs. I walk past a tangle of bikes affixed to a nearby bike rack, each wedged in so tight they've become a single mass of spokes and seats.

And then, there's heaven. At least, my kind of heaven: Savers.

A second-hand superstore.

I enter through the big sliding doors and inhale the ever-present scent of mothballs. Savers is always busy but since it's a Monday afternoon, the crowd is slightly thinner. I make my way over to the men's section, purposefully ignoring a fur-lined camel jacket on a mannequin. I am here for one reason and one reason only: to look hot as fuck on this date.

Browsing through the racks of clothes, I find a few gems, including another oversized retro eighties geometric shirt, a pair of barely worn faux leather loafers and a cool Nike hoodie that'll be perfect for cool summer days.

'We meet in the sunlight at last,' says a familiar voice. A blond man approaches me; he's tall and well built, with large lips and a smear of mascara on his lashes. As he reaches me, he glances at my basket and pulls out the geometric top. 'Another one to send them wild, hey?'

I stammer, caught in that awful moment of feeling like I know someone but struggling to place them. 'I'm sorry, I—'

'Babes, it's me.' The man laughs and I immediately twig.

'Peaches!' I reach forward and give Peaches an awkward hug. 'Didn't recognise you without your layers of makeup.'

'After everything I've done for you, you're still so cruel to me,' she says, nudging me out of the way and grabbing a black silk shirt before I can.

'I can't believe I've never seen you outside of work,' I say as she admires the top. 'Do you come here often?'

Peaches shakes her head. 'We're rehearsing an act over at the Playroom, and I have drag karaoke at ten at the Flamingo Bar in Fitzroy. You should swing by.'

'Maybe. I've got a date tonight.'

Peaches raises an eyebrow. 'Oh! Is it who I think it is?'

Shit, I definitely should not have said anything. 'I—'

Peaches must clock my worry because she nudges me good-naturedly. 'I get it. But if you feel like coming by afterwards, I'll put your name on the door.' She hands me the black silk shirt. 'You should wear this. Leave a few buttons undone and put a bit of oil on your chest, he won't be able to look away.'

I feel my cheeks go red, but I place the shirt in my basket anyway.

♪

Peaches was right—I am loath to even *think* those three words—because the silk shirt looks divine, clinging to my collarbone and shoulders but billowing out around my waist. Leaving the two top buttons undone, I loop an old gold chain around my throat and admire it as it hangs delicately on my clavicle. Finally, I spritz on a splutter of cologne, slide on my new pair of disinfected loafers and manage to run a dollop of wax through my hair just as my doorbell rings.

I'm a jumble of nerves as I go to open the door. God, what if I'm *too* dressed up? What if the amount of effort I've put into this night just makes everything feel awkward?

As I open the door, all my anxiety melts away. Gabriel stands on my doorstep in his white linen shirt, dark jeans with rolled cuffs, a pair of well-worn brown leather loafers and a flashy gold watch. His glossy hair bounces around his shoulders, washed and styled to let his natural curls shine.

Not for the first time, I'm in awe of just how beautiful he is—and how, just for this moment, he's all mine.

Before I can say hello, Gabriel captures my mouth with his.

It's not a polite kiss or a greeting. It's hard and wanting and consuming. In a matter of seconds, I'm pressed against the doorframe, his hands in my hair and his mouth hungry on mine.

'Babe, we'll be late for our booking,' I gasp as he kisses down my throat. Somehow, I manage to get my foot around the door to push it closed—quite the feat if I do say so myself.

'I can't go to dinner,' he mumbles against my throat. For a moment, I panic over the non-refundable booking fee at the stupidly fancy Italian place. Why hadn't he called ahead? 'Not when you look like this. I won't be able to focus.'

I feel his fingers begin at my shirt buttons and it takes everything in me to stop him. 'It's all a part of the Noah experience. Trust me.'

I can't say it's not thrilling to know he wants me just as much as I want him, especially after the afternoon we spent in the locker room and given the dwindling time we have together before the tournament ends.

'I promise, I've heard their *spaghetti nero* is better than sex.'

Gabriel scoffs even as he steps away from me. 'I doubt it.'

♪

La Cucina—'the kitchen'—is one of those beyond-small, busy Italian places along Lygon Street. I've requested a private table and it's certainly that, wedged between the bar and a wall. The restaurant is dim, but a tea light flickers in a small dish between us.

Gabriel and I take a seat across from one another. His dark eyes shimmer in the candlelight as he glances around the restaurant.

'Thanks for bringing me here,' he murmurs, reaching out to take my hand. His calloused thumb brushes over my knuckles. I flex my fingers, and he laces his with mine.

'And to think, you didn't want to come fifteen minutes ago.'

Gabriel grins, casting his eyes down to the menu. 'I disagree, I very much wanted to come fifteen minutes ago.'

I laugh, scandalised, and pull my hand away.

He gives me a teasing smile as his gaze takes in the menu. 'So, you recommend the *spaghetti nero*?'

When the waiter swings around, we order our meals. I get a glass of wine, and Gabriel orders sparkling water. We play footsies under the table, hiding our smiles like complete children when the waiter comes back with our drinks.

I take a sip of the wine, enjoying the complex taste. With Dad being the way he is, I'm always careful not to overdo it. As much as I despise the thought that I'm anything like him, I'm half of him—the bad stuff that's in him is in me, too.

'My mum texted me,' I tell Gabriel. 'Well, I texted her, and she finally replied.'

'Really?' Gabriel says, his face lighting up. 'Where is she?'

'Around three hours from here, in a regional town. She says she's coming to Melbourne this weekend. We're going to make plans to meet.'

'Noah, that's wonderful,' he says, reaching forward to take my hand again. 'I'm really happy for you.'

I look down at our entwined hands and the phrase *What are we?* pushes against the back of my teeth. As much as I want some clarity, is it worth potentially ruining what could be our last night together? I glance up at Gabriel and he smiles, then brings my hand to his mouth and kisses my knuckles. His eyes smoulder as he looks up at me beneath his lashes. How could anyone not fall for this man?

And how am I going to pick up the pieces when he leaves?

When the bill comes, Gabriel hands over his credit card.

'I want to split it,' I protest even as the waiter whisks the bill away.

'I don't,' Gabriel replies, and I guess that's that. No arguments.

The late evening is unusually bright; the sky is deep crimson as the sun sets over the city. Whatever rain was predicted hasn't eventuated, and what remains is one of those perfect, lazy, long summer evenings.

'Gelato?' Gabriel suggests, pointing to a gelato shop across the road.

'Twist my arm, why don't you?'

Gabriel gets a rich chocolate fondant, and I choose *dulce de leche*. Tipping my cone towards Gabriel, he licks the swirl off the top.

'That's good—here, try mine.'

Sitting like this, under the fairy lights of Lygon Street, it's easy to imagine a future together—Christmas markets in Paris, cups of hot chocolate warming our hands as we walk arm in arm down the cobblestoned streets, laughing and seeing our breath turn to mist in the air.

'What's the next part of the Noah experience?' Gabriel says as we bite down to the end of our cones.

I check my watch. It's almost nine. 'It's a surprise.'

Gabriel quirks a brow. 'Are you going to get me in trouble?'

'The best kind of trouble,' I say. 'Come on, it's a few blocks.'

We leave Lygon Street and cut across the suburbs. Sure, we could have caught the tram to Fitzroy and been there in under ten minutes, but then Gabriel would not have been bold enough to hold my hand between Barkly Street and Brunswick Road. Our fingers interlace as we weave through quiet streets lined with Victorian townhouses, tiny local bars and the odd convenience store.

We come to the town centre of Fitzroy and Gabriel lets my hand go—we're back in public view, and the rules of our relationship as set out by Victor's guidelines are back in full force.

Across the road, the Flamingo Bar is painted a garish, well, *flamingo* pink. Party lights flash along the rafters, and house music pumps through the speaker system. The line curls around the block. Gabriel pauses beside me.

'I can't go in. If it gets back to Papa that I was out *partying* the night before a match, he'll kill me,' he says. 'The media will go into a frenzy.'

'But you're not even drinking,' I say. 'And we'll be home before twelve.'

'It doesn't matter. It's how it *looks*.'

I get it. I do. But I think I have a workaround.

'Wait here,' I tell him, and then I scurry over to the security guard managing the line, a plan slowly forming in my head.

25

GABRIEL

When I agreed to go out with Noah, I'd pictured us enjoying each other's company over a candlelit dinner and, hopefully, spending the rest of the evening naked in Noah's bedroom because, well, frankly, I just want to have sex. All night. In various positions. And the three condoms that are burning a hole through my pants pocket right now attest to that fact.

I had *not* expected to be dragged into a drag queen's dressing-room, stripped out of my clothes and asked to choose between a sapphire sequined gown or a shimmery emerald cocktail dress with a long fringe.

The drag queen in question, a tall, broad-shouldered queen named Peaches O'Plenty, presses the dresses against my collarbone, one after the other, assessing them. 'What do you think, baby?' She turns back to Noah.

'Emerald, for sure,' Noah says.

'You heard your man, love,' Peaches says as she thrusts

the emerald dress into my hands. 'Let me know if you need help with the zip.'

'Why am I the one in the dress?' I mutter as I step into the neck and shimmy the fringe up my hip.

As I slip the dress over my shoulders, I reflect on what would be worse: getting photographed in a nightclub the night before a match or being recognised in drag, in a nightclub, the night before a match.

'You said it yourself,' Noah replies from behind the screen. 'You don't want anyone recognising you.'

'Help me zip up,' I demand. Noah slips behind me, his hands finding my hips.

'Green was a good choice,' he whispers as the zip rises.

'And now for the wig!' Peaches declares as I step around the screen. I glance apprehensively at a wall full of wigs, wondering if it's too late to back out.

'Look at you! Put your arms down and walk properly. It's a dress, not a shackle, Gabriel,' Peaches says as I shuffle forward. 'Gosh, I *love* you baby gays.'

Leading me to a seat in front of a large mirror, Peaches plucks a dark afro from her wig wall and places it loosely on my crown. 'No?'

I shake my head, unsure when I started forming opinions about the kind of drag queen I want to be. 'Longer.'

Noah hands Peaches a poker-straight black wig that screams Cher *à la* 'Don't Go Breaking My Heart'. Peaches places it on my head, fanning the hair around my shoulders.

'Not feeling it?' she asks.

'I want to go blonde.' If I'm going to do this, I want to do it right. Go all out.

Peaches smiles. 'Sassy queen knows what she wants.' She reaches over me and grasps a styled blonde wig that could just as easily belong in Dolly Parton's wardrobe.

'We've created a monster,' Noah agrees.

I slip on a hair cap and follow Peaches's instructions on how to put on the wig. Adjusting it around the hairline, I flip the wig over and let the hair fall around my shoulders. It's bouncy and bright and *everything*.

'Well, well, well,' Peaches hums beside me.

I don't look anything like myself and yet—

I feel *so* free.

I'm not Gabriel anymore. His concerns, his issues, his limitations—they simply don't exist for this person. If only for a few hours, I can be someone else; someone completely different.

Peaches picks up an eyeshadow palette full of vibrant pinks, yellows and greens. 'Time to make you a woman, honey.'

'Keep it subtle, she has to go home at twelve,' Noah instructs behind me.

'Noted, sweetness,' says Peaches as she gets to work applying a dark eyeliner on my lower lash line. Then, she directs me to look to the ceiling as she swipes a wand of mascara over my top and bottom lashes. 'You have the most gorgeous eyelashes, lovely.'

'Um, thank you,' I say. No one's ever complimented me on my eyelashes before.

After a long while in the chair, Peaches drops her tools like she's just finished surgery. 'My masterpiece.'

I open my eyes, not sure what to expect, and for a second, I'm not even sure the person in the mirror is me. But it is.

Noah appears behind me, wrapping his arm around my shoulder.

'What do you think?' he asks.

'Well, I don't think anyone will recognise me.'

The Gabriel in the mirror has flushed, soft skin that glows like I've just got out of the sauna. My eyes are bright and large, framed by long black eyelashes. I've never thought I have particularly nice lips before, but now they're coloured a dusky pink and look glossy and full.

'I look ridiculous,' I mutter, but even I know I don't sound convinced.

'You'll be wearing skirts on the court before we know it,' Noah trills. 'A versatile, gender fluid queen.'

A scandalous idea.

Peaches gives me the once-over, admiring her work. 'Enjoy, you two. I'll see you during the show.'

Noah thanks Peaches again, and we go out to the bar. It's dark, and the unique smell of club fog fills the narrow hallway. Whatever confidence I'd mustered looking at myself in the mirror disappears as soon as I emerge onto the pumping dance floor. I can't bring myself to go out there; step out of the darkened doorway we've found ourselves in and be *seen*.

Noah's fingers lace through mine and he gives me an encouraging smile. 'No one here knows who you are, promise!' he yells over the thumping music. 'Come on.'

I wish I could believe him, but as we make our way towards the bar people seem to turn to me, like moths to a flame. Something deep in me twists with fear. Of all the times to be recognised, it's going to be in a dress, heels and a wig.

'People are staring.'

'Yeah, because you look *fucking hot*,' he says, and oh, I hadn't considered that. 'Seriously, Gabi, you look bloody amazing.'

Another woman—another drag queen—looks me up and down, and the darkness in her gaze is . . . hungry.

'Looking good, sweetie,' she practically purrs.

We grab a drink as more people enter the bar. Soon, I'm just another person in a sparkly dress and wig in the crowd—and we're practically a dime a dozen.

On the main stage, a man slowly slides down a pole to a Saweetie song, his long, muscular legs perfectly horizontal. This place isn't at all what I expected—it's risqué and confronting and *thrilling*; it's everything I shouldn't be doing right now, but the sheer rebellion of tonight is everything I didn't know I needed. Tomorrow, I'll be back to drills, diets and match-day prep, but tonight I can just be.

Noah claps as the dancer flips and lands elegantly on his heels. He finishes his performance with a flourish before prancing backstage. The lights dim, the music dies down, and then Peaches O'Plenty appears to the rapturous applause of the crowd.

'Friends and enemies of Flamingo Bar,' comes an announcement, 'welcome to Drag Queen Karaoke! It is my esteemed honour to introduce the despicably sexy, devilishly handsome and all-round singing superstar, Peaches O'Plenty!'

The audience erupts into cheers and hollers. Confetti falls from the ceiling as Peaches makes her way onto the stage. The frilled hem of her hot-pink baby doll dress flares as she twirls and dances and her long scarlet hair falls over one shoulder, vibrant and glossy under the stage lights. She grabs the microphone with a gloved hand.

'Come on, cunts, you know this one,' she says in a comically harsh Australian accent, and then launches into a rendition of Whitney Houston's 'I Wanna Dance with Somebody'.

Noah looks wonderfully stunned beside me, but the crowd behind us is dancing and singing, and their enthusiasm is infectious. I pull Noah closer to the stage, feeling the music wash over me.

Tonight, I'm not Gabriel. For this brief, beautiful moment in time, I'm just a guy dancing with a guy, quietly and desperately in love with him.

'I never knew she could sing,' Noah says as he huddles against me. He's quite drunk and I'm incredibly, painfully sober. Still, he insists on riding back to my apartment with me, which is very sweet. It's just after eleven and the city is bustling. We order an Uber and wait the fifteen minutes it'll take for the driver to pick us up on the corner of the next block—away from the crowds that spill in and out of the Flamingo Bar.

'She's an excellent singer.' I nudge him as he begins to slump against me. 'So are you.'

Somewhere between his second gin and tonic and the round of Jägerbombs, Noah had leapt to the stage during the open mic break in the set. His rendition of 'Memory' had both surprised and moved me, and the club had stood, in stunned silence, as he'd belted out the final, haunting chorus, before breaking into rapturous applause.

'Did you have fun?' he slurs. 'Do you like the Noah experience?'

'It was the best night of my life,' I say, and mean it. Really, really mean it.

'Really?'

'Yes.' I reach over and take his hand. 'You're the best thing that has ever happened to me.'

'Even better than winning the Monte-Carlo Masters?'

'*Salaud*,' I huff, pushing him away. 'You said you would not google.'

'I didn't! You mentioned it on *Hot Ones*—what, like I'm not going to watch your *Hot Ones* episode?'

'I was being sincere.'

Noah's hand rises to cup my face, his gaze a little hazy and unfocused. 'I know you were,' he says, so tenderly it makes my chest feel tight.

Noah's phone pings. Our ride's approaching.

We find the Toyota Camry and both slide into the back seat. As soon as the car pulls away from the kerb, the magic we'd experienced this evening feels . . . broken, somehow, and now we're being chauffeured back to our boring, careful, normal lives.

I don't want that. I want to live in this moment forever; to be who I was in that club, with Noah, forever. Or maybe not *forever*, but longer than a few hours.

The bar at my hotel is quiet but still open, so I deposit Noah in an armchair and order two glasses of sparkling water from the bar. We still have thirty minutes until I technically have to go back up to the room, and I want to sober Noah up before putting him in a cab.

But the moment I step away from the bar, drinks in hand, I realise Noah's disappeared.

Glancing around the foyer, I spot him quickly; he's talking to the night receptionist, hands planted firmly on the counter to stop himself from swaying.

Apparently happy with whatever the night receptionist has said, he swaggers back over with a smile on his face. He ushers me to follow him and understanding dawns when I see where he's headed: the grand piano in the corner of the bar.

So drunk it makes my heart ache, Noah flips back his imaginary coat-tails and takes a seat on the piano stool. He pats the space next to him, gesturing for me to sit down too.

'This . . . this is a Kawai,' he says groggily, caressing the glossy top like one would a lover. 'She's *very* expensive and,' he plays a few notes, 'pretty much in tune, actually. Any requests?'

'The maestro's choice,' I reply, taking a seat beside him. I feel his thigh press against mine, hot through our clothes.

Noah positions his hands over the keys. 'Very well.'

And just like that, his fingers take off. Nimble and precise, he plucks out a gorgeous fast-paced melody. I catch the eye of the bartender, who stares at me with a look of joyous wonder, and I shrug in reply. I knew Noah loved jazz, loved the piano at the old bar he used to work at, and after his karaoke tonight, I've discovered he can sing like an angel.

But I didn't know he'd be *incredible*.

He plays for a short while, totally lost in the music, until he fumbles a note, falls off the melody playing in his mind, and swears, stopping.

'I messed up,' he mutters.

'It's okay. Have a drink.' I hand him the water glass and he takes a long sip. 'Where did you learn to play?'

'School,' he replies. 'It was the one place that wasn't complete shit.'

The last thing I want is to bring up those memories, so I direct his attention back to the piano. 'Would you keep playing for me?'

'Requests?'

'What, you know everything off by heart?'

He shrugs. 'No. But I spent a lot of time playing.' To show me his extensive repertoire, he plays the opening notes to 'My Heart Will Go On' and seamlessly weaves it into 'Hotline Bling'.

'Play something you like,' I suggest.

Noah's fingers are still for a moment, poised in a way that reminds me of a spider ready to strike. A second later, they fall onto the keyboard, fast and messy and beautiful. Even if he made a mistake, I don't think I'd notice it. He's so masterful it's just a privilege to watch him be *good* at it, and I wonder if that's how he feels watching my tennis matches.

I loop my arms around his waist and press my forehead against his shoulder. Noah shifts slightly, angling his body towards me, and switches to a gentle repetitive melody with his left hand as his right comes to rest on my upper thigh.

'Darling, cameras, public,' he says, barely audible over the music.

I kiss his cheek and feel his surprise against my lips. I desperately want him to turn his head and find my lips, but he keeps playing.

'What was that for?' he asks, clearly amused.

Because I love you. Because I want to keep you after all this is over; because you know me better than anyone else, know me better than I even know myself, sometimes.

But Noah has such a full life here; I've seen a glimpse of it tonight. How can I ask him to leave? To give it all up—for me? Someone who's in Paris for less than four months a year; someone who might not be able to kiss him on his birthday or take him out for a drink on a Friday night, or do all the wonderfully simple, beautiful, mundane things people do when they're in love.

'I don't want this to end,' I say. 'Any of this.'

Noah stops playing and turns to me. 'I don't—'

'I know there's a lot of . . . *shit* here,' I interrupt before he can say something. 'That I still have to talk to Papa, and I know my life is anything *but* normal . . .'

'Gabi, I—'

Realising I can't stomach his rejection right now, I squeeze his thigh. 'Just say you'll be there at the end of the Open.' That's enough for now; it has to be.

Noah pauses, swallows, nods. 'Of course I will be.'

I take his hand. 'Will you come and watch tomorrow?' It might be the last match I play in this tournament; it might be the last match Noah sees for a while.

He nods. 'If you want me there, I'll come.'

'I do. I want you, badly.'

For more than a match, more than a tournament, more than a summer.

'*Gabriel.*' He says my name as though it hurts him, then he pulls out his phone and checks the time. It's barely past midnight. 'I should go.'

I sit on the edge of the piano stool, trying to untangle my feelings as Noah orders an Uber.

'You played beautifully,' says the night receptionist as we make our way out to the street.

'Thank you for letting me,' Noah says bashfully.

When we get outside, a car pulls into the half-circle drive, and Noah turns to me. 'See you tomorrow?'

'See you tomorrow.'

He reaches forward and squeezes my hand. 'This isn't the end, I know it isn't.' I don't know if he's talking about the tournament, or us.

I nod, swallowing. 'Okay.'

26

GABRIEL

My alarm blares at eight-thirty the next morning. When people think of professional athletes, they often think of 4.30 am wake-up calls, of hours spent in the gym, of restrictive diets and supplements. While that might be true for competition time, it's not the reality for most of us. Occasionally, I'll train before six if we have to travel during the day, or if there's a meeting or engagement early in the morning, but most of the time, I train for a few hours either side of lunch and then focus on recovery, or strategy, before getting a full eight to nine hours of sleep. Sleep is just as important as training.

Blearily, I reach over and turn off my alarm. After the magic of last night, I'm still achingly tired and since there's no hurry to get up, I close my eyes and sink into the pillow a while longer. My match isn't until six this evening.

Beside me, my phone buzzes.

And again.

And then *again*.

Rubbing my eyes, I pick it up, and to my horror, I realise *all* the notifications are Google Alerts, sending me emails because my name's appeared online.

BREAKING: Gabriel Madani's loved-up date night with another man!

Gabriel Madani and #retrotennisguy rumours heat up! Brand new evidence!

New Queer on the Block? Tennis star Gabriel Madani seen on romantic date with Melbourne friend.

'FUCK!' I scream before I can stop myself. My fingers shake as I click on one of the articles. There's a photo of Noah and I sitting side-by-side on the piano, head crooked towards one another, shoulders brushing together.

Gabriel Madani's loved-up date night with another man!

Tennis star Gabriel Madani enjoys a loved-up romantic date night with his mystery lover, who recently attended one of his matches at the Australian Open.

The pair returned to their Southbank hotel at approximately eleven-thirty last night, at which time Gabriel's partner performed a piano solo for him in the lobby. According to witnesses, the pair seemed 'very loved-up'. Shortly after midnight, a car arrived to take Madani's partner home.

Gabriel Madani, ranked ninth in the world, faces world number two, Lukas Froebel, in the quarter-final tonight.

Gabriel Madani has never dated publicly, though he has been linked to tennis player Phoebe Song, singer Grace Love, and British influencer Louisa Wright in recent years.

I burst out of my bedroom, phone in my hands. I'm not sure what I'm doing, I'm not sure what to say. Everything's a rush of pain and anger. I don't even know what's happening until someone grabs me and pulls me into their arms.

My phone falls from my hands and clatters to the floor, but I can't seem to bring myself to care. I sob into his shoulder.

'I'm sorry.' I heave the words out. 'I'm so sorry.'

'It's okay, Gabriel,' Papa says, pulling me closer. Papa. My *papa* is hugging me.

I try to pull away, but I can't. He holds me closer, and I cry until it feels like I might throw up. Papa just holds me. I feel his hand rub my back, feel him stroke my hair.

When, after a few minutes, I've calmed to hiccups, he leans back to look at me.

'I love you,' he says, his tone even and sure, and everything shatters. Within a matter of moments, everything's changed and nothing, *nothing*, will ever be the same again.

'I'm sorry I didn't tell you.' I raise my hands to wipe at my face, but I can't stop the tears. 'What are we going to do?'

He leads me to the lounge suite and sits me down. Then, he retrieves my phone from the floor. His hands are shaking too.

'I need you to bring Noah here now. Do you have his phone number?'

I nod and find it. 'Can you talk to him?'

'Put him on speaker,' Papa says.

I call him, and the phone rings for two, three, four rings until—

'Gabi?' Noah answers sleepily. Good, maybe he hasn't read anything.

'I need you to come to my hotel,' I say. 'As soon as possible.'

'I will meet you on the street,' Papa says.

'What?' Noah mumbles. 'What's wrong? What's happened?'

'Someone's printed a story about me—about us. They've told people I'm gay, they've—'

'Oh, fuck, oh, *fuck*.' I hear Noah's bedsprings creak. 'I'll be there as soon as I can.'

He hangs up and the enormity of the situation descends on me like a wave, suffocating and overwhelming. Someone has taken a photo of me without my permission. Someone has published it online without my permission; has outed me to the public, and everything, *everything* that I've been working up the courage to do in my own time has been taken away from me—just like that.

I feel powerless, and overwhelmed, and *angry*, but mostly, like I'm going to throw up.

When I thought about coming out to my parents, I'd expected it to be on my terms. I'd imagined I would go over what to say, prepare and memorise my words and answers. But now, no words come to me. There's nothing I can say.

'You're going to be okay, Gabriel,' Papa says.

'I didn't want to tell you this way, I—' I swallow down my emotions. 'I had a whole *speech* planned. I wanted to do it *right*.'

I wasn't brave enough, I want to tell him. *I was scared for so long.*

Wordlessly, Papa goes into the kitchen and pulls two mugs from the cupboard before running the coffee machine. I want to tell him not to bother, I don't think I can stomach anything right now, but I lack the energy even to do that.

Papa comes back and places the coffee on the table in front of me, but I don't reach for it.

'This tournament has not been easy on you,' Papa says.

I scoff. Understatement of the year.

'*But*,' he continues, 'I hope it has shown you that, regardless of what happens, I will always be there for you. I will always support you. I will always love you. I don't want to say that your being gay doesn't matter to me—' I turn to him, unsure what he's about to say. 'Because it clearly matters to you.'

'Papa, I—'

He raises one large palm, silencing me. 'Let me finish. I thought that you just hadn't found anyone special, that you were like me and focused on your career. I can see now that keeping this side of you a secret has weighed heavily on you. I'm sorry it took me so long to see that; to offer you the support you needed.'

I sniff and wipe the tears from my eyes.

'I know you aren't homophobic,' I say. 'But I can imagine it's different when it's your son.'

'Not different,' Papa assures me. 'Never different.'

My phone vibrates on the coffee table. Another Google Alert.

'Ignore it,' Papa says. 'Victor's meeting with our lawyers. This will go away, Gabriel, I promise.'

Papa throws an arm around me, and I curl into his side, resting my cheek against his chest. We haven't done this since I was a kid. I can hear his heartbeat through his t-shirt, and he smells like Old Spice and deodorant. Comforting. Like home.

A few minutes later, Victor bursts through the door carrying his laptop. He's still dressed in his plaid pyjama shorts but wears a grey suit jacket over his white t-shirt. He grasps my coffee mug and takes a big mouthful of lukewarm coffee.

'Gabriel,' he says, slightly breathless. 'We're working on getting the photograph and the article taken down, and the lawyers are looking at avenues of legal action. Adidas called, the Open's called—' He pauses. 'They want to make sure you're okay.'

Okay? 'I'm . . . fine.'

Papa's arm tightens around me. 'They're concerned for you.'

The Open. I have to play tonight, I realise. Against *Lukas*.

'We'll understand if . . . you want to retire,' Papa says carefully.

'What? No!' My immediate reaction is so visceral; it even surprises me. If I retire now, they'll know they got to me. I'm not naïve. I know there are people out there who will dislike me—hate me—for who I am, and some will see my bowing out of the Open as a victory. 'I'm here to play. I just need to get my head right.'

Papa looks to Victor and they do that weird 'talking without talking' thing they always do. 'If you think you can play,' Papa says eventually.

'I can.' The reality is I have to.

'We'll get on top of this, Gabi,' Victor says. 'I'm sorry it had to be this way.'

As I remake my coffee, I check Instagram. Big mistake. Huge. The photo is *everywhere*. It's weird to see candid photographs of yourself. Aside from the rage I feel at my privacy being violated like this, I'm awed at the way we lean into one another, how even as I kiss him, the corners of my mouth are turned up into a smile; how very . . . in love we look. As far as scandalous pictures go, this is one of the best.

'It was the night receptionist,' I say, noting the angle at which the photograph was taken as memories of last night come back to me in pieces. It dawns on me that some of this is, at least partly, my fault. I'd been careless last night, too lost in the magic of the night to worry about the risk.

Papa steps out of the room and everything goes quiet again. Victor is furiously typing into his laptop, even as I hear the *ding ding ding* of emails hitting his inbox. I can't stand hearing him work, so I take my coffee out onto the balcony and sit in the bright morning sun.

It's done.

Everyone knows now.

I'd hoped that when it finally happened, I'd feel free. Vindicated, even. Celebrated.

But all I feel is sad. Betrayed. My relationship, my sexuality, everything I've struggled with for the past few years, all used just to get site traffic.

My phone's blowing up. There are a dozen unread messages in my inbox; among them are messages from Phoebe and Lukas, but also Nathan Derbin and Alanzo Ruiz, and other players on the tour, even those I'm not necessarily close with, all reaching out to see if I'm okay and to offer their support.

I wish I could call *Maman* or Claudia, but it's two in the morning in Paris. They might not have seen the article yet. I still might be able to tell them on my terms.

I don't hear Noah enter the apartment, but around ten, the door to the balcony slides open and he steps into the bright morning light.

'Gabi,' he breathes. I get to my feet and pull him in for a hug. 'Gabi, baby, I'm so sorry.'

'Don't be,' I say into his shoulder. 'I'm glad you're here.'

Out of the corner of my eye, I see Victor standing by the door. 'Now that the team's here, we need to talk,' he says.

27

NOAH

The moment I saw the photo, I knew it wasn't just going to go away. These kinds of things don't just disappear. Not off the internet. Bernard places a coffee mug in front of me as we gather around the dining table. Victor's face is grave as he types out a reply to yet another email. Beside me, Gabriel's leg jiggles nervously and I suppress the impulse to reach across and take his hand. I'm not sure how well that would be received right now.

'*D'accord, les enfants*, I have good news and bad news,' begins Victor as he hits send on the email. 'The major newspapers have agreed not to print the article. They're not interested in a forced outing scandal. Apparently, the night receptionist was studying journalism and knew a good story when he saw one. Management assures me he's been let go.'

Ethics class must be next semester, then.

'What's the part I'm not going to like?' Gabriel replies evenly.

'Two parts,' Victor says. 'One: social media's already got their talons on the story. It will be impossible to kill it.' Victor's mouth presses into a long thin line. 'And two, I want you to make a statement. To camera. Today.'

'No,' Bernard says without a moment's hesitation. Suddenly, Victor and Bernard launch into a flurry of French. It sounds heated, passionate. Gabriel doesn't say anything. He just stares into the dregs of his coffee, his brow furrowed, and in that moment, I'm aware of just how different our worlds are; how much this has affected every part of his being. Not just the personal side, but the professional—his very career is at risk. Not just how he plays, but the sponsorships, his fan base, everything.

'Speak English,' Gabriel says eventually. 'Noah can't understand what you're saying.'

I reach across the table and take his hand. Fuck it. He gives me a half-hearted smile, one that doesn't touch his eyes, and it kills me to see him so miserable.

'Sorry,' Bernard replies, switching back to English. 'I think you should wait until the end of the tournament to make a statement.'

'I can't,' Gabriel says. 'It's all anyone will want to talk about. I can't continue without addressing it on *my* terms.'

I guess Gabriel feels he needs to take his power back; to control this betrayal any way he can.

'We'll release a written statement,' Victor says, trying to find middle ground. 'No cameras. We'll do it this morning, and then that's it. We'll focus on the match.'

'Do you want to be named in the media release?' Gabriel asks, turning to me. 'Think of your father.'

My dad. My dad who's spent most of my life weaponising fear to control me.

'You can if you need to,' I say. Gabriel looks dubious. 'It's okay.'

Victor closes his laptop and leans across the table. 'This is the not-so-fun part,' he says seriously. 'I need to know what you two have been up to. Especially what you've done in public.'

Gabriel gives me a loaded look. I've always scoffed when couples say they have an almost telepathic connection, but in that moment, I know exactly what Gabriel's thinking. *There's no way in hell I can tell him I was in drag last night.*

'We only went out to dinner—' I say at the exact same time Gabriel says, 'We hooked up in the locker room at the rental tennis courts.'

Shit.

Bernard lets out a long sigh, like this is the last thing he wants to deal with. Sexuality is all fine and good but, clearly, mucking around during a tournament is where he draws the line. 'I'll leave you to it,' he says to Victor, pushing his chair back from the table.

'Okay,' Victor says. 'Let's focus on last night. You said you went to dinner?'

Gabriel looks at me. 'We have to tell him.'

Victor looks between us, clearly unimpressed. 'Well, then? Explain.'

'We went to dinner, and then we ate gelato across the road,' Gabriel begins, looking to me for backup.

'I thought it would be nice to unwind for a bit, and a

friend was hosting karaoke nearby.' I feel my face go red. 'Drag Queen Karaoke. At a place called the Flamingo Bar.'

'The drag queen is Noah's friend,' Gabriel interjects. Victor looks like he can't believe what he's hearing.

'I had a few drinks, but Gabi was definitely still sober, and the next thing I knew, I was on the stage singing a rendition of "Memory", and—'

Victor gives me a strange look. '. . . The cat song?'

'Heaps of people recorded it; I suppose it might even show up on the club's social media page.' Saying it out loud, I realise we definitely were not as careful as we thought we were last night and that possibly a fair chunk of the shit that's gone on this morning is mostly my fault. 'Gabriel was there, but, well, he was in disguise.'

'*Disguise*.' Victor looks to Gabriel. 'What does that mean?'

'I was dressed up like a woman.' He says it very, very quietly.

It's clear Victor doesn't know whether to be amused or scandalised. 'As in . . . you dressed up like a drag queen?'

'We didn't want anyone to recognise him,' I say.

Victor runs his hands over his face. 'Let me get this straight. Last night, the night before a match, you went to a club, and dressed up as a woman to watch a drag show in which the person you were with sang a song from the musical *Cats*. And everyone recorded this. Am I up to speed?'

'Pretty much, yeah.' Gabriel looks as if he wants the floor to open up and swallow him whole.

'You're earning your salary this tournament, Victor,' Gabriel's manager mutters to himself as he turns back to his computer. 'The good news is that no media have mentioned the club scene, and I suppose, technically, you *were* in disguise, so it looks like you weren't recognised. I'll just need to monitor social media for a few hours to ensure any videos don't surface.' He looks at us both expectantly. 'Is there anything else?'

'Most of it was pretty tame,' I explain.

'Other than hooking up in the locker room and a brief stint as a drag queen, it was pretty tame,' Victor says dryly. 'No scandals; no drug use, no public sex, nothing that could possibly get out to make this story live any longer?'

Gabriel shakes his head. 'Nothing else.'

'Okay.' Victor tilts his neck back and forth, cracking it. 'I can work with that. Now, how serious is this thing between you two?' His finger waggles between us.

Shit. I look at Gabriel. He looks at me. Our conversation last night is pretty hazy, and I still have no idea how to navigate how I feel about him. The only thing I know is that Gabriel occupies my every waking thought, and that in a matter of days he's upended my life so spectacularly, I don't think I can go back to the way it was before, and that I hope, desperately, that he feels the same way.

'Have you not—' Victor begins.

'It is—' interrupts Gabriel, his eyes never leaving mine, '—serious. Isn't it?'

I look into those stupidly beautiful brown eyes and just want to leap across the table and kiss that stupidly beautiful brown face. 'Gabriel, I—' God, the *I love you* is right there but it's not the right time. Not when he's dealing with all this. 'I'm so serious about you it hurts.'

Not my most eloquent love declaration, but I'm pretty sure he gets the point.

Victor mock gags beside us. 'Gross.'

Gabriel turns to him, spitting a barrage of French words that only make Victor smile, but when he turns back to me, Gabriel is grinning like a fool as well.

'You are serious about being with me—even when all this is over?'

I nod. 'I mean, it's gonna be fucking hard, but yeah, I'm in.'

Gabriel brings my knuckles to his mouth, kissing them, and every anxiety about who we are together and what will happen after the tournament melts away. I want this, want him, want to find a way forward together.

'Right,' Victor says. 'New rules are in place. No more hooking up in semi-public places as a general blanket rule. No talking to the media without my permission. Any question that isn't about tennis, you will both respectfully decline to comment.'

'And no sex before the match,' Bernard says, reappearing in the living room. 'At *all*.'

Gabriel's face flushes a deep red. Consider us both suitably chastised and completely mortified.

Bernard's gaze turns to me. 'Come with me.'

'Papa—' Gabriel says, standing up.

He raises a hand to quell Gabriel's protest.

'*Maman* is awake. You should call her.'

Gabriel nods soberly. I've rarely heard him talk about his family back in Paris—his sister, his mother. It must be hard being apart from them for so long; only seeing each other through the other side of a screen. *That'll be you, soon*, a small voice reminds me.

I don't want to risk Bernard's ire, so I follow him out the door. Gabriel mouths the words *I'm sorry* as we leave. What have I got myself into?

There's no one in the hotel pool as Bernard swipes us in, grabbing a few towels from the rack by the door. He hands me one.

'Get undressed and join me in the sauna,' he says.

He opens a locker a little way away from where I'm standing and undresses. Holy *shit*, my lover's father is undressing in front of me. I avert my eyes. Not only is he *actively* undressing right now, but Bernard expects me to get naked too, and join him in a hot room to sit and get sweaty.

'Relax,' Bernard says as he opens the door to the sauna. 'I will not murder you.'

'Well, now that's all I'm gonna think about.' I pull off my shirt and kick off my shorts.

'If I did, Gabriel would be upset, and he wouldn't win the tournament,' Bernard replies, deadpan, and I realise a beat too slow that it's a joke. A joke! So, he's got a sense of humour after all. Great. Lovely.

I follow Bernard into the sauna and take a seat opposite him. The little thingie—oven, stove, grate?—shoots out steam.

'I've never been in a sauna before.'

'They're good for recovery and relaxation,' Bernard says, closing his eyes.

And for interrogating-slash-torturing your son's boyfriend, too, I consider.

Bernard, like Gabriel, has crops of thick hair across his arms, chest and legs. Unlike Gabriel, his dark hair is styled in long locs that fall around his shoulders and down his back. I can tell he's careful to maintain them.

'So,' he says after a long while.

'So,' I echo.

'Who are you?'

Fear prickles up my back. 'What do you mean?'

Bernard cracks one eye open. 'We ran background checks, social media checks, but nothing comes up. No accounts. No history.'

'I'm a man of mystery.'

He doesn't smile. Okay, no jokes now, then.

'Noah. My son is worth twelve million dollars. He is the jewel of French tennis. If he was not so attached to you, I would have ended your relationship as soon as I'd run those reports. No one on my team knows who you are. Therefore, you're a risk. If you want to keep seeing my son, you'll tell me everything there is to know about you.'

Jesus *fucking* Christ on a cracker, what have I walked into?

'Gabriel knows everything about me.' I recall our 'no Google' pact and how, at the time, I felt it protected him more than it protected me. 'The short story is that my dad was abusive to me and my mum. He was a cop and he always told me he had ways of finding us if we ever left, so I've always been careful to keep my online presence hidden. Mum and I got away from him when I turned eighteen. I moved here. Got a job at the bar where I met Gabriel. My driver's licence expired and reapplying for it means I need an updated address, which gets stored on their system. A system the cops have access to. No passport, but that's mainly because I'm too broke to fly overseas.' I pause. 'That's it.'

Bernard's body language is putting me off. I'm already skimming so close to the surface of a full-on breakdown, the last thing I'd thought I'd do today is relive my shitty childhood trauma, or justify it to anyone. 'Look, you don't have to believe me but I actually give a fuck about your son, and not because he's rich, or famous, or whatever you think—I didn't even know who he was when I met him!—but because he's actually amazing and so caring, and passionate about what he does. And he *loves* you so much.'

Immediately, I regret letting my emotions get the better of me. The stove hisses out more steam. I suck in a lungful of humid air, and try not to shift uncomfortably as Bernard considers my words in silence.

'My father was an angry man,' Bernard says eventually. 'He hit me when I was growing up. It was normal to hit for discipline, but he did it more than that—when he was upset, when I lost a match. When Gabriel told me he wished to become a tennis player, to turn professional, I told him he must always play with dignity and calmness. Never hit the racquet on the ground or throw your things. Never be violent or angry. Sometimes the media, they think that is just bad behaviour, that it is interesting and fun to the game, but how do we know the people who hit their racquets on the ground do not go home and hit their dog, or their wife? We cannot condone violence of any kind.' He looks at me, his expression neutral. 'I believe you, Noah.'

My relief is immense. 'Thank you,' I say.

'As much as you distract Gabi, it is clear you also make him very happy. Before you met him, he was questioning if tennis was the right choice. He has given up so much to get to this level, and I began to worry if I had allowed him to give up too much. The drive he needed to continue was waning. I was losing him, and I did not know how to get him back.' He pauses. 'It is hard for a father to accept he might have failed his child.'

I can't comment, so I don't.

'He mentioned he wishes to stay in Australia after the tournament. I think it is a good idea. Perhaps afterwards you can come to Paris. Gabriel will play at Roland-Garros in May; I'm sure he would love to show you around Paris.'

It feels weird making plans so far in advance, but it's kind of Bernard to think of me. 'That'd be nice.'

I'm proud of the progress we've made together. Not having a proper dad has fucked me up in more ways than one, but seeing the way Bernard cares for Gabriel is, well, heartwarming.

'We should get back,' Bernard says just as the stove spews out more steam.

Oh, thank god. I can't leave the sauna fast enough.

When we return to the apartment, Gabriel gives his father a suspicious look. He's still at the table with Victor, the laptop between them.

Bernard heads into the kitchen and I mouth *sauna* to Gabriel when he shoots me a questioning look.

'Ah. It's his favourite torture chamber,' Gabriel explains. 'Whenever we have fights, he wants to talk in the sauna. I hate it. I told him to take you to a coffee shop.'

Bernard reappears from the kitchen with two glasses of water in hand. Surprisingly, he places one down in front of me. I suppose it's to replenish the shit-ton of water I just lost.

'We spoke,' Bernard summarises. 'It's all fine.'

Gabriel reaches out and grasps my hand. I squeeze back. 'We're just about to post the statement.'

'Oh!' I'm not exactly sure what I should say.

'Pressing *Send* now,' Victor says. 'One . . . two . . . three, posted!'

There's a pause. A silence. Maybe a minute, or less than, where no one moves or says anything, and nothing happens—and then Victor's phone begins to ring.

The rest of the morning is a blur. Gabriel and I spend it on the couch, me down one end, him up the other, with our legs tangled together. We watch a bit of TV as Victor fields questions and phone calls around us. Gabriel watches TV with a hollow, tired gaze. I'm not sure he's really, fully here with me—and that's okay.

My phone buzzes around eleven-thirty, and I lean over to see Margie's name flash up on the screen. Gabriel looks at me, frowning.

'Is everything okay?'

'Not sure,' I reply as I pick up the call. 'Hey, Marg, are you okay?'

'I'm fine.' She sounds a little breathy on the phone. I hear the *ding ding ding* of a tram in the background and realise she must be on her bike. 'Are you home right now?'

'No. I'm with Gabriel. Why?'

♪

It's hard to leave Gabriel, but Margie sounded slightly panicked on the phone, and he has to prepare for his match tonight. As much as I want to be there for him, that also means giving him space to get his head right. I've already established I'll be there after the game, and for whatever comes next.

Despite the absolute shitshow of a morning, hearing Gabriel say we're serious has lifted a weight off my shoulders.

As I get home, I see Margie out the front of the house talking to our neighbour over the fence. Sadie sees me coming and bounds up to the gate.

'Fei was just saying that someone rang the doorbell a few times, then tried to go around the side,' she says as I step through the gate. 'She says he stuck around for a while. Sadie was barking like mad.'

Fei is around the same age as Margie and of Chinese descent. She's wearing an old grey top flecked with mud, and gardening gloves. 'It was very strange behaviour. I've never seen him around before.'

'What did he look like?' I ask.

'He had a cap on, but he was wearing a pair of jeans and a white shirt. I don't think he was looking to break in,' Fei says. 'I think he wanted to see if anyone was home.'

It could have been a journalist looking to spring an interview on me as I stepped out of my home. After this morning, I'm not surprised at the lengths people will go to for a story.

'I'm going to get a security system installed,' Margie says. 'Even if this is just a one-off, I don't want to take chances. I'm only getting older, and if you're not here, Noah, the house feels lonely.' She looks down at Sadie and snorts. 'You were supposed to be a guard dog.'

'Kill 'em with kindness, that's Sadie's motto.' I lean down to ruffle Sadie's fur.

28

GABRIEL

Lukas Froebel.

I adjust my sports bag on my shoulder and take a deep breath. Lukas Froebel is a few metres in front of me, jogging on the spot to keep his calves warm. We're waiting to be called to take the court, and my nerves are so bad it feels like there are worms chewing through my gut.

It's not just because this is a quarter-final.

It's not just because I'm playing against Lukas, one of my oldest friends.

It's everything. It's the journalist reminding me I've never won a grand slam at the grand old age of twenty-five; it's knowing Noah's watching me and that there's a very good chance he'll watch me lose; it's the fear of having to swallow that defeat and pull myself together for our next tournament. After what happened this morning, I'm not in the headspace to compete or have cameras on me.

But I have to.

This is the biggest match of my career.

Lukas turns to me. His blond hair is perfectly styled: shaved at the sides and back and chopped haphazardly into spikes on the top of his head. He looks cool, calm and frustratingly effortless. I've pulled my hair back into a ponytail and spent five minutes debating whether or not to wear a headband, because I worry it makes my ears stick out too much.

Lukas claps me on the back. 'Let's just focus on the match today, hey?' he says. 'You got big balls, man.'

'Thanks,' I mutter. It doesn't feel like I have 'big balls'. It feels like I'm going to throw up.

Clearly unsatisfied with that answer, Lukas grabs my shoulders and makes me turn, forcing me to look into his eyes. 'Hey, look at me. You're gonna go out there and smash it, you hear me, Madani? You're going to go out there and play the best tennis of your goddamn life.'

I don't meet his gaze. The last thing I want is to be reminded that we're friends right now; it's easier if he's just someone else. Some faceless opponent. 'To do that, I'd have to beat you.'

'Hell, I hope you do,' he says fiercely.

Tears well in my eyes again, but I blink them away, shrugging Lukas off. 'Stop it.'

'I won't,' he replies. 'Now tell me you're gonna kick my arse. *Tell me*.'

'I'm gonna kick your arse,' I say, wiping my nose on the back of my hand.

'With *conviction*.'

I suck in a deep breath. 'I'M GOING TO KICK YOUR ARSE!'

'Fuck yeah you are!' Lukas bursts out laughing, making a staff member turn at the commotion. Outside, the stadium goes dark. Static crackles through the speaker system.

Lukas turns away from me. It's time.

'Welcome to the first quarter-final of the Australian Open,' a man's voice booms through the speaker system. 'First, please give a big welcome to your number two seed, from Sweden, Lukas Froebel!'

Lukas steps into the stadium lights. The audience erupts around him. He looks like a fucking rock star. So confident, so sure of himself. I do not know how he does it.

'And now, the fourteenth seed, from France, Gabriel Madani!'

With a deep breath, I adjust the bag on my shoulder and step out onto the court. There's applause, but I can tell it's not as rapturous as the applause for Lukas. Raising my hand to wave at the crowd, I look to my player's box. I need to see Noah, I need—

A poster catches my eye.

The word *ALLEZ* is in big black writing over a rainbow flag. The Pride flag.

I stop in the middle of my walkout. Lukas is looking at it too, shielding his eyes from the stadium lights. The fan holding the poster is close enough that I can see her face: she looks young, maybe fifteen years old, and she waves the poster vigorously when she realises she's been noticed.

'*ALLEZ*, GABI!' the girl shouts. The crowd erupts into applause, and then they begin to get to their feet. The match hasn't even begun but they're standing for me.

Allez, allez, allez.

More flags appear, dotted across the crowd, waved proudly under the stadium lights.

Maybe this is what Phoebe meant, all that time ago, when she said that my coming out could help people. I never wanted this; I never wanted to carry this weight on my shoulders. I'd always worried I wasn't strong enough, wasn't *good* enough, that I'd make too many mistakes and let people down. But that's not what this is about at all.

I take a breath before raising my hand to thank the crowd, to show my love, and receive it right back.

It's time to play.

It's two sets apiece.

6–4, 6–7, 6–7, 7–5.

My breath catches as I stare at Lukas across the net. This is the hardest match I've played in a long time. We've fought tooth and nail for every single point, with tie breakers on two sets. I almost had him in the fourth and the nerves that come from being so close to a win jostled in my stomach—and I squandered my advantage. Before I knew it, he had called on something deep within him, some power, and bested me.

He's still dangerous. He's still hungry. And I'm still in trouble.

Lukas wipes his brow on his towel and sets up by the baseline, awaiting my serve.

Taking a breath, I bounce the ball once, twice, and then send it across the net. He returns with incredible force. I lunge for it but don't make it.

Love–fifteen.

I shake out my hair and sweat drips down my neck and onto the astroturf. Grabbing another ball from the ball kid, I set up to serve again.

Ace.

The crowd cheers. Scores are level again.

Three quick points later and I win the service match, taking a small lead.

I look to my player's box. Noah's watching intently, hunched over with half of his face in his hands. Papa and Victor are talking to each other, leaning in close.

If I can break Lukas here, I might out-serve him on my next service game and have him 0–3.

But it's never that easy. Not with Lukas. Lukas fights me in his service match. He's a grubby, dirty player who has an annoying habit of convincing you to play fast and loose. Unlike Ruiz, he likes to play long volleys. He likes the trick shots, he likes the performance, but above all, he likes the mind games.

He doesn't know I've been working on my slow game, on ways to convince him out of his play style. He hits the ball back, but it's smothered by the net. The score changes by fifteen points.

Every single point is a fight.

Even as I take the lead, racking up five games to his three, he chases.

We're neck and neck. There's no clear winner. We're as well matched as we've always been.

I suck down a lungful of air, but it's warm and damp. My chest feels tight and my legs ache. Glancing at the clock, I realise we've been playing for close to four hours.

Lukas pushes back his hair, wipes his sweatband across his forehead and serves the ball. It flies across the net but lands short. My legs burn as I lunge for it, but my racquet hits the ground a second too late. The ball bounces twice and the point falls to Lukas.

I look up to my box, to the crowd, trying to keep my mind and body in the game. Papa's staring down at me, arms crossed over his chest. Close it, he'd say if he could, *close it.*

There's only a handful of points between me and the semi-finals. Lukas is down a game and it's his service.

I know what the commentators would be saying on TV right now: this is my chance to break on service, and win the set 6–4, but there's a small part of me that says, *If you just lost, this would all be over.*

Having made the finals, I would leave the tournament satisfied with my performance. I'd be able to spend a week or two with Noah, rest and recharge.

I'd be happy to see Lukas move to the next round.

I turn and position myself to recieve. Lukas bounces it once, twice, and then sends it flying over the net. I manage to return and the ball just barely scrapes the line as it hits the back of the court. A lucky shot for sure. The score levels again.

Lukas sets up for serve. Faults.

'Fuck,' I hear him mutter from across the net. He bounces the ball and prepares to serve again.

Double fault.

The crowd cheers.

Gabi, Gabi, Gabi.

It's 30–40. I'm one point away from closing this set. The tingle of winning starts again, the surge of adrenaline. I swallow down the thickness in my throat, the nerves, the fear, the excitement. I focus on the bounce of the ball on the other side of the net—the one-two bounce that Lukas does before he serves—and return it as best I can. It's a struggle. I lunge for the ball and barely have time to scramble my way back to the centre before Lukas hits it back. It falls into the far left-hand side. Lukas is almost immediately opposite, leaving his right side bare. I see an opportunity, an expanse of space. He won't be quick enough. We're both already so fatigued.

It's a hard angle. My backhand might not be good enough, but it's worth a shot. With a grunt, I push my arm back and return the ball. For a terrifying second, I think I've put too much into my backhand and overshot the mark. The ball barrels over the net. It curves, twisting in the air, before landing on the baseline.

I don't need to hear the umpire's call to know it's in. Lukas sags in defeat.

I've won the match.

The crowd roars. They're up on their feet celebrating as I drop the racquet and fall to my knees. The hardest match of my life is over. It's done.

I beat Lukas.

All these years I've come up short.

All these years I've had to smile through my tears as he went on to the next round and I went home.

All these years, a part of me accepted that he was better than me—that he would *always* be better than me.

'Great match, Gabi.' Lukas pulls me to standing and wraps his arms around me. We're both sweaty and smelly and exhausted. 'I'm proud of you.'

'Thank you.' I sob into his shoulder, no longer able to control my emotions. He hugs me a little longer, a little tighter, than what's normally acceptable on camera, and I dig my fingers into the meat of his shoulders.

'I love you, man,' he says, pulling away.

We thank the umpire and I run over to my player's box and launch myself up to hug Papa, Victor and Noah. It feels like I've just won the final. Fuck the cup; this right here is a career-high win.

Percy Jones is on the court as I return to gather my things. Throwing my bag over my shoulder, I walk out to greet him. Today, he's wearing tan chinos and a white shirt; there are large sweat patches under his armpits.

'Great game, Gabriel,' Percy says. 'Earlier this tournament, I said you were playing with the skill of a second- or third-seed player, and here you are, advancing to the semi-final after defeating the second seed, Lukas Froebel. How are you feeling right now?'

'Tired,' I admit, and laughter vibrates through the stadium. 'It is always hard playing Lukas; I think I had very good luck to beat him tonight.'

'You received a lot of love for your statement this morning,' Percy says, and the crowd erupts again. Rainbow flags flutter around the stadium. 'What's it been like to come to play and receive this sort of response from the crowd?'

'Incredible,' I reply, emotion making the words catch in my throat. 'Obviously, this situation was beyond my control, but love is love, and I'm pleased to have such a warm welcome from my fans and the people of Australia. I wanted to try to come out here tonight and put on my best performance . . . and to have such a good reception after an unfortunate event is . . .' My voice wavers. 'It makes my heart feel very light.'

The crowd cheers again.

'And finally, before you go,' Percy says. 'What can you tell us about your mystery man over there—is he an Australian? Will we be seeing you Down Under more often?'

I risk a glance at Noah, and he smiles back. 'He is Australian, but it's still new and very private, so for now I cannot answer those questions.'

Percy pats me on the shoulder, though I know I've not answered the question to his liking. 'Good luck in your next match, Gabriel; you've certainly wooed many with that performance.' He turns back to the camera. 'That's fourteenth seed, Frenchman Gabriel Madani, into the semi-finals of the Australian Open.'

Lukas is waiting for me in the hallway and immediately pulls me into a headlock.

'I knew you could do it!' he says, ruffling my hair. I push against his rib cage, trying to free myself. We wrestle in the hall just off the court, laughing so hard it hurts. Finally, he lets me go, and we lean against the walls, catching our breath.

'See you in Brazil, then?' Lukas asks, wiping the sweat from his brow.

I shake my head. 'I'm taking a break. No Brazil for me. I'm going to focus on Roland-Garros.'

Lukas gives me a knowing smile. 'I remember being in love. We give up a lot for tennis, but so do our partners.'

'Gabriel.' Victor appears at the end of the hallway, pulling me away from Lukas. 'They're ready for you.'

'Go,' Lukas says. 'Don't let those journalists get to you. You beat me fair and square today and you'll beat the next sorry bastard who has the misfortune to come up against you.'

I hug Lukas goodbye. 'See you in Paris?'

'You know it. Won't let you win so easily next time.'

I meet Victor at the end of the hallway and he takes my kit from me. 'Let's get this over with,' I say.

'You spoke well. Even when Percy threw you the hairy ones.'

Clearly, now that I'm embroiled in scandal, my press conferences are the place to be. People even line the back wall, unable to get a seat in the main gallery.

Sucking in a deep breath, I steel myself and take a scat at the table, grabbing one of the complimentary bottles of water and cracking it open. 'Hi, everyone,' I say into the microphone. 'I won't be talking about personal matters, so please do not ask me about my relationship.'

The questions come in a flurry:

How do you feel you played tonight?

'Very well. It was a rough match; Lukas plays very good tennis consistently, so I knew I had to be in excellent form to beat him.'

Pejo Auer is the first seed—you've never played against him. What're your thoughts about that possible final?'

'If I get to the final, I think it will be an excellent match for me, experience-wise. Pejo is a great player. I would have a lot to learn from playing against him, but I am not focusing on the final. I am focusing on my next match.'

Speaking of the next match, you're either playing Aleksis Dimitriou or Mikhail Stepanov in the next round; what's your mindset going into that match?

'Both opponents present their own challenges, but I have played both many times in the past. I'll do what I always do; recover well and do my best to prepare mentally and physically.'

What's your downtime like? Have you been enjoying the sights Melbourne has to offer?

'Yes, I have been to the Melbourne Zoo and a few restaurants around town. Little things. Obviously, I am here to play a tournament, and I am serious about my tennis, but I am happy to experience Melbourne. Last question, please?'

The press conference comes to an end with little issue. As Victor and I make our way back to the player's room to meet up with Papa and Noah, I feel my right knee grab.

Stopping, I attempt to stretch it out.

'You okay?' Victor asks.

'Feels weird,' I mutter. I probably should have spent more time cooling down instead of jumping straight into media, but I like getting it out of the way. 'It's fine.'

Papa and Noah have our gear ready to go outside the player's room, but as I lean down to grab my tennis bag, I feel something *pop*.

I'm falling before I can stop myself and faceplant into the cold cement floor. Fire shoots up my leg and into my spine, like someone's just kicked me in the kneecap.

'Someone get a medic,' Victor cries, his voice echoing through the hall.

'Where's the pain?' Papa says, and I try my best to pinpoint it, gasping, 'My knee,' between clenched teeth.

'ACL?' Victor asks over Papa's shoulder. 'Yes, we need a medic *right now.*'

I take in deep breaths as the pain subsides. Noah's behind me, holding my head off the cement floor. 'I felt something like a pop, and then just . . . pain.'

A medic comes running with a first-aid kit and two icepacks. Another comes soon after with a wheelchair. Papa wraps both icepacks around my knee, curving the frozen gel against the joint, and then I'm hauled into the wheelchair.

That's it. I'm done. Tournament over. I won't realise any grand dream of making it to the final or holding the cup. I've just played the best match of my career and hurt my knee walking out of a press conference.

'Noah,' I say, grabbing his hand, but I can't seem to say anything else. Can't tell him that I've seen this play out before with Phoebe; can't tell him that it looks bleak at best, and career-ending at worst. 'Don't go.'

'I won't,' he says. 'Promise.'

'It's going to be all right,' Papa says. 'Don't get worked up. We'll manage this.'

Victor arranges for a doctor to meet us at the apartment, and I suffer through yet another ice bath—this time, medically recommended. Noah sits beside me on the cold bathroom floor, his hand holding mine. At least this time, we don't have to pretend to be just friends in front of Papa and Victor.

'I can't imagine the pain you're in right now,' Noah says.

'Take my mind off it.' Just in case Noah gets the wrong idea, I add, 'Tell me what you want to do after the tournament is over. Where do you want to go?'

'Go?' Noah echoes. 'Where would we go?'

'On holiday. I want to book somewhere nice and hot. Somewhere where we can lie on the beach all day if we want to.'

'That sounds lovely,' he says, pressing his cheek against the lip of the bath. The hand that isn't holding mine pushes around a little chunk of ice in the water. 'Well, first, I want to buy a book at the airport. It feels like you're going on holiday if you buy a book at the airport. Then, we'd have a coffee in the café—or if we're flying in the afternoon, we'd get a beer—and we'd complain about how overpriced it is and how we can't believe that we bought it. They'd call our flight. We'd board. You'd hold my hand as we took off because it's my first flight ever. You'd give me the window seat.'

'Where are we going?' I ask.

'Somewhere by the sea but close by because I don't have a passport. Somewhere with palm trees and long stretches of coastline. We'd find a shady spot and call it ours; we'd go there every day to swim and lie down. That's where I'll read the book. On the second day it'll rain because no holiday is perfect, and we'll get breakfast in bed and resolve to stay in there all day. But you can't do that. You get restless around three in the afternoon and by some coincidence, the rain lets up. We go for a walk around the hotel grounds and find a little trail that leads to a waterfall. It's secluded and the water's clear. I convince you to go for a swim. At first, you're not sure but then I take off my clothes—'

'I like where this is going.' Though I'm far too cold and in way too much pain to do anything about it.

'I take off my clothes and jump in the pool beneath the waterfall. We swim until sunset. No one disturbs us. It's perfect. We barely get back to the hotel before the sun sets, worried we'll trip over something in the dark. After we shower, we go to dinner. We're both ravenous. You order a lobster because I haven't had lobster before—'

'I don't like lobster.'

'A steak then.' He huffs out a laugh. 'You order a steak. It's amazing. We go to bed and sleep in until eight the next morning. The sun is shining. You're full of energy and somehow, it's infectious. You ask me to play tennis with you and, like a fool, I accept.'

I laugh and it hurts my ribs. 'Would not be much of a match.'

'I beat you in three sets.'

'Now I know this is a fantasy.'

Noah's fingers twist around mine. 'It sounds great, though, doesn't it?'

'Yeah,' I reply. 'It does.'

'It's bursitis,' the doctor says later that night. 'Rest, rest and more rest. It might take one or two days, or one or two weeks to heal, there's no way to know. You were good to get it iced immediately.'

Noah looks at my father. 'What does that mean for the tournament?'

'We wait and see what happens,' Papa replies. 'We'll have to make a call by tomorrow . . .'

'It's already feeling better,' I assure everyone but mostly myself. 'Honestly.'

The doctor stands and gathers his bag. 'If you develop a fever, or chills, go to the hospital. Otherwise, you can take an anti-inflammatory to ease the pain and rest it for at least a few days.'

'You can't do anything else? Cortisone shot?' Victor asks. 'Numb it up and Gabi will play all night.'

The doctor hesitates and looks at Gabriel. 'I understand how important this sport is to you, Mr Madani, but it's important to take injuries like this seriously.'

We don't have a few days. We have thirty-two hours at best before I'm expected on the court. I scrub my hands over my face and sink further into the lounge.

'Right,' Victor says. 'I'm ordering Chinese. Nothing bad has ever happened while eating Chinese food. Noah, are you staying?'

Noah looks at me and then nods. 'Thanks. For a little while at least. But then I should go home to Margie. Someone was trying to get into our house earlier today, and I think she's a bit rattled by the whole thing.'

'What!' I say, sitting up. 'Why didn't you tell me?'

Noah shrugs. 'You were busy, Gabriel, and it's fine. It was probably a reporter. I can handle it on my own.'

Noah's right. Of course he can. 'I didn't want to drag you into this.'

'Well, I've been dragged. Willingly,' he replies in a tone that implies not to argue.

'Right—chicken with cashews or Mongolian beef?' Victor calls from the kitchen. 'Oh hell, I'll get both. And two fried rices, and a bag of prawn chips.'

29

NOAH

I don't hear from Gabriel the following morning, though I do send him a message before I go to work; it's simply *<3 gotta work. Thinking of you.*

I'm an incredible sap. Who would have thought two weeks ago I'd be in love! Going serious with my tennis superstar boyfriend! Working a new job!

My shift at the Rosewood starts at ten-thirty, just before the lunchtime rush. Bella swings into the office as I'm about to loop my apron over my head.

'Hey, stunner, time for a photo.' She grabs the polaroid camera from the top of the bookcase. 'Against the wall.'

I run my hand through my hair, taming it, before posing awkwardly. A second later, the polaroid spits out a photo. Bella grabs a Sharpie and writes NOAH in big black letters on the polaroid.

'You're official now,' she says as she pins the photo up on the board. 'And assigned to the main bar. It's gonna be a busy one.'

Bella's not wrong: it's a busy shift. There's a steady stream of customers throughout the day, and I think I make approximately one million mimosas. At two o'clock I scoff down a sandwich made by the chefs and check my notifications in the back office.

Hungrygabriel73: *My knee feels better today but i still rest it. How are you?*

NoAgenda: *Just working. It's so busy—don't these people have jobs?*

I send him a photo of me biting down on a sandwich.

Hungrygabriel73: *I have been thinking on where to book a holiday. What does your work look like for next week?*

NoAgenda: *No shifts yet. I can call in that I'm unavailable. Where do you want to go?*

Hungrygabriel73: *Not sure. Doing research now.*

NoAgenda: *Anywhere is fine with me—gotta go back to work.*

Hungrygabriel73: *Be safe x*

The rest of the shift is a blur. At four, a woman named Nadia comes to relieve me, and I take the polaroid photo off the board. Nadia replaces it with hers.

'Noah, huh?' She looks me up and down. 'You look familiar. Have you worked here long?'

'No, not long.' I grab my satchel, give her a quick wave before I'm accosted with any further questions and slip out the door.

The day is bright and hot: a classic late-January afternoon. The streets of Carlton are full of people enjoying the long days; browsing bookshops, drinking coffee alfresco, shopping in local grocers.

'Hey! Hey, Noah!'

Fear shoots through me. I don't know if that feeling will ever go away. *He can't find you, Noah. You're in a city of four-fucking-million people; he can't find you.*

I turn. It's not my shit-stain of a dad. It's Peaches. She's running after me in a hot-pink sequinned mini-dress and a pair of fluffy heels.

'Blend in much?' I say as Peaches reaches me.

'God, you're impossible to get hold of,' she snaps. 'Why didn't you reply to my text?'

Shit. 'I changed my number, sorry. I'll message you my new one.'

'You should be sorry,' she says, exasperated. 'I've had people calling me nonstop about your little performance the other night.'

'What?'

'"Memory"—or were you too shitfaced to remember?' I recall being encouraged up on the stage, but honestly the rest is a bit of a blur. 'Do you know how long I worked to get a gig at the Flamingo? Now all everyone can talk about is you.'

'What, really?'

'You'd know that if you could be contacted,' Peaches says. 'One of the managers at the Flamingo Bar wondered if you might be interested in a gig. I told them you could play the piano too.'

Horror shoots through me. 'What? I can't do that!'

'But you can play!' Peaches replies, clearly not seeing the issue.

This is a nightmare. 'I said I could play, not that I could *perform*. There's a difference.'

Clearly bored with the circular conversation, Peaches crosses her arms over her chest. 'So, you want me to say no?'

'Shit, no, of course not,' I reply. 'I just need some time to think.'

'Well, think about it until Friday and for god's sake, text me your new phone number.'

I promise I will, and Peaches goes back to rehearsing at the Playhouse, and I take a minute to process the conversation. Playing music because I enjoy it is one thing; but performing it for people—performing for money and being consistent in my craft—is another.

But if I'm serious about music, serious enough to consider studying it for a not-at-all-small amount of money at university, shouldn't I take this opportunity?

Margie's not home when I get back to the house, so I feed Sadie, put on a podcast, and start making dinner. I don't cook often and, to be honest, I'm not a fantastic chef (there's a reason I'm behind a bar and not in a kitchen), but the one thing I can make is a mean Bolognese sauce.

I cut onions and carrots, sear the mince, and try to keep up with the hosts on my favourite true crime podcast. Not sure how I ever got into true crime podcasts, to be honest, and I loathe the ones that try to make crime funny. This podcast, luckily, has trigger warnings in the description of their episodes and I'm always careful to avoid the ones flagged with intimate partner or family violence.

I've just added tomatoes to my Bolognese sauce when I think I hear the front door open. Normally, Margie comes home like a storm, carrying bags and books, calling out as soon as she steps over the threshold.

Turning down the gas stovetop, I crane my neck around the doorway. The front door's still closed, though I swear I'd just heard it open. 'Marg, is that you?'

But there's no Margie.

I lock Sadie in the walk-in cupboard while I investigate, lest she run out the front door and out the gate.

I step into the hallway, my senses on high alert, but it's empty. I try to listen for anyone walking through the house—it's not hard, our floorboards creak something fierce—but all I can hear is Sadie whining and scratching at the cupboard door.

I make sure to lock the front door. That's the second time today I've felt paranoid, and the mental strain from being so on edge is real.

'I'm so fucked up,' I tell Sadie as I let her out of the walk-in. 'Even the bloody wind makes me freak out.'

Margie gets home later that evening, announcing her entrance like she always does.

'That smells nice, Noah! What a treat!' She places her tote bag on the dining table and boxes of CCTV cameras spill out.

'You're really doing it?'

'It's a shame,' she says, lining the cameras up one by one. 'Carlton used to be such a safe place.'

'You bought enough to cover every inch of this house,' I say as I inspect a camera. It's about the size of my fist, dome-shaped and completely conspicuous.

'That's the point. Except for the bathrooms. And the bedrooms. You just won't be able to sneak anyone through the windows anymore.'

I raise my eyebrows. 'Excuse me, I brought him in through the door, I introduced him to you. I acted like a completely respectable gentleman.'

In the end, the cameras don't take long to install, so we do it while my sauce is simmering. We have most of the entry and exit points covered. It all loops into a recording system that feeds into a cloud app we each download onto our phones. There's also an emergency call button, which Margie thinks should go under her dining table like a bank alarm.

I look at the camera by the back door while we eat dinner. 'You don't think it's the kind of system people can hack, do you?' I ask her. 'Like they'll see us if we walk around naked?'

'Do you walk around naked when I'm not at home?' Margie laughs as she adds more parmesan on top of her Bolognese. 'Your sauce is better, but it needs more garlic.'

I poke out my tongue in mock protest. I think it tastes good. 'You think everything needs more garlic.'

♪

Mum texts me that night.

Mum: *I'll be in Melbourne Sunday and Monday. Are you free to catch up?*
Noah: *Sure! I might be busy Sunday night but I could meet for coffee on Monday.*
Mum: *Anywhere close to you?*
Noah: *There's a cute coffee shop near my work—fox and pen?*
Mum: *Sounds good.*

30

GABRIEL

Since I turned pro, Papa and I have had an agreement: I don't get up before eight-thirty. I'm not a morning person, and never have been. This agreement, however, clearly doesn't apply to Victor. I hear him open the door to my room in the early hours of Friday morning—the day of the semi-final—whispering, 'Gabi, Gabi, Gabi, are you awake?' He comes closer. 'Gabi!'

I open my eyes, but I'm not at all ready for what I see: Victor standing at the end of my bed, his thin body cast in the shadows, with only the light of his mobile phone illuminating his face. He looks like a godforsaken undertaker on a house call.

I gasp, fear shooting through me. 'Victor!' I hiss. 'You can't just sneak into my room!'

'I have great news,' he says gleefully, ignoring my complaint. 'Aleksis has pulled out.'

'What?'

'Abdominal tear. Can't go on. Isn't that great? You're into the final!'

I run a hand down my face. 'Victor. Get *out*.'

His smile drops. 'You're not happy?'

'Victor, it's,' I grab my phone and check the time, 'it's six in the morning.' The information wouldn't have been any less relevant at 8 am.

'Yes, well, right,' Victor mutters and heads for the door. 'You do have a final to rest up for. Shall I leave the door open or—'

'Closed,' I reply firmly. Victor closes the door.

With a huff, I fall back onto the mattress. Flexing my knee, I am relieved to find that while it still feels a bit tender, the pain, thankfully, is mostly gone. Still, there's no way I could have played on it today and not risked further injury. With Aleksis out, I now have another two rest days until the final.

Final.

I'm in the final.

The realisation strikes fear through me. God, I'll probably play Pejo Auer. He'll play tonight against the seventh seed, and probably win in straight sets. Auer's the reigning champ, the first seed, the best damn player to come out of Peru possibly ever—and the fact that I'm going to have to face him at less than my prime is terrifying.

I want this so badly. I want my body to *know* how badly I want this, and perform, damn it.

It's clear I won't get back to sleep, so I grab my phone and see Phoebe's called me. I call her back, and she picks up on the fourth ring.

'Hey you,' she says; her voice sounds tired, warm. 'I just heard the news about Aleksis. Congratulations.'

'Is this a bad time?'

'What? No! I just woke up from a nap.' She laughs. It's so nice to hear her voice. 'Growing an entire human is exhausting. So, how are you?'

I settle back onto my pillow. 'Fine.'

'*Gabi.*'

'Not so fine,' I admit. 'This tournament has been . . . hard.' It feels like such an understatement.

'Do you remember when I played Anna Kocourek in the final at Roland-Garros in 2019?' she asks. How could I not? I'd sat courtside to cheer Phoebe on, but at the end of the three sets, it was Anna who raised the trophy above her head. 'After the match, I almost quit. Like, quit tennis. For good. All anyone kept telling me was that Wimbledon was only three weeks away—I'd get another shot at a grand slam. But I'd trained my guts out for *months* to play Roland-Garros, and suddenly it was done and dusted, and it was onto the next one? It almost broke me.'

'Pheebs, I—' I don't know what to say.

'I know our situations are not exactly the same,' she continues. 'You're dealing with things I can't even begin to fathom, but it's not all about tennis, you know? Sometimes it has to be about you.'

'When you announced your retirement, it felt like my world was going to end,' I say abruptly. 'All I kept thinking about was how your decision affected me. You've been my lifeline for so long, Phoebe. In tennis, in life. In everything.'

'And I'll always be there. I'm not gone, Gabriel, I'm just a little farther away than before.'

A little farther away. 'I like that,' I admit. 'Noah and I are going on holiday after the final. I think we could be something outside of all this.'

'I know this isn't how you wanted any of this to play out,' Phoebe says. 'But I'm proud of you. Like, really proud.'

'Me too,' I reply, and realise I actually mean it.

Phoebe and I talk for a little longer before she declares she has to pee, and we agree to check in again after the tournament's over. Papa's watching the television in the main room when I get up. Victor's typing away at his laptop, furiously answering emails.

'How does it feel?' Papa asks as I place my mug under the coffee spout.

'Good. Tender, but better.'

'We'll work it gently. Ice bath after.'

I groan. The two things I hate hearing before coffee are *get up* and *ice bath*.

'So Aleksis is out,' I say as I take a sip of my latte.

'Abdominal tear, hernia,' Papa confirms. 'Needs surgery, so you've been granted a free pass.'

'Feels strange not earning it.' I should send Aleksis a message of support.

'I know, but a win is a win,' Papa confirms. 'Especially in your condition.' He finishes his coffee and gets up, making those noises all old men do. 'I'll make you breakfast.'

Papa's breakfasts are prescriptive and boring: yoghurt, granola, supplements, powders and vitamins. I choke them all down and remind myself there's less than three days before this tournament ends and I can eat whatever I want – for a short while, anyway.

After breakfast, I hit the bike to warm up my knee. Papa looks pleased enough, so we take to the court and play loosely for about an hour before I'm back on the bike, warming down the knee while Papa calls for ice.

While he's distracted, I pull out my phone and text Noah.

Hungrygabriel73: *Want to come over this afternoon? We could watch a movie.*

NoAgenda: *Sounds good. How is the knee?*

Hungrygabriel73: *Doctors have recommended amputation.*

NoAgenda: *Oh no ☹ it was my favourite knee*

Hungrygabriel73: *Joking it still needs rest, but it's better.*

NoAgenda: *I'll be there at 1. Want a coffee on my way in?*

Hungrygabriel: *Yes pls.*

NoAgenda: *Want me to sneak a doughnut past your dad if I go to our favourite shop??*

Hungrygabriel73: *I will not say no.*

As predicted, a bellboy waits outside our apartment door with four buckets of ice on a trolley. He almost looks sympathetic as he's directed to dump it all in the bath. Once the tub's full of icy water, I strip down and climb in. Hate does not even describe how I feel about this side of the job.

I'm two minutes into my fifteen-minute session when there's a knock on our apartment door. My body has acclimatised to the water, but I can't stop my teeth from chattering.

'That better not be more ice,' I call out. 'And I'm naked.' Hopefully, that'll deter them.

'It's me,' Noah says as he opens the door. 'Back in the ice bath, hey?' He takes one look at me and pointedly says, 'Poor little guy, I bet this is rough on him too.'

'Please don't refer to him as little.' Noah hands me the coffee and I take it, my fingers pale from the cold. 'Stupid ice actually works but god, it's torture.'

'Especially in the nipple area, hey?'

'Very much in the nipple area,' I say through gritted teeth.

Noah closes the door and reaches underneath his billowy shirt, pulling out a bag of loaded doughnuts. 'I bought the goods. Tiramisu and Lavender Fields.' He pulls apart the lavender doughnut, cream spilling onto his fingers. 'Mind the fingers.'

I lean forward and use my mouth to take the doughnut from him, my tongue darting out to lick the filling from his fingertips.

Noah moans softly as I suck on the tips of his fingers. A part of me revels in his blown-out eyes and flushed cheeks. I sit back in the bathtub and enjoy the doughnut, the flavours of lavender, citrus and musk not something I'd pick for myself, but it's nice. Doughnuts are like pizza and sex—always pretty good.

'How much longer do you have in the water?' Noah asks when he finishes his doughnut. I glance down at my phone. I'd jumped in just after one. 'Ten more minutes.'

'How can you stand it?'

'I can't. I'm sitting,' I reply. It takes him a moment and then Noah groans.

'God, I'd drown you if you weren't in literally four inches of water.'

'And if I wasn't far stronger than you,' I reply. Noah's all bone and lean muscle. I'd take him in a fight any day.

'Have you thought about the holiday any further?' Noah asks.

'I've booked somewhere.'

'Really? Where?'

'It's a secret.' Noah's face scrunches. 'Not good with secrets?'

'It makes me feel all itchy not knowing.' He laughs. 'Is it by the water? Oh god, you're not one of those people who thinks climbing a mountain is a holiday, are you? Gabriel, I'm not climbing a mountain. I'll go as far as *looking* at one from the deck of a bar, but that's it.'

'No mountain climbing,' I promise.

31

NOAH

Bella from the Rosewood calls me just after three. Gabriel and I are curled up on his bed watching a French movie. At least, we had been until Gabriel nodded off and I'd found more interest listening to the little noises he makes in his sleep than anything happening on the screen.

Gabriel must feel the phone vibrate between us, though, because he wakes and stretches his body like a cat, his joints cracking and popping as he flexes.

'Don't go,' he mumbles against my shoulder. Fingers find their way under my shirt, caressing my stomach. I try to wiggle away but he wraps one strong arm around me, pinning me against him.

I find my phone in the folds of blankets and pick it up.

'Hey, Noah, sorry to bother you,' Bella says. 'Ashley called in sick. Could you come in for a shift tonight?'

I don't know who Ashley is but fuck her.

'Sure, I can be there in an hour,' I reply. As much as I don't want to leave Gabriel, I need the money. 'Do you have a spare shirt? I won't have time to go home and change.'

She says she does, and I promise to be there soon. I hang up and kiss Gabriel's temple, his cheek, the corner of his mouth.

'I will pay you double to stay and cuddle me more,' he murmurs.

'Tempting,' I reply. 'But a bit too sugar baby for me. Let's just stick to the "free companionship and sexual favours" deal we have going already, yeah?'

Gabriel rolls onto his back, pillowing his head on a crooked elbow. 'Agree, it could get very expensive for me very quickly.'

He looks divine spread out on the white linen of his hotel bed. It's almost a sin to leave him there, but I pull on my shorts and sneakers and give him a kiss goodbye.

He holds me by the collar of my shirt. 'Will you come to the final?'

'Of course,' I say. 'I wouldn't miss it for the world.'

Gabriel kisses me again, hard and passionate. 'I want to look up and see you there. Whatever the outcome.'

'You will,' I promise.

♪

'It's a buck's party,' Bella groans as I swipe in for my shift. 'Keep an eye on them and call me if it gets too rowdy.'

The bucks are obnoxious and completely take over the beer courtyard, playing round after round of cornhole.

Each time, the bet gets a little bigger; a little more dangerous until one of them has to scull an entire litre of beer. Bella then kicks them out for bad behaviour, and the litre of beer is regurgitated just outside our front door.

I finish my shift just before seven. At home, Margie and I split two pizzas between us, curling up in the lounge room to watch the quad wheelchair tennis semi-final between Austrian Lars Webber and Italian Matteo Salvatore. Webber is up one set, and has won the first game in the second. It's his service game, so there's a possibility he will hold, and lead two-love.

God, listen to me. If you told me two weeks ago that I'd be watching tennis for *fun*, I would have said you were dreaming. But here I am, knowing terms like *service game* and *unforced error*.

We're on an ad break when my phone rings. It's Gabriel.

I take the call in my bedroom. 'Hey.' I fall onto my bed and the springs groan in protest. 'I was just watching the match.'

'Salvatore and Webber?' He sounds surprised.

'Yes. I like other players as well as you. Salvatore has quite the rugged look to him.'

'I think you're being quite unfair. First Lukas and now Salvatore. Where do I rank on the list of favourite players?'

'I'm yet to see anything *particularly* impressive.'

'I'll show you impressive,' he teases. A part of me feels like a high schooler, holed up in my room talking to my crush on the phone. Never thought I'd have that feeling, and it's exhilarating.

'Where are you?'

'In bed. Thinking of you.'

Instantly, my face heats up. 'What, really?'

'Yeah,' Gabriel breathes, and I can almost hear the smile on his face. 'Sorry I fell asleep on you today.'

'Sorry I bailed on you to go to work.'

'It's okay.' He pauses. 'Match is back on; you want to watch it?'

'No, I'll catch up online.'

Fabric rustles. I picture him getting comfortable in bed. 'Can I tell you a fantasy, then?'

'Is this an explicit fantasy?'

Gabriel laughs. 'If you want. But I think we'll save the explicit fantasies for when we're apart.'

It feels like this tournament will never end, and frankly, I don't want it to.

'Tell me about that,' I say. 'Tell me about what will happen when we're apart.'

'Well,' he says, 'I'll be travelling the world, living a life of luxury, as one does. Private jets, expensive hotels, deals with major designers.'

'A humble existence, truly.'

'We'd make a FaceTime schedule, but we'd have trouble sticking to it because I'm somewhere different all the time and you're on shift work, so we'd decide to send each other little video messages when we could.'

'I feel like that's something we'd definitely do.' I roll onto my back and stare up at the ceiling. 'I'd watch your matches back here. Wish I was there.'

'I'd wish you were there, too.' Gabriel sighs. 'It can be . . . lonely on the road, I guess. Horny, too.'

'Now I really want to hear about these fantasies.'

Gabriel laughs on the other end of the phone. Hearing his laugh feels like downing a shot and feeling the warmth spread slowly through your insides.

'Why do you laugh like I'm joking?'

'I feel weird saying it out loud,' he replies. 'I'm bad with words. Not like you.'

I prop myself up on my elbows. 'When we're on holidays, do you want to, you know—' God, now I'm bad with words. 'I mean, we should talk about sex.'

'Very romantic.' Gabriel's voice is warm and teasing. 'I don't have any viruses if that's what you mean. You already know I've never been with anyone.'

'So, let's talk about that,' I say.

'Let's not. It's not something I'm proud of,' he replies—and I get it. Even though it's nothing to be ashamed about, I understand he doesn't want to elaborate. 'When was the last time you had sex with someone else?' he asks.

'Over a year ago. I got tested a few months after. I could get tested again if you'd like but I promise I haven't been with anyone else.'

'I believe you,' Gabriel says.

'Should I *sign* something?' I ask, because isn't that something you're supposed to do with celebrities? Victor's already sent me his exhaustingly long rulebook about dating Gabriel, so maybe that suffices.

'It's not necessary. I trust you. You're the only one I've ever trusted to—' He pauses, clears his throat. 'Well, do this with.'

'Sex?' I clarify.

'A *relationship*,' he says exasperatedly and then spews out a string of French words, sounding truly vexed over my confusion. 'Stop thinking with your dick, I was being sincere.'

'You're such a sap,' I reply. 'But I trust you too. Even with the very bad parts of me.'

'Me too,' he whispers on the other end of the phone. 'I'm afraid I can get a bit hard to handle at times.'

Gabriel, my veritable cinnamon roll of a boyfriend, who doesn't like swearing because it makes him *feel* bad, thinks that being slightly difficult is enough to scare me off? Bless him. Bless his little cotton socks.

♪

It's the day of the big match and I'm belting out ABBA's 'Gimme Gimme Gimme' in the shower and considering whether to shave my balls—and if Gabriel has any strong opinions about pubic hair. Probably not, I decide. I can't be bothered with the effort, so I trim the area and leave it at that.

Shutting off the water, I go to my wardrobe and grab my latest geometric cotton shirt, tossing it on the bed as I rummage through my drawers for a clean white tank top.

It's barely one in the afternoon, but I'm already excited. Tonight, I'll *hopefully* watch my lover win his first grand slam and then tomorrow, I'll reunite with Mum at a café in the city, then Gabriel's taking me on holiday on Tuesday—and wow, if you'd told me I'd be doing all this just two weeks ago, I would have laughed in your face.

But it's real. It's my life.

My phone plays a mix of the queerest energetic hits: Dua Lipa, the Pointer Sisters, Lady Gaga, Elton John. Suddenly,

Lady Gaga's voice cuts out and is replaced by the ringtone I've reserved just for Bella.

No!

I know I used to complain about not getting enough shifts at Mark's Place but being the Rosewood's flavour of the week makes it almost impossible to plan around shifts. I've already picked up an extra shift this week. Still, Bella has been nothing but welcoming and I'd feel guilty if I ignored her call.

'Hey, Bella,' I say, wedging the phone between my ear and shoulder.

'Noah, we're swamped!' she yells over the phone, so loud it makes my ear hurt. 'Is there any chance you could come in?'

I check the time. I have to leave for Gabriel's match in less than four hours . . .

'You'd be doing me a huge favour,' Bella insists.

'Fine,' I relent. 'But I've got tickets for a match at seven. I gotta leave at six.'

A part of me hopes the offer of a short shift will make her reconsider.

'Yes, yes, that's perfect,' she gushes. 'Thank you!'

Clearly not, then.

I hang up and toss my geometric shirt back on the bed, pulling on a clean black shirt and a pair of black dress pants. Gabriel will be pissed if I'm late to his match, but I'm so new at the Rosewood, a part of me still wants to make a good impression, and I've just told them I'm unavailable all next week for Gabriel's 'surprise' getaway, so it's not like I can really say no. Besides, I want to be trusted and, hell, *liked* by Bella and the team.

I want to fit in.

When I get to the Rosewood, I realise Bella's not joking. It's as busy as I've ever seen it, absolutely teeming with semi-drunk and slightly sunburnt customers. One of the bouncers is trying to help a lady in a sundress into a taxi, but the taxi driver is straight-up refusing to take her. I slip past the argument, drop my bag into the office behind the bar, and swipe in.

'Thank *youuuu*,' Bella says, the relief evident in her voice as she walks past with a tray full of empty glasses. 'Totally not glamorous, babe, but I need you to run dishes in the kitchen.'

Stepping into the kitchen is what I imagine hospitality hell to look like; there are at least four trays of dirty glasses waiting to be washed, three trays on the drying rack that need to be taken back to the bars, and a bucket half-full of cracked and chipped pint and midi glasses that need to be recycled.

For at least an hour, I process tray after tray of dirty pint and cocktail glasses, running them through the dishwasher until my fingers go prune-like and my back hurts from lifting.

'Noah, babe.' Bella pokes her head into the kitchen. 'Great work on the dishes. Michelle needs help in the beer garden—can you switch?'

I grab a fresh apron to meet Michelle in the beer garden, secretly thankful to be out of the steaming heat of the kitchen.

'Don't think I'm not looking at that clock,' Bella says as I leave. 'As soon as it hits five fifty-nine, you're out of here.'

32

GABRIEL

'Is Noah here yet?' I ask Victor as I grab my game bag.

'Not yet.' Victor hands me my racquet. 'I'm sure he's on his way. How do you feel?'

'Fine,' I say, even though I don't. Cheers echo through the tunnels of Rod Laver Arena, and I swallow down my nausea. I wish I could have seen Noah before I went on the court; I wish I could have hugged him and found that blissful peace that comes when I'm in his arms.

'Gabriel.' Victor places his hands on my shoulders, grounding me. 'You've got this. Say it to me.'

'I've got this,' I repeat.

'You're going to walk out on that court and play the best tennis you can,' he says. 'And if you win, it won't be because the cards predicted it, or because you wore the right kind of underwear, or because Noah was there to see it. You'll win because you played well.'

'But if I—'

'And if you lose, who cares?'

'*I* care. It's the entire reason I'm here, Victor, I—'

'Gabriel, look at me.' I do. 'We are so proud of you. You will not disappoint anyone today. Not yourself, not me, or your father, or Noah, or your country. Emmanuel Macron heart-eyes all your Instagram stories, and I've never told you that before because I don't want you to get a big head, but we are all so proud of you.'

A laugh bubbles out of me before I can stop it. 'Thank you.' I shrug Victor's hands off me so I can pull him into a hug.

'I'll call Noah, I'm sure he'll be here any second,' Victor says into my shoulder. 'Go. You have a match to play. Remember that match point. Remember Arnie and the Championship Point.'

I don't tell Victor that I'll be lucky to even see a single match point, let alone convert one. The odds are clearly in my opponent's favour. Pejo Auer is the reigning champ and most expect he'll be able to win the title again, especially over me, a low-seeded player in his first grand slam final.

The only thing I can rely on is the feel of my body, and how ready it is to play. After a few days rest, my knee feels good enough to play while strapped, and I've taken a small cocktail of anti-inflammatories to keep the pain down.

I shield my eyes from the bright stadium lights as I step onto the court. There's not an empty seat in the house. Rod Laver himself sits front and centre, attending the men's final in the arena named in his honour, and the emotion of it all makes my throat catch.

This is it.

Pejo Auer is five-foot-five. For years he shaved his hair into a buzz cut and sported a very well-groomed beard. A fiery man, he famously argued with Wimbledon about his right to wear a cap during a night match.

I know everything about my opponent. I've watched him play for almost ten years, seen him reach his peak and never, ever back down from it. There's no doubt Pejo Auer is one of the greats, and it's a true honour to play against him. Right now, he's on an eighteen-match winning streak; practically unbeatable.

And yet, I've just won the first set, 6–4.

As I walk back to my station, I glance up at my player's box. Papa's leaning over the railing, his face solemn and unreadable. Behind him, Victor sits beside Lukas. But no Noah.

Closing my eyes, I will my mind to *stop thinking about him*. Stop thinking and worrying and wondering. Focus on the match. *Focus on the match*.

I glance to the match timer in the far corner. We've been playing for almost an hour and my strapped knee feels tight, but not painful, which is a welcome relief. I won't mind losing if I know I've played my best and put on a good show, but having to retire due to injury would be heartbreaking.

'Time,' the umpire says beside me. '*Madani*.'

The umpire directs us back onto the court. As hard as it is, I push Noah from my mind. There's no use being distracted. I have a grand slam to win.

33

NOAH

It's just after six when I finally leave the Rosewood, dashing the few blocks home to change. Thanks to a stumbling tradie who spilt half his schooner down my back, I stink of apple cider and sweat. He had the audacity to ask for a free refill, too.

I grab my phone from my satchel as I half walk, half jog, and am immediately flooded by messages from Gabriel.

Where are you? I need you here.

Please get back to me.

Are you on the train?

I only live fifteen fucking minutes from the Rosewood, and yet, it feels like I catch every bad traffic light and get stuck behind every slow Sunday-afternoon walker on my way home.

Quick as anything, I duck down the alley and dash through the narrow backstreets, avoiding milk crates and narrowly slipping past a delivery truck that goes into reverse just as I dart behind it. It brakes hard and someone swears at me, but I don't care. I keep running.

I'm at the end of our block and making good time when I notice something on the road. Something golden.

The golden thing bounds closer and, horrifyingly, I realise it's Sadie. I swallow down my dread as I call her to me, my voice high and saccharine so I don't scare her. When she gets close enough, I loop my arms around her neck and hold on to her collar.

'You okay, girl?' I rub my hands over her face. She seems fine. Maybe she just got out. She's lucky I was here when I was. Hell, *I* was lucky I was here when I was. Margie's street isn't that busy, but if Sadie had got to the end of the block, she could very easily have run onto the tramline.

I walk her back to Margie's place, hunching over to keep a hand on her collar, and realise the front door's wide open.

There's no one else around. The street is quiet. Perhaps Margie's just left it open and didn't realise? She could be engrossed in a book or a podcast or thinking about how many papers she still needs to mark, and it's just slipped her mind. Just this once.

I lead Sadie into the yard and close the front gate. Down the road, a tram rattles past.

'Margie?' I call into the house, dropping my keys on the hall table.

Sadie hangs back by the fence.

That makes me stop in the threshold. Sadie always pushes past me to get in the door first.

'Sades?' I call, patting my leg. 'Come here.'

She doesn't move. Fear—cold, sickly fear—runs down my spine. I don't know what to do. There's something stopping me from going into the house, but I also can't turn away. My phone is a heavy weight in my pocket. I should take it out. I should call someone. Anyone.

'Margie?' I manage again.

Heavy footfalls echo down the hallway. I feel the vibration through the floorboards before I see him.

The first thing I think when I see my dad is that he's shorter than I remember. If we were standing side by side right now, I'd be a bit taller. He's always been such a huge, terrifying presence in my life that I'd always pictured him physically bigger. Wider. Stronger.

His beard is long and wiry with wisps of grey hair. There are dark circles under his eyes and a bruise on his cheekbone, and his nose is crooked from when he broke it after a bar fight one night.

'Come in.' Dad's voice is deep. Raspy. 'Close the door. Sit down.'

I turn to Sadie and call her in. She hesitates, pawing the ground.

'Now, Noah,' he thunders. That's the voice I remember and the trauma sparks, burning in its intensity. Immediately, I'm back there. Back in that house. Back under his thumb, terrified of defying him.

As I walk down the hallway, I run my hand over the hallstand to find something, *anything*, I can use to defend myself. And then I think—defend myself? *What are you going to do, Noah, murder your father on your lounge room floor?* Am I really capable of that? Even if I was, all that's on the nightstand are

Margie's and my keys, Sadie's leash and a half-eaten tennis ball. No weapons I could use in a break and enter.

All those cameras and yet we forgot the baseball bat by the front door. Classic.

The *cameras*. He must have noticed them. I hazard a quick look up to the one stationed by the front door; the little red light is off. In fact, all the lights are off. The house is dark and quiet. Clearly, Dad's turned the electricity off at the mains.

'You've been a tough one to find.' Dad's hot breath hits my face. He stinks of rum and smokes. 'I knew it was only a matter of time before you tried to contact your mother.'

I see Margie sitting at the dining table, back straight and eyes rimmed with tears.

'Sit down,' he says again, grabbing the back of my shirt and throwing me against the table. My head hits the wood and when I push myself up, there's blood on the varnish. Running my tongue over my lip, I taste blood and realise I've bitten it.

Dad paces around the kitchen, rifling through the cabinets.

'What are you looking for?' I demand. Is he after booze? Money? Whatever he wants, I tell myself I'll give it to him if he'll leave us alone.

Dad draws a knife from the knife block near the stove. It's a sick threat.

'There's booze in the cupboard,' Margie says. 'Take it and leave.'

Dad grins, slinking towards the walk-in cupboard. He grabs the half-empty bottle of vodka on the top shelf—bought for Moscow mules on warm summer days and to accompany pierogi during long frosty winter nights—and downs a mouthful like it's water.

'Why are you here?' I ask Dad, reaching across the table to take Margie's hand.

'Thought I'd send a message to your mother,' Dad says. 'I don't know where she is, but I'm sure she'll hear about this.'

Kill me. He wants to *kill* me. I feel vomit rise in my throat, and it mixes with the blood in my mouth. I swallow it down, feeling the bile burn as it slides into my stomach.

I'd been happy to hear from my mum. Ecstatic even.

All this time, I'd been telling him things about my life. What I was doing. Where to find me.

And he'd played along with it. The *sick fucking bastard.*

Margie's hand squeezes mine and that's when I feel it. Something hard and smooth against her palm.

The emergency alarm to our home surveillance.

Thank god for Margie and her batshit idea to hide it under the table like we were a fucking bank. Oh my god, I could reach across and kiss her. We just gotta wait this out. Someone's coming.

Dad swallows, wiping his mouth on the back of his hand. 'Knew you couldn't have fucked off far, but your mother disappeared after the trial. Even my retired buds couldn't help me track her down—but they found you no problem. After that photo of you at the tennis, we found his hotel—'

Shit. Gabriel could have been in danger.

He puts down the bottle of vodka. 'It wasn't hard to track you from there; you led me straight to your home. It's not hard to find someone, Noah, not in this day and age.'

God, I thought I'd been so careful. Dad pulls out Mum's phone from his pocket; still the same phone with the old fluffy key chain on it. 'She's always been able to disappear,' Dad says, flipping the phone over in his hands. 'Been a good trick of hers for a while now.'

'Maybe it's because she despises you, like I do. You're fucking disgusting.' I spit at his feet before I can stop myself.

Anger bursts from my father. It flows up his body and through his shoulder, his arm, his enclosed fist and finally erupts against the side of my face. The world spins. Suddenly, I'm falling. I put out my hands to catch my fall and the emergency alarm skids across the kitchen floor. I try to grab it before he notices, but I can't move. Everything's all fuzzy and far away.

Dad looks at the alarm. He was a police officer for twenty-five years. He knows exactly what it is as soon as he sees it. He raises one boot and stomps on it, breaking the plastic casing and destroying the transmitter inside it.

I groan against the floor tiles, feeling blood start to pool around my cheek. Dad grips me by the collar and hauls me to my feet. 'Up.'

With a final feat of strength, I push against him, kicking, clawing, doing whatever I can to get him to let me go. Distantly, I hear Sadie barking in the front yard, and I wonder if Fei's called the cops.

Dad twists suddenly and his arm comes in range of my mouth. I bite down, hard, and he screams. There's slack on my collar and I realise he's let me go. I dash forward, running down the hallway. His boots thump behind me. Closing in.

'RUN, MARGIE!' I yell back. Dad grabs me just before I open the flyscreen door. The neighbours never helped when I was a kid, but this isn't fucking Bendigo. 'HELP ME!' I scream out onto the street. 'CALL THE COPS!'

'Shut the fuck up!' Dad bellows as he drags me back down the hallway. The nails in the old floorboards cut against my shins. I kick and scream, making as much noise as I possibly can to wake up the quiet neighbourhood.

In the scuffle, Margie's disappeared—she's probably run out the back door and out the back gate. Good. She's out.

But suddenly Dad buckles. He cries out. I turn. Margie has the iron poker from the fireplace and she's thumping it against his back, a deranged look on her face.

Dad rears up as if the beating doesn't even hurt. I try to get between them, but he shoves Margie hard, and she falls against the wall. The poker clatters to the ground. I lunge to grab it, but I'm too slow. Dad kicks it across the room.

Sirens. I hear sirens outside now, and I think they're getting closer. On the floor, Margie clutches her shoulder, pain evident on her face.

Dad grabs the knife as I scramble to my feet. I watch him warily, waiting for him to lunge. He glances over his shoulder at the backyard, to the gate beyond it, and for a moment, I think he's going to bolt.

No.

He's not allowed to get away, not this time.

I'm sick of living in fear; sick of thinking I'm crazy every time I feel something's not quite right.

I see the red and blue lights flash outside as a police car pulls up. Dad drops the knife and bolts towards the back door.

I lunge towards him, wrapping my arms around his waist and pulling him to the ground.

His boot sinks into my side as he tries to get away, but my rage makes me stronger than him. Somehow, I keep him pinned to the ground as the front door opens.

'POLICE!'

'Help!' I call out. 'Down here!'

I let Dad go just as a female officer steps into the room. She's got her taser drawn. 'Hands up now!' she demands.

I rise to my knees, putting my hands up. Dad's heaving as he rolls onto his side, showing his bloodied hands.

'It's fine. He's my son. We were having a disagreement, that's all,' Dad says. More sirens sound in the distance. 'It got out of hand.'

'Get on your knees.'

Dad laughs a little, like it's all a big joke. Just a misunderstanding. But the officer's face doesn't crack.

'I won't tell you again,' the officer says. 'Get on your knees. Hands behind your back.'

Dad gives me one final look of absolute hatred before he lets out a long, laboured sigh and does as he's told. The police swarm.

34

GABRIEL

6–4, 5–7, 4–3 . . .

I'm cramping.

6–4, 5–7, 4–6.

The set ends. Auer's leading two sets to one, having clawed his way back from a game down in the third. I'm cramping up badly. The muscles in my knee and calf spasm as I sit down at my bench. As I chug a mouthful of electrolyte water, I check the strapping on my knee and then return to the court.

I haven't looked at my player's box since the start of the second set. If I look, and Noah's not there, I'm going to spiral. If I don't look, there's every chance he *could* be there. Schrödinger's Noah.

It's almost ten o'clock at night and Auer and I are both dripping with sweat. Somewhere between the second and third sets, the southerly sea breeze dropped and ever since, the arena's felt like a hotpot, and I'm a piece of meat cooking in my own juices.

Auer glares at me from over the net as he raises the ball to serve. I soften my knees, preparing to lunge.

It hits the net.

Fault!

With a huff, Auer sets up again. I've never been able to get a read on this guy. He's a complete machine on the court but couldn't be nicer off it. Where other tennis players will go on training camps together, he trains alone with the same coach he's had since he was ten years old. You'd think his game would get stale but it never does. I've watched hundreds of his matches over my career, and I can read his playing style—but watching him play and playing him are two different things.

All I know is I'm losing control of this match.

I can feel it.

35

GABRIEL

6–4, 5–7, 4–6, 7–5 . . .

It's come down to the last set. It's almost midnight. The blisters on my palm weep and stain the thick bandage I've put on it. Every swing, every hit, every serve hurts. Every *step* hurts.

My socks are soaked with sweat and there's probably another blister forming on the bottom of my foot, right where it's rubbing against the insole of my shoe, but I ignore it. I ignore everything. There will be time to recover after this match.

I'm so close to glory I can feel it.

Pejo Auer sizes me up from across the net, bounces the ball once, twice, three times, and then serves.

My body protests as I lunge forward to return the ball and feel my muscles instantly fatigue. I can't play these long rallies anymore. All my points are short, sharp and quick, and I know Auer's noticed it. He's playing me hard, making me run.

Auer steals the first game; the score's 1–0, but now it's my service game.

The racquet handle catches a blister the wrong way and I flinch on my first serve, sending the ball into the net.

Adjusting the bandages on my hands, I try to bite back the tears. The match has slipped away from me, and I'm physically and mentally exhausted. Risking a glance up to my player's box, I meet Papa's eyes. Noah's still not here. He was my person, and he's not here.

I needed him here.

'Allez, Gabriel!' Papa calls back. I know he must be able to read every emotion on my face; he understands the exhaustion, he's dealt with it before.

Play restarts and I fight Auer for every point. I chase the ball across the court, send it along the line, but he's there, every time. Finally, a drop shot causes him grief and he loses the game. 1–1.

The crowd cheers. I can barely take it in; two weeks ago, I'd never made a grand slam final. Now I'm being watched by millions of people across the globe.

Auer serves. Every point, every game, is hard won. We're pushing each other to our limits. When, at the end of the third game in the fifth set, Pejo hits the ball out of the court, my player's box erupts. Lukas gets out of his seat, shouting as I take the lead. Papa's smile is so wide and bright, it looks unnatural on him. Hope flutters in my stomach. I'm close. Closer than I've ever been.

Why isn't Noah here?

God, I wish I knew where I'd gone wrong about tonight; what I'd said. Did I push him too far? Was this . . . all of this . . . too much for him? I can't blame him if that's true. The fans, the tour, the gruelling hours, the distance—it's a lot for anyone. And maybe I just wasn't worth it.

Glancing up at the stadium lights, I blink back tears and force myself to turn my attention back to the match.

Pejo mutters on the other side of the court, clearly beating himself up about the break. I wipe my hands on my towel and notice the red streaks on the fabric. I quickly re-tape the blisters bleeding through the bandages, strapping them firmly before taking the court again. A soft breeze flows through the arena, bringing with it a small amount of relief. Above me, seagulls squawk as they hover around the roof.

Taking a deep breath, I set up to serve. We've been playing for almost five hours now, so my serves aren't what they used to be, but the sudden force with which Auer sends the ball back shocks me. I try to return it, but the newly strapped bandages have compromised my grip on the racquet and it falls to the ground with a clatter. The ball careens away, bouncing into the media seats.

Auer, clearly riding a second wind after his one-sided pep talk, steals my service game. My control's fraying. Then, Auer hits a killer serve and aces me in the next game. I claw back another two points but it's not enough. I'm not good enough. In a handful of minutes, our scores are level.

Three games each.

I adjust my bandages and prepare to serve again. The blister that was forming on the sole of my foot is now a full-on fluid bubble. I feel it pinch with every step, but I have to keep playing.

I serve decently; not my best, but it sails across the net. Auer returns. I try a drop shot that doesn't work. Lose a point. Gain a point. Back and forth, back and forth. We desperately try to one-up each other, neither of us willing to give in.

My ball skims the top of the net. It falls forward, hitting Auer's side. The crowd erupts, applauding the stamina, the skill, the point. Even Auer claps his hand against the strings of his racquet, and I give him a tight smile.

Panting, I take my place back at the baseline as the scoreboard registers one point. I'm exhausted. All that effort for one point.

My first serve is a fault, and the linesman's call echoes around the stadium as he confirms it. Behind me, the serve clock ticks down. I take a breath, steady myself and serve again.

Double fault!

Auer's fans applaud my mistake and I try to get out of my own head. *You can do this.* This time, my serve is weaker, but it makes it over the net. Auer sends it sailing back with a driving backhand and I stumble to meet it, scooping it up underneath my racquet. It hits the net. Another point gone.

Another serve. I try to ace him, and fail. A stupid decision so deep in the fifth. A softer serve only means Auer will use his backhand, and he does. I try to meet it with a forehand—weaker but a little more precise—and aim for the back corner, crosscourt. In what can only be described as an absolutely mad act, Auer intercepts it in midair and slices the ball down the line. It hits the far back corner, mirroring exactly where I'd hoped my ball would land. The absolute ease with which he hits the shot makes my shoulders sag. What's the point anymore? I'll *never* be at his level.

The set point ticks over. Auer's now in front. Only two games lie between him and the title.

I look up to Papa in the player's box. He's literally on the edge of his seat, resting his chin on his hand. He looks deep in thought, anxious. He mouths *Are you okay?*

Nodding, I re-tape my bandages. I put on an extra pair of socks to cushion the blister on the bottom of my foot and stand, testing the padding.

I'm so wrecked. So sore and defeated and aching. I could call it now, and it would be done.

Eight points and you finish this match with dignity and pride, I tell myself even as my body protests.

I shove the bloodied bandages into my pack, ignoring the *whir-click* of a camera behind me. Injury porn. The media loves it. They like to know how we suffer and hurt for our passion. Like gladiators.

Pejo Auer waits for me, grim-faced and focused, and it feels like I'm facing my executioner. There are no mind games here. It's just one player outplaying another. He sets up his serve, sweat dripping down his angular nose, and sends it flying across the net. I hit it back, and without moving, Auer digs down and sends a forehand straight across the other side of the court. It bounces past before I've even taken a step. An excellent shot. And he didn't move an inch.

For every point I claw back, Pejo gains two. He closes the fifth; now he's two games ahead. The crowd is going wild for him: the reigning champ; one of the best of the game; the person people come to these tournaments to see. I wonder if they'd have the same energy for me if I were ahead. It's hard enough to fight your way to the final, and it's even harder when you're facing a crowd favourite.

Auer takes a deep breath on the other side of the net, and I know that he's trying to steady his nerves, to tell himself this game isn't over just because he's got a sizeable lead. That I could still come back and take this from him. Strangely, that makes me feel good. It's nice knowing your opponent still sees you as a threat, even after playing tennis for five hours.

It's his service game. He has all the momentum to convert this and win the championship. I tell myself to play like it's just another game, but of course, it isn't. Nerves get the best of Auer in the first point; he double faults. It's an easy point for me.

Auer rolls his shoulders, stretches his head from left to right and then sets up to serve again. This time, it's a stronger serve and the ball flies down the middle line. I hit it back, he returns it, I hit it back again. Neither of us backs down. Auer plays a drop shot and it lands close to the net. I manage to reach it, lobbing it back. It's not the most refined shot but it's the only shot I can make. Of course, Auer, the incredible freak that he is, rears up and spikes the ball back down. I fumble for it, but the ball hits the edge of my racquet and lands back in my court.

15–15.

Auer serves. Back and forth, back and forth, until my shoulder buckles from fatigue and I hit the ball into the net.

30–15.

It's almost 1 am. The audience falls silent as Auer bounces the ball. Even I can hear the *tap tap tap* on the astroturf.

The ball flies past me before I can even comprehend it. Incredible. How does he still have enough energy?

40–15.

Pejo's face breaks into a smile. It's the championship point.

I've always wanted to experience this once—a grand slam championship point—and I suppose now I am. It's just not for me.

I've thought about losing as much as I've thought about winning these past couple of days. I knew what I'd expect to feel when faced with a championship point—elation, nerves, that final serve of adrenaline, like when you've only got a mile left to go in a marathon. You push through because the end is so close.

The feeling of losing the championship was harder to pin down. I thought maybe I'd feel dread, loss, sadness. I'd feel that I'd let myself down, my team, my trainers. My papa.

But now, as I face down Pejo Auer on the championship point, I don't feel any of those things.

I don't feel bad at all.

A serve, a few hits, my ball lands just outside the baseline, and it's all over. In the end, the championship point is a point like any other; there's nothing special about how he wins it, no big rallies, no trick shots.

He's won. I've lost.

Pejo Auer falls onto his back as the crowd roars around him.

I collapse on the baseline. Whatever strings have kept me up for so long have been cut, and I'm like a wobbly puppet as people rush onto the court, TV cameras celebrating Auer's win. Beside me, a medic leans down to offer me an electrolyte drink and a towel.

Sitting up, I glance towards the crowd to see Pride flags intermingle with French and Peruvian flags, posters that say *ALLEZ GABI!* and *VAMOS!!!*. I sit and take it all in. Mostly because I can't walk, but also because it's such a beautiful sight.

A hand touches my back and I turn, expecting to see Papa. But it's Pejo.

He kneels beside me, sweat shining off his bald head. 'Are you okay?' he asks.

'I'm fine,' I assure him. 'I'll be okay.'

He takes my hand and helps me to stand. 'You played like a lion out there. It was incredible. We gave them a match they will *never* forget.'

And that's still something, isn't it?

We thank the umpire, and all the spectacle turns back to Pejo and his victory. I return to my station, place my tennis racquet back in its cover, and drink another mouthful of water. I need to get off this court before I pass out, but as I grab my bag, my hand spasms.

'Let me,' Papa says as his hand covers mine. I choke back a sob, too overwhelmed with emotion.

'I lost, Papa.'

But Papa mustn't hear me because he says, 'You played so well.'

We find a seat inside the hallways of Rod Laver Arena, where it's private and mostly quiet. Papa kneels beside me and unlaces my shoe. As soon as the cool air hits my foot,

Papa makes a small, concerned noise in the back of his throat.

'How bad is it?' I ask.

'Good thing we are not going to Brazil,' he mutters and then calls over the medic. They unwrap the bandages on my fingers and hands, fussing over them.

'They're just blisters,' I say as officials begin to prepare for the awards ceremony out on court. 'They don't even hurt anymore.'

'We'll have to take you downstairs,' the medic tells me—as if what I just said doesn't matter. 'Don't put any pressure on your foot.'

Suddenly, I'm hauled up. The medic is under one shoulder and Papa's under the other and I'm being dragged—literally dragged—down the hallway.

'You tennis players can play through anything, can't you?' laughs the medic as I'm seated in a sterile-smelling first-aid room.

'You should have called for a medical timeout, Gabriel,' Papa berates me.

'Where's Noah?' I ask.

Papa's expression darkens. 'He couldn't make it. He contacted Victor. We'll talk after the presentation.'

'Did he tell you why?' My phone's still in my bag which I think is still on the court but I need to know now. 'Did I do something?'

Papa takes my head between his hands. 'You didn't do anything, Gabriel. You played so well. He will be very proud of you.'

'I need to talk to him.'

'You can call him once we're back at the hotel,' Papa says firmly. There's no arguing with him. 'Focus, Gabriel. You're not finished here. You've still got to do the presentation. Have you thought about what you're going to say?'

36

NOAH

There's one flickering fluorescent light in the corner of the hospital waiting room and it's fucking annoying. I close my eyes, take a deep breath through my nose and think about what's around me. I can hear the gentle chatter of nurses at the ward desk, footsteps on linoleum, a cleaning cart rattling its way down the hallway, the tinny voices of commentators as they chat about why Gabriel Madani had to be helped down to the medic's room after his nail-biting loss to Peru's Pejo Auer—and if he'll be well enough to accept his trophy at the presentation ceremony.

Worry has lived with me for so long that the concern I feel for Gabriel is just another guest at an already at-capacity party. The psychologist I saw two hours ago told me that eventually this sort of thing breaks; that I'm less like a bucket emptying and filling and more like a dammed river at the point when the water overflows.

They're still setting up for the presentation on the big

TV I'm watching when Lucy, Margie's eldest daughter, steps into the waiting room. I recognise her from photos around the house. She's pretty, maybe thirty-five, with long blonde hair and Margie's upturned nose. Despite living over an hour away in Rosebud, she'd got in the car as soon as the police contacted her. It's almost two in the morning. It must be nice to have someone like that, someone who will put down everything just to be with you; to come running when they're called.

Lucy sits beside me, smoothing her hands over her jeans. 'You're Noah, right?'

I nod. 'Nice to meet you.'

I haven't seen Margie since we disembarked from the ambulance. She'd been lucid but high on pain meds, and I was dealing with my own shit with a split lip and what was soon confirmed as an orbital fracture.

Lucy looks pointedly at the IV drip beside me. 'Shouldn't you be resting?'

'TV in my room doesn't work,' I reply, gesturing to the large flat-screen in the waiting room. 'Tennis.'

I missed so much of the match, but I saw how close it was. I saw how wrecked Gabriel was, how well he fought in the last few games, saw the pain in his eyes even as he stood up and kept going.

As soon as I'd got to the hospital, I'd contacted Victor with a lengthy recount on what was going on and why I wouldn't make it to Gabriel's match. He'd replied between sets with *We'll call you after this is done.*

The TV replays match highlights. I wish I could be there for him; to hold him in those narrow corridors and feel his body thrum against mine; to tell him everything's going to be okay and that he played *so, so* well.

'I'm going to stay with Mum for a bit, help her get back on her feet,' Lucy says. 'Mum mentioned you were planning to go away with your boyfriend.'

'We were going to leave on Tuesday.'

Suddenly, Gabriel appears on the TV. He hobbles back onto the court. He has a clear limp, and as the camera pans down, I see that his entire foot is wrapped in bandages. Bernard hovers behind him, staying close as Gabriel ascends the staircase and stands beside Pejo Auer on the podium.

'Where are you going?' It's clear she's making light conversation to make me feel more comfortable, but I just really want to watch the ceremony. The lights have darkened in the arena and the president of the tennis association speaks into the microphone.

'I'm not sure,' I reply, and then get up to manually increase the volume on the television. 'Sorry, I just really need to watch the ceremony.' At Lucy's strange look, I clarify, 'That is my boyfriend.' I gesture at the screen.

Lucy looks at me like my broken eyelid came with a side of concussion, which, well, it did. 'I'm being for real. Gabriel is my boyfriend.'

'Oh, yes, sure,' she says, clearly humouring me.

Lucy gets up and fills two paper cups of water from the large bottle in the corner, handing one to me just as Gabriel takes the stage. I'm not really thirsty, but as soon as the camera zooms in on him, I swallow down a mouthful to dislodge the sudden ball that's formed in my throat. He looks so incredibly beautiful. Curly hair sticks to his forehead and neck and his skin glows under the arena lights. It reminds me of the way he'd looked as we'd driven home from the beach, how he'd smiled as he'd placed his hand on my thigh while I drove, how he'd smelt of the sea and sunshine and happiness.

Gabriel accepts his trophy—a massive plate—and shakes the presenter's hand. Then, with a big breath in, so deep I see his chest rise under his shirt, he steps to the microphone.

'English is not my first language, so please forgive me if I don't make sense,' he begins. 'For a long time, I have dreamed of this moment. I have dreamed of playing on a court like this and standing up at the end of the night with a trophy, and tonight, my dream came true.'

The crowd cheers. Gabriel continues, 'Tomorrow, the newspapers will write that I lost the match. They'll write about the scores and the play, and the number of trophies Pejo has won and how few I have. But what they won't write about is how proud of myself I am right now.'

And then, Gabriel begins to cry. Fat, rolling tears. He looks at his trophy and says, 'I am so proud of myself right now. I am so proud of who I have become in this tournament.'

The crowd cheers and I feel Lucy's hand on my back, rubbing back and forth. Am I crying? God, I hope it doesn't fuck up my stitches.

'Thank you to my team, to my papa and my media manager, Victor. You had a lot to deal with this tournament.'

The camera pans to Victor, who is laughing through his tears.

'Thank you to my friends and family, to my sponsors and, of course, to the Australian Open and Tennis Australia for putting on the tournament. Thank you to everyone who watched me play this year. I love playing in Australia, and I can't wait to come back next year. Finally, thank you to Pejo. I grew up wanting to play you, and it was an honour to meet you in the finals. Next time, maybe you will not be so lucky, eh?'

Pejo claps his thanks as Gabriel lets out a deep, steadying breath and hitches the trophy on his hip. 'This has been the hardest tournament of my life. I'm tired and I'm sore, so I'm going to take some time off for a bit. I don't have anything else to say, so I guess I will see you next time.'

He lifts the trophy once more, and it must be heavy because his arms clearly tremble with the effort. Immediately, Bernard steps forward to help him down the steps off the stage. He's probably in more pain than he's letting on, but he stands, holding his second-place trophy, as Auer steps up to the microphone. He turns to look fondly at Gabriel, warmth shining in his brown eyes.

'How to follow up a speech like that, huh?'

'Stay right there,' Gabriel says, even though I'm still hooked up to an IV and being monitored for a concussion, so I won't be going anywhere for a few more hours, at least. 'I'll be there as soon as I can.'

'Gabi, you don't have to,' I say quietly into the phone. 'I'm fine, I promise. Get some rest.'

'I'm coming, Noah,' he says, so fiercely it leaves no room for argument. 'You need someone to be there for you. I'll be there in fifteen minutes.'

Gabriel hangs up on me, and I lean back onto the hard pillows of my hospital bed. The ward's quiet save for the quiet chatter of the staff around the nurses' station. Margie's somewhere down the hall, and the police have already taken both our statements. I'm tired, but way too hopped up on adrenaline and whatever drugs they gave me when they stitched my brow back together to sleep.

Gabriel bursts through the door like a hurricane twenty-five minutes later, with his frizzy hair pulled into a bun on the top of his head and bandaged feet shoved into Adidas slides.

He looks horrified when he sees me.

'I promise it's not as bad as it looks,' I say, easing off the bed. Gabriel takes my chin in his grip, eyes roaming over my face, taking it all in.

'It was him?' he asks.

I nod. 'Yeah.'

'I will *kill* him,' Gabriel snarls and *wow*, that's a lot. 'You do not deserve this, Noah. You don't deserve to *live* like this; in fear, in pain.'

My eyes prickle with tears, and it *hurts*—physically hurts—to cry. 'I know, okay?' I say, my voice wet with emotion. 'I don't want this either. I don't want *any* of this.'

'Move to Paris with me,' Gabriel says, sliding his hands down my shoulders. 'Come home with me.'

I can't do that. He's asking way too much of me right now. 'You're away most of the year, you said it yourself. I have a life here; friends and a job that I like.'

'But you would be safe with me!' he almost shouts. Suddenly, Gabriel takes a step back, his chest heaving. 'I'm sorry.' He looks away. 'I just—I'm angry, and I don't know how to say the right things. All I know is that I wanted you to be there tonight, and I kept wondering why you weren't, what I had done that meant you weren't there and I—' He takes in two fast, deep breaths, struggling to keep control of his emotions. 'I feel so stupid and selfish and—' Gabriel presses the ball of his palm into his eye socket as a sob escapes his mouth.

Without a word, I pull him towards me and feel him settle against my collarbone.

Gabriel wraps his arms around me, clutching my shirt. 'It feels like I'm being torn apart. I am . . . I have fallen in love with you. I want to do everything with you, and I hate knowing that I can't.'

I pull him closer, crushing him, my heart faltering at his words. This isn't just about my dad, or anything that's happened in the last twelve hours. The tournament's over, and that means our relationship, in its current form, is over too. Soon, no matter what we decide to do, Gabriel will be on a plane back to France, preparing for the next tournament, and I'll be here, doing whatever comes next.

I smooth a hand over his hair. 'Oh, Gabi. Me too. We just have a lot of shit to work through.'

'I know,' he murmurs weakly, then pulls back, sniffing. 'You really stink of apple cider.'

I laugh, pushing him away. Gabriel takes my chin in his hand again and, mindful of my split lip, kisses the very corner of my mouth.

37

GABRIEL

Somehow, I manage to sleep for a few hours in the armchair beside Noah's bed until we're discharged.

Despite feeling like death warmed up, I have a full morning of media appointments. But with my throbbing knee and blistered foot, I'm barely able to walk. As I'd re-wrapped my blisters this morning, I'd felt a bit like Victor Frankenstein's monster, held together by twine and bandages, my limbs not quite my own.

'I feel like I'm about to go play tennis,' Noah says as he emerges from the hospital bathroom in a pair of Nike shorts and a loose cotton shirt, sourced from my suitcase.

I roll my eyes. 'Sorry it's not off the two-dollar rack.'

'I won't hear you talk badly of the two-dollar rack.' Noah slips his hand into mine. That's something we can do now, I realise. Hold each other's hands. Kiss in public if we want to.

Margie's room is down the corridor. Her bed is positioned

beside a big window, and the early-morning sun streams into the room.

'It's Noah and Gabriel,' Noah calls ahead as we enter the room, and I realise I like the sound of our names together, the way the vowels sound, the ring to it. Margie sits up in bed, smoothing her hands over her curly hair.

'Oh, what a treat.' She reaches out her right arm to pull Noah in for a hug. Her left, I notice, is in a sling. 'Noah, my boy, look at your face.'

He presses a hand to his cheek self-consciously. 'Don't worry about me. I'm made of strong stuff.'

She smiles sadly. 'We both are.'

'I came to say see you later,' he says. 'Gabriel's got a thing on at eleven, and then we're going on our trip tomorrow. You can call me anytime, but—'

Margie tuts, brushing off Noah's concern. 'Now, don't you worry,' she says in the stern but warm way only grandmothers can. 'Lucy's staying for a few days. She's going to take good care of me. Go on your trip. Enjoy it. Relax.'

Noah looks unsure. It must be a lot for him to let this go, to leave Margie in the hospital while he jets off on holiday. It's easy for me to tell him he deserves it, but it's harder to make him believe it.

'I'll call you on Wednesday, okay?' he says to her. Then, he looks at me. 'You're taking me somewhere with reception, right?'

I nod. At least, I think there will be phone reception.

The taxi ride back to Southbank is quiet. Neither of us knows what to say but I realise that maybe we don't have to talk; that what's happened doesn't need to be gone over a million times. Noah told me enough last night. Maybe he just needs to know that I'm here for him, and will be, in whatever way he needs me.

Papa meets us at the car, his eyes darting between Noah and me, clearly unsure where to start. Finally, he settles on, 'Gabriel, you need to shower before the photoshoot. They've sent clothes across.'

I suppress a groan as I step under the warm spray of the shower; my muscles are clearly telling me they'll keep me upright today, but nothing more.

There's a pressed linen shirt and a pair of sage green shorts waiting on the bed when I step out of the shower, along with a pair of buttery-soft brown leather loafers.

'Wow, fancy,' Noah says as I step out of the bedroom.

'Let's get a coffee, Noah,' Papa says as we walk the short distance to Southbank. 'It looks like you could use one.'

Leaving Papa and Noah to sort themselves out, I hobble towards the waterfront where Pejo's waiting among a crowd of makeup artists, hairstylists and photographers.

'How do you feel today?' Pejo asks.

'Like I've torn every muscle in my body,' I admit. 'You?'

'Similar,' he chuckles. 'It was a hard match.'

We have our photos taken, pose with our trophies, kiss them, bite them, raise them above our heads (very painful), pose together, pose apart: the whole deal. We stop to do a few TV interviews; get our photos taken by a few other newspapers and pose for our myriad sponsors and their products.

I've always pictured doing a media blitz after winning a big tournament and having that 'famous' feeling. Now that I'm here, and cameras are in my face, I realise it's a little bit shit.

I'm tired, sore and grumpy. It's hot, my feet are killing me, and pain shoots through my knee every time I walk.

'See you in Paris,' I say to Pejo as we wrap up. 'Won't be so easy in my home town.'

Pejo laughs. 'I have won on clay more times than I can count. Rest up, Gabriel.'

If he wasn't so genuinely lovely, I'd hate Pejo's guts.

I find Noah and Papa eating on the balcony of a waterfront café. Well, Noah's eating—halfway through a breakfast omelette—and Papa's drinking an espresso. I pull out a seat beside Papa and place the giant silver plate on the seat beside me, as if it is dining with us.

'No trophies at the dining table,' Noah chides.

Victor joins us and we all order coffees, sitting and chatting and going over plans—while Noah and I will leave for our break tomorrow, Papa and Victor will return to Paris to rest and begin preparing for the clay season.

'Monte-Carlo,' Papa says after a long while. 'Let's aim for Monte-Carlo.'

A cool breeze flows off the Yarra River. Trains slip in and out of Flinders Street Station every few minutes, full of busy people on their way to do a million things. People pass us on the footpath, eyes on their screens or talking on their phone, or with their earbuds in. Everyone else is moving. It feels weird to stop.

I don't remember the last time I stopped.

'You okay?'

Noah's thumb brushes mine under the table. I turn to him, embarrassed to have been caught in my own head. 'Just thinking about our break,' I say, because it's true.

We spend the rest of the afternoon in bed. Unfortunately, it's not sexy. We put an episode of the baking show on my laptop, but it's soon forgotten.

'I need one more recommendation,' I tell Noah. 'One more thing for the Melbourne experience.'

'Hmm?' he hums groggily.

'I need to know the *best* burger place in the city.'

Later that night, I fulfil my promise to myself and order the most obscene burger Melbourne has to offer; plus a side of fries. Victor and Papa decide to go out for dinner; a thinly veiled attempt to give us some space. Noah and I watch *Jurassic Park* on the hotel TV while we eat dinner. As the velociraptors burst into the kitchen, I loop my arm around Noah and feel him relax against me.

The last thing I think about before I fall asleep is the feeling of Noah's warm breath on my shoulder, the brush of his fingers on my bare thigh, and how he still, very slightly, smells like apple cider.

38

NOAH

There's something special about waking up in Gabriel's arms. I'd slept fitfully all night until he'd rolled over and, in his sleep, wrapped his arms around my middle. I'd drifted off into that warm, lazy kind of sleep where you wake up feeling the cosiest you've ever been—at least until your alarm blares on the bedside table.

Bernard and Victor's flight to Dubai leaves at nine-fifteen. Ours, to wherever we're going, leaves at ten-thirty. Even as we make our way to the airport, Gabriel refuses to tell me.

At the international terminal, we stack Gabriel's luggage—all five large suitcases—onto a trolley.

Bernard steps towards me, his arms outstretched. For a second, I don't know what's happening, but then he pulls me against his chest. Hug. Bernard Madani is giving me a hug.

'See you soon, Noah,' he says. I feel his voice rumble against my cheek.

'See you again soon, Mr Madani,' I say, awkwardly looping my arms around the expanse of his back.

'You can call me Bernard,' he says. 'We're past formalities.'

'You have seen me at my highest highs and my lowest lows,' I concede. Bernard laughs, that stone face finally cracking.

Barely two weeks ago, I was terrified of Gabriel's father. I saw so much of my own dad reflected in the stories that Gabriel told me: a man who controlled his life, who pressured and fought with him. Now, I look at Bernard and I understand they are nothing alike.

In a way I can't really describe, Bernard feels like home.

Once they've gone through the departure gate, we get back into the van and take the short trip to the domestic terminal.

Gabriel checks us in at a self-service booth. The machine spits out our tickets. I lunge to grab them, but he blocks me, laughing. He directs me to wait near the security gates while he takes our suitcases to send them to wherever the hell we're going.

'You going to tell me now?' I ask as we wait in line for security. We've both packed light. I take out my wallet and phone and place them in the trays.

'No.'

As we stand in front of the departures board, I look over all the destinations to figure out which one could be ours.

Gabriel nudges me. 'Come on, we have a bit of time before we board.'

'Darwin?' I ask as he walks away, excluding the flights departing in the next half an hour from my guesses. 'Hobart? Alice Springs?!'

Gabriel and I walk through the food court, past the Victoria's Secret shop, and into a large bookstore.

'This is what you wanted, isn't it?' Gabriel asked. 'It's not a holiday unless you buy a book from the airport bookshop.'

Emotion swells, and I swallow it back down. 'Yeah, I said that.'

Gabriel's hand touches mine, just enough to bring me back to reality.

'I need to go to the pharmacy. Meet you back here in ten minutes?'

I nod. It seems a bit personal to follow him into the chemist, plus he's got all those nasty blisters on his hands and feet. I hang out in the bestseller section, trying to decide if I should get a novel or go non-fiction. Like a moth to a flame, I'm drawn to the shiny covers of the young adult section, with their wizards and queer romances and stories about teens fighting serial killers.

'Find anything?' Gabriel asks as he re-joins me. I'm deep in the first chapter of said serial killer book.

'I like the sound of this,' I say, flashing him the cover. 'Are you going to get anything?'

He looks around the bookshop. 'No, I can't read in English.'

I look up from my book, unsure if I've heard him correctly. 'You can't? I never realised. You read the menu—'

'I can *read*,' he corrects, 'in French. In English I can read words. Sentences. Short articles. But I'd never be able to comprehend a whole book in English. Maybe that's a better way to describe it.'

I close the book. 'I get that. It's your second language and all.'

'Third,' Gabriel corrects. 'I also speak Arabic. Did you really not look me up online at all?'

'I remember promising that I wouldn't, and it being quite a big deal for you at the time. Romantic even.'

He pretends to look offended. 'Still, I thought by now you would have.'

'I'm buying this book,' I tell him. 'I'll read it out loud to you.'

'Will you do voices?' he asks. 'I like it when the audiobooks do voices. Like Stephen Fry.'

'I'm no Stephen Fry, but I'm sure I can give it a go.'

I take our book—the first book on our first holiday—and pay for it. In a few years, maybe we'll have an entire shelf of holiday books. Stories that mark our trips; memories locked between printed pages.

We get a coffee and find a place to sit in the food court. It's busy. People stare as they pass us. I wonder if it's because they recognise Gabriel from the TV, or because I have five stitches and two black eyes.

Gabriel fishes our boarding passes from his pocket. 'I guess it's finally time.'

I wriggle with anticipation as he hands me mine. The journey, printed in smudged ink, says MEL > HTI.

'HTI?'

'Hamilton Island,' Gabriel supplies. 'But from there, we're getting a charter to Daydream Island.'

Daydream Island. These last few weeks have been like a dream. An incredible dream that I know, eventually, I'll have to wake up from. It's stupidly perfect and I am stupidly in love with this man, and everything, from the way he looks at me across the table to the price of the coffee we just bought, is *stupid*.

A week on Daydream Island with nothing to do but do nothing. It's perfect.

'I've never been on a plane before,' I say later as we find our seats.

'That will be repaired a hundred times over,' he promises. 'Paris in summer, New York in the fall. We'll go all over the world.'

I hold Gabriel's hand as we take off. The plane rocks and shudders as it ascends into the clouds. Gabriel hands me an earbud and shows me a playlist he's compiled for the two-hour flight.

Melbourne spreads out below us; the Yarra winds like a serpent through the city. The country is a patchwork of yellow and brown, fields dry and burnt off after the end of harvest.

Gabriel's thumb rubs over my knuckle but then he lets go of my hand to raise the armrest between us. He slides across the seat slightly and pulls me to lean against him and . . . it's nice. He smells like expensive cologne, which he's obviously sampled at the fragrance department. And he's so warm. Comfortable. I don't know how—because between the noise of the engine and the occasional turbulence, it really shouldn't be possible—but I fall asleep somewhere between the seatbelt sign going off and refreshments being served. Gabriel, bless him, grabs me an extra muesli bar.

♪

A parrot chirps through the open window, rousing me from my sleep. As far as morning wake-ups go, one can't sniff at a tropical parrot replacing a phone alarm.

Distantly, I hear waves rolling and then, closer to home, Gabriel's sleepy huffs.

Opening my eyes, I find our bedroom bathed in the grey glow of early morning. The clock on my beside table says it's just after seven. From the briefing last night, I know breakfast has already started in the main hall.

Gabriel's hand snakes around my waist and tugs my back flush against his chest. 'I don't get up before eight-thirty,' he murmurs, voice heavy with sleep.

I turn in his arms. His eyes are still closed, so I take the opportunity to run my fingertips over his brow, the curve of his nose, his cupid's bow. He puckers his lips and kisses my fingertips lightly.

I feel something press against my thigh. 'Your body says otherwise, Gabi.'

'He betrays me.'

I lean forward and kiss his slack mouth. 'They always do.'

After we'd got to the hotel, we'd both been too sore and tired to do anything but fall into bed, accidentally missing dinner and the chance to order anything to our room.

Gabriel's hand caresses my neck and shoulders as he drifts back to sleep. It's fine with me. It's nice just to lie with him, to feel his skin against mine.

Eventually we do get up—at eight thirty-two exactly—dress and make our way to breakfast, where we spend a leisurely hour eating.

It's a beautiful day, if a little humid, so we gather our things and go to the beach. The water's crystal clear and so warm. Gabriel and I slosh through the shallows until we leave the hotel behind on the other side of the island, and there's no one else to be seen.

We find a shady spot under a tree and spend the morning coming in and out of the water, smelling like sunscreen and salt.

While we dry off, I read the opening chapters of the crime book to him, explaining the harder language as best I can while his hands get increasingly distracting.

Eventually, I put down the book. 'Do you want to go back to the hotel?'

Gabriel laughs and rubs his nose against the sparse hair on my stomach. 'Yes. Definitely. Yes.'

When we get back to our room, I take a quick shower. Then, still naked, Gabriel presses me against the mattress and maps every inch of my body with his mouth. When he crawls on top to kiss me, I taste salt on his tongue. Soon we're tangled in each other, lost in the feel of each other's bodies.

That's the good thing about dating a professional athlete: it's their job to be incredibly ripped at all times, and while I'll relish a day when Gabriel's regime relaxes, feeling the ripple of his abs under my fingers is a novelty I'll never grow sick of.

He kisses me, open-mouthed and hungry. There's no need to guess what he wants. I want it too. Heat prickles along my skin as I feel him press against my thigh, feel his heaviness.

'Baby,' I groan into his shoulder as he bears down, finding that perfect friction. His hand grips my hair, just on the right side of being too hard, and everything starts to spin.

'There are condoms in the drawer. Lube too,' I say. I'd put them there last night; hadn't wanted to fumble through our suitcases when the mood hit us.

Gabriel sits up, dazed and red-faced.

'Gabi.' I place my hand against his flexed thigh. 'Everything okay?'

'Do you want to—'

Oh. 'Well, I thought—'

With all our careful planning, there still seems to be something we haven't spoken about.

'Don't you like it, you know?' His face gets redder. 'A certain kind of way?'

'I like it lots of different ways,' I admit. 'But I thought for your first time, it might be easier if you're on top. Then we can start figuring out what you like later.'

Gabriel nods and reaches forward to open the drawer, grabbing the box of condoms and the lube. He tries to open the box, but his shaking fingers can't get underneath the seal. Frustrated, he thrusts it at me.

'Are you sure you want to keep going? We can just do what we did before—I liked that too.'

He scrubs a hand down his face. '*Fuck*, yes, okay. I'm just—' He lets out a long, shaking breath. I think that's the second time I've ever heard Gabriel swear. 'Nervous.'

I reach forward and cup his face. 'Nothing to be nervous about. Touch me for a bit. The rest will happen.'

'Oh,' Gabriel mutters, as if it dawns on him that he's not the only one nervous about sex with a new partner. 'I can do that.'

Gabriel can, indeed, do that. In fact, he is very good at kissing; he's firm and demanding and it's not long until I'm mindless. He takes control, pinning my hands beside my head, and then his hands are in my hair, on my hip, grabbing the fat of my thigh, pulling me closer and closer, until we're flushed against one another, chest to chest, hip to hip.

'Tell me if I hurt you,' he murmurs against the shell of my ear, and then he's touching me; really touching me, his fingers hot and slippery. I open my eyes and he's right there, wide, and open and loving, looking at me like I'm the centre of his fucking universe.

'Baby.' It's all I can muster, so caught up am I in his focus. I slide my hands over his shoulders, and feel the muscles in his back ripple.

'I just want to make you feel good.' His voice wobbles at the end.

'You are, you are.' I kiss him, sliding my mouth against his. 'You make me feel so fucking good every single day.'

He kisses my chest, my throat, sucks on my earlobe before finally, finally, slipping in. My legs curl around his hips, ankles finding their place on his hip bones, drawing him closer, and somehow deeper. The bottle of lube falls off the bed and hits the floor, rolling somewhere out of reach.

It doesn't take Gabriel long to find a rhythm; or to take control. He's strong and precise and *consistent* in his lovemaking and my toes curl every time he slides in the right way. Our bodies press together, the heat of him like a searing brand and god, it's wonderful. I'd never thought Gabriel would be like this in bed—so dominating and passionate, but I love it. Fucking love it.

Gabriel grips my thigh, driving into me. The bedframe hits the wall behind us, but neither of us cares.

Everything is so good and before I know it, I'm speaking, rattling my pleasure mindlessly, 'So good, so so good, Gabi, baby, so good.'

Then comes that same narrowing pleasure—everything I feel becomes focused, almost overwhelming, and then it bursts. I hear myself cry out as my body snaps like a band.

A few seconds later, Gabriel groans into my shoulder, jaw clenched, overwhelmed and blissed out. I hold him as pieces of the room come back to me; the dampness of the sheets beneath my back, the soft roll of the waves through the open window, the way my knee creaks as I lower it from Gabriel's hip.

Gabriel rests his head on my chest, and I kiss his sweaty hairline. He slurs something in French. Or something resembling French.

'Weirdly, Duolingo doesn't cover pillow talk,' I murmur against his temple. Gabriel just chuckles in response.

'Brain broken. Try later,' he sighs, and then rolls to lie beside me.

I take the condom because that seems like the gentlemanly thing to do, wrapping it and throwing it in the rubbish bin. Then, I return to Gabriel and pull a sheet over our bodies.

'You okay?' I push his hair away from his face. 'Blink once for yes. Twice for no.'

Gabriel smiles against the pillow, still blissed out and a little loopy. 'I'm okay. That was great.'

I laugh, running the backs of my fingers over his cheek. 'You were pretty fantastic.'

39

GABRIEL

Just over two weeks ago, I'd sat next to Phoebe in her hospital bed as she'd told me her injury was career-ending. That her time playing tennis was over.

I'd sat and listened to her, but all the while, I could only think about myself. What would happen if I was in the same situation? If the game was ripped away from me? Who was I if I wasn't a tennis player?

I love tennis so much that it was hard to face that something, eventually, could take it away from me. An injury, illness, an accident beyond my control. One day, despite my best efforts, my body will decide it has had enough, even if my mind has not.

But tennis will always be a part of me, at least in some form, whether it's playing professionally, or coaching, or commentating, or something completely different. I know this because on the fourth morning we spend in the Whitsundays, I wake up with a burning desire to play tennis.

'You've got to be joking,' Noah says as we eat breakfast on the patio. Yesterday it rained and we'd spent the entire day in our villa. No prizes for guessing what we'd done. Even now, Noah only wears a robe. The tie of his robe is loose, revealing a long sliver of skin. 'Hey, eyes up here.'

I look up.

'You just played two weeks of tennis,' Noah says soberly. 'Your blisters have barely healed and you still have a limp.'

I look down at my hands; at the calluses. The bandages are off and the blisters have scabbed over and the bursitis that afflicted my knee has subsided with a few days rest. 'Yesterday was far more taxing than a round of tennis. Besides, it's just you and me. It's not like I'm playing the world number one.'

'Fine,' he relents. 'One game.'

'One *match*,' I clarify.

'I know what I said.'

Noah grabs his sneakers and changes in the bathroom. I'm not sure why he bothers. We've seen so much of each other, there's no need for privacy.

'Is this fine?' Noah asks as he steps out of the bathroom in a pair of my shorts, a black t-shirt and—

'Get that off!' I gasp as he pulls my headband onto his forehead.

'I'm just trying to look professional.' He steps back as I try to swipe the headband from him.

'Fine, wear it,' I say. 'But I don't think I've washed it since the tournament.'

'Oh, *gross*, Gabi!' Noah rips the headband off and flings it towards me. I dodge it and it lands squarely in the middle of our messy bed.

We rent two racquets from the leisure shack near the pools. The courts are on the other side of the resort, so we walk through the gardens, narrowly avoiding a peacock's wrath, only to find two poorly maintained grass half-courts.

'Guess they don't get a lot of use,' I say as we swing open the rusted gate.

'Most people don't like playing competitive sport on their holidays,' Noah replies. The net, limp and full of holes, has seen better days. 'You know, we should make a bet in case I beat you.'

'You've never played tennis before and you're wearing Converses,' I reply. 'Sure, I'll take a bet.'

Noah sniggers as he kicks a few stray rocks off his baseline. 'Best of three gets a massage off the other person.' He looks at the net apprehensively. 'So, I just hit it back over the net?'

'That's the idea,' I say as I prepare to serve.

Noah crouches slightly. 'Be gentle with me, this is my first time.'

I look up from the ball to give him a hard glare across the court. He laughs, a wicked smirk forming on his face. A moment ago, I'd considered going easy on him, but now—

I serve hard. Noah yelps and curls away as the ball rockets towards him. It hits the meaty part of his thigh with a smack.

'*OW!*' he hollers. I didn't serve it hard enough for it to hurt. Much. 'Not fair.'

'I didn't say I'd play fair. Just that I'd take the bet.'

We play for two and a half sets. 'Play' is a strong word when really, we're just hitting the ball over the net and shit-talking each other, but eventually Noah forfeits the match, complaining of an impending blister.

'You of all people should be sympathetic,' he says, limping for show as we return the racquets.

He gets the massage that night, purely out of pity.

'Gabi.' Noah says a string of words after my name, but I don't catch them. I'm lying on the beach with Noah beside me, his head on my chest, and my brain's too slow to translate and process what he's just said, so I agree with a little hum and hope the conversation ends.

'I'm serious.' Noah's head rises and he looks up at me. 'Gabi, are you asleep?'

'Just resting my eyes.'

'Did you hear what I said?'

'Not really.'

He shifts so that he's sitting up. 'I want to talk about what's gonna happen when you go.'

'What do you want to happen when I go?' I ask, hitting the metaphorical ball back into his metaphorical court like it's my profession.

He's silent for a while—a long while, actually—as his fingers trace patterns on my chest and stomach.

'I want to be with you,' he says finally. 'Do you want to be with me too?'

I bring his fingers to my lips, kissing his fingertips. 'I don't want anyone else. But you know, it might be a while before we see each other again. Months, even.'

Noah doesn't say anything, so I continue. 'I'm worried I can't give you what you want. Routine. Time. Commitment.

I feel like there's a lot we have to work out for ourselves in the next few months.'

'But I love you.'

He doesn't look at me as he says it, his dark eyelashes downcast as he fidgets with a loose strand on our beach towel.

'Noah, look at me.'

He doesn't.

I catch his chin with my hand. He looks up, his mouth twisting into a grimace, lower lip wobbling. Tears hug his lashline.

'I love you. I knew it sitting on the banks of the river eating doughnuts with you, I knew it when you sang *Cats* in a drag queen's nightclub. I know it now, and I'll know it tomorrow, and the day after that, and the day after that.'

'Tomorrow and tomorrow and tomorrow,' Noah agrees. 'I knew I loved you when I saw you eat a gyros in less than five minutes, and when you signed to Alanzo on the court, and when you walked me to my door just to make sure I got home safe.'

'I broke that door trying to kiss you.'

He laughs through the tears. 'I know.'

I touch his face again, run my thumbs over the tear tracks running down his cheeks. 'You have changed me so much. Every day, I become a better person with you. But I think we both know there are things we need to do once we leave here.'

Noah takes my hand from his face and laces our fingers together. This tournament has been a whirlwind but there are still so many things unresolved; this holiday is exactly what I needed, but I know it won't fix my burnout, and I need to focus on getting fit for clay season. Noah just started a new job and is still trying to figure out university. Not to mention the issues with his own family. It's selfish to ask him to leave all of that for me.

My battle with Pejo Auer will go down as my best performance ever; I was so close to a grand slam title; so close to holding the cup. As hard as this tournament was, it proved I could make it to the end. There are still three more grand slams up for grabs this year; I have to keep trying. Right now, I have to make tennis my priority in the same way Noah needs time to figure his own shit out.

'I want to give us the best shot,' I say. 'But we both know it is not the right time.'

Noah turns my hand over and kisses the back of my palm. 'What if we give this long-distance thing a chance? We give each other twelve months to sort our shit out. If we still want to be together, we meet at the Flamingo Bar when you come back for the Australian Open.'

'The Flamingo Bar?' I echo. 'Will I have to be in drag?'

'If you'd like.' Noah kisses the corner of my mouth. 'One year. Barely fifty weeks if we're being pedantic. If we still feel the way we do, then we'll know it's a good thing.'

I reach up and kiss him in earnest.

'I love you, Gabriel Madani,' he says against my mouth.

'Careful,' I reply. 'Love means nothing to me.'

'Can I keep your hoodie?' Noah asks as we pack our bags on the eighth day, readying for checkout. It's drizzling outside, a perfect representation of our mood. Neither of us wants this holiday to finish.

But it has ended. I have a flight to Paris departing Sydney at six o'clock tonight. Noah has a flight from Sydney to Melbourne at midday.

I cross the room, kneeling where he's sitting in the desk chair, one knee pulled to his chest. 'You want me to wear it for a while and give it to you just as you leave?'

He scrubs his hands down his face. 'What about your hot-pink swimmers? Can you give me those too?'

I scoff. 'I would, if I didn't think you'd throw them out as soon as I left the country.'

'Rats, foiled again,' he mutters, and rises from the chair.

I'll be honest, the goodbye sucks. We fly back to Sydney. I've still got six hours until I need to be at my terminal, so I stay with him in a quiet corner of the gate until the final call for boarding.

'Twelve months,' I tell him as he kisses me.

'Make sure you text me every time you see something funny,' Noah mumbles, wiping his face on the inside of my hoodie.

'Every time,' I promise. 'Will you send me a recording of you playing? You will keep playing, won't you?'

Noah sniffs and nods. 'Yeah. Yeah, for sure.'

I pull him into my arms, inhaling the smell of warmth and sweetness, like cutting into warm, fresh bread. 'You're the best thing that's ever happened to me.'

'Oh fuck, Gabi,' he says over my shoulder. 'You won't

make this easy for me, will you?' He pulls away, shaking off the melancholy as he wipes a hand down his face. 'I love you, you awful man.'

'I know. I love you too.'

He picks up his backpack and with a tight smile, fishes out his boarding pass, handing it to the patient flight attendant.

'See you in twelve months, then, I guess.'

Noah steps to the other side of the desk. A small movement, but now he's out of reach, in a different construct of space.

Our time is up.

This chapter of my life is over.

I cry all the way back to Paris.

EPILOGUE
ONE YEAR LATER
NOAH

'There's a snowstorm,' Margie says four days before the Australian Open is scheduled to start. 'It's causing havoc across France, Switzerland and Austria. That's probably why.'

'Causing havoc with my life, that's what it's doing.' Gabriel's supposed to be getting here *tomorrow.* In less than twenty-four hours. 'What if they can't get out? How long are snowstorms supposed to last?'

Margie pats my shoulder as she steps back into the kitchen. 'Try not to think about it,' she says, like it's a switch I can flip. 'Do something to take your mind off it. Don't you have an assignment due on the weekend?'

'Sunday night and I'm stuck on it,' I say as I take Sadie's leash instead. Margie gives me a disapproving look. 'The walk will help me work it out.'

'Can you get milk while you're out?' Margie asks. 'Lamb chops for tea—that all right?'

'Sounds good,' I half shout back over Sadie's barking.

Opening the flyscreen door, Sadie launches herself onto the porch. I barely have time to grab the spare keys and a library book that needs returning before she's pulling me towards the front gate. Luckily, once she's on the footpath she chills out a bit and doesn't pull as hard.

We pass Carlton Library and I slip *The Count of Monte Cristo* through the return slot. We've been on a real classics binge for some reason. Last month we read *Little Women* together, and the month before was *Pride and Prejudice*. I tie Sadie to a pole outside while I collect this month's book, *The Call of the Wild*, and the newly published sequel to the book in the young adult crime series I'd started reading on Daydream Island. Gabriel hadn't rated it, but I'm sucked in.

I hadn't really been a reader before Gabriel. Sure, I read in school, but English wasn't my favourite subject and I'd never read a book for fun. Since I've started reading them to Gabriel—whether our schedules allow us to jump on a call together or I record segments for him to play back—I've been reading more and more. Gabriel's English has also improved. He says words like 'benevolence' now. Unfortunately, it's given him ideas about helping me improve my French—which still isn't great. I'm learning via an app because I don't have the money to pay for classes, and occasionally Gabriel will try to speak to me just in French, but we always revert to English. There are only so many times we can talk about my favourite fruits, or what we had for lunch, or name different kinds of animals. I think it must be like talking to a toddler. Gabriel says it's cute.

Every second Thursday is jazz night at the Flamingo Bar. Gabriel's never seen me perform, and tomorrow was supposed to be our night—the big return. I keep checking the weather apps. Apparently, a couple of planes have managed to fly out of Paris, but otherwise the wild weather is supposed to stay.

The snow hadn't been that bad when I'd been in Paris over Christmas, but Gabriel had loaned me one of his puffer jackets and I was loath to give it back to him by the end of the trip.

When I get back to the house, I make good on my word and finish my assignment before bed. Only two more assignments before the end of the summer bridging term—and then I'll have officially graduated high school. We've already researched French universities where I could take courses in English. Or online universities where I can study from wherever. Wherever Gabriel is, I suppose.

Leaving Australia is something we've discussed all year. It'll be hard but I think it's the right choice for me—and Margie agrees. Dad's in prison on federal drug charges for an operation that happened right under my nose, and the officers handling the case say Mum's in witness protection. It explains why, after all this time, she's never contacted me.

There's a chance she might come out of protection soon, but I was also given the option to move into protection with her. It would mean giving up *everything*—Peaches and Margie and the Rosewood and Melbourne and, most importantly, Gabriel. I know Mum wouldn't want that for me. I know we'll be together again, eventually.

I still work at the Rosewood, and have become friends with a lot of the team. I don't say no to after-shift drinks, and a few months ago, we went out partying in Chapel Street. I'd walked past Mark's Place for the first time since January and seen the For Sale sign in the window. A part of me had wanted to tell Gabriel, but he'd likely come back with some ridiculous answer like 'Let's buy it!' Hopefully the new owners treat the place with the respect it deserves.

I wake up to see Gabriel has sent me a message—*We made it to Dubai! Be there soon*—along with a photo of Victor and Bernard looking how one would expect them to look after twelve hours of delays. My heart swells at the thought of seeing them all again, though we'd just spent Christmas together. I suppose this is what it feels like to be a part of a family.

When I arrive at the Flamingo Bar, Peaches is in the middle of warming up. I'm not really sure how it happened, but we've become a thing. She's a bloody good singer and we've developed a strong backlist of jazz, blues and swing covers, and hey, if sometimes we lean closer to the Michael Bublé versions than the originals, that's no one's business. The man knows how to entertain.

'Where's this boyfriend of yours then?' Peaches teases good-naturedly as I set up my sheet music. 'Today's the big reunion, isn't it?'

Technically we saw each other in September—and again last month for the week over Christmas—but this is the *big* one. The thing we'd always said we'd do if we were serious about a future together.

'He's on his way,' I mumble as I pull the stool from beneath the piano. 'There's a snowstorm in Europe but he made it to Dubai.'

'If he doesn't show up, at least there's booze close by,' Peaches replies. 'Anyway, I was hoping we could start with a bit of Frank Sinatra this evening, and I'd love to try an Elvis number . . .'

GABRIEL

Every year, I forget how hot it gets in Australia.

Like, I know it's hot. But getting on the plane in sub-zero temperatures in Paris to be greeted in Melbourne by thirty-eight-degree heat is enough to send anyone loopy.

It's late, too. Later than I thought, but a snowstorm grounded planes at Charles de Gaulle, and we'd missed our connection in Dubai. I'm overtired, grumpy and my phone's dead.

'He can wait a little longer,' Papa says as I pace back and forth, willing my phone to turn on. 'Go have a shower. It'll have some charge by the time you're out.'

Victor laughs from the apartment kitchen and mutters something that sounds like, *Même merde, autre année.*

Except it's not the same as last year. The person who I was a year ago was scared, afraid to say what he wanted or be who he wanted to be. It's taken a lot—a grand slam title, long conversations with Papa and *Maman*, time spent away from tour and, perhaps most importantly, the help of a therapist—to get where I am today.

I wash the plane off me, the sour sweat and body odour, and Papa's right; when I get out my phone's charged to almost twenty per cent.

'Leaving! Bye!' is all I offer them before I'm out the door, navigating the familiar halls to find the elevator. It's too slow, so I take the stairs. I connect to the wi-fi and order a car, plugging in the address for the Flamingo Bar.

Wait for me, wait for me, wait for me.

The city looks the same. Green trams rattling along their old tracks, the dense streets teeming with outdoor shoppers. Rain comes over in the fifteen minutes it takes the driver to cross Melbourne's CBD.

'Typical Melbourne,' the driver laughs. He slows to a stop at the corner of Lonsdale and Russell streets. 'Looks like there's a crash up ahead.'

I check the maps. The Flamingo Bar is only a couple of blocks away. If I run, I could be there in a few minutes. Grabbing my wallet, I give the driver a five-dollar tip and bail out of the car.

'Go!' he cheers, but I don't look back. I'm sprinting down the rain-slicked pavement, weaving through the crowd and dodging umbrella spokes.

The Flamingo Bar is busy. The tables are full of patrons, happy to finish off their pints while waiting out the rain. Music floats down from upstairs; a woman is singing gentle blues. There's no line, so I rush towards the door, only to be blocked at the last second by a burly man.

'ID, mate,' he demands.

Quickly, I fish out my wallet and flash him my passport. He looks at my photo. Then at me. Then back to my photo. Finally, he presses his hand-held clicker once and hands my passport back. 'In you go. They're finishing in ten minutes, though.'

I push my way towards the stage, feeling the momentum of the music push me back and forth. On the stage, light dances off the sequins of the woman's dress, and the effect throws small bursts of rainbow onto the walls, the roof, and the piano beside her. Someone's blocking my view of the pianist.

'Excuse me,' I yell before forcing my way through. Someone spills a bit of their beer on me. I don't care. I make it to the front of the crowd as the song finishes, just in time to see his back straighten and his eyes slide towards the crowd.

He sees me.

And smiles.

NOAH

'We could have met tomorrow, you know. I would have understood.' I place a Coke in front of Gabriel.

'This was our thing. We promised each other. And I wanted to see you play.' Gabriel looks tired. Deep bags hang under his eyes. I wonder when he last slept, and for how long.

The sincerity of it all makes me laugh. It's so Gabriel. 'I'm glad you made it.'

The Australian Open starts in a few days, and he has a charity match on tomorrow night. I'm not going to say he needs to take the tournament seriously—I'm sure his dad's made that incredibly clear—but after winning the US Open five months ago, he's got a reputation to uphold.

'Seems like a long time since we made that promise,' I reply. 'We're different people. In the best way. You're a grand slam champion; I'm a high-school graduate who plays in a jazz band with a drag queen.'

'It's my favourite drag queen jazz band, if that counts for anything,' he says. 'And you also forget that you can now speak French with the proficiency of a seven-year-old.'

My heart swells at the teasing. 'I missed you.'

'I missed you, too.'

It feels like everyone always says long distance doesn't work. Even Margie had her doubts about our arrangement—but here we are, together, almost a year later. Who knows what the future holds for us. Travel, definitely. Hopefully more grand slam wins. I plan to be courtside as much as possible. Maybe eventually we'll get married, have kids.

His pinkie finger reaches out to snag mine. 'So, have your affections for me waned?'

'Hmm, good use of the word "waned".' I loop my fingers to interlock with his and bring his hand up to my mouth, pressing a kiss onto the smooth skin on the back of his hand. 'Never. Yours?'

He laughs, and the little crow's feet at the edges of his eyes wrinkle. 'Not at all.'

I pick up my beer and clink the rim against his Coke. 'Well, then, happy anniversary, baby.'

ACKNOWLEDGEMENTS

The initial idea of this book was born in the summer of 2015, when I was a broke university student who spent a summer making milkshakes in a tiny café at the Australian Open. I'd use my work pass to catch matches on either end of my shift, watching whoever was playing on the general access courts, or holding a training session. One day, a colleague of mine rocked up to his shift with a t-shirt signed by Rafael Nadal, who had just held a practice session. As a fan who'd stayed up past midnight watching his incredible matches with Novak Djokovic, my jealousy was *palpable*. All that to say—I love tennis.

Like many people isolated during the pandemic, I decided to use the time to dust off an old idea. Quickly, this manuscript became the book of my heart—a queer sports romance that didn't hide away from the hard realities of life but also celebrated the very best of Australia; diverse, accepting and sport-loving.

Thank you to the team at Pan Macmillan Australia: you saw what this book could become from the start, and you championed it the whole way. I am so lucky to have the opportunity to work with you.

Thank you to my family who always believed I could do this, even when I didn't. Thank you for encouraging me to study my passion at university, even if you thought it was a bit of an off choice. Notably, thank you to my dad, who is always up for a hit down at the local courts and whose passion for tennis inspired so much of this novel.

Rebecca Cox—you are the sister of my soul. My best friend. Neither time nor distance will stop us from messaging tennis scores in the middle of the night. I always said your book would be published, and here it is.

Rebecca Lim—you are the champion every writer needs in their corner. Thank you for the early feedback on this manuscript, the encouragement to keep going even when things got hairy.

To my friends, Scott and Ellie, Clair, Kimberly, James, Clare, Will and Amanda; and to my critique group: Bea, Shelley, Maree, Ella, Amelia, Claire and Deborah. Thank you.

To my incredible colleagues, Vanessa, Tracey, Geraldine, Nurul and Vrinda, thank you for tolerating my relentless enthusiasm for this book, for over a year, without ever telling me you were sick of hearing about it, even though I'm sure, at times, you were.

Finally, thank you to the Canberra School of Tennis, Tennis NSW & ACT, and the West Wyalong Tennis Club—and particularly thank you to the lady who always asks when my next book is coming out. The answer: right now.